Highland Storms

Highland Storms

Christina Courtenay

First published 2011 by Choc Lit Limited
Penrose House, Crawley Drive, Camberley, Surrey GU15 2AB
www.choclitpublishing.com

A CIP catalogue record for this book is available
from the British Library

ISBN-978-1-906931-71-1

Printed and bound by CPI Group (UK) Ltd, Croydon, CR0 4YY

For my mother
Birgitta Tapper
With lots of love

Acknowledgements

It is truly amazing how helpful people are whenever an author needs to know the answer to some particularly tricky question! This proved to be the case when I was unable to find out what an ordinary Scottish woman would have worn in the second half of the 18th century. I contacted the lovely Eileen Ramsay with a plea for help and within half an hour she'd put me in touch with author Maggie Craig (whose wonderfully titled book *Bare-Arsed Banditti* is a must for anyone who wants to read about the Jacobites) and their mutual friend Naomi Tarrant, retired Keeper of Costume at the National Museums of Scotland. Huge thanks to all three for helping me!

A massive thank you once again to the brilliant Choc Lit team who continue to be a joy to work with, to the other Choc Lit authors (love working with you guys too!), to my two critique partners Gill Stewart and Henriette Gyland for their unfailing encouragement and support (and special thanks to Gill for correcting my Scots!), and as always, to my family for putting up with me in 'author mode' and to all my friends in the Romantic Novelists' Association who continue to inspire me.

Finally, I'd like to say a very special thank you to the cover artist for giving me this vision in lilac – love it!

Chapter One

Marsaili Buchanan was pulled back from the brink of sleep by the soft growling of her deerhound, Liath. It started as a low rumble inside the big dog's chest and throat, and grew in volume while the animal raised his head and stared fixedly at the door. Since Liath was snuggled around Marsaili's feet, the vibrations could be felt all the way up her legs. Her heart skipped a beat as she held her breath, waiting to see who was coming up the stairs to her tower room this time.

'They never give up, do they, boy,' she whispered and sat up, putting her palm on Liath's flat skull. She felt the rumbling more strongly there and stroked the dog's wiry neck, keeping her hand near his collar in case she needed to hold him back. It was a distinct possibility.

She'd been plagued with night-time suitors like this for a while now, even though she never encouraged any of the men in the household or on the estate. Her face and figure seemed to inspire lust in any male between the ages of fifteen and fifty, no matter how much she covered it up. She silently cursed fate for giving her this dubious blessing. It brought her nothing but trouble.

The latch moved softly. Since it was well-oiled and silent, Marsaili wouldn't have heard it if she hadn't been forewarned. The door didn't open though, the bar she'd had installed recently saw to that. The latch dropped with a clink and she heard a snort of frustration. This was followed by a muted thud, presumably a shoulder pushing against the door. When this didn't produce the desired result either, a man's voice muttered an oath. A harder shove which made the wooden planks quiver seemed to conclude the assault. Marsaili bit her lip hard to keep from making a sound.

'Marsaili? It's me, Colin.' The whisper was clearly audible and seemed to hang in the air for a moment.

Marsaili almost gasped out loud. That was one voice she'd never thought to hear outside her door. She'd believed Colin Seton, the estate manager, too proud to go sneaking around at night.

'Mr Seton? What's the matter?' she asked, trying to sound as if she'd just been woken up. 'Is something amiss?'

'Come now, girl, you know why I'm here. You've been holding out for long enough, it's time you were rewarded.'

His voice was slightly louder, but still low. Marsaili didn't know why he bothered trying to keep it down. Her room was at the top of one of the towers of Rosyth House and there was no one immediately below her at the moment. He must be aware of this.

'I beg your pardon?' she sat up straighter, glaring in the direction of the door. *Holding out for what? Him? How on earth did he reach that conclusion?* She just wanted to be left alone, not be importuned by a widower old enough to be her father.

'The finest looking woman in all the Highlands deserves only the best. Can't blame you for setting your sights high. Let me in now, you can trust me to look after you right.'

Rage bubbled up inside Marsaili's throat and threatened to choke her. The words she longed to hurl at Seton were so stacked up, she couldn't spit them out. All that escaped her was a noise of frustration, but Liath felt her wrath and gave voice to it on her behalf. His growling grew into a crescendo of menace that reverberated around the small room.

'Marsaili?'

She managed to control her vocal chords at last. 'Please leave, Mr Seton and I'll forget we ever had this conversation.

2

I'm sorry, but you've misunderstood.'

'Eh? You're just being stubborn now and you know it. No need to be coy, you've made your point.' His voice was beginning to sound strained, as if he was keeping his temper in check, but only just.

Marsaili didn't know what to reply. She didn't want to antagonise the man, but on the other hand she had to make him understand she wasn't available to anyone. As if to emphasise her thoughts, Liath gave a short bark, and although she couldn't see him, Marsaili knew he was probably baring his fangs as well. She felt her heart beating harder, the sound of her pulse almost drowning out the dog's noise inside her ears. She took a deep breath. 'I meant what I said. Anyone who wants to court me can do so in daylight.' *Not that it would do them any good since I don't want any of them.*

'Who said anything about courting? Your mother –'

She cut him off abruptly. 'What my mother chose to do was up to her. It has nothing to do with me and I'll live my life as I see fit. I'm a respectable woman.'

'Rubbish! You're no better than you should be. Hoity-toity by-blow of a –'

'Mr Seton! You've said enough.' Marsaili was shaking with fury, but was determined not to enter into a lengthy argument with him.

Seton cursed long and fluently. Finally, he hissed, 'That dog isn't allowed in the house, you know. I'll see it's put where it belongs from now on, in the stables.'

'You can't! I have the mistress's express permission to keep him in here. The dog stays,' she said firmly, trying not to let her voice tremble the way the rest of her body was doing. It was true after all, but would he leave it at that? She waited again, holding Liath's collar in a tight grip, while Seton made up his mind.

The door was stout, but she knew Seton was both strong and determined. Fortunately, so was Liath. Marsaili was reluctant to let the dog loose on anyone because she'd seen what those powerful jaws could do, but if she was cornered, she'd have no other choice.

'We'll just see about that,' Seton snarled before giving the door a vicious kick. Soon after, she heard footsteps disappearing down the stairwell. She breathed a sigh of relief and threw her arms around the dog's neck, burying her face in the shaggy fur.

'Thank you, Liath, good boy. You're the best.' He licked her hand in acknowledgement of this tribute and leaned against her until her limbs stopped shaking.

They'd won this time, but Marsaili knew that from now on she'd have to be on her guard at all times, both for herself and for Liath. There was no saying what Seton would do and now he'd put all his cards on the table, there was no going back. He wasn't the type to give up easily and she'd probably wounded his pride. He would use every means at his disposal to have his way.

Well, she'd be ready for him. *Just let him try!*

Chapter Two

'Brice, are you awake?'

'Hmm?' Brice Kinross lifted his head from the pillow and blinked, wondering for a moment where he was. The small movement was enough to make him wince and he swiftly registered all the signs of a monumental hangover. Before he closed his eyes again, he had time to notice that he was in his own bed, probably for the first time in a week. He had no idea how he'd got there. Not that it mattered.

Nothing mattered any more.

His father, Killian, knocked once more on the bedroom door and Brice gritted his teeth against the pain this caused. 'Come in,' he muttered, his voice hoarse as though he'd done too much shouting the night before. He half remembered raucous singing and guessed that he'd joined in, perhaps a little too enthusiastically.

Killian entered quietly, as if he knew his son's head was too delicate to withstand even the smallest of sounds. He went straight to the window and opened it wide, then pulled up a chair next to the bed and sat down. 'Smells like a taproom in here,' he said with a smile. 'I'm surprised you actually made it into bed. I expected to find you curled up on the floor next to the chamber pot.'

Brice was still too befuddled to reply to such teasing, so he stayed silent.

'I reckoned you must have drunk the town dry by now, so perhaps you're ready to listen to a proposition?' Killian's smile turned into a more serious expression.

'Uhm, what kind?' Brice struggled into a sitting position,

then groaned and put up his hands to cradle his aching skull. At the same time he tried to disentangle himself from the covers. It was August and as hot as it ever became in Sweden and since he'd apparently slept with the windows closed, the linen material was sticking to him in a most uncomfortable way. The sheets weren't too fragrant either. Or perhaps that was him? He made a face.

Killian pulled a hip flask out of his pocket and held it out. 'Here, hair of the dog, but it's the last drop of anything stronger than tea you're having this week. Understand me? This has got to stop.'

Brice grimaced as the liquid burned a path down his throat. Normally his Scottish-born father preferred whisky, so Brice was surprised to find the flask contained *brännvin*, the pure spirit favoured by the Swedes. Although this particular one was flavoured with herbs, it was still vile so early in the day. He shuddered and gulped down a sudden bout of nausea.

'It's none of your business if I want to have a night on the town with my friends,' he began, but Killian cut him off.

'A night, is it? More like an entire week. Enough is enough, don't you think?'

Brice had already reached this conclusion for himself, but that didn't mean he wanted to be lectured like a naughty schoolboy. He was nearly twenty-two, not twelve. 'It's my choice,' he reiterated. And if anyone had cause to drown their sorrows, he did, he added to himself.

'Maybe so, but it doesn't change anything.' Killian's voice was gentle, but firm.

Brice clenched his fists around the sheet as the memories came flooding back again. No amount of drinking could lessen the pain of betrayal. 'I trusted Jamie,' he said. 'My own brother. With his looks and charm he could have had any girl in the country, but he had to take the only one I wanted. The one he knew was spoken for. Why? And as for her ...'

6

He couldn't find the words to express how he felt about Elisabet now.

Brice had been in love with her for as long as he could remember. There had never been any doubt in his mind she was the woman he was going to marry. She had the kind of beauty that seemed almost unreal, her features delicate and perfect in every way like those of some other-worldly creature. Although young boys don't normally notice such things, he'd been bewitched from an early age. Since she was four years younger than him, however, he'd had to wait for her to grow up, but he didn't mind. It gave him the opportunity to try and make something of himself before settling down and he wanted her to have the best he could provide.

Obviously, it wasn't enough and I waited too long.

'You've made your point and believe me, I'm not much happier with your brother than you are,' Killian told him. 'I thought better of Jamie, but accidents happen and he's paid the price now. You should pity him, rather than waste your energy on useless anger.'

'Pity him? When he's married the most beautiful girl in all of Sweden? *My* girl. You can't mean that.' Brice handed back the flask, his stomach curdling at the mere thought of any more. It only deadened the pain for a few hours anyway, but then the agony returned tenfold afterwards.

'I'm perfectly serious. You may think Elisabet is the loveliest girl on earth, but I doubt Jamie would agree with you. He was nowhere near ready to settle down with her or anyone else and he doesn't love her. To him she was just like all the others. The difference is, he's now stuck with her for life, whereas you're free. Free to find someone else, someone better.'

Brice made an angry noise, but Killian raised his voice. 'Look at me, Brice. Even you must realise that if she didn't want you enough to wait, then she wasn't the girl for you. Any marriage with her would have been one-sided. Is it what you want? Being shackled to a woman who doesn't love you?'

Brice knew his father was right about that as well, but he wasn't ready to admit it yet. Perhaps he never would be. 'No, but she did until Jamie decided to have her,' he muttered. 'No girl can resist him when he puts his mind to it.'

'Rubbish. Besides, Jamie swore to me he never deliberately tried to entice her and I believe him.'

'Right. That must be why she's with child then.' Brice felt his mouth set in a mulish line. His father could believe what he liked, he'd never convince Brice of Jamie's innocence.

I should never have gone to China again, he thought, knuckling his eyes as if it would take away both the tiredness and the image of Elisabet with Jamie, which seemed to be burned onto his eyelids. *But I did it for her!*

He'd been barely eighteen when he sailed to Canton for the first time on board one of the Swedish East India Company's ships. It was both the worst and most wonderful thing he'd ever experienced. On the one hand, eighteen months of hard work and having to endure one of the toughest journeys imaginable. On the other, the joy of seeing strange sights he'd only ever dreamed of, plus enormous gains on his share of the cargo. And so he'd set out for a second time, hoping it would give him enough capital of his own to ask Elisabet to be his wife.

It had, but he shouldn't have bothered.

Killian sighed. 'Whatever the case, you have to face facts. Elisabet wasn't the right one, which means your soul mate is yet to be discovered. Trust me, you won't find her at the bottom of a keg of ale or barrel of wine. You're young, you have plenty of time.'

'Soul mate? There's no such thing,' Brice scoffed.

'Yes, there is. I used to be like Jamie until I found your mother. I thought women were just put on God's earth for my enjoyment, never anything else. I was wrong. Luckily for me, I realised it before it was too late. Now you have the chance to look for yours.'

Brice knew he and his five siblings were lucky in that their parents were prepared to allow them to choose their future spouses for themselves, but at the moment he wasn't in the mood to feel grateful.

'And how do you suggest I go about it? Join the riveting social scene here in Gothenburg?' Brice knew he was being overly sarcastic, but he couldn't help it. He wasn't sure he was ready to face the reality of his situation. He still wanted to forget.

'No, that's not at all what I had in mind. I think it's time you went to Scotland to take up your birthright.'

'My what?' Brice sat up straight and stared at his father, then drew in a sharp breath when the sudden movement jolted his sore head. 'Ouch.' He rubbed his skull, trying to lessen the pain, but didn't take his eyes off Killian, who was heading for the door. 'What did you say?'

'Get yourself washed and dressed, then come downstairs to the study and I'll explain.' Killian turned, his stern expression softening into a grin. 'And eat something. You look awful and no respectable Scottish lass will give you so much as the time of day in that state.'

'Who says I want them to?'

But Killian had already left, so the question remained unanswered. Brice scowled in the direction of the closed door, but his father's words had intrigued him and he knew he wouldn't be able to go back to sleep now.

'Damn it all,' he muttered, but for the first time since he'd found out about Jamie and Elisabet, something had penetrated the fog of pain and piqued his interest.

Ignoring his aching head, he went in search of food and hot water.

Balancing a heavy tray on one hand, Marsaili knocked on the door to the estate office.

'Come in.'

'Sit. Stay,' she ordered Liath in a stern whisper. As usual, he'd padded behind her as she went about her daily work, but she knew this was one room he couldn't enter. She managed to open the door and manoeuvre her way through without dropping either the tray or its contents. Leaving it slightly ajar, she went across to the desk and deposited Seton's breakfast in one corner where there were no papers or ledgers at present. Porridge with thick cream and buttermilk, two bannocks and a quart of ale, as well as some honey and cheese. Nothing but the best for the factor.

'Thank you,' he said, without looking up at her.

Marsaili's stomach churned. As housekeeper, it wasn't really her job to serve Seton, but the maids were all terrified of him so she'd taken over the task a while back. Now she wished she hadn't. She'd been dreading this encounter after what had happened the night before, but he seemed to be acting as if she didn't exist. *Well good,* she thought. The less notice he took of her, the better. *What on earth was he thinking? He's much too old for me.* But she knew there was nothing rational about men who lusted after women. And he was good-looking for his age, she'd give him that, so perhaps he'd genuinely thought she would welcome his advances.

As he pulled the tray over and started on the porridge, she turned to go, but before she'd taken more than a few steps she heard him spit loudly. 'What the devil is this?' he grumbled.

'I beg your pardon?' She looked over her shoulder, bracing

herself for an eruption of wrath. His temper was volatile, to say the least.

'I always have the great oats, not this pap, you know that well enough.' He threw down the silver spoon borrowed from the laird's cabinet and it landed in the cream, splashing globules all around. This made him visibly more irritated as he then had to mop the mess off his papers with his handkerchief.

Marsaili drew in a steadying breath and replied as calmly as she could. 'There were none left, Mr Seton, only these. I informed you just the other day that we were running low on provisions. You said we'd have to make do as there's no money for more.' The so-called 'black oats' were an inferior type, usually given to the servants, but it was all they had now. Times were hard, or so Seton claimed, and the harvest still a good month away at least.

'You're the housekeeper, you should have rationed it better,' he accused.

'No one has been given any except you, Mr Seton, I assure you. I kept it under lock and key, as you instructed.'

'Huh, this is what comes of giving a slip of a girl responsibilities above and beyond what she can manage. Housekeeper, indeed. It's a position for older and more experienced women.'

Marsaili decided not to answer. She was nearly twenty-two and didn't consider herself a 'slip of a girl' any longer, but since Seton was probably in his mid-forties, perhaps that seemed very young to him. Either way, they'd had this conversation before and she'd learned that maintaining a dignified silence worked better.

'Well, what are you waiting for? Find me something decent to eat,' Seton snarled.

'But the bannocks ...?'

'Are all well and good, but won't keep hunger at bay till

11

dinner time. I need proper victuals – eggs, mutton, something I can sink my teeth into. See to it.'

'Yes, Mr Seton.'

Turning to leave again, she was halted once more by his parting shot.

'And if I catch your dog inside the house again, I'll personally shoot him, is that clear?'

Drat, she thought, *he must have heard Liath's claws clicking on the flagstones outside the door.* 'But the mistress said –'

'Devil take it, woman! He's to stay where he belongs and there's an end to it.'

Marsaili closed the door behind her without a word.

Brice joined his father downstairs at last, clean and presentable, and slightly less hung over after a cautious breakfast of rye bread, cheese and ale.

Killian waved him to a seat and came straight to the point. 'I want you to go to Rosyth. Something's not right there and we need to know what it is.'

'Why me?' Brice asked. 'Can't you send someone else?' The last thing he wanted was to go gallivanting across the North Sea when he'd only just come back from the long journey to Canton.

'I could, but the estate is yours anyway, so it should be your responsibility. I've tried to look after it from a distance on your behalf, but it's impossible. Since I can't go myself to see what's happening, you'll have to sort it out.'

Brice frowned. 'I don't understand. It belongs to you. Has done for ages.'

Rosyth House was his father's Scottish property, inherited some ten years earlier from old Lord Rosyth, Killian's grandfather. Although technically Killian was now the laird and chief of clan Kinross, he hadn't been able to set foot in

Scotland since taking part in the Jacobite rebellion on the side of Prince Charles Edward, the man the English called 'the Young Pretender'. Brice had been brought up to think of him as the true king's heir, but most people had now given up hope of him ever gaining the throne. Rosyth House had remained in Killian's possession, however, despite him being branded a traitor to the crown. He'd had the foresight to become a Swedish citizen and was therefore outside the reach of English law. Since the uprising, he'd lived in Sweden where he and Brice's mother Jessamijn ran a prosperous trading company.

Killian shook his head. 'No, I signed it over to you before I declared for the Prince. Apart from the fact that you're Swedish, you were too young to fight so no one could accuse you of being a Jacobite. It seemed the best thing to do at the time and it worked. The English couldn't confiscate Rosyth, no matter what. Other lairds did the same, or so I've heard.'

Brice was having trouble taking this in and squinted at his father. 'So you're saying it's been mine all along?'

'Since 1745, yes.'

'Why didn't you ever tell me?'

'I was going to when you were legally old enough to run it yourself, but you were in China when you turned twenty-one. I'm telling you now.'

'Well, what's wrong with it?' Brice asked. 'I thought you had a steward looking after matters. And what about your late cousin's wife, Aunt Ailsa? Isn't she keeping an eye on things? Why do I need to go there?'

Killian stood up and began to pace back and forth, his hands behind his back. Brice knew his father's barely perceptible limp was a constant reminder of how close Killian had come to losing his life for the Jacobite cause, just like his father and two brothers before him. He'd been lucky though. He had lived to return to Gothenburg, together with a number of other Scotsmen whose lives he'd saved by allowing them to board his merchant ship before the Redcoats caught up with them.

'Ailsa's not in good health and I haven't heard from her in ages. But there is a factor, yes, Colin Seton,' he said now. 'He sends me regular reports and the income that is your due. I've kept it for you and I'll hand it over before you leave. Lately, however, there hasn't been so much as a farthing and Seton's letters are full of tales of woe. The tacksmen are insolent, they don't pay their rents, the sheep and cattle are dwindling in numbers, the house has needed repairs, the crops are failing … The list is endless and as a result he's asking me for money instead of sending any. I want to know why.'

'Isn't it possible he's right though? I mean, the Scots have suffered since the forty-five and I've heard tell there's a lot of hardship. Why not at Rosyth?'

Killian shook his head. 'My grandfather ran it with an iron fist. It's always been prosperous and in my youth, when he was teaching me all about it, he showed me that even during hard times, Rosyth ought to do reasonably well. Some losses are always to be expected, certainly, but not to this extent. I'm telling you, there's something seriously wrong. I want you to get to the bottom of it.'

'Very well. I suppose it's no worse than sitting around here brooding. And the whisky is good, I hear.'

Killian shot him an impatient look, his blue eyes darkening with anger. 'This is serious, Brice. You're the new Lord Rosyth, it's your concern.'

'Me, a Scottish laird?' Brice almost laughed. He hadn't been to Scotland since he was a boy and considered himself Swedish through and through, despite his father's antecedents. Even though he'd known about it, becoming the next laird had always seemed like something that was too far away to bother thinking about.

'It's not a laughing matter. The oldest son always inherits and that's you, whether you like it or not. Sooner or later, it would have been yours. It's a very important position, but one which brings with it responsibilities. A Highland chief is almost like a father to his clan – less so now the accursed new English laws are in place, but the people will still expect things from you. And Scotland is beautiful. Who's to say you won't like it and want to stay? You used to love it there as a boy.'

Brice snorted. 'Right now, going back to bed sounds more appealing to be honest.' He caught another dark look from his father and held up his hands. 'But fine, if you want me to go to Rosyth, I will. Just tell me what to do. Shouldn't be that difficult.' He knew his father was trying to help him forget about the recent marriage *débâcle* and to a certain extent he'd succeeded. Thanks to Killian, Brice now had a purpose and an excellent excuse for leaving Sweden. The more he thought about it, the more he realised it was a good thing.

'Right. Then let me tell you my plan ...'

Chapter Three

Edinburgh, August 1754

Brice stepped off one of his father's merchant ships at the port of Leith and looked around with interest. He hadn't set foot in Scotland for nearly ten years, but Killian had been right, he remembered now how much he'd always liked it here. In fact, there was no denying he felt almost as at home as he did in Sweden. The voices all around him spoke in a mixture of tongues, mostly Scots, Gaelic or English, but he understood them all for the most part, although his Gaelic was a bit rusty. He'd spent some time at Rosyth House every summer until the age of twelve and by mixing with the local children he soon picked up their speech.

He stood still for a moment while his mind adjusted to the unaccustomed sounds. He was sure the Gaelic would soon come back to him and he'd be fluent again in no time. He had an ear for languages since his mother had spoken to him in Dutch, his father in English and Scots, and all his friends in Swedish. Somehow his brain absorbed them all.

'You must go and see Rory Grant,' his father had told him. 'I've already written to him and he'll help you sort out the legal documents so you can officially take over the running of the estate. It's important for you to be able to prove your ownership if you're to avoid any problems.' Brice thought this sounded like sensible advice.

He left orders for his possessions, including his horse, to be brought later and set out to walk the two miles or so into the town of Edinburgh. It felt wonderful to be able to stretch his legs after the week-long sea journey and he didn't mind the exercise. He'd never been one for sitting still any length of time, which was probably another reason why he'd gone to China. It put off the moment when he'd have to start helping his father to run the family's merchant business, something which entailed being perched at a desk for hours on end.

Edinburgh was much larger and noisier than Gothenburg, and Brice found it exciting to be there. The mostly stone-built tenement buildings rose all around him as he walked up the High Street. Closely crowded together, some were as tall as twelve storeys and he marvelled at such height. Wynds and closes snaked off at irregular intervals on either side, dark, narrow and noxious. The main street, with the imposing castle at the top, was teeming with people and he had to push his way through the throng, but as he was tall, he had no trouble keeping his bearings. Killian had told him how to find Rory's lodgings and Brice was soon there. He was shown into a small parlour, sparsely furnished but comfortable, where his host greeted him with genuine pleasure.

'Welcome back to Scotland, young man. You've changed a bit, I must say, but you remember me, I take it?'

'Yes, of course. How could I forget my own godfather?' Brice embraced his father's oldest friend heartily. 'Although it's been too long. You should have visited us in Sweden. Father is forever talking about you.'

'Alas, the sea is not for me.' Rory ushered Brice to a chair and settled himself in another after calling for refreshment to be brought. 'I turn green at the mere sight of it, so I'm afraid the thought of a whole week was too much to contemplate. I'm not as intrepid as the members of your family, I fear. Going to China ...' He shuddered in exaggerated fashion.

'Foolhardy, you mean?' Brice grinned.

'Well, now you come to mention it, entrusting your life to what really amounts to a very large bucket does seem a bit reckless, but to each his own.' They both laughed.

Brice knew Rory was no coward though. He'd been a supporter of the Jacobite cause as well, fighting bravely alongside Killian. Rory's father, however, had been a Whig and somehow managed to keep his son from suffering any consequences of what he called his 'rash actions'. Now, almost ten years after the uprising, Rory was once again an upright member of society 'with some clout', as Killian had put it.

'Yes, don't worry, I won't have any problems helping you find a reliable lawyer,' he told Brice when the subject was raised some time later. 'He'll soon have all the paperwork ready, then the estate will be yours. It will take a week or two at the most, I should think.'

'Excellent, thank you,' Brice replied. 'Then if you don't mind, I'll go and do a bit of reconnaissance while we're waiting. I take it my father put you in the picture when he wrote to you?'

Rory smiled. 'Indeed he did. I wish you luck.'

Marsaili heard the yelp of pain through the half-open doorway to the kitchen and immediately set off in the direction of the sound. A high-pitched bark spurred her into a run and she sprinted into the stable yard at breakneck speed. She took in the scene at a glance and didn't hesitate to intervene. Instinctively using the broom she'd been wielding, she struck Seton a heavy blow on one arm. It made him miss the kick he was aiming at Liath, whose collar was held in a firm grip by one of Seton's minions, and he turned towards her instead.

'What the ...?'

'Stop that this instant! You have no right to touch him, he's mine,' Marsaili snarled and raised the besom to thwack Seton across the shins before advancing on the stable boy with it. The youth let go of the dog and made a run for it, leaving Liath free to rush to her side and bare his fangs at

Seton. There was no mistaking the menace in the growl that accompanied this stance.

'You don't understand. I was defending myself.' Seton was red in the face and for an instant his normally handsome features were twisted with anger, but his expression quickly changed to one of conciliation. He backed up a couple of steps, keeping a wary eye on Liath. 'The dog attacked me. I can't allow such behaviour. He's vicious and needs to be put down.'

'That's not true and you know it. He'd never hurt anyone unless he was threatened. Besides, how could he be attacking you with someone else holding onto him?' Marsaili looked around to see if anyone was listening, then added in an undertone, 'You have your own reasons for wanting him out of the way, but I've told the mistress and if anything should happen to Liath, she'll know who to blame.'

'I don't know what you mean.' Seton's tone was dismissive, as if she was talking rubbish.

'Really?'

His face relaxed, then he smiled at her suddenly, his eyes glittering with suppressed amusement and something suspiciously like condescension. 'Besides, do you think I'm afraid of the mistress? Locked in her tower, away with the fairies most of the time. Hah, much good her support would do anyone.'

Marsaili clenched her fists on Liath's collar, trying to stay calm. Although she disliked Seton, she knew it was irrational. Apart from that one night-time visit, he'd always been polite to her and he never tried to touch her surreptitiously the way some of the other men did. His general air of superiority grated though. *He carries himself like a king*, she thought, *or as if he owned the place.*

He didn't, but there was no denying the fact that he was in charge of the Rosyth estate and she wasn't.

'The mistress still has the final say in how matters are

run here until the laird comes back,' Marsaili insisted, even though Seton was probably right. Ailsa Kinross, widow of the laird's cousin, was nominally the head of the household in Lord Rosyth's absence, but everyone knew it was Seton who decided everything. Ailsa was seldom seen.

He shook his head at her foolishness, as if she was a deluded child. 'The laird's not coming back, at least not as long as the Sassenachs still want Jacobite scalps. It'll be years yet, mark my words. When was the last time he was here, eh? Ten years ago? No, the coward won't set foot on Scottish soil any time soon, trust me.'

'It's been eight years since Culloden. Things have changed.' *Though perhaps not enough*. The English would still be interested in a laird who'd been a confirmed Jacobite, even if they'd given up persecuting ordinary people after the Indemnity Act of '47 had guaranteed underlings wouldn't face further punishments.

Seton stepped closer, ignoring the increased growling coming from Liath, and whispered, 'Never mind the laird. You really ought to think about your own future, Marsaili. If you want to retain that dog of yours, you should be nice to me and keep him under control. Putting on airs and graces won't change where you came from, but your life could be so much better than it is at the moment. Your own cottage, fine clothes, trinkets ... It's your choice. Think on it.'

With that parting shot, he sauntered off, leaving Marsaili simmering with rage. She wanted to tell him he was the last man on earth she'd be 'nice' to, but knew she was better off keeping her sentiments to herself.

She'd just have to continue to stay out of his way.

The plan Killian had come up with was for Brice to travel to Rosyth House under an assumed name at first, in order to see how matters stood.

'That way, you'll be able to see the true state of affairs and hopefully catch them unawares. Make an assessment of all the goods and equipment that's needed in order to put the estate back on its feet, if indeed it's as bad as the factor claims. Then you can go back to Edinburgh and order everything to take with you, along with the title deeds. If there really is something underhand going on, it'll hopefully rattle the people responsible as well.'

'What if they recognise me though?' Brice had protested. 'My second cousins or aunt Ailsa?'

'I doubt it.' Killian laughed. 'You're not exactly a scrawny twelve-year old any longer. From what I understand, Ailsa is an invalid so you might not see her at all, and the girls should be married and long gone by now. I sent over their *tochers* ages ago.'

'Their what?'

'*Tochers*, dowries. With five thousand merks each, I'm sure they were snapped up quickly, although strangely enough Seton never told me who they married.' Killian shrugged. 'Mind you, he never writes about anything other than estate matters and as I said, I haven't heard from Ailsa for some time now. Anyway, with a bit of luck, you'll find some things out before you're unmasked. It's worth a try.'

Consequently, Brice left Edinburgh behind after only one day. The fact that he'd brought his own horse from Sweden and therefore didn't need to hire one saved time. However, he was sure Starke would baulk at crossing the Firth of Forth by boat at South Queensferry, having just endured the North Sea for a week, so he took the longer route west by land. They were soon trotting happily through the countryside, past Linlithgow and almost as far as Stirling, before heading north in the direction of Drummond.

At first, the landscape was fairly flat, with fertile farmland all around, spread out like a rippled quilt. Crops ripening in the sunshine, mostly golden oats or barley, interspersed with the dusty green of late-summer meadows. Once they'd crossed into Menteith though, low lying, rolling hills came into view, with higher mountains in the distance and copses of trees which sometimes turned into small woods. The area had a natural beauty that was undeniable and somehow it called to Brice, even though it was so different from the deep pine forests he was used to in Sweden.

Although the landscape itself hadn't changed, Brice immediately noticed that the country he was riding through was altered. He'd heard about the reprisals carried out throughout the Highlands during the summer and autumn of 1746, when the Government forces wreaked their terrible revenge on those who had dared to oppose them. There were horrifying tales told of people being shot out of hand, women raped, houses and crops burned, but Brice had thought they were probably exaggerations. Now he wasn't so sure.

Although nature had covered the tracks of the looters, there were still quite a few houses which were nothing but burned-out shells. And Brice saw overrun gardens and former orchards where every single tree was nothing but a stump. The main change, however, was in the faces of the people he met en route. Most of them looked downright miserable, there was no other word for it, especially the further north he travelled.

Scotsmen in general and Highlanders in particular were a proud race, but polite and hospitable to a fault, as Brice well knew. Or they used to be. Now they seemed introverted and reluctant to talk to him. Whenever he stopped at an inn for some refreshment, he was regarded with suspicion, even when he addressed the landlord in Gaelic or Scots. It was as if they didn't trust their own eyes and ears and thought him a spy of some sort, merely because he was better dressed and rode a fine horse.

After a long day in the saddle, he stopped for the night at a traditional inn near Crieff. It didn't look very inviting from the outside, being nothing more than a crude hut built in the Highland manner. This consisted of a low dry stone foundation, topped by a turf wall and a timber frame to hold up the roof beams. The roof itself was made up of turf as well, laid grass side down so the soil wouldn't fall on anyone's head, and covered with thatch of heather. The floor was nothing but beaten earth and there was no chimney, just a hole in the middle of the roof to allow the smoke to escape.

Poor Starke had to be tethered outdoors as he was too tall to fit through the door of the nearby hut which served as a stable, but Brice made sure the horse had something to eat and plenty of water.

'You'll be all right, old boy, at least it doesn't look like it'll rain,' Brice whispered to the big stallion, who only snorted in reply.

Brice himself had to duck to enter the main room of the inn and immediately walked into a cloud of peat smoke. Belatedly, he remembered it was best to sit down quickly on one of the low stools that were the room's only furnishings. The 'reek' as the smoke was called in Scots tended to rise, which left only the air nearer the ground fit for breathing.

'Here ye are, guid sir, sit yersel doun. What's yer will?' The landlord was friendlier than most and indicated a vacant stool. Brice lowered himself onto it, while the 'guidwife' ignored him and continued to stir the contents of a huge cauldron, hanging over the central hearth by means of a thick iron chain coming down from the roof beams. When he tried to follow its length with his eyes, Brice saw instead several hens roosting in the rafters, which made him duck instinctively.

'Some broth would be welcome,' he said, not sure whether this was what the cauldron contained.

'Aye, it'll be ready the noo, and we've some bannocks to go wi' it.'

While they waited for the food to be served, the landlord sat next to Brice and offered him a cup of whisky, then filled one for himself. Brice had no doubt he'd have to pay for the both of them, but he didn't mind. At least the man didn't seem averse to talking to him.

'Yer health, sir.'

'Thank you, and yours,' Brice countered politely.

The man was more outspoken than most and regarded Brice with his head to one side. 'Ye look like ye're newly arrived, laddie,' he said, as if taking pity on the newcomer. 'Dinnae expect a friendly wealcome here if ye're onything tae dae wi' the 'cursed Redcoats.' He spat on the floor for emphasis, causing his wife to mutter under her breath about his dangerous behaviour. 'We'll no' ferget wha' they've put us through.'

Brice hastened to assure the man he was nothing to do with the English forces. 'My father fought at Culloden,' he confided in a low voice, in case there really were Sassenach spies around. 'Won't you please tell me more? I've been abroad, and it's hard to separate fact from tall tales.'

The landlord nodded, perhaps swayed by the sincerity in Brice's voice and gaze. He accepted the offer to share a meal and some more whisky with Brice and moved his guest as far away from the smoking peat fire as possible once the food was served.

'Weal,' the man said, 'onyone suspected o' bein' a Jacobite suffered terribly.' The man shook his head sadly. 'Them Redcoats treated everyone the same, e'en the bairns. They took all we had an' more. Nae mercy, nae pity. It were an ootrage.'

The man proceeded to regale him with several horror stories and Brice believed him. Killian had told him the

Duke of Cumberland had been set on nothing but total humiliation. The threat to the crown had to be dealt with once and for all, the country and its people completely broken. It looked to Brice as if the hated man had succeeded only too well, apart from the odd spark of defiance.

He couldn't help but wonder what he'd find at Rosyth House. Although it hadn't been sacked because no Jacobite connection could be proven, were the people there as dejected as the ones he'd met so far? He hoped not, for his sake and theirs. It would make his task that much harder.

Chapter Four

'So what's this I hear about you attacking Mr Seton with a broom, sister dear?'

This question and the accompanying giggle almost made Marsaili miss her step and she had to put out a hand to steady herself against the thick stone wall of the stairwell. She was on her way up to Ailsa's quarters for an afternoon session of sewing and hadn't heard anyone come up behind her.

'Kirsty, you gave me such a fright! And you shouldn't call me sister, you know.'

'Of course I should. It's the truth and everyone knows it.' Kirsty grinned, unrepentant.

Marsaili didn't reply. Kirsty was right in a way, but they were only half-sisters and Marsaili felt she had no claim to kinship really. Kirsty's father Farquhar Kinross had seduced Janet Buchanan, his wife's maidservant, and Marsaili was the result. She didn't find this out until she'd turned fourteen, however, and her mother had died. Although Janet had been forced to stand on the stool of repentance in the kirk for three Sundays in a row, she'd always refused to reveal the name of her child's father.

Farquhar was long dead by then as well, but the local minister had taken it upon himself to inform the widow, Ailsa. Apparently he'd sworn that Farquhar admitted fathering the child just before he left Rosyth for the last time to go abroad, and he'd even signed a paper to this effect.

'He wanted to make sure that if the bairn was a boy, he'd be taken in by the old laird,' the minister explained. Marsaili had been given to understand her father had been obsessed with siring a son. She thought to herself it was just as well he never returned from his journey to find he had yet another daughter.

She had an older half-sister too, Flora, who spent most of her time looking after Ailsa, and Marsaili knew there had been a third, younger daughter, Mairie, who'd died.

Marsaili shook her head at Kirsty. 'They might know it, but they're also well aware that I was born out of wedlock. And kin or not, you're as powerless as I am against Seton, so please don't add to your mother's worries by mentioning the incident with the broom to her. If he chooses to complain about it, fine, but I have a feeling he'd rather keep the altercation to himself.'

Kirsty frowned. 'Very well, but you must promise to come to me for help if he attempts to go too far. I heard what he tried to do to Liath and he had no right. He may think he's the one running things around here, but even he would have to obey a direct order from my mother. I'm fairly sure I could persuade her to issue one should the need arise.'

Marsaili wasn't convinced, but nodded all the same. As the two of them entered the bedchamber cum sitting room in the north tower, occupied by the Kinross ladies, Marsaili was struck anew by the amazing kindness and forbearance Ailsa had shown. Not only had she accepted her husband's infidelity with equanimity, but she'd taken the orphaned Marsaili in, fed and clothed her, and made sure she received some education. She would have done more, had Marsaili allowed it, but the latter felt that being treated as a daughter of the house was too much. Although Ailsa meant well, it would have felt like taking charity, which was something Marsaili could never contemplate.

'I'd rather you give me a position of some sort, if possible, so I can work for my keep,' she'd told Ailsa, which was how she came to be the housekeeper, responsible for the day to day running of the household. This suited them both, since Ailsa could never be bothered with such matters and neither of her daughters wanted to take on these tasks. Flora was too busy looking after her mother and Kirsty – well, she was hoping to get married, although as yet there had been no announcement.

'Ah, there you are girls. Come in, come in. We've only just started.' Ailsa was sitting at a round table by the window, together with Flora, working on a huge quilt which was spread out between them. It was made up of dozens of tiny squares of material, all scraps left over from other projects or cut up old garments. Since there was no money with which to buy new lengths of silk, they'd had to make do with whatever they could find. To Marsaili's mind, this in no way detracted from the beauty of the quilt, which was a piece of art in itself. The ladies were now in the process of embellishing it even further by adding embroidery to some of the squares. They had decided on a theme of flowers, since this allowed for individuality yet a uniform appearance.

She and Kirsty took their places at the table and picked up one side each, continuing with the motifs they'd been working on the previous day. Marsaili was creating a sprig of heather, the purple and lilac hues vivid against the pale cream square she'd chosen to embroider on. Kirsty had just started on a rose, the bright yellow of it making another splash of colour on her side of the quilt.

'How are you today, madam?' Marsaili asked the older woman politely. Ailsa had asked her to call her by her name, but somehow it didn't feel right.

'I'm very well, thank you, my dear. It's such a lovely, sunny day. How can one not be in good spirits?'

'Indeed.' Marsaili smiled, but thought to herself that it would have done Ailsa the world of good to actually go outside and enjoy the sunshine and fresh air, rather than stay cooped up in her tower. Unlike Seton, Marsaili didn't think Ailsa was 'away with the fairies', as he'd put it, but she was frail and nervous.

Small and birdlike, she looked as though she'd blow away in a strong wind. Her face was remarkably unlined for a woman of her age and the ash blonde hair mixed with grey suited her, but some exercise might have put roses in her pale cheeks. Marsaili had a feeling Ailsa would be pretty with a bit of colour, but she refused even to come downstairs for meals.

'How is your lovely hound? I thought I heard barking earlier?'

Ailsa's remark seemed innocuous, but Marsaili sometimes wondered if the woman knew more about what was going on at Rosyth House than she let on. Her pale blue gaze gave nothing away, however, so Marsaili replied with the lie she thought was required.

'Fine, thank you. He was probably just answering some of the other dogs. You know how they love to make a racket.'

Ailsa smiled. 'Yes, of course. And has he acted as a deterrent to the determined suitor you were telling me about?'

Marsaili had concocted a story about a love-sick groom, who she claimed was pestering her, in order to obtain the necessary consent to keep Liath with her at all times. Ailsa had been in favour of this and had given her permission.

'So far, thank you. Liath is a wonderful guard dog.'

Ailsa nodded. 'Good, I'm glad.' Then, as if her mind flitted from one thing to another, she changed the subject and began to talk about some gossip she'd heard from Flora. Marsaili breathed a sigh of relief. She had sensed many times that Ailsa was afraid of Seton, and after the woman's many kindnesses to her, the last thing she wanted was to force her into a confrontation with the man.

Stabbing her needle into the material with unwarranted viciousness, she swore she'd handle him herself. She just didn't know how yet.

'Wishin' ye guid weather,' the landlord called after Brice as he left the inn the following morning, feeling slightly bleary. Although the heather mattress he'd slept on was comfortable enough, the little inn hadn't afforded much in the way of privacy and someone's snores had kept him awake a good part of the night.

'Thank you.' He knew this strange farewell was a legacy from the old days when a man's safety depended on the weather as he travelled through the Highlands, and it made him smile.

He was soon riding along the military road built by the English General Wade in the 1730s. It was at least five yards wide, a lot better than most Highland tracks and properly constructed of stone and gravel. It headed north-west towards Glenalmond and here he'd reached the edge of the Highlands proper. The heather-covered hillsides, steeper than any he'd passed the day before, were a lovely sight to behold. Rich blossom in shades of mauve, lilac and purple spread out before him, and he breathed in their fresh scent. The tops of the hills were bare rock, which for large parts of the year would be covered in snow, but were now dark and imposing.

In the valley, the River Almond wended its way into the distance like a long glittering snake. At one point, a beautiful waterfall made its way down to join it and Brice stopped for a while to admire it. The sun was beating down, but flurries of wind danced around, keeping him cool. It was quite simply glorious.

'Are you thirsty, Starke?' He guided the horse towards the edge of the fast-flowing burn and they both drank their fill.

Once through the long glen, Brice didn't continue north to Aberfeldy. Instead he turned left onto a fairly wide, but rough, track constructed by his great-grandfather Kenelm. The old man had lived to a good age and as he'd wanted to travel in some comfort, he'd seen to it the journey to Rosyth could be done by carriage if need be.

'Just as well for us, eh?' Brice patted the neck of his horse and received the usual snort in reply. 'You're too big and heavy for the normal Highland paths.' He reflected that he probably shouldn't have brought the horse at all, but he'd hated the idea of leaving him behind again when he'd only just come back.

Brice had fond memories of Rosyth House and now he was closer, excitement built inside him. Would it look the same? And how would he feel about it now he was older? He had his answer when he rounded the final hill and saw the strath – the wide, shallow valley – which surrounded the small Loch Rosyth. The big house was still intact. However, there were clear signs of neglect and dilapidation even from a distance.

It was situated right next to the loch, dominating a peninsula that jutted out as if pointing towards a small island in the middle of the water. It was more like a keep of many towers than an ordinary manor house. Built of grey stone hewn from the surrounding hills, it looked forbidding, but Brice knew the interior was comfortable and welcoming. *At least, it used to be, but perhaps things have changed?* The loch's surface was almost still today, reflecting the summer sky and the surrounding hills perfectly. Brice felt an unexpected jolt of pride as he gazed down at his new domain – as far as the eye could see was Rosyth land and it belonged to him now.

'I can't quite take it in, Starke,' he muttered. It felt slightly unreal.

He approached down a half-mile-long dirt road flanked by the twenty-odd rounded huts which made up Rosyth township. They had always been poorly constructed, but Brice couldn't remember ever seeing them in such a dismal state before. They were all smaller versions of the inn he'd stayed at, made of timber, turf and stones, with turf- or heather-thatched roofs. From a distance, they blended in with the surroundings, except for the fact that there were little wisps of smoke escaping through the roofs.

It looked as though most had been patched and mended as best the owner could manage, although some had gaping holes. There was no regularity in the way they'd been set out, and what passed for gardens, divided by dry-stone walls, were all different sizes. Brice could see most contained patches of kale and a few other vegetables, but it didn't seem to be enough to feed one person, let alone a family of ten or more, which was what some of the huts contained. He'd spent enough time in them as a child to remember how crowded they could be.

As he passed, he saw old men and women sitting in doorways, their faces dark and wrinkled, with skin like smoked herrings and eyes which could no longer see clearly, if at all. This was the legacy of years living round a peat fire, he knew. They gazed at him impassively, although he caught the occasional fearful glance. Children played in the dirt of the road, but even they seemed subdued. The only interest he received came from a group of girls walking along carrying farm implements. They were pretty, in a rough sort of way, but dirty and poorly dressed with bare feet.

'Good afternoon.' Brice returned their sidelong glances with a bow, which sent them giggling into the nearest hut without replying to his greeting.

The door of every cottage was flanked by a stack of turf on one side and a midden on the other. The noxious odour of these made Brice hold his breath as he passed. A few huts had a lean-to at the back to shelter a cow or a goat, but most had a byre incorporated into one end of the house, divided from the human living quarters by a wattle wall. There was also a corn-drying kiln and a few barns which presumably contained the community's grain and hay stores. These were in a sorry state as well.

Brice shook his head. 'This isn't how I remember it,' he murmured, as Starke shied away from a dog that looked as though it hadn't been fed in years.

Nearer the main house, there were a couple of slightly larger and more substantial dwellings, both built entirely of stone, apart from the roof. One was clearly the smithy, since the sounds of hammering on metal carried along the road. It was also distinctive because it had a slate roof, rather than thatch, in order to reduce the risk of fire. The other, Brice recalled, had traditionally always belonged to the estate manager. He assumed it still did, which meant it was where Colin Seton lived. The thought made him wonder again what sort of man he'd be dealing with. Hopefully he would soon find out.

Entering the courtyard of Rosyth House, he dismounted and looked about for someone to take his horse. Although several lads loitered in a corner, no one stepped forward or even greeted him. A swarthy, middle-aged man was the only one who cast him more than one glance and eventually he ambled forward, his steps slow and reluctant.

'Good day to you,' he said, the words coming out in a grudging fashion as if he didn't really want to utter them. There was no welcome in his dark hazel eyes.

Brice nodded. 'Good afternoon, my name is Aaron. I'm travelling north and wondered if I could have a bed for the night, please? The inns around here aren't exactly what you would call comfortable as I found to my cost last night.' He lessened the sting of his criticism with a smile, so as not to give offence, but the swarthy man didn't smile back or acknowledge the comment either way. Brice added, 'And my father knows the Kinross family so he said to stop by here.'

'I'll inform the housekeeper,' was all the man said. 'The laird isn't at home and the mistress is indisposed.' He turned to shout in Gaelic at one of the loitering youths. 'Ewan, take the man's horse. You know what to do.'

A surly boy came forward and led Starke away without much enthusiasm. Brice decided he'd better go and check on the horse himself later, but for now he followed the taciturn man into the house.

A steep outside staircase led up to the main door, which in turn opened directly onto the great hall, situated on the first floor. Brice had spent many an evening in there, playing with his siblings and second cousins, and was pleased to be taken to this room first. He remembered it as vast, but warm and welcoming. That plainly wasn't the case now.

The huge fireplace halfway along one wall had cobwebs hanging in the corners and a pile of old ash littered the hearth. All the wall hangings were faded, their once vibrant colours washed out and drab, not to mention dirty, and all the cushions on the furnishings were in the same sorry state. A few rugs were scattered over the stone-flagged floor, but nowhere near as many as Brice recalled and most of them looked threadbare and in need of replacing.

He frowned. His father was right, Rosyth House was not being looked after.

'If you'd wait here, I'll send for someone,' the swarthy man said, indicating one of the chairs by the hearth.

'Thank you, Mr …?'

'Seton.'

'Seton, that's very kind.'

A curt nod was the only reply Brice received as Seton turned on his heel and left.

Brice sat down. 'Well, this should be interesting …'

Marsaili hated washing days with a vengeance. Not because the work was hard and mind-numbingly boring, but for the reason that most of the male inhabitants of Rosyth House always seemed to find some pretext for coming to watch.

She wasn't stupid, she could see why. With their skirts hiked up and their bare legs on display, she and the other girls were no doubt an enticing sight as they stood in the tubs up to their knees in washing, trampling it clean. Not to mention the way the steam from the hot water made their other garments cling to them and the rhythmic trudging jiggled certain parts of their anatomy. It was a wonder the men's eyes didn't grow stalks, Marsaili thought crossly.

She was now struggling across the back courtyard of Rosyth House with two heavy pails of hot water to add to yet another batch of dirty linen. Her arm and back muscles strained in an effort not to spill any. The day was warm and sultry, but the soft air didn't soothe her raw knuckles. She tried to ignore the pain. The washing was nowhere near finished and sore hands were par for the course. She was used to it. And since Seton claimed there wasn't enough money to pay more servants, Marsaili had no choice but to help out.

At the back of Rosyth House's thick-walled towers, lower buildings had been added which contained stables and all manner of store-rooms. The washing didn't take place indoors, however, but close to the edge of the loch, since it was more convenient for rinsing. Six young women, including Marsaili, shared three large tubs between them, singing as they worked. Marsaili headed for the nearest one to add the hot water, the steam from which was making her tawny hair curl even more than it usually did.

'Now there's a pretty sight and no mistake.'

Marsaili turned too quickly and swore under her breath as some of the water sloshed out of the buckets. She glared at Seton, but didn't dignify his remark with an answer. His attentions were becoming more marked by the day now, his whispered comments more pointed, but she knew as long as she kept out of his way after dark, he couldn't hurt her. She wished he'd tire of this game and find someone else to hound, but it didn't seem likely.

She put the pails down and stared him in the eye. 'Was there something you wanted, Mr Seton?'

'Oh, aye,' he said slowly, his gaze taking in every last part of her dishevelled appearance in the disconcerting fashion that made her skin crawl. Marsaili suppressed a shiver and was grateful she'd lowered her skirts for the moment.

'I'm in the middle of washing,' she told him, 'so if you wouldn't mind coming to the point? I can't stand around here all day. The water's getting cold.'

His mouth tightened. 'Hoity-toity,' he said, then added, 'We have a visitor. A Mr Aaron. You'll need to find him somewhere to sleep and organise a meal. Nothing fancy though, if you know what I mean. Remember what I said last time someone stopped here.'

Marsaili frowned. 'Another Sassenach, come to check on us?' she asked. 'Aren't they satisfied yet? You've shown them enough of those letters from the laird in Sweden.'

Seton shrugged. 'Most likely, yes. Some of our hospitality should see him on his way right quickly though. We don't want the likes of him hanging around any longer than he has to.'

'Very well, I'll see to it in a minute. Will you put him in the great hall?'

'Already have. He's waiting.'

'Fine.' She turned her back on Seton and continued to the loch.

'I'm sorry, but I'll have to leave you to it for now,' she told the other women working there. 'Seems we have a visitor. I'll be back as soon as I can.'

She hurried back towards the house and into the kitchen. It was large, with a brick floor, and even warmer than the steam from the tubs. Cauldrons of water were being heated for the laundry in a never-ending stream and the cook, Greine Murray, looked hot and frazzled.

'You've only just been in here. This won't boil for a wee while yet,' Greine said.

'I know, I haven't come for more water. Apparently we have a visitor. Are there any of those old barley bannocks left?'

Greine nodded towards the larder. 'Aye, there'll be some in there. And the wine that's turned sour.' The cook smiled wryly. 'Another Sassenach visitor, eh? Don't fash, I'll fetch 'em and prepare a tray while you go and greet the guest.'

Marsaili returned the smile. 'Thank you. The sooner he leaves, the better. But not the wine, give him watered-down ale instead.'

Chapter Five

After giving orders for a small bedchamber to be readied for their guest, Marsaili made her way to the great hall. She hadn't exactly rushed, but although she knew it was rude to keep the guest waiting, it was part of the instructions Seton had given some time ago.

'Any strangers turning up out of the blue are bound to be Redcoats in disguise, trying to prove we're all rabid Jacobites,' he'd said. 'They deserve no consideration and none of the usual hospitality. Let's hope they take the hint and don't return.'

Marsaili privately considered Seton overly cautious, even verging on paranoid, but kept her thoughts to herself. Culloden and its aftermath were in the past now and she doubted the English were interested in Rosyth House any longer. Still, there was barely enough food to feed the current inhabitants, let alone anyone else, so the fewer guests that returned, the better.

She entered the great hall without knocking and walked over to the two high-backed chairs in front of the huge fireplace. All she could see of the visitor was a pair of very long muscular legs encased in travel-stained breeches and dusty riding boots. She opened her mouth to announce her presence, but didn't get a chance since the visitor turned to look at her and spoke first, his clear, unaccented English proclaiming him a Sassenach of the worst kind – gentry.

'Ah, I thought I'd been forgotten,' he said. 'Whatever happened to the famed Highland hospitality I've heard so much about? A man could die of thirst here, I should think.'

Marsaili realised he must believe her to be a maid servant, which was no wonder since she was still wearing the old clothes she used on washing days. She drew herself up straight and found her tongue. 'I'm the housekeeper here and I apologise for keeping you waiting. I was detained, but I was under the impression you were being looked after.'

'Haven't been offered so much as a drop of water.' The man stood up and put his head to one side to regard her critically. 'You're the housekeeper? You look far too young, if you don't mind me saying so.' His piercing gaze travelled the length of her from head to toe, a scowl marring his brow.

Marsaili felt her cheeks flame. Men had stared at her since her early teens and she hated it. It made her feel very uncomfortable. Although she knew she should have been pleased that they found her beautiful and desirable, it had been nothing but a source of annoyance. This man was assessing her too, but he didn't seem impressed with her looks. On the contrary, he continued to frown as if he found her wanting, which baffled her. It wasn't the reaction she usually got. Either way, she knew there wasn't a thing she could do about it except glare at him. He stared right back, his eyes startlingly blue.

Disconcerted, but determined to stand her ground, she deliberately looked him over in the same way. Unfortunately, she found nothing to criticise, as he was quite the best-looking man she'd ever encountered. Not conventionally handsome perhaps, but unbelievably striking. On first impression, he seemed like a gilded statue, with deeply tanned skin and hair so blond it was almost pure white. Dead straight, some of it fell from a middle parting, caressing his high cheekbones, the ends just brushing a square jaw covered in at least a week's worth of golden stubble. The rest was tied back in a somewhat messy tail which hung down past his shoulder blades. A strong nose, straight and sharp with a slight upwards tilt at the end, a firm but full mouth and a determined chin added character and made for an arresting face.

Marsaili's gaze moved down to take in broad shoulders dressed in nothing but a linen shirt, with the sleeves pushed up to show sun-kissed, well-muscled arms. The man wore no waistcoat or neckcloth and had left the shirt open at the throat so she glimpsed an equally tanned chest as well. It was a most unsettling sight.

'Do I pass muster?' he asked somewhat sarcastically. 'Because if so, perhaps I could have that drink now?'

The man's words brought Marsaili back to her senses and she looked away. 'I don't know what you mean, sir,' she murmured, feeling her cheeks heat up again. She couldn't believe she had done to him the same thing she was usually subjected to herself. Now she'd been just as rude, and to the only man on earth who apparently wasn't attracted to her.

She took a deep breath and wondered if she should apologise, but then, out of the corner of her eye, she suddenly caught sight of Liath. The big dog was lounging on the other side of the chair the man had been occupying, seemingly at ease with the stranger. In fact, his tongue was lolling and he looked ridiculously happy. Marsaili gasped and looked around to make sure no one else had seen him, Seton in particular.

'Liath!' she exclaimed. 'You know you're not allowed in here. Back to the kitchen with you, now.' She pointed towards the door, but although the dog sat up on hearing his name, he didn't move. Marsaili blinked. Liath had never before disobeyed a single command from her, not since he was a small puppy.

'Oh, leave him be,' the man said. 'He's been keeping me company and he's been most welcoming.' He bent to scratch the dog behind the ears, earning himself a lop-sided grin from the hound. 'So you're Liath, are you? Pleased to meet you.' Then he looked up at Marsaili. 'And might I know your name?'

Marsaili gritted her teeth and swallowed her anger. The

sooner she served this man, the faster she could escape from his presence. 'Marsaili Buchanan. If you wouldn't mind waiting for a short while longer, I'll fetch you some victuals then I'll show you to your room.'

'Thank you. Don't rush on my account, by all means.' Again the sarcasm that made Marsaili want to hit him, but she knew he was right and they hadn't treated him as they ought, so she contented herself with marching off towards the kitchen.

Brice was pleasantly surprised to only be kept waiting a few minutes before the woman returned with a tray. He was less pleased with what was on it – some sort of tiny, stale-looking biscuits. At least these were accompanied by a large tankard of ale and he immediately took several gulps before realising it was watery beyond belief. He hid a grimace. If it hadn't been for the fact that riding on dusty roads made a man thirsty, he would have refused to drink this brew.

'Hmm, what a treat,' he murmured, then quickly disposed of the meagre meal without commenting further. Perhaps the house genuinely couldn't offer him anything else. From what he'd seen so far, there was no prosperity here. In fact, most of the people looked as if they could do with a square meal. This made him frown because it wasn't right. As his father had said, the Rosyth estate ought to be a prosperous one, despite the recent conflict. So why wasn't it?

He glanced at the woman – *Marsaili, odd name* – and found her waiting by the door with an impatient look on her face. Perhaps he was keeping her from her duties, but surely in that case she could have delegated the job of showing him to his room to someone else? He looked her over again, although not as blatantly this time. He'd already noted earlier there was nothing wrong with either her face or figure, although she was tall for a woman. In fact, she was most definitely a beauty, but he was so used to comparing all women to Elisabet and finding them wanting, he'd automatically done the same here.

Besides, her hair, which hung in a thick plait over one shoulder, was made up of various shades of red and gold and she looked at him as if he was some sort of repellent insect. He'd never liked red-heads and had heard they had tempers to match their colouring, which he could do without. A woman should be soft and biddable – *like Elisabet pretended to be, damn her!* – and not sharp-tongued and glaring like this one was.

He stood up. 'I'm ready,' he declared.

The housekeeper nodded. 'Then follow me, please.'

Brice and the dog both did, Liath bringing up the rear despite being told once more by the woman to go to the kitchen. 'I don't know what's got into him,' she muttered. 'He's usually very obedient.'

Brice smiled at the dog when she wasn't looking their way and received a tail-wag in return. He somehow felt the creature was trying to make up for the lack of hospitality and he was doing a great job. Much better than any of the humans in this place, Brice thought ruefully. Although perhaps the hound wasn't usually treated with kindness and revelled in the attention the newcomer had bestowed on him. Brice loved dogs and animals of every kind, and Liath had obviously sensed this immediately.

'Here we are, sir. I hope you'll be comfortable in here.'

Brice walked into the room Marsaili indicated, while she remained by the door putting a detaining hand on Liath's collar as the dog tried to sneak past her. Brice stopped after two paces, since that was about as far as he could go without bumping into the narrow bed which took up almost all the space. This wasn't so much a bedchamber as a closet, he thought to himself. And it was situated in what he'd always thought of as the servants' part of the house too. Taking a deep breath to contain his anger at what he perceived was a deliberate slight, he gritted out a curt 'Thank you.'

At least the bed had fresh sheets and a blanket without holes, and Brice spotted his saddle-bags in one corner. He turned around, deciding to goad the housekeeper just a little more. 'I'd like a bath, please, if that's not too much to ask? The roads around here are unbearably dusty this time of year.'

Marsaili, who had been on the verge of leaving, swivelled round and frowned at him. 'I'm sorry, but there's no hot water to spare – it's laundry day. Why not just jump in the loch like everyone else? It's warm enough.'

She walked off, dragging the dog with her, and Brice stared after her. What was going on here, he wondered. *Go and jump in the loch?* She may as well have told him straight out to go to hell, since it was obviously what she and everyone else was thinking.

Well, they weren't getting rid of him that easily. Now he was even more determined than before to find out what had happened to his father's once-prosperous estate and its surly inhabitants. *His* estate.

'We'll just see who has to take a running jump,' he muttered. 'I'd wager it won't be me.'

Marsaili dragged an unwilling Liath back down to the kitchen. The dog gazed at her with big eyes as if to say she was being mean in not letting him stay with the stranger. But even if she'd wanted to allow it, there would have been no room for both him and Mr Aaron in the tiny room. And if Seton caught Liath anywhere in the house except the kitchen, he'd have a fit.

A twinge of guilt pierced her and she wondered if they were making a huge mistake in treating a possible government spy with such blatant inhospitality. What if it made him even more determined to find something to charge them with? It wasn't up to her, however, she left such decisions to Seton. He was in control of estate matters and if he thought this was the best policy to adopt, then so be it. It was his problem, he'd have to deal with any bad consequences.

She went back to the laundry, but her mind wouldn't give her any peace. An image of the golden-hued Mr Aaron kept invading her brain and she felt strangely unsettled. There had been something about him that didn't ring true and she couldn't work out what it was. He'd been easy-going enough, despite his barbed comments, and she should have been grateful he didn't give her the kind of hungry looks she was used to receiving. For some reason she wasn't though. Instead she couldn't help but wonder if there was something wrong with him.

Why else had he virtually ignored her?

Faith, but he was more interested in Liath than in me! It was a sobering thought. *Well, perhaps you've grown too used to male attention,* she told herself. Not everyone was like Seton and there were a few others, like Kirsty's suitor for example, who also seemed able to resist Marsaili's charms. Still, even he looked.

She shook her head at herself. *Just forget the man. Tomorrow he'll be gone and hopefully you'll never see him again.*

Why did that thought suddenly depress her?

Brice didn't know whether the housekeeper had expected him to stay in his room for the rest of the afternoon, but it certainly wasn't his intention. He took matters into his own hands and decided to have a look around. If he was to find out what was going on, he might as well start now, he reasoned.

He gazed out of his window and was momentarily distracted by the sight of half a dozen young ladies standing in tubs full of washing with their skirts hiked up almost to their hips. Although they were some distance away from him, he had no trouble picking out the housekeeper, whose shapely limbs were working just as hard as anyone else's. He remembered this strange way of doing the laundry from his visits as a child, but he'd never before realised how enticing a tableau the women made, especially her.

He blinked and turned away, trying to erase the image from his mind. He had more important things to do than gawp at indecent females.

First of all, he needed to check on Starke. Since he was familiar with the layout of the house, he was able to use a back door and thereby avoid being seen. On reaching the stables, he found them deserted and apart from his own horse, there were only two others in there. They were small, of the type most common in the Highlands, nothing but ponies really, sturdy and strong. Usually they'd be referred to as *garrons*, Brice remembered. He and his siblings had often ridden them and he knew they were sure-footed when travelling along difficult tracks, but also used for ploughing. You'd need teams of four for that though. Brice wondered what had happened to the rest?

As he'd suspected, Starke had been left in a stall, tethered to the wall with only a token handful of hay to munch on and no water. The horse's coat was still covered in sweat and grime from the journey and it was obvious no one had even attempted to rub him down. Brice swore under his breath and untied the rope.

'Sorry, my friend,' he murmured, stroking the silky muzzle. 'I should have insisted on seeing to you myself straight away.'

He turned abruptly to go in search of a currying brush, more fresh hay and some water, and came face to face with a small boy who must have been spying on him. Possibly around nine or ten years of age, with shaggy brown hair and dark eyes, freckles on his nose and skinny legs covered in bruises and dirt, he looked like a proper urchin. His eyes opened wide in alarm when he realised he'd been rumbled. Before he had time to scarper, Brice reached out a hand and grabbed the back of his shirt.

'Not so fast, young man,' he said. 'I have need of your services.'

The boy was clever enough not to struggle. Instead he lowered his gaze and tried his best to look apologetic. He spread his hands and said in Gaelic, 'I'm sorry, but I don't understand.'

Brice smiled and replied in the same language, 'Oh, don't you? That's a shame. I could really do with some help.'

Startled, the boy blinked at him. 'You speak the Gaelic? I thought Mr Seton said you were a –' There he stopped short, obviously realising he probably shouldn't have mentioned anything about Mr Seton or his theories.

'A what? Sassenach?'

The boy shook his head and mumbled something that sounded like 'spy' and Brice chuckled. 'He may be right, but not in the way he thinks. Now are you going to help me or not? My horse needs seeing to and it will be faster with your assistance. He's waited long enough, poor beast.' Without waiting for the boy's assent, he walked along the stalls until he came to the tack room, where he quickly found the implements he needed. As he turned to go back to Starke, he found the boy right behind him looking unsure.

'I, uhm, I'm not supposed to. Mr Seton said not to touch your horse.'

'Well, I tell you what, if you take this curry brush and use it you're not actually touching the animal, just the brush. What do you think?' He grinned at the boy and watched as an answering smile spread across the tiny features when he understood the subterfuge. The urchin nodded and didn't waste any more time.

'What's your name?' Brice asked as they worked together companionably. It was clear the boy had done this kind of work before, although he was still so short he had to stand on an upturned food bucket to reach higher than halfway up the horse's side.

'Archie.'

'Pleased to meet you, Archie. I'm Mr Aaron at the moment.'

A startled Archie reverted to Scots for a moment, thus proving that he'd understood Brice well enough earlier. 'Just the noo?' Puzzled brown eyes stared at Brice, who smiled again and winked.

'I'm a spy, remember? We don't give our real names.'

'Oh, o' course.' Another conspiratorial grin, but then Archie grew serious. 'Ye woan tell Mr Seton though, will yer? Aboot me helpin', I mean.'

'No, but you'll have to promise to keep a secret in return.'

'Aye, onythin'.'

'I don't want anyone here to know that I speak Gaelic, at least not yet, so don't say anything about that. Agreed?'

'Absolutely. I swear on the edge o' my dirk.' The boy produced a tiny knife from his pocket which was hardly worthy of the name dirk, and laid his hand on the rusty blade.

'Me too.' Brice put his own hand next to Archie's on the knife's edge. He knew that to a Highlander, swearing something on your dirk was the most solemn oath you could take and was more binding than any other. It amused him that someone so young should invoke this, but he wouldn't dream of laughing out loud at the boy. To Archie, it was serious and Brice had a feeling he was going to need every ally he could find in this place, of whatever age and size.

The boy was a good beginning.

Chapter Six

During the summer before his tenth birthday, Brice had been initiated into a Kinross family secret – the fact that there were hidden doorways and passages built into the thick walls of Rosyth House. His father had taken him on a tour one evening after everyone else went to bed and Brice still remembered the excitement of that night.

'You're old enough to be trusted now,' Killian told him, 'but you must swear never to reveal this to a living soul unless you have to. One day, it could save your life or those of the people you love. But not if it's common knowledge. Understand me?'

'Yes, Father.'

'I'll tell Jamie too when he's old enough, but no one else. It's a secret only for boys as long as there's an heir to carry on the name, although when you marry, you may tell your wife too.'

Having made his way back into the house unseen, Brice decided to make use of the hidden passages to try and glean some more information. Luck was with him and he found old Lord Rosyth's book room, which was at the back of the house, deserted. In one corner, he pushed his finger into a small hole in the wainscoting and opened a secret door. A rush of stale air hit him, but he quickly stepped inside and closed the panel behind him.

I remembered correctly, he thought, although he'd never really doubted it. Killian had made him memorise every hidden door and the layout of the tunnels behind in minute detail. They'd spent hours criss-crossing the house until he could have done it blindfolded and he'd been exhausted by the time he fell into bed.

He made his way along the narrow space which seemed a lot smaller now he was an adult. Every so often he stopped to listen. There were tiny holes drilled through the walls at intervals in order to provide some air and also the chance to hear your enemies. On the side facing the outer walls of the house, there were grilles which gave some light. Not much, but enough for the tunnels to be navigated without the use of a torch if need be.

He was walking parallel to a corridor that led from the great hall to the kitchen stairs at the back of the house when he heard familiar voices.

'Marsaili, a word if you please.' Colin Seton, Brice thought. There could be no mistaking those abrupt tones although the man was now speaking Gaelic rather than English.

'Yes?'

'Did you tell the Sassenach to stay in his room? We don't want him wandering about, looking for the family heirlooms or some such fool's errand.'

'He'd be wasting his time if he did, wouldn't he. I didn't exactly order him not to wander around, but last I saw, he was sitting on his bed so I'm assuming he'll have a nap before supper.'

'Never assume anything with those whoresons. They can't be trusted.'

The vehemence in the man's voice startled Brice. He knew the English weren't well liked, but this seemed personal somehow.

'Really, I don't think one man is a danger to any of us. He seemed harmless enough.'

'Much you know about it. Well, serve him supper in his room. I'll be damned if I'll entertain him all evening.'

'As you wish.'

Seton's voice changed timbre abruptly and he murmured,

'Actually, I'd rather spend time with you. I hope you've given some thought to what I said?'

Brice thought he heard a sharp intake of breath and assumed Seton was taking liberties with the housekeeper. For some reason that bothered him, but he knew it was none of his business. It sounded as though they had an understanding, and she was obviously perfectly willing to help the man in treating their guests badly. It was clear the two were in agreement about that. Perhaps they were colluding in other ways too? Brice pitied the woman's husband.

'Mr Seton –' she protested, belated guilt perhaps rearing its head.

'Call me Colin, when we're alone.'

Brice heard the proprietary note in the man's voice and also what sounded like gloating. It was understandable, he supposed. Marsaili was a price worth winning, if you liked tall statuesque women with lissom legs and – He pulled his thoughts up short, but couldn't blame Seton for wanting her.

Before either of them could say anything else, however, footsteps approached from the direction of the kitchen below and someone called out, 'Marsaili? Are ye there? Ye're wanted oot back.'

'I'm coming.'

She disappeared quickly, leaving Seton to amble off at a slower pace in the other direction. Brice remained where he was for a while mulling over this exchange. It was plain there was some sort of conspiracy going on with regard to visitors, but quite what they hoped to gain by it he didn't know.

'Interesting though,' Brice muttered. Seton's observations regarding the English made him realise he'd have to tread very warily indeed. The man was apparently a loose cannon and quite possibly unhinged in certain respects. Not to mention full of hatred.

A dangerous combination.

Marsaili personally brought Mr Aaron's meagre supper on a tray to his room. It consisted of a couple of stale bannocks and some mutton broth, together with a glass of the vinegary wine Greine had mentioned earlier. The broth was very watery and had barely any bits of meat in it, only some overcooked kale. She saw the surprise and anger in his face when he glanced at this offering and she couldn't blame him. He was obviously a gentleman of some means and entitled to better treatment.

But he was also, most likely, the enemy.

'I'm sorry to be serving you here,' she told him, 'but the Mistress is unwell so she cannot receive you. I'm sure you'd rather not eat with the servants.'

Mr Aaron didn't reply at first, just gave her one of his penetrating looks which made her want to squirm like a maggot. She turned and headed for the door, but stopped when he suddenly shot a question at her.

'So do I gather the crops haven't been too good in recent years around here?'

Marsaili raised her eyebrows at him, wondering why he was suddenly making small talk about their harvests. And to her, of all people. 'The crops? No, as far as I know they've been fine for the last two years. We had a scarce year in '51, but since then we've done all right.'

'I see.' He glanced at his food and she immediately took his meaning. He was asking why she was serving him such a paltry meal if there were no shortages. She felt her cheeks heat up and cursed herself for not seeing it coming.

'You should discuss such matters with Mr Seton,' she said tartly. 'As factor, that's his domain. Now if there's nothing else I can do for you, I have duties to attend to.'

A slow smile began to tug at the corners of his mouth while his blue eyes sparkled with sudden amusement. 'I didn't realise you were offering anything other than food,' he commented.

Marsaili was so distracted by that smile she didn't register his words at first. She felt the full force of it wash over her. For some unknown reason it was making her limbs weak and her heart beat faster, but then she realised what he'd said and gasped.

'How dare you?' she spluttered. 'I'll have you know I'm a respectable woman.'

His smile widened. 'Those are usually the best.'

Marsaili wasn't sure if he was being deliberately provocative or just teasing, since he was still smiling. Either way, she was determined not to let him rile her. She didn't know what it was about this man that stirred her up so, but she mustn't let him affect her equanimity. Under cover of her apron she clenched her fists tightly, then headed for the door. There was no point dignifying his comments with an answer. Her silence would speak volumes more.

As she closed the door with a distinct snap, she heard his laughter, low and rich. It rumbled through her stomach, unsettling her even further, but she ignored the feeling and ran down the stairs. Someone else could serve him his breakfast, she'd had enough.

Brice stared after the fiery housekeeper for a moment, before picking up the horn spoon to make a start on his supper. He had enjoyed teasing her and although she probably wasn't the one responsible for the ill treatment he'd received so far, she wasn't helping either. *She deserved a little shock*, he told himself.

When he'd first seen her that afternoon, she had been dishevelled and in working clothes, presumably because of helping with the laundry. This evening she had dressed with more care in a skirt and bodice which, although threadbare and not of the latest fashion, showed off her perfect figure and flawless skin. Not to mention a pair of very fine green eyes, outlined with dark lashes. He would have had to be made of stone not to be affected by the sight of her, red hair or not.

He wasn't interested in finding a wife any longer, but that didn't mean he intended to live like a monk. He'd spent enough time in his brother's company to know there were plenty of women who were willing to offer more than flirtatious glances. And he'd been perfectly serious when he told Marsaili the so-called respectable ladies were the best. They were usually starved of real love-making by husbands who only used them as breeding cows. A man who knew how to pleasure them could reap the benefits without risk of being leg-shackled. As long as said husband didn't find out, of course.

Brice didn't want to think about his brother, but had to admit he was indebted to Jamie when it came to such matters. And since he'd found out about Elisabet's betrayal, he'd decided to make good use of this knowledge. He should have listened to Jamie on that score as well – women were only there for temporary enjoyment. They were all treacherous bitches, especially the beautiful ones.

He swallowed down a gristly lump of mutton and tried not to choke on it or the feelings of anger that welled up inside him yet again. *They can never hurt me now*, he thought savagely. *I won't let them.*

Use the ladies who were willing, but don't get caught, that would be his motto from now on.

As Mr Aaron rode out of the gates and down through the township, Seton stared after him for as long as he was visible, then spat into the dust.

'Good riddance,' he muttered and headed back towards the house. His son Iain had been hovering behind him, and fell into step beside him. In his mid-twenties, the boy was slightly taller than his father, but not by much. *Thank goodness he doesn't tower over me like that Englishman*, Seton thought. *That would be unbearable.* He added, 'I'm getting tired of these Sassenach's snooping around. They've nothing to find here.'

'Are you sure he was English?' Iain asked. 'I heard him put on quite a creditable Scots accent.'

Seton sneered. 'Not creditable enough. You could hear quite clearly he wasn't from around here. No, I'm sure.'

Mr Aaron had set his teeth on edge. The man had eyes that seemed to see all too much and Seton mistrusted the easy charm and pretended good humour. These were all the tricks of someone who was after something.

'I wonder why he came,' Iain said. 'I mean, no one's been here for ages now. I thought they'd lost interest in the Rosyth estate.'

Seton shrugged. 'Who knows? Mayhap they've passed some new law whereby they can annex the holdings of absent landlords. It makes no difference to us though, we'll soon have our own back. Then the Kinross family can fend for themselves.'

Iain frowned at this comment. 'You're not still hoping the government will give us back Bailliebroch, are you? It's not going to happen.'

'I know that well enough. Naturally I'd have preferred to be given it for nothing, but we'll soon be able to buy it back and I doubt they'll refuse to take our money.'

'*Our* money?' Iain raised an eyebrow at his father.

As Iain knew, Seton had been siphoning off profits from the Rosyth estate for years now. Very soon he'd have enough to buy back his own family's lands. The lands his idiot older brother had gone and lost because he didn't have the foresight to sign them over to someone who wasn't a known Jacobite, the way the Rosyth laird had done. *Damn him!* If the dolt hadn't fled to France, Seton would have wrung his scrawny neck himself.

No, Bailliebroch was his by right, especially now Duncan had died without an heir. He *would* get it back, whatever it took.

'Yes, ours,' he said firmly. 'The Rosyth laird doesn't need it. What does he care for this place? Hasn't set foot on Scottish soil for years and isn't likely to either. That's played right into our hands and besides, I've been busy garnering support from a certain quarter. When the time comes, which it will soon, there will be no objection to us buying Bailliebroch.'

Iain frowned again. 'I hope you know what you're doing. Those Redcoats can't be trusted, you've said so yourself.'

'With the right incentive, they can. Gold is a powerful motivator. Either way, we don't need the likes of him,' he nodded in the direction Mr Aaron had gone, 'sticking his nose in where it's not wanted.'

'Well, I doubt he'll come back,' Iain said with a grin. 'After the way he was treated here, he'd be a fool to.'

'Amen to that. I sincerely hope I never set eyes on him again.'

Marsaili also breathed a sigh of relief when the stranger left. After stripping the bed he'd used – *more washing, blast it!* – and straightening the covers, she retreated to the kitchen. There Greine was in a slightly better mood since she was allowed to get on with her normal duties, rather than heating endless cauldrons of water.

'Did our guest enjoy his parritch?' she asked with a grin. 'I seem to have accidentally spilled a mite too much salt into it.'

Marsaili laughed, but she regretted that such measures were necessary. It seemed cruel, but she remembered what the Redcoats had done to a lot of the Highlanders in the not so distant past and hardened her heart. 'I've no idea. I sent Isobel up with the tray and she's so shy she probably dumped it next to him and fled.'

Kirsty came down the back stairs and peeked round the door frame. 'Is it safe for us to come out now?' she asked, her pale blue eyes searching the room.

Marsaili smiled. 'Yes, all clear. The ogre is gone.'

'Thank goodness for that. I hate skulking upstairs all day long. I don't know how Flora puts up with Mother's endless chatter. I mean, she doesn't actually say anything. She has nothing to talk about since she never goes anywhere.'

Kirsty sat down at the big, scrubbed pine table in the centre of the kitchen. She picked up a paring knife and began to help Marsaili peel onions. 'So was he really that bad then, the visitor? I heard tell he was rather good-looking.' She threw a twinkling glance in Marsaili's direction.

'If you like brash, self-centred men, certainly.' Marsaili tried her best to adopt a nonchalant expression. If she let on that Mr Aaron had rattled her in more ways than one, she'd never hear the end of it. Kirsty was a determined match-maker who wanted everyone to be as in love as she was herself. She could never understand Marsaili's reluctance to even consider the candidates she promoted.

'It sounds like a perfect match for you,' Kirsty teased.

'Kirsty,' Marsaili warned. 'I've told you before, I'm not interested.'

'Oh, come now, just because your mother was ill-treated by your step-father doesn't mean all husbands are like him. And with your looks, I'm sure you could find one you can wrap around your little finger.'

Marsaili gave her a scornful look. 'What would be the use of such a weakling? If that's what Iain's letting you do, he's not half the man I took him for.'

'Oh, there are ways and means.' Kirsty smiled smugly. 'Besides, it's give and take, you know.'

'Hmm, well, it's not for me.'

She made her voice sound firm, but even so an image of Mr Aaron's smiling features rose up in her mind's eye.

Thank goodness he was gone.

Chapter Seven

Brice headed north at first, since that was the direction he'd said he was going in, but once he reached Aberfeldy, he turned and rode south-east, towards Dunkeld. From there, the road led back to Stirling via Perth and although it was longer than his previous route, he wasn't delayed too much. He needed to get to Edinburgh to prepare for the next phase of his father's plan and he found he was actually looking forward to the challenge.

He still hadn't quite grasped that he was now the owner of a huge Highland estate. He wasn't even sure he wanted to be, since he'd always imagined himself living in Sweden for the rest of his life. Still, if it was his birthright, then the least he could do was to make it profitable before he sold it, he reckoned. Besides which he needed to find out what Mr Seton was up to. Or not, as the case might be ...

There had been a lot to learn in quite a short time before he left Sweden. Although Brice knew how his father's Swedish manor house, Askeberga, was run, he was well aware a Highland estate was different in many ways. For one thing, it was much larger. The agriculture was also mainly based on rearing cattle, Killian had told him, unlike their Swedish acres which produced mostly grain. But with a bit of guidance from his father, Brice was sure he could manage.

'Tell me exactly how things *should* be done, please,' Brice said. 'Then I'll be better able to see whether the factor has been negligent or not.'

Killian handed him a notebook. 'It's all in here, everything I can remember. I thought it best to write it down since I won't be there to answer your questions on the spot.'

'Thank you. So what's he like, this Colin Seton?' Brice asked.

Killian shrugged. 'I don't really know him very well. His brother Duncan owned the neighbouring estate of Bailliebroch before the forty-five, but it was confiscated and Duncan fled abroad. Colin, who didn't take any part in the uprising, was hoping it would be given to him to look after at the very least, but the authorities thought otherwise. The house was burned to the ground and the family fled before the Government forces came.'

'What, all of them? The tenants too?'

'No, the tenants were allowed to stay on. The ones who weren't suspected of being Jacobites, that is. Those were shot or taken prisoner. Then a factor from outside their clan was appointed and Colin and his family sought shelter at Rosyth. I only heard about it afterwards, but apparently my grandfather had been great friends with Duncan's father, so he appointed Colin factor at Rosyth in my absence just a few months before he died. It seemed a good solution, so I didn't challenge this decision.'

'But now you suspect him of cheating you … us?'

Killian nodded. 'Something's not right, that's for certain. I can't believe the estate would yield so little year after year.'

Brice thought for a moment. 'What about aunt Ailsa and my cousins? Surely they'd keep an eye on things?'

'Well, I've not heard from them in a while. Ailsa has always been frail and to be honest, I don't think she knows the first thing about running a household, never mind an estate. And the girls, as I said, should be married and gone by now. The eldest will be about twenty-eight if I'm not mistaken.'

'So what do you suggest? Shall I go in and take over the reins and fire Seton?'

'No, not right away. We need to be able to prove he's not

doing his job and that may not be easy. I think a little stealth is called for.' Killian had smiled and outlined his plan. 'What do you say?

Brice had smiled back – his first genuine smile for weeks – and agreed.

Thinking back now to everything he'd seen at Rosyth, Brice had no regrets about the spying mission. It had been clear just by looking out of his window that the place had been mismanaged. He'd seen dilapidation everywhere, a garden overrun with bushes and weeds and a dovecote which didn't seem to be in use. All the men had been lazing about and although he'd caught a glimpse of cattle in the pasture beyond the fields, there weren't nearly as many as there ought to be.

The women had been busy with the washing, but even from a distance he'd noticed the sheets they were hanging out were threadbare and patched. Children playing in the yard wore an odd assortment of clothes, as if they were hand-me-downs or remade from bigger garments. And the women themselves had on faded skirts and shawls with holes in.

It seemed as if Killian's worst fears were realised.

'Time for a change,' Brice muttered. 'I'd say some people need a wake-up call and no mistake.' He smiled again at the prospect and nudged Starke into a canter. 'Come on, my friend, we have work to do.'

Brice rode into the courtyard of Rosyth House almost exactly two weeks after he'd left it, but this time he wasn't alone. Two so-called *kellachs* followed in his wake, laden with all manner of goods. They were primitive carts with solid wheels, well suited to use on the rough Highland tracks, but they weren't able to take very heavy loads so

Brice had also brought six *garrons* carrying as much as they could. A small herd of black cattle, twenty goats and some sheep came next, driven by two youths he'd hired for the purpose. It was a slow procession and therefore he wasn't surprised to find Seton and what seemed like most of the house's inhabitants waiting for him. There would have been ample time for one of the villagers to run over and alert them to his arrival.

He came to a halt directly in front of the scowling man and smiled. 'Good morning, Mr Seton. I trust I find you well?'

The man's frown deepened and Brice imagined that if Seton had been a dog, his hackles would have been well and truly up by now. 'You're out travelling again? Or did you forget something?' Seton said, none too graciously, his eyes widening slightly at the sight of the cavalcade entering the courtyard in Brice's wake.

'Yes, as a matter of fact I did.' Brice widened his smile. 'I completely forgot to tell you I'm the new Lord Rosyth.' He dismounted with a graceful jump and landed only inches in front of Seton. 'Brice Aaron Kinross is my name. I believe my father might have mentioned me in his letters?'

At least twenty pairs of eyes were fixed on them and Brice could almost feel the weight of those stares as something tangible. There was a susurration of surprise from the onlookers, but he ignored everyone else and kept his gaze trained on Seton. He knew very well the others would take their cue from the factor, as they had on his previous visit.

Seton had stilled upon hearing his announcement, his mouth falling open a fraction. He stood as if paralysed by lightning for a long moment. When Brice continued to stare into the man's eyes without wavering to show that he was serious, Seton finally drew in a long breath and blinked. 'You have proof of this, I take it?' he said, his voice not quite steady. 'I'm sure you don't expect me to accept such a claim otherwise.'

Brice nodded. 'Of course.' He'd come prepared and reached into his saddle-bags to retrieve the documents Rory had procured for him. 'Here's the legal documentation.'

Seton took the papers reluctantly, as if he was afraid they'd burn him, and unrolled the official looking missives. *And metaphorically speaking, they might well singe you*, Brice thought to himself. Outwardly, he remained calm while the factor glanced at the first one. A long silence ensued, but Brice waited patiently.

'I'll have to read these more carefully,' Seton said at last and folded them again.

'Certainly.' Brice held out his hand for the papers; he wasn't about to let them out of his sight. 'You may peruse them at your leisure later. For now, I'd be grateful if someone could see to my horse and ...' He gestured to the rest of the convoy as it came to a halt behind him. 'I'll need the *kellachs* unloaded and the animals put in a pen or enclosure. All the goods can just be stowed in the great hall for now, I suppose, then we can sort out where it's going later. It's probably a task for the housekeeper, in any case.' He glanced around, but couldn't see her among the bystanders, which was a shame. He'd been looking forward to surprising her almost as much as he had Seton.

The factor handed back the documents and looked as if he wanted to protest against these orders, but although he opened his mouth, no words came out. After a moment, his expression became shuttered and he bowed, wisely choosing not to dispute Brice's authority in this instance. '*Fàilte* then, my lord,' he said, even though Brice was sure the last thing Seton wanted was to welcome him. 'I shall look forward to working with you.'

Brice noticed he said 'with', not 'for', as if they were

equals, but let it go. He'd shocked the man and it wasn't his intention to take away all his dignity in front of everyone. Until he could prove that Seton was guilty of gross mismanagement, he had to tread warily. It was even possible the factor was innocent and the blame lay elsewhere. It would be best to make sure before flinging any accusations about, Brice thought.

'Thank you,' he replied.

Seton turned to shout, 'You heard the man, move yourselves!' Then he strode off without offering any assistance.

Brice took a deep breath and smiled when he noticed Archie peeping out from behind another, taller, boy. He beckoned him forward and held out Starke's reins. 'Here, you can be in charge of my horse. You know what to do, right?'

Archie beamed at him and stroked Starke's muzzle. 'Aye, sir ... er, my lord, I dae.' He glanced over his shoulder to make sure everyone else was out of earshot before whispering, 'And right glad I am ye're back and ye're no' Mr Aaron ony mair.'

Brice laughed and ruffled the boy's hair. 'Me too, Archie. Off you go now. Get someone to help you, eh?'

He watched the boy lead the huge horse away, summoning the taller lad to join him. Brice knew they wouldn't come to any harm because Starke was the gentlest horse in Christendom and wouldn't hurt a fly, despite his size. Satisfied the animal would be looked after this time, he turned his attention to overseeing the unloading of the goods. He didn't just observe, but carried in his fair share. This resulted in some surprised looks, but he pretended not to notice. The inhabitants of Rosyth House would find out soon enough he wasn't the kind of master who'd sit still and watch others do all the work.

Just as the last of the *kellachs'* contents were being carried indoors, a woman came round the corner of the house and stopped to stare at all the commotion. She was clearly a lady, although her gown was faded and worn. Ash-blonde hair framed a heart-shaped face and Brice glimpsed pale, but sparkling blue eyes. She was shorter and plumper than the housekeeper he'd met on the previous occasion, but still attractive. When her eyes came to rest on him, she let out a shriek and came running over to throw her arms around his neck.

'Brice! By all that's holy, what are you doing here? It is you, isn't it? My, how you've grown!'

He grinned at her and returned the embrace, kissing her on the cheek before lifting her up and swinging her round like a child. She gurgled with laughter, but didn't protest.

'You've grown a bit too, Kirsty, but maybe not as much as me,' he said with a smile. 'I didn't think you'd still be here, but it's wonderful to see you.'

She was four years older than him, but even so she'd joined in with games of tag and the like when they'd been younger. The last time he'd seen her she had been sixteen and already becoming a young lady, but when no one else was looking, she'd been quite the hoyden. He put her down and was about to make some teasing remark about that, but before he had time to do so, a hand grabbed his shoulder from behind and spun him around. The next thing he knew, someone punched him on the side of the face and for a moment, he saw stars.

'What the …?' He danced out of the way in case of a second blow and blinked to clear his head. He vaguely heard Kirsty cry out, but his concentration was all on the man who'd hit him.

Shorter than Brice by half a head, he was nevertheless compact and well muscled. With his dark hair and complexion he would have been quite handsome if it hadn't been for the mammoth scowl that currently marred his features. Brice guessed the light hazel eyes would likewise be attractive if they hadn't been filled with rage. He didn't have time to speculate further, however, as the man charged him again. This time Brice was ready.

He reacted instinctively, without wondering why he was being attacked. As boys, he and Jamie often resorted to fisticuffs so he'd learned to defend himself from an early age. It had become a reflex to just fight back and ask questions later. Killian had taught them both a few tricks when their mother wasn't about – she would have been horrified, but Killian reasoned that it was part of their education. 'Of course I don't want you going round picking fights,' he'd told them, 'but if it's unavoidable, I want you to be able to give a good account of yourselves.' Brice set about doing exactly that now.

Being taller, he had a longer reach, and he was able to land quite a few blows without being hit in return. The dark-haired man, whose name he gathered was Iain since that's what Kirsty was shouting, didn't give up easily though. He seemed able to take everything Brice aimed at him, without faltering. Brice didn't want to prolong this, so went in close and allowed the man to get in a few hard punches, lulling him into false complacency. Then, when Iain let down his guard for a moment, Brice hit him hard, aiming up under the man's chin.

He saw the surprise in his opponent's gaze and quickly followed up with a couple of powerful blows to the stomach and torso. Iain stumbled and would probably have fallen if Brice hadn't reached out to grab one arm. This had gone too far and he was just about to say 'Enough!' but before he had a chance, he suddenly found himself drenched to the skin by a deluge of cold liquid that appeared out of nowhere.

Brice whirled around and came face to face with Marsaili Buchanan, the housekeeper. She was glaring at the two men and she was clutching a large pitcher which must have contained ale just a moment earlier. Its contents were running down Brice's face and clothes and he wiped some out of his eyes, clenching his jaw to contain the fury. The pungent smell of it already clung to him and he felt the stickiness oozing inside his shirt.

'What in Hades do you think you're doing, woman?' he snapped, breathing hard both from the recent fight and having to control the urge to shout at her for interfering.

'Stopping you from hurting Iain.' She stood her ground, green eyes defiant, although he could see her pulse flickering wildly at the base of her throat. He admired her spirit, but just then he was too angry to appreciate what a magnificent sight she was in full battle mode.

'It's none of your business,' he said through clenched teeth. He glanced at Iain to make sure the man wasn't going to attack him from behind, which by the look in his eyes was all too likely. He was about to tell him to back off, but was forestalled by Marsaili.

'Iain Seton, have you no sense in that small brain of yours?' she scolded. 'Fighting with the new laird on his first day here. Is that any way to behave?'

Brice noticed the resemblance to the older Seton for the first time and wondered why he hadn't seen it before. Iain was plainly his father's son, perhaps in more ways than one.

Iain turned his glare on Marsaili. 'New laird or not, he was kissing Kirsty. I'll not have anyone poaching on my territory in such a blatant fashion.'

'She's my cousin,' Brice said, understanding dawning. 'I was only greeting her.'

'Oh, aye, a likely tale,' Iain scoffed. 'Besides, she doesn't have any cousins.'

'We're second cousins really, but kin all the same.' Brice didn't see that it made any difference.

Kirsty, who'd been silent up to this point, joined the conversation. 'If you must know, we haven't seen each other for ten years. We used to be close so is it to be wondered at if we're pleased to see one another again?'

'Very close, I'm sure,' Iain muttered.

'Oh, for heaven's sake, there's no reasoning with you. I'll not argue with such a pig-headed man. Honestly, I've had enough of your jealous tantrums.' She turned her back on Iain and grabbed Brice's arm. 'Come, cousin, we'd better find you some soap and water.'

Brice allowed her to lead him towards the house, but sent a glance over his shoulder at Marsaili and Iain, still standing where they'd left them. He nodded at Marsaili, 'I want a word with you, madam, as soon as I'm clean again. Await me in the great hall, please.'

'Very well,' she replied, but her expression was still mulish.

Damned meddlesome woman, he thought. He'd been well on his way to winning his first battle here at Rosyth and if she hadn't stepped in, he would have shown everyone he wasn't to be trifled with. He was going to have enough trouble asserting his authority as it was. He didn't need her to take away a prime opportunity to show them what he was made of.

Well, he'd make sure it never happened again.

Chapter Eight

Marsaili could have kicked herself, but she'd honestly thought the big blond brute *was* going to hurt Iain badly. He was bigger and undoubtedly more powerful and he'd been fighting like he meant it. Throwing the ale had been the only thing that sprang to mind, but she could see now she should have restrained herself. No doubt she'd find herself out of a job and banished from Rosyth thanks to her over-reaction and then where would she go?

But perhaps it wouldn't have mattered. After the treatment she'd meted out to the new Lord Rosyth on his previous visit, he'd be well within his rights to dismiss her anyway. She gritted her teeth, a surge of irritation shooting through her. *What an underhanded ruse!* To pose as a stranger and trick them all like that. What manner of man did such a thing? It was beyond belief. Although to be fair, none of them had asked him any questions or given him the opportunity to explain why he'd come. They couldn't wait to be rid of him.

Her stomach muscles clenched. That had been a mistake and now they'd pay for it.

'Haughty bastard,' Iain muttered next to her, rubbing his ribs which were no doubt smarting from some of the punches he'd received. Marsaili had little sympathy for him, however.

'You have only yourself to blame,' she told him roundly when he stared at her in hangdog fashion. 'If you can't get it into your head that Kirsty only has eyes for you, you're a bigger fool than I took you for. There's no need for these theatrics every time someone so much as looks at her.'

She left him to mull this over and headed back into the house. Somehow she had to make amends to Lord Rosyth, even if it went against the grain. She simply couldn't imagine living anywhere else and she had no wish to try and find herself another position. This was where she belonged.

When Brice strode into the great hall a short time later, she was already there waiting for him. On a table by one of the armchairs she'd placed a tray with fresh ale, newly baked oatcakes and some cheese and butter. She gripped her hands together hard as he walked towards her and tried to read his expression. He was still frowning, and his blue eyes were dark and stormy. Her heart sank.

He was mad as a hornet.

'Sit down, please,' he said, surprising her. He seated himself in the chair next to the tray and indicated she should take the other one.

'But – I'm the housekeeper, your servant,' Marsaili protested, flustered by his command.

'That remains to be seen,' he murmured, making her draw in a sharp breath.

'Really, my lord, I apologise if I acted hastily, but you're so much bigger than Iain and I thought for sure you'd –'

He held up a hand to stop the flow of words and pointed at the chair. 'Please. Sit down and let me do the talking for a moment, Mrs Buchanan.'

She perched on the edge of the chair, uncomfortable with this strange request. It seemed too personal somehow, sitting next to him as if they were acquaintances instead of employer and employee. In fact, his mere presence made her unaccountably flustered again. 'It's *Miss* Buchanan. I'm not married,' she blurted out, then added the word 'yet', although she didn't know why since she had no intention of letting anyone lead her to the altar. On reflection, it might have been better to allow him to think her a widow, she thought, but it was too late now. She was very conscious of the fact that Seton wasn't the only one who considered her too young to hold a position of such responsibility. Then again, the new laird would find out her marital status soon enough.

He gave her a measuring stare. 'Really? Are the men around here blind then?'

Marsaili blinked, then felt her cheeks heat up at what must have been a compliment. He was confusing her, angry one minute and praising her looks the next. 'I ... no,' she stammered. 'But I am a very capable housekeeper and if you're worried about my respectability because I'm not married yet, then you can ask the mistress. I'm sure she'd vouch for me and –'

'*Miss* Buchanan,' he interrupted. 'That is not the issue at the moment. I am more interested in what happened outside than in your marital status. I'd like to make it absolutely clear I will not tolerate any interference from you whatsoever in future if I'm engaged in a brawl. Understood?'

'But ...'

'*None*, Miss Buchanan. It would be most unwise of you to get involved and I can assure you it wasn't my intention to seriously hurt young Mr Seton.'

'That's not what it looked like,' Marsaili muttered.

'You'll have to take my word for it.'

She nodded reluctantly, but couldn't resist adding, 'Do you intend to "brawl" often, then?'

His mouth twitched slightly as if her remark had amused him, but it was gone so fast she might have imagined it. 'No, not if I can help it,' he said. 'It will depend entirely on whether the rest of the males here are as hot-headed as young Seton.'

Marsaili had to admit he had a point. Iain had over-reacted and it wasn't the first time this had happened. She hoped it was the last. She returned her gaze to the new laird whose eyes seemed to have lost some of the martial light in them.

'Now, if you wish to keep your position as housekeeper, I'd like some straight answers to a few questions please,' he said.

Marsaili gasped. 'Of course I do, but ... what sort of questions?'

'Well, you could start by telling me in what capacity Iain Seton is employed here?'

'Wouldn't you be better off asking the factor about such things?'

'Maybe, but I'm asking you.' He steepled his fingers together and leaned his chin on them, his blue gaze fixed on her in a most disconcerting fashion. Marsaili didn't understand what game he was playing now, but decided she might as well humour him.

'Very well. Iain is one of the men in charge of the cattle, among other things.'

The new laird looked thoughtful for a moment. 'I see. Shouldn't he be up on the shieling then, instead of loitering in the courtyard attacking strangers?'

'Well, no, everyone's come down from there by now, but I suppose he ought to have been in the pasture, making sure the cattle don't get into the crops.' Marsaili felt a flush spread across her cheeks, although why she was embarrassed on Iain's behalf she had no idea. It wasn't her fault if Kirsty's intended shirked his duties to spend time with his beloved. That was for the young man's father to sort out.

'I take it he's Kirsty's husband? And yet he's merely a cattle herder. That seems a bit odd.'

'Oh, they're not married yet. She lives here with her mother, of course, and Iain has been here since his father took over as factor. He's learning how to be one as well. Factor, I mean. Perhaps that's why he was around.' She saw Brice frown.

'But Kirsty must be getting a bit long in the tooth, if you'll pardon my saying so. She's, what, twenty-six?'

Marsaili shrugged. 'Yes, but sadly they can't afford to marry. Soon, hopefully, but Iain's father controls the purse strings so they have to wait until he agrees.'

'What about Kirsty's dowry? Wasn't that enough?'

Marsaili looked at him. 'Have you forgotten, my lord? She has no dowry. This house and everything in it was your father's and now I gather it's yours. Her own father had nothing to leave her.'

For some reason this explanation seemed to make him very angry, although Marsaili had no idea why. His expression darkened as before and she saw him clenching his jaw. 'I see,' he said, his voice clipped and cold.

He was silent for a while, as if mulling this over, and Marsaili ventured to ask, 'Will that be all then, my lord? I have duties to attend to.' She sincerely hoped this was true and he wasn't intending to replace her with someone else.

He took a deep breath and fixed her with his piercing gaze again. She felt the palms of her hands grow moist and wondered if he was about to dismiss her. She drew in a deep breath and let it out slowly in order to stay calm.

'Ah, yes, your duties. How long have you been the housekeeper here, if I may ask?' he said.

She lifted her chin a fraction. 'For four years,' she said. 'And no one's complained so far,' she added for good measure. *Except Mr Seton, but he doesn't count as he complains about everything.*

'Really? Perhaps this room is never in use then,' he commented, a sarcastic note in his voice which she took exception to.

'What do you mean?'

He pointed to the fireplace. 'Cobwebs. A pile of old ash that hasn't been swept up.' He indicated the rest of the room. 'Hangings which haven't been taken outside and

72

beaten for what looks like years. Dirt everywhere. A general air of neglect. If this is how you take care of your duties, I'll need a very good excuse to keep you on.'

Marsaili swallowed hard. He was right, damn him, but she couldn't tell him the real reason the hall had been allowed to get into such a state was that Seton thought it better if Rosyth House didn't look too prosperous to any visitors. He'd reasoned that the shabbier it seemed, the less likely it was anyone would want to appropriate it. Looking around her, she wasn't so sure any longer.

'This room hasn't been used for many years,' she said finally. 'The mistress takes her meals upstairs in her private quarters with her daughters, so everyone else eats in the kitchen.'

'Daughters? Are you telling me Flora isn't married either?'

Marsaili blinked. 'Well, no, she isn't. Like I told you, there was no money for dowries. Flora looks after her mother.'

'Damn it all to hell,' he swore and shot to his feet, startling her into standing up as well. 'Someone will pay for this.'

Marsaili didn't know what he meant, but she was sure of one thing – she didn't want to be on the receiving end of his wrath.

She wondered how soon it would be before she could escape from his presence?

Brice took a deep breath and tried to calm down, running a hand through his hair distractedly. He noticed Marsaili's startled look and realised she must think him a madman or at the very least, exceedingly rude.

'I apologise,' he said curtly. 'I didn't mean to swear in front of a lady.'

But damn and double damn! He was sure his father had told him he'd sent dowries for the girls years ago. Five thousand merks each, wasn't it? So why hadn't they arrived?

It was one thing for the estate to be mismanaged, that could be pure laziness on the part of the factor and others. But for a large sum of money to go missing, that was altogether different.

It was outright theft and punishable by law.

Marsaili watched him with wary eyes as he paced in front of the fireplace and Brice forced himself to return to the matter at hand. The dowries could wait, the great hall couldn't. 'Whether Aunt Ailsa chooses to eat downstairs or not, I'd like the rest of us to use this room from now on,' he stated. 'I want it cleaned and made ready for supper today, if possible. You may hire extra help from the township if needed. I'll make sure they're paid. Can you also ask the cook to prepare a feast for everyone, please? And I mean everyone, from the township or anywhere else on the estate, if they've a mind to come. There should be victuals aplenty over there, so none of her watery, tasteless broths, if you please, or she'll find herself without employment and all.' He gestured towards the huge pile of goods stacked by the front door.

'As you wish. Do I take it I am still employed then?' Marsaili's gaze challenged him, but he'd had enough of fighting for one day. He was tired of being angry, especially after recent events.

'Yes. For now.' Before she had a chance to protest at this caveat, he motioned for her to follow him. 'Shall we make a start on sorting out the provisions I brought? Some of it should probably be stowed where it's cooler and the doves will need to go to their new home.'

'Doves?' Marsaili goggled at the many crates, barrels and sacks as if she hadn't seen that much food stuff in a long time, if ever.

'Yes, I saw the empty dovecote out back last time I was here and I thought it a shame there were no inhabitants.

They make a tasty pie every once in a while, don't you think? But I'm guessing it will need to be cleaned as well.'

'Indeed. I'm surprised you noticed. You've been very thorough with your purchases.'

Her eyes opened even wider as she took in the rest of what he'd brought. Now he'd calmed down, Brice noticed again how green her irises were. The colour of new moss in the forest, he thought. He remembered that they'd seemed magnificent when she was in a temper, but even without the extra sparkle, they were beautiful. And unlike most redheads, she had dark lashes which further emphasised their perfection. He shook his head and pushed these thoughts aside, telling himself he wasn't interested in her undoubted charms.

He had been thorough when planning what to buy, that was true. Apart from sacks of oats, barley, rye and dried peas, he'd bought several sugar cones, a dozen smoked hams, salt, spices, root vegetables, brandy, wine and even some chocolate. A crate with a grille at the front contained the doves and there were four more with two dozen hens, clucking distractedly. Last, but not least, there was an exotic looking wooden chest.

When Marsaili spied it, she exclaimed, 'Is that ... it's not tea, is it?'

'Yes, but only one chest. I can always buy more if it's not enough,' Brice replied.

She stared at him as if he'd grown horns. 'Are you mad? I mean ... begging your pardon, but that'll last us for ever.'

'Really? My mother drinks it by the gallon, I swear. I thought all you ladies were the same.' Brice didn't mind the odd cup with honey added, but he much preferred ale.

'But it's so expensive,' Marsaili protested.

Brice couldn't help but smile at her awe. 'Not if you bring it from China yourself,' he said. 'Which I did.' He picked up the chest and hefted it onto his shoulder. 'But if you think it's so valuable, you'd better keep it locked up somewhere. Shall I take it to your room?'

'My room?' She turned an interesting shade of pink. 'No, no that won't be necessary. The cook keeps the larder locked, it should be safe enough in there. Or I can have it taken up to Mrs Kinross later. It will be for her to dispense it.'

'Very well, lead the way.'

'You want to go to the kitchen?'

'Why not? It will be done faster this way. Or is the kitchen in an even sorrier state than this room?'

She sent him a withering look. 'No, it's spotless. Follow me.'

She picked up a heavy sack without much effort and Brice was impressed with her strength. It would seem she actually did her fair share of the housework and didn't just oversee things, the way Elisabet had always done in her father's house. He almost laughed out loud at the thought of his former beloved ever doing anything so strenuous. She would never have been able to lift a sack such as the one Marsaili was carrying, but then again, she wouldn't have wanted to. He frowned as he realised he'd never thought about this before. It wasn't a side to Elisabet he would have tolerated when they were married, but why had he assumed he'd be able to change her? He was no longer sure it would have been possible.

Oh, what does it matter anyway? He should forget all about Elisabet.

Marsaili headed for the kitchen and Brice followed. He could have found his way there by himself, but he decided the view was better from behind her and he must learn to appreciate such sights if he was to have any chance of burying the past. He gave himself a pat on the back for noticing the graceful swing of her hips as she walked and the perfect proportions of her body. For so long he had been blind to the charms of other women, but he was a free man now. There was no harm in looking at the housekeeper, even if she was already spoken for. As long as he didn't act on the lascivious thoughts she evoked.

Besides, anything was better than dwelling on what might have been.

Chapter Nine

Marsaili couldn't understand this man at all. One minute he was giving orders and telling her off for interfering in his business and the next he was helping her carry goods to the kitchen. From what she'd been told, the old laird had never so much as set foot in any domestic part of the house, let alone helped with anything. It would have been far beneath his dignity. But this one didn't seem to care.

She was further confounded when Liath came bounding over to Brice and greeted him like a long-lost friend with a series of happy barks. The dog had been occupying his usual spot in an alcove near the cooking range, but jumped up the moment he spotted Brice and danced around with excitement.

'Liath, behave!' Marsaili said sternly, but just like the last time, the dog ignored her. He focused all his attention on Brice, who put down the chest and knelt to make a fuss of Liath, scratching behind his ears.

'Hello there, my friend,' he said to the dog, ignoring the cook and two kitchen maids who all goggled at him. 'How nice to see you again. You missed me, eh?'

Liath seemed almost beside himself with joy, his tail wagging so hard it made his entire back end wiggle. Marsaili muttered 'Traitor' under her breath. She couldn't understand why her faithful hound was behaving in this fashion, he'd never done so before.

When Brice stood up again, she performed the introductions. 'This is Mrs Murray, the cook, and her helpers Isobel and Fionna.' They all curtseyed and he bowed back.

'Forgive me if I don't remember everyone's names at first,' he said with a disarming smile. 'I'll do my best.' He picked up the tea chest again. 'Now where would you like this Mrs Murray?'

Greine looked as flabbergasted as Marsaili had felt at the sight of so much tea, but managed to unlock the larder. 'In here, if you please, my lord.'

'You'd better send for a stable lad to help you carry the rest in here,' he told her. 'And we'll need someone to take care of the doves and chickens. Please leave half the sacks of oatmeal behind for the moment though, I have other plans for those.'

'Very well, we'll see to it,' Marsaili said.

'Thank you. Then I'll go and find out what's happened to the livestock.'

Marsaili had seen the cattle, goats and sheep on her way to the courtyard earlier, after Seton had given her the news of the new laird's arrival. She'd wondered why he had brought them and without thinking, she voiced her thought out loud. 'What are they for? Slaughter? I'm not sure we'll have space for so much extra meat all at once.'

He looked surprised. 'Not yet, no. Just a few at a time. I thought the herd here looked a bit small so I decided to add some more females to it.'

'But winter is coming. Most of the creatures will be slaughtered or sold soon. And the ones you've brought won't have time to fatten up much.'

'They shouldn't need to, they've been well cared for. I selected them myself. Besides, as I said, they're not for killing. We're going to keep most of them over the winter to increase the herd for next year. For now, they'll need to go into the nearest fields I expect. Do you mind if I take Liath outside with me? He looks as though he would like a walk.'

Marsaili was so stunned by his words that she lost the power of speech, but she managed to nod her assent to his request. By the time she'd recovered, he and the hound had gone. She turned to Greine. 'Did he just say what I think he said?'

'Aye, he did that.'

'But where will he get the hay to feed cattle over the winter? There's hardly any been mown.'

Greine shrugged. 'Perhaps he'll have some cut? There's still grass in the meadows that's not been touched.' She smiled. 'Hah! Wish I had time to go and listen when he tells the men that bit of news, if it's what he's got in mind.'

'Indeed, they won't like the extra work. Well, it's none of our business I suppose. We've got our own tasks to do and we'd best make a start. His lordship wants a feast, and he's given orders we're all to eat in the great hall. I don't know how he thinks things can be arranged so quickly.'

Greine smiled. 'We'll do fine. It'll be grand to cook a proper meal again without having to stint. And I'll enjoy it even more if it puts Mr High-and-Mighty Seton's neb out of joint as it surely will.'

Marsaili laughed. 'Yes, good point.'

Seton felt as if his well-ordered world had suddenly turned upside down. Only that morning, he had been counting the money he'd saved up. He came to the conclusion it wouldn't be long now before he had enough to buy back the Seton lands. A few more months and he'd be able to leave Rosyth, a place he'd come to hate.

But his plans had all been scuppered by the arrival of a man he'd thought never to set eyes on. *Damn his impudence!*

Seton hadn't stayed to see young Kinross lording it over his clansmen. It was bad enough he had to greet him civilly and pretend he was going to work with him. *Hah! Over my dead body!* But he realised he'd have to tread warily, or everything he'd worked towards would disappear in the blink of an eye.

He can't prove anything, he thought. The estate's accounts all tallied, he'd made sure of that. Kinross would never know Seton hadn't recorded even half of the true amounts. Nor that he had the extra money stashed away in a secret hiding place. But how was he to obtain the rest of the sum he needed? Seton had no idea at the moment, but he would think of something. He always did.

One way or another, he'd deal with the new laird.

Before Brice left Gothenburg, Killian had explained the system of clanship to him, adding, 'Although I gather it's mostly been abolished by the English after Culloden, old habits die hard.'

As far as Brice understood it, a clan chief owned the land and it was rented out to tacksmen, the local term for the main tenants. Most of them were related to the chief, so there was an additional bond between them that made the relationship stronger. They, in turn, allowed others to farm parts of the land they rented. These common labourers performed most of the work and the tacksmen were responsible for paying everyone's dues to the laird. Then there were skilled craftsmen, like blacksmiths, joiners and weavers. Apart from the people who lived and worked at Rosyth House itself, the rest were congregated in the small township or in smaller settlements in neighbouring valleys.

'The laird is more like a patriarchal figure than anything else,' Killian had said. 'In my grandfather's time, he'd have expected unswerving obedience and loyalty, but these days I think you'll have to tread more softly. And don't forget, until you prove yourself a worthy chief, you'll be on trial as it were. They don't have to accept you.'

Brice had no intention of forgetting this.

'So the tacksmen will pay me rent?'

'Yes, but not necessarily in ready money,' Killian replied.

'You're more likely to receive payment in kind – butter, cheese, oatmeal and perhaps the odd calf, sheep or some lengths of home-made linen. If there's a surplus, you sell it and that's where the money comes from, just like at Askeberga.'

Both Brice and Jamie had been taught how to manage the Swedish estate, so he wasn't unduly worried about taking on Rosyth. The produce might vary slightly, since here cattle rearing seemed the main objective, but the principles were surely the same.

The most important thing Killian had impressed upon him, however, was that a chief had to be seen to be hospitable. He was therefore determined to show everyone he wasn't stingy, which was why he'd ordered the feast to be prepared for the evening meal. It would also be a subtle reminder of the lack of hospitality shown him on his previous visit. He was sure he didn't need to spell it out to those responsible.

He'd arrived mid-morning, which admittedly didn't give the housekeeper and cook much time. His request hadn't seemed to ruffle them, however, so he was sure they'd do their best. What he needed to do now was invite the guests – every member of the clan he could find – and after he'd given orders for the new cattle to be taken to a nearby field, he decided to tackle this task. He wasn't at all sure they'd come, but he had to try.

To that end, he made his way down to the stables to retrieve Starke. He could have gone on foot, but he reckoned he could cover a lot more ground by riding. It would also give him the advantage of height, which would come in useful when trying to assert his authority. The Lord knew he needed all the help he could get.

'Guid mornin', Mr ... I mean, my laird.' The bright little face of Archie popped up from behind a wattle partition. The stables had seemed deserted so the boy's appearance

82

startled Brice, but he smiled at him. There was something very appealing about the freckled nose, sparkling eyes and tousled hair.

'Oh, hello there. Are you playing a game of hide and seek?'

'No, I was lookin' after yer horse, like ye told me tae. I've fed and watered him. I … I hope that was a'right?'

Brice nodded. 'Absolutely, you did well, thank you. But I didn't mean you had to be in sole charge of him. Where's your friend?'

'He had tae help his father.' Archie nodded in Starke's direction. 'And hisself was hungry. I could tell.' The horse snorted loudly as if agreeing with the boy.

Brice laughed. 'Yes, he's a stomach on legs, that one. Don't let him fool you into giving him extra rations. He'll get fat and lazy.'

'Beggin' yer pardon, sir, but there's nae more food tae give 'im. Did ye bring aught?'

'Yes, a bit, but we'll need to gather hay for the winter, and not just for the horses. I'll ask the men to cut as much as they can.' Brice knew natural hay was rare in the Highlands and had to be gathered wherever possible, a tiresome task at the best of times. It wasn't usually planted, since all the available land was needed for crops. A distant memory surfaced. 'Actually, when I was here as a boy, we children used to help by collecting grass from the waysides and from under bushes and such. Could you spread the word among your friends that I'll pay them a groat for every armful? Might fire up their enthusiasm.'

'I'd say! Should I dae it the noo?'

Brice laughed. 'Later is soon enough. Remind me to have a look at the barns though. From what I saw during my previous visit, they may not be in a fit state to keep anything dry.'

'Shuir an' I will.'

Archie nodded and came closer, and Brice took in the tattered state of the boy's clothing. He saw that Archie was in dire need of a new outfit. His breeches were way too short, showing off thin legs and bare feet. His shirt was darned in quite a few places and looked as though it had been fashioned out of a much larger one and cut down to size. It hung off the boy's spare frame and stuck out at the back from under a threadbare waistcoat, also too large. Brice made up his mind there and then to do something about this sorry state of affairs.

'Are ye goin' fer a ride?' Archie dared to ask.

'Yes, I'm going to invite everyone to a feast tonight. At the same time, I thought to go and have a look at the cattle. Do you want to come with me?'

Archie's expression turned from astonishment to pure joy in the blink of an eye. A huge smile spread over his features and he nodded enthusiastically. 'Aye, I do, please!' Then his smile dimmed a little. 'But there's only Mr Seton's *garrons* and I daren't borrow those. The ones ye brought this mornin' will be tired oot.'

Brice grabbed Starke's saddle from where it had been slung over a beam. 'It's not a problem. Starke's name means "strong" in Swedish and he is that. He'll easily carry us both I should think. You can sit in front of me and be my guide.'

'Braw!' Archie's eyes shone and Brice reflected that the poor boy obviously never received any attention if it took so little for him to be happy. Perhaps he could rectify this from now on.

It was a lovely, sunny morning, and Starke seemed happy to be out in the open again. So was Liath, who bounded along behind them. The big horse covered the ground with easy strides, the extra weight of the small boy no problem for him. Brice held the reins in one hand and laid the other one loosely round Archie. The boy didn't seem afraid, even though the horse was so high off the ground. He held on casually to Starke's mane.

'Would you mind if we speak only in Gaelic?' Brice asked. 'I need to practise, you see, it's been a while.'

Archie nodded. 'Fine with me.'

'You've ridden before, I can tell. You're keeping your back straight and your knees tight, very good.'

'Aye, I've always loved horses and my auntie's man was head groom here before he died last year. He taught me to ride.'

'What happened to him?'

'Congestion of the lungs. Weren't nothing they could do for him.'

'What about your own father? What does he do? And your mother?'

'They're dead too. I live here with Auntie Greine, the cook.'

'Ah, I see. A shame about Mr Murray then. Do you miss him?' Brice thought the man must have been a father figure to the boy, but Archie shook his head.

'Not really. I only miss helping with the horses. He had a fearsome temper and didn't always want me around.'

Brice decided a change of topic was called for. 'So have you lived on the Rosyth estate all your life?' he asked instead. 'I'm guessing you were born after my last visit, which would make you about nine or ten, am I right?'

'I'm eleven,' Archie said, then added glumly, 'but no one ever thinks so on account of me being small and puny.'

'I wouldn't say you're puny,' Brice replied. 'You may not be very tall yet, but you're strong and tenacious, which counts for a lot. And you'll soon grow, don't worry. Not everyone does so at the same pace, you know.'

'You think?' There was hope in Archie's voice and he glanced over his shoulder at Brice with big, trusting eyes.

'I don't just think, I know.' Brice felt something shift inside him. He realised he could make a difference to this child's life by being here. As laird of Rosyth, it would be his responsibility to make sure Archie and all the other children had enough to eat so they could grow the way they should. It put things in perspective somehow and although he knew it would be an uphill struggle for him to become accepted, he was suddenly filled with even more determination to succeed. He'd do it for Archie and all the people who were now his tenants.

And for himself.

'I wasn't born here though.' Archie interrupted his thoughts.

'No? Where then?'

'At Bailliebroch.' The child's voice had taken on a very serious note and he sounded as if he had to force the words out.

Brice frowned. 'Oh, so you came with the factor then?' He'd been told that when Seton was given the position as manager, a few of his clansmen had followed him and settled on Rosyth land.

'Not exactly. Auntie Greine took me in when ... after the soldiers came.'

Brice saw Archie's hands tighten on Starke's mane. His grip was so hard the small knuckles went white and the boy's head bent forward, the shaggy brown hair falling down to cover his face.

'What are you saying?' Brice asked gently. 'The Redcoats ransacked your home, which was on Bailliebroch land? Because of Mr Seton's brother fighting for the Jacobites?'

Archie nodded. When Brice tightened his hold around the boy's waist to show his support, the whole tale came out in bursts. 'I was only little, but I remember it. Th-they came to our hut, shouting. Said my dad was a traitor. S-said we were too. They … they grabbed Mother and she screamed at me to run. I didn't know what to do, but … then I did what she said. I ran, fast as I could. Found a hiding place. Stayed there till they'd gone. They never found me, but M-Mother …'

Brice could guess the rest and it made his heart ache. No one so young should have to witness something like that. In fact, it ought not to happen to anyone. Red hot fury coursed through him and he cursed the Government forces for their unwarranted brutality. It was one thing to wage war on grown men who had chosen to take sides, but women and children? That was nothing short of an outrage.

'It's all right, Archie, you don't have to tell me if you don't want to,' he said.

Archie drew in a deep breath. 'I want to, but I don't remember much after that. I sat down next to Mother, but she never woke. Someone took me away and then I came here.' He half turned to stare at Brice with anxious eyes. 'Mr Seton said as how you were like those men, but you're not, are you?'

Brice shook his head and silently damned Seton. 'No, Archie, I'll swear to you on my dirk I'm not.' The boy managed a small smile at the reference to the oath he'd taken the first time they met. 'Not all Englishmen are like that anyway, I've met some very nice ones during my travels. There are good and bad people in all countries. Either way, I don't have a single drop of English blood in me, as far as I know. Even if I did, I would never behave like that. Do you believe me?' He held Archie's gaze and the boy nodded.

'Aye. I knew he was wrong.'

'He is wrong in many ways, but perhaps together you and I can do something about it. What do you say, will you help me?'

'I'd like to, but how?'

'Well, for a start, you can introduce me to everyone. Perhaps with you by my side they'll talk to me more readily. If Mr Seton's been telling them I'm their enemy, it's no wonder I get some funny looks. We have to convince them I'm on their side. Can we do that, do you think?'

'I'll do my best.'

And Brice was sure the boy would. He may be small, but he was as full of determination as Brice himself.

Chapter Ten

They made their way up a well-trodden path to the lower hillside pasture, where the cattle were being watched over so they wouldn't stray into the crops in the infields and wreak havoc. The animals had only recently been brought down from the shielings, the higher ground where they spent most of the summer, but where the sweet grass would now all be gone. To Archie's delight, Brice made Starke jump the dry-stone wall which separated the pasture from the fields on lower ground. The horse cleared this obstacle easily and Brice made sure he was holding the boy in a secure grip so there was no danger.

'Can we do that again on the way down?' Archie asked eagerly.

Brice hid a smile at this childish request. 'Of course, if you wish.'

Their ride proved to be the most enjoyable part of the day. Even with Archie as facilitator, Brice found it an uphill struggle talking to his tenants and clansmen. The men loitering around clearly thought he'd come to check on them and were surly and evasive. He had, but not in the way they thought.

During his previous visit he had seen the herd of cattle wasn't as large as it ought to have been for an estate of this size. Before the new stock was added, he wanted to know exactly how many there were so he could see if the figure tallied with the ledgers Seton presumably kept. Since he couldn't get a straight answer out of any of the herdsmen nearby, he and Archie counted the beasts for themselves.

'I wish these damned cows would stand still,' Brice

muttered when he'd added them up for the third time and come to yet another different total.

Archie laughed. '*Kyloes*, not cows,' he corrected, using the local word.

'I know, but they're cows to me if they produce milk and bullocks if they're turned *into* meat in the autumn.'

In truth, the black shaggy creatures with long horns looked nothing like the cows Brice was used to. The Highland ones were small and obviously hardy though. With their long, wavy hair, he knew they could survive outdoors most of the year and they seemed to eat just about anything. Just as well, he thought, since they had to make do with whatever they could find half the time.

Mingled with the cattle were goats and a few sheep, although not as many as Brice had expected. White with black faces and curling horns, they too were tough and resilient, but he'd been told they needed a lot more grazing than the *kyloes* and therefore large herds couldn't be sustained. He was still convinced there could have been quite a few more than he could see though.

When he was satisfied he'd counted all the sheep and cattle and had made a mental note of the number, he returned to the nearest cluster of men. One of them, who hadn't been there earlier, stood up, and to his relief, Brice recognised him.

'Mr Ross?' he asked, the name surfacing the moment he caught sight of the man's face, then added tentatively, 'Sandy *Mor*?' As a child, Brice had always heard him referred to in this way as 'Big Sandy' and most men in the Highlands had nicknames of this sort since so many of them had the same surname. As one of the tacksmen and a distant relative of Killian's, Sandy would no doubt act as spokesman for the others, which was probably why he'd been fetched. Brice dismounted and held out his hand. He knew Scottish tenants genuinely believed themselves the equals of their chief since they all shared a common ancestry and they usually took the laird by the hand whenever they met.

Sandy took Brice's hand after a slight hesitation. 'MacCoinneach,' he said with a nod. Brice frowned, confused at first, then another memory fell into place. Chiefs descended in a direct line from some illustrious ancestor were often addressed as 'son of' that man, even though there were countless generations in between. In Brice's case, his most famous ancestor was one Coinneach, who'd apparently been a friend of Robert the Bruce. He smiled cautiously at Sandy.

'So you remember me then?' he asked in Gaelic, to show he hadn't forgotten his summers at Rosyth either.

'Aye, I can still see the skinny lad who played with my Rob.' Sandy glanced at one of the younger men standing nearby and Brice recognised his former playmate.

'Well, good, at least you won't take me for an impostor then,' Brice said.

'No.'

The clipped word told Brice that even if they didn't, they weren't prepared to accept him as laird straight off. *Fair enough*, he thought. 'Sandy, I realise some of the men have to stay up here at all times, but those of you who can be spared for a while are welcome to come down to the house for supper this evening. The lad's aunt,' he nodded briefly at Archie, who was still perched on Starke's back, 'is preparing food enough for everyone. Will you send word to anyone within walking distance, please?'

He saw surprise in Sandy's eyes, but it was quickly masked. 'Very well,' he said, but Brice could tell the man was reluctant. He sighed inwardly. It wasn't that he'd expected to be liked or respected immediately, but he hadn't realised quite how much enmity there would be. Surely these men must understand Killian had been unable to return to

Scotland to run the estate? But perhaps they'd counted on Brice to come earlier in his stead?

He hid his thoughts, however, and nodded. 'I hope to see you later then,' was all he said.

As well as counting livestock, Brice decided it would also be useful to know how far his domains reached, how many people the land had to support and what was being grown where. In short, he needed to take stock of his possessions properly. He and Archie therefore took a long detour around the fields, leading Starke behind them at times as the big horse found the ground hard going. They checked on the various types of grain – oats and barley mostly, with some peas and also flax for making linen – before they returned to the township. Here Brice again dismounted and made a point of stopping at every hut along the road to introduce himself personally. There were mostly women around and although wary, in general they were slightly more welcoming than the menfolk. Archie did his best to break the ice and it also helped that some of the older women remembered Brice as a boy.

'A harum-scarum little bantling you were, my lord,' one of them said with a smile. She reminded him of her name, Bridie Ross, and the fact that she was the wife of Sandy, the tacksman he'd met earlier. As soon as she said it, he recalled being told off by her on several occasions.

Brice smiled back, shaking his head ruefully. 'I know, I caused my mother a few grey hairs, I believe. Not as many as my brother though.' It still hurt to even think about Jamie, but Brice knew he'd worked his charm on everyone at Rosyth even when he was young and they were likely to remember him. This proved to be the case.

'Oh, aye, a right hellion he was, to be sure.' But this was said with an indulgent smile, as so often was the case when people talked about Jamie. It made Brice want to grind his teeth and hit something, but he'd long ago accepted that

Jamie could get away with murder and still be liked. *Only not by his brother, not this time.*

He buried the thought, however, and tried to emulate his brother's charming manners. 'I hope you'll all honour me by joining us up at the house for a wee feast this evening,' he said. 'Mrs Murray will be sorely disappointed if you don't come and sample the tasty dishes she's working so hard on.'

It took him a while, but in the end he reckoned he had persuaded most of them to come. He exchanged a look with Archie and winked at the boy. 'Right, we'd better get home then and make ourselves presentable. Although how we're going to manage it with you, I've no idea. Some soap and water might help though. Ladies, we'll see you later.'

Marsaili was proud of her abilities as housekeeper and the new laird's criticism had stung, even though the state of the great hall wasn't directly her fault. She therefore set to with a vengeance, determined to have the room spotless come evening. To that end, she rounded up as many women as she could find, even recruiting Kirsty.

'I'll be damned if I let the man find a single speck of dirt anywhere,' Marsaili muttered to her half-sister.

Kirsty sent her one of her teasing glances. 'Oh, aye? Want to impress him, do you? I wonder why.'

Marsaili gave Kirsty what she hoped was a withering look. 'That's the last thing I want to do, but I'll not have anyone say I'm incompetent, because I'm not. This is all Seton's fault and I'm not going to take the blame. I want to stay here.'

Kirsty smiled. 'I doubt Brice would dismiss you. He's much too nice for that. Now if it had been his brother … well, anything could have happened. But Brice was always the level-headed one.'

'That's not what you were saying this morning when he beat up your beloved Iain.'

Kirsty's expression darkened. 'The dolt deserved it. Honestly, you'd think he'd have learned by now. Why would I stay true to him for so long if there was any likelihood I'd prefer someone else?' She shook her head. 'I hope Brice knocked some sense into him.'

'We'll see, won't we. In the meantime, take out your anger on these hangings, if you don't mind. They could do with a good beating.'

Brice was secretly impressed to find the great hall much improved by supper time. The last of the sunlight shimmered in through newly cleaned windows. The hearth had been swept clean of cobwebs and ash, and both furniture and wainscoting gleamed with a polished sheen. There wasn't a speck of dust to be found anywhere and someone had even gathered bunches of heather and put it in makeshift vases on the window ledges.

The fresh smell of flowers and beeswax mingled with the mouth-watering aromas from the long table, where an array of succulent dishes had been set out. Joints of mutton and beef, large sides of salmon, pots of broth and plates of onions and cheese, together with fresh bannocks. Interspersed with these were bottles of claret, pitchers of ale and some whisky. It seemed like a feast fit for a king and Brice was very pleased.

Meanwhile, what seemed like an enormous group of people milled around aimlessly, looking out of place and ill at ease. They brought with them the smell of peat smoke and wool, but these odours were quickly masked by the other clean scents. Brice decided he'd better take charge before they all thought better of it and bolted. By banging a silver spoon against the pewter tankard which had been set out for him, he achieved silence. 'Welcome, everyone, and thank you for coming,' he said as loudly as he could. 'Please be seated according to custom.'

Killian had told him everyone would know their place and, surprisingly, this turned out to be the case. He was just about to take the seat at the head of the table, as was his due, when an exclamation of surprise hissed through the diners and everyone turned to stare at the door leading into the northerly part of the house. There stood a tiny, middle-aged woman with rather mousy hair and pale features. She looked incredibly frail, but nevertheless walked into the room with purposeful steps and her head held high. Brice left his chair and went to meet her halfway.

'Aunt Ailsa,' he said, smiling at her and bending to kiss her porcelain cheek. 'I was told you were resting earlier and you weren't to be disturbed, so I thought I'd visit you later. And Flora, how lovely to see you too.' He greeted his cousin who hovered behind her mother, adjusting the older woman's shawl and generally fussing over her.

'And you, Brice. Welcome back to Rosyth.'

Brice had always liked Flora, who was kind and gentle, but since she was six years older than him they had never played together. She'd acted more in the role of mother hen to him and his siblings, although usually without much success as the Kinross brood ran wild. He was pleased to see she was still passably pretty, with strawberry blonde hair, the same pale blue eyes as Kirsty and a neat figure. Unfortunately though, her face was marred by pock-marks and he wondered when that had happened. Some time during the ten years since he'd last seen her, poor girl.

'Thank you,' he said, and took Ailsa's arm to lead her to the table. He seated her on his right, with Flora next to her, and Kirsty took the chair opposite her mother. Everyone else adjusted their seating accordingly. Brice looked around and noticed Seton was about to sit down by Kirsty. As the highest ranking member of the household after family members, this would have been his due except for one fact. Brice hid a smile and called out to Iain, who was much further down the table.

'Iain, you're in the wrong seat, man. I hear you're to be part of the family so your place is next to Kirsty.'

Iain only hesitated for a fraction of a second. Brice guessed the man in no way wanted to be beholden to the new laird, especially after their altercation that morning. But on the other hand he'd never pass up a chance to sit next to his beloved. Brice caught the look of annoyance which flickered across Seton's features, but since this was an honour for his son at the same time, he couldn't very well say anything.

When everyone was finally in place, Brice stood up and they all fell silent without being told this time. 'Thank you again for coming this evening,' he began. 'I'll only keep you from your food for a moment while I thank Mrs Murray and Miss Buchanan for their sterling efforts today. Organising this so quickly was a tall order, but they managed it, so thank you both and all your helpers.' He saw Marsaili look down while a blush of pleasure spread over her cheeks. 'I want to apologise on behalf of myself and my father for leaving you to fend for yourselves for so long. Circumstances made it impossible for us to reside here, as I'm sure you all know. But I'm back now and it is my intention to improve the estate, not just for my own gain, but for all of you. I hope you'll help me in this endeavour so that from now on, no one need go hungry or cold at Rosyth. I promise I will do my very best if you do the same. Now, let's eat!'

His words were greeted with quiet murmuring and some sceptical glances, but no exclamations of appreciation. He hadn't expected universal approval straight away, but couldn't help but feel disappointed at such a lukewarm reception. Still, he had to start somewhere and he'd prove his words soon enough. With a jolt, he realised he really did feel responsible for these people already and he was determined to make sure they never went hungry again. They were his people, his clan.

Killian had been right – he belonged here and he wanted to stay, so they'd all better get used to him.

Marsaili was exhausted from the day's endeavours, but unaccountably pleased at the praise she had received from the laird. The great hall did look wonderful, or at least as good as it could, given the state of the soft furnishings. It was amazing what water, soap and some polish could achieve in a short space of time.

She listened to the little speech their new master gave and had to concede he sounded sincere. Whether he would be able to follow through on his promises, only time would tell, but it seemed as though he meant every word. She didn't want to like him, after the ruse he'd practised on them and their exchange of words that morning. A part of her had to admit he'd been well within his rights though. Especially given the fact that she suspected Seton had been swindling him for years. The estate Brice Kinross had returned to was not what it should have been.

Only a fool would have failed to notice something was seriously amiss at Rosyth. Marsaili had been a witness to many encounters between Seton and the tenants over the years.

'We need more food, extra rations for ourselves and the bairns,' they'd begged. 'We're starvin' and it's our right.'

They were invariably turned down. 'There's none to be had,' was Seton's usual reply. And yet the harvests hadn't failed for several years and the cattle thrived. So where did all the surplus go, Marsaili wondered?

It was true the estate didn't yield as much as it had in the old days by all accounts, but Marsaili was sure the crops ought to be able to feed everyone adequately. Somehow there was never enough grain and no money for repairs, however. It simply didn't add up.

She glanced diagonally across the table at Seton, who was a few places away from her on the other side. His face was like a miniature thunder cloud. Everyone else was loosening up a little and the combined volume of the voices all around them rising. Seton said nothing, just ate in silence.

Once, he looked up, turning his head to fix his hazel eyes on her. Marsaili suppressed a shudder. If he was unhappy, he'd brought it on himself. It was nothing to do with her and she had no sympathy for him. His expression grew even darker when, after the meal, Brice announced there was a sack of oats over by the door for each family to take home.

'I hope it will be enough to keep you fed until harvest time, but if not, please come and tell me,' he said.

Marsaili saw Seton's mouth set in a grim line and he left as soon as everyone else stood up, barging a few people out of the way in his hurry to reach the door.

'Hmm, that went well, don't you think?'

The voice just behind her, low and slightly sarcastic, made Marsaili swivel round so fast her braid swished across the laird's chin. 'Oh! I'm sorry, I ...' She felt her face turn warm, but he didn't seem bothered. 'Er, you were saying?'

'The meal wasn't quite as much of an ordeal as I'd thought,' he said with a wry smile. 'It would have been nice if they'd talked to me, but at least they didn't all try to skewer me with their dirks. Or not yet anyway.'

Marsaili watched with him, as the last of the clansmen shuffled out into the balmy evening, the men hefting a heavy sack of grain each. 'You matched your deeds to your words,' she commented. 'People who have children to feed can't be too hasty.' She looked up at him and added, 'Besides, haven't you heard? Dirks are forbidden.'

Brice shook his head, the smile widening. 'I may be

considered an outsider, but even I know they're not going to abide by that rule. I doubt very many dirks were handed in to the authorities, at least not the best ones.' He held up a hand to stop her protesting. 'But I don't want to know. It's none of my business.'

'Perhaps not. If it's any help, I'd say they've reserved judgement for now. If you want to win them over, you're going about it the right way.'

'Thank you. That was exactly what I needed to know and I'll keep it in mind.' He bowed to her. 'Goodnight, Miss Buchanan. I trust you'll sleep well after all your hard work.' With a twinkle in his eyes, he added, 'For someone who wants to keep her own position, you're going about it the right way too.'

Marsaili was torn between wanting to hit him and laughing. In the end, she just shook her head after his retreating back and took herself off to bed, muttering, 'Dratted man. I hope they do skewer you, and soon.'

But she knew she didn't mean it and that worried her.

Chapter Eleven

Marsaili slept badly. A combination of too much rich food, which her stomach wasn't accustomed to, and an unseasonably warm night, had her tossing and turning. In the early hours of the next morning she decided there was no point staying in bed any longer. After all the previous day's hard work, she felt in need of a complete cleansing, so she gathered together what she required and headed for the loch. With Liath trotting at her heels, she felt safe to go for a swim. The women usually used a small bay secluded by trees when they wanted to bathe. Since it was so early, she didn't think anyone else would be about in any case and Liath would warn her.

It was the first day of September and the water almost too cold, but she steeled herself and ran in quickly. She let out a shriek, but only under water so it wouldn't be heard, then swam as fast as she could back and forth until her body had accustomed itself to the temperature. It wasn't easy to swim wearing a shift, but she managed it. There was no way she'd risk being seen without a stitch on, like some of the others. That, to her mind, was courting disaster. Finally, she set about washing herself and her long hair with the home-made soap which was Flora's speciality. This took quite some time.

Emerging from the water, she dried herself and changed to a clean shift, bodice and skirt. Further along the shore, closer to the house, there was a small jetty with a magnificent view across the loch and Marsaili decided to go and sit there while she tried to comb out her wet hair. Untangling the unruly curls was always a mammoth task and it helped to have something else to distract her from the frustration of it.

'Come, Liath,' she called to the dog, although this wasn't strictly necessary since he always followed her anyway. She stroked his shaggy grey fur when he came up beside her, shoving his muzzle against her affectionately. 'Good boy. What would I do without you, eh?' She smiled at him and humoured him by picking up a stick to play a game of fetch.

Once seated at the end of the jetty, she took out her comb and began the laborious task. She'd often cursed the fate that gave her such a curly mess instead of the lovely wispy waves her half-sisters had been blessed with, but she was used to it now. She worked methodically, dividing the hair into sections and combing out each one before attempting to join them up. About halfway round one side of her head, however, she was startled into dropping the comb when a face popped out of the water right in front of her without warning.

'Oh!' She stared, enthralled, at the vision before her.

The new laird, naked to the waist, rose to stand half submerged only yards away from her. His tanned torso gleamed in the early morning sun as the water ran in little rivulets down his chest. She followed their course with her eyes, but blinked and looked away when they reached the edge of his breeches. She couldn't resist another peek from under her lashes at him though – he was truly magnificent.

Hard muscle under sun-kissed skin, with a trail of golden hair leading downwards from his navel to wet breeches that clung to him. Powerful arms and shoulders which looked like they'd make short work of swimming all the way across the loch. A stomach that was both flat and ridged at the same time in the most fascinating way. Marsaili felt a thrill race through her at this sight.

Then she realised he was grinning at her.

'I'm sorry if I startled you, Miss Buchanan,' he said, pushing wet hair out of his eyes. 'That was not my intention.'

'Well, you did a good job of it even so,' Marsaili snapped, annoyed with herself for being caught staring at him again. 'And now I've lost my comb too.' It had bounced off the end of the jetty and straight into the loch.

'That, at least, I can rectify,' he said and dived back under the water. A moment later he came up with her comb in one hand. He held it out to her and she had to swallow a gasp as he was now so close she could have reached out and touched his smooth skin had she wanted to.

Which she definitely didn't. Or so she attempted to tell herself.

'Thank you,' she murmured, and tried not to show her surprise that his fingers felt so warm against hers despite the cold water. A jolt shot through her at the small contact between them and this made her even more flustered. What was the matter with her?

'You're very welcome.'

His voice was a bit hoarse this morning. The husky timbre sent shivers down her spine though, so she wasn't complaining. She realised she was still staring and pulled herself together.

'What are you doing out here so early?' she asked. She sounded a bit grumpy, but she couldn't help it. He seemed to have a knack for rubbing her up the wrong way at the same time as making her feel attracted to him. It was rather unsettling.

He crossed his arms over his chest, which showed off the muscles to great advantage. Marsaili gripped the comb tightly to stop her fingers from touching his taut biceps. It was incredibly tempting and she'd love to know if they were as hard as they looked.

'Just having a bath,' he replied with a smile, 'like you told me last time I was here. I was given to understand hot water was scarce.'

Marsaili was sure her face turned bright pink at this reminder of her ungraciousness during their first meeting. The teasing glint in his eyes didn't help either. He knew he was discomfiting her and he was doing it on purpose. *The scoundrel!* But she wasn't really angry with him and had to hide a smile. 'Only because it was laundry day,' she defended herself. 'Any other time, you've only to ask.'

'That's good to know.' He changed the subject. 'You're up early too,' he commented. 'Should you be out here all alone? You might be abducted by a kelpie.'

'What nonsense. And I have Liath to protect me. Although ...' She turned an accusing eye on the hound who'd come to lie next to her, wagging his tail furiously at the laird. He hadn't given her any warning that anyone was approaching. She sighed. 'It would seem he's not much use where you are concerned,' she admitted.

Brice's smile widened and he reached out to rub the dog's head. 'That's because he's a clever fellow who knows you've got nothing to fear from me.' Liath took the opportunity to lick his arm, as if confirming this.

'Hmph.' Marsaili didn't know whether to be pleased or annoyed with his assertion. On the one hand, she should feel reassured if the laird had no designs on her virtue, but on the other ... She felt her cheeks heat up again as her brain refused to continue that line of thought. So the man was handsome, what of it? There were many others like him and she was better off without a husband. She'd seen the way her mother was treated when she finally married someone. It had been hell.

Besides, a man like Brice Kinross would never be interested in marrying a servant, even a high-ranking one. No doubt his parents would choose him a bride from among their rich acquaintance. The most he'd want from Marsaili would be a tumble in the hay. And tempting as that might seem when she glanced at his gilded chest yet again, it wasn't worth the consequences. As her mother had also found to her cost.

She'd do well to stay away from his lordship altogether.

Dear God, but his eyes are so blue! You could drown in them ...

Brice couldn't take his eyes off the woman this morning. He didn't know why, but somehow she seemed different today. Softer and more vulnerable. Or perhaps the long swim in the lake had relaxed him and mellowed his mood.

He took in the glorious hair, a riot of honey, gold and copper curls, mixed with hints of ochre and flame. He had never seen hair like that before and he'd been wrong to dismiss it as plain 'red'. It was no such thing. It was beginning to glint in the sun where a few wisps were drying in the morning breeze. A large part of it was still wet and tangled, however, and she was plying her comb as they spoke. Not an easy task, judging by the occasional tightening of her mouth as she fought to pull the comb through the long tresses.

That mouth was generous, but not overly so, with a dimple to one side. He'd only glimpsed it when she smiled at something Kirsty said the night before. So far she hadn't smiled much around him, which was understandable, he supposed. The sun had only tanned her skin a little, mostly it was creamy and flawless. And those green eyes of hers seemed more vivid outdoors than inside the gloomy rooms of Rosyth House.

Without asking her leave, he hoisted himself onto the jetty beside her and held out a hand. 'Here, give me the comb and let me help you or you'll never finish.'

She turned a startled gaze on him and he heard her draw in a sharp breath. 'What? No! I mean, you can't ...'

'Of course I can. I have four younger sisters. You'll see, I'm a dab hand at disentangling stubborn knots.'

'Four?' She looked at his outstretched hand and hesitated, then put the comb in it. He closed his fingers around both the comb and her hand for a moment and her eyes flew to his once more. He felt a surge of desire shooting through him, but suppressed it. She was promised elsewhere and she'd made it quite clear during his last visit that she wasn't interested in being propositioned. He didn't want to scare her away. Not just yet.

'Turn around and I'll soon have your elf-locks sorted out,' he ordered, and she did as she was told.

'What do you know about elf-locks?' she muttered.

'Only that they're very tangled, but beautiful nonetheless,' he replied.

He began to comb out her hair, working methodically the way she'd done herself. The only difference was he could do it faster, since he didn't have to do it by touch. He found that he liked handling her hair. Even when wet it was silky and smooth, and the colour continued to astound him as more of it dried. From where he sat, he also had a perfect view over her shoulder into her loosely fastened bodice. The top half of the perfect curves which were displayed made his fingers itch to reach around her and touch them for himself. Again, he resisted.

'I see you're a practical woman,' he commented.

'How so?' Her voice sounded slightly dreamy, as though she was enjoying having her hair combed.

'You wear a bodice which is fastened at the front so you don't need anyone's help to don it. A shame, I could have acted as your lady's maid.'

She sent him a suspicious glance over her shoulder, one eyebrow raised. 'And I suppose you're well versed in that skill as well, what with all those sisters?'

He grinned at her. 'Of course. Where else would I have learned?'

She snorted. 'Where else indeed. Do you take me for a complete fool, my lord?'

'Call me Brice, please. At least when no one else is around. All this lord business still sounds strange to me. I've been plain Brice or Mr Kinross all my life until now.'

'But that would be … improper.'

She was still looking at him and bit her lip. He had a sudden urge to bite it himself, or nibble the soft flesh at any rate.

'No,' he said, 'it would be a kindness.'

'Hmm, perhaps I will then.'

He finished the last tress and pulled the comb through her hair from the crown of her head down past her nicely rounded *derrière* onto the jetty. 'There, all done.' He couldn't resist picking a handful up and inhaling the flowery scent. 'Mmm, lovely. What did you put on it?'

She pulled the hair gently out of his grasp. 'Really, my … Brice, you shouldn't do that. And it's a mixture of heather and lavender soap which Flora made, if you must know.'

She was blushing and he realised for the first time that Elisabet had never done so even once when he paid her compliments. She'd always taken them as her due and just thanked him prettily. It made him wonder whether his father had been right after all. Had Elisabet ever loved him? Cared about his compliments? Perhaps he just hadn't understood this before. He shook himself mentally.

Forget Elisabet. She's irrelevant. Concentrate on enjoying life, living for the moment. But it wasn't easy. Still, he had to try so he pushed all thoughts of her away.

Marsaili was gathering up her things and he jumped off the jetty into the water to stand in front of her again. 'Wait there,' he said, 'and I'll fetch my drying cloth so I can escort you back to the house.'

'It's not necessary. I have Liath.'

'Ah, but has he ever chased away a kelpie? You've no idea how he'd react to one.'

A gurgle of laughter escaped her and she shook her head at him. 'You're quite mad, you know. Either that, or you're still drunk from last night.'

He laughed too. 'Neither. Now stay put, that's an order from your laird.'

'Yes, master,' she replied sarcastically, but when he returned from fetching his drying cloth, which he'd left on a stone further down the shore, she was still there.

He held out his arm and bowed, as if he was a gallant escorting his lady to a ball. She smiled, but shook her head. 'Come Liath,' she told the dog. 'I'm not walking anywhere with this madman on my own.'

Liath obeyed, but only after Brice started walking.

'Good dog,' Brice said with a chuckle.

Colin Seton didn't live in the big house. As factor, he had his own house in the township, although it was larger than any of the others with a stone flagged floor and proper furniture. That suited him fine. He barely noticed his surroundings in any case. His mind was always focused on the future, when he'd be the laird of Bailliebroch and in possession of a huge estate with suitable dwelling. The fact that there wasn't much left of his former home didn't daunt him – he'd soon have it rebuilt. He remembered every last detail of its architecture and had no doubt he'd be able to recreate it.

But it required money and his scheme for obtaining enough of that seemed to be going awry. He clenched his fists as he walked towards the entrance to the courtyard on his way to the estate office. Something had to be done about the new laird, that was for sure. His mere presence stopped Seton from achieving anything.

His brows lowered even further as he remembered the

slight he'd received the night before. To put his own son higher up the table than himself, it was the outside of enough. The boy wasn't even formally betrothed to the penniless girl he coveted. Seton had hoped that by delaying matters, he'd be able to talk Iain out of it altogether, but his son had proved surprisingly stubborn. Well, perhaps Seton would have to put up with Kirsty as a daughter-in-law, but in his own house he'd be the one highest up the table until the day he died.

He entered the house and walked along a corridor, glancing out of the windows now and then. Movement caught his eye and he stopped to stare when he realised what he was looking at. The new laird and Marsaili, walking close to each other, strolling up from the loch. *At this time of day?* Seton blinked in shock.

What was the whoreson up to now? Wasn't it enough that he was interfering with the running of the estate? Did he have to try and insinuate himself into the ladies' good graces as well? It was not to be borne.

They were laughing, he'd swear to it, even though he had trouble seeing clearly from a distance. And the laird wasn't even fully clothed. It was a disgrace.

Seton felt bile rise up in his throat and his chest heaved. Marsaili was his. He'd wanted her from the first time he'd set eyes on her, when she wasn't even fully a woman yet. He'd waited patiently and he was going to have her. No foreign whipper-snapper would take what was his, he'd make damned sure of it.

Yes, the laird had to go and then the damned dog. But how?

'Thank you for the escort, my ... Brice. And your efforts as a lady's maid.'

Marsaili felt suddenly embarrassed, standing so close to him, especially since the drying cloth only partially covered his still half-nude form. He'd made her laugh with nonsensical tales of Swedish trolls and other magical creatures, which he claimed were much worse than any Scottish kelpie. It made her realise he wasn't always the stern taskmaster she'd seen before. He had a lighter side to him, one she couldn't help but admire.

'Not at all, it was my pleasure. And although I enjoy being called "your Brice", it might be best if you don't say that within earshot of anyone else,' he teased.

'It was a slip of the tongue, as well you know,' she said and held up a hand in a mock threatening fashion, as if she was going to punch him.

He laughed. 'Hmm, now don't go giving me ideas.' He wiggled his eyebrows at her and stared pointedly at her mouth.

Marsaili felt heat flooding her cheeks. 'For shame, my ... Brice. I won't listen to you any more.'

'Oh, you wouldn't have to listen,' he said, eyes twinkling mischievously. 'Just close your eyes and I'll show you.' His voice was still husky, filled with some kind of promise that made Marsaili's insides melt and actually almost persuaded her to do as he asked, but she pulled herself together and shook her head.

'I'll do no such thing. And now you'd better go and dry yourself or you'll catch your death.'

He sighed dramatically. 'Very well, you cruel woman. I'll see you at breakfast then. Make sure it's not watery porridge this time, please, or I'll tip it over your newly washed hair.'

He walked backwards a few steps, grinning at her, and she couldn't help but smile in return even though he was again reminding her of her previous misdeeds.

'Lots of butter and honey, please, with cream,' he added. 'And I'll need two helpings at the very least. Combing hair as long as yours is hard work.'

'Away with you!' She shooed him off and turned towards the kitchen entrance, determined not to pay him any more heed. She couldn't resist one last glance out of the corner of her eye, however, and was treated to the sight of his broad back, bare in the sunlight.

She sighed. He really was magnificent.

Chapter Twelve

'Right then, Mr Seton, I think we have a few things to discuss regarding the running of this estate.'

Brice had postponed the inevitable meeting with Seton until the second day in order to see how the man responded to his presence at Rosyth. So far the factor hadn't countermanded any of Brice's instructions, but he hadn't helped by making sure they were carried out either. His expression at the supper table the night before had been anything but joyful and he seemed, if possible, even grumpier this morning, as if Brice had mortally offended him. *Perhaps I have, just by being here*, Brice thought, but he had no intention of mistreating the man so his anger was a little premature.

Seton had already been sitting at the desk when Brice arrived, but at a sharp look from the latter, the factor vacated the chair. Instead, he had to sit down on the opposite side, while Brice took his place. Brice was aware this might make the man feel uncomfortable, but perhaps that was all to the good in this case. Seton had a few questions to answer.

'I've been having a look through the ledgers,' Brice said, 'and everything appears to tally.'

'Aye, and so they should. I've kept them myself,' Seton answered, his gaze stony and his eyes narrowed slightly as if he was on the defensive.

'I'm not doubting your abilities to add up or keep accounts, Mr Seton. What I'm wondering, however, is why the amounts are so small. There seems to be no profit whatsoever for the last few years.'

Seton shrugged. 'As you may have heard, we've had some hard times here in the Highlands. The Redcoats saw to that.

What with wrecking homes, then taxes and more taxes. There's never an end to them.'

'Even so, it's been nearly eight years since the forty-five and as I understand it, the last two have been relatively good as far as harvests are concerned. And yet Rosyth's yield is ludicrous. How do you explain that?'

Seton's cheeks took on a somewhat ruddier hue and Brice saw a muscle jumping in the man's cheek, but he kept hold of his temper. 'After the bad harvest in '51, we didn't have much grain to sow, therefore no yields either. The people had to eat and the families just keep growing. Too many damned bairns to feed.'

'Surely you could have bought more grain for sowing? And what about the cattle? I reckon the pasture here ought to be able to sustain a herd of at least three hundred, half of which could be sold at market each year. Last year you sold twenty.'

The factor attempted a look of unconcern, but Brice could tell the man was rattled. Perhaps he hadn't thought the new laird would know anything about farming or even be interested for that matter. 'We'd had to sell a lot of cattle in the previous years, so there weren't enough calves being born,' Seton said. 'I sold the ones we could afford to lose. The rest have been slow to mature. Perhaps, being from another country, you're not familiar with the Scottish beasts? The *kyloes* take up to four years to grow to full size and there's no point selling them before that. Not all of them make it through the winter either.'

'So how many are left now exactly?' Brice checked the ledger. 'According to this, there were only eighty-five making up the herd after the rest had been taken either to slaughter or the market last autumn. Assuming most of those were female and the bulls were doing their job, we should have had some seventy or eighty calves born in the spring. By my reckoning, that would make a hundred and sixty five *kyloes*.'

'Ye-es.' Seton drew out the word, as if he wasn't quite agreeing with Brice.

'Hmm, strange there seem to be about fifty more up in the pasture then,' Brice commented. 'Two hundred and sixteen. Were there a lot of twin births?'

Seton's dark eyebrows came down and he glared at Brice. 'How did you arrive at that figure, my lord?' He said the last two words in a slightly offensive way, but Brice decided not to take any notice. He smiled instead.

'I counted them.'

'I beg your pardon?' The factor's eyes opened wide and he sat up straighter.

'I went up there yesterday to invite people to last night's supper. As I was there anyway, I took the opportunity to count the beasts. And I made it two hundred and sixteen.'

For a moment, it seemed as if Seton wasn't going to reply. His mouth opened and shut again. Finally, he drew in a deep breath and said, 'You must be mistaken. They move around a lot after all, which makes them hard to count. And there are always a couple of extra belonging to the tenants themselves. Yes, that must be it, they've put theirs in with the rest.'

'You think? Well, we'll see when we bring them down later in the month I expect. I can assure you my eyesight is excellent, however, and if there are any less than the number I counted, I shall want to know what happened to them.'

The factor didn't reply to this, which made Brice suspect the man had intended to remove a few animals at a time, perhaps at night, and send them to market. He was satisfied he'd nipped that scheme in the bud.

'As you may have noticed,' he continued, 'I brought some more females, so the total number ought to be two hundred and fifty now. I think we should sell fifty bullocks this year and slaughter about five to begin with.'

'To begin with? Why that would leave a hundred and ninety-odd to feed for the winter. Impossible!'

'Not if we buy some fodder and also start haymaking now. I'd like you to find some men for that job straight away please as a priority. I'll help them myself this afternoon if you have a spare scythe. The cattle will be able to stay outside most of the year, I understand, but we'll need extra feed for when they have to be brought indoors.'

'That's not how we do things here,' Seton protested, his gaze darkening.

'Why not? Come spring, I'd like at least a hundred and twenty animals alive so we'll have a decent sized herd next year. As I said, the pasture should support upwards of three hundred.'

'But where will you house them if the weather is bad? The townspeople can only take between three to six each, depending on the size of their huts, some only one.'

'I'm sure we can build a new barn for the purpose. At a pinch, some of them can go in the stables, since they seem sadly empty with only four garrons and my horse in there. It shouldn't be a problem. Also, I gather we need a new building for the hay. I think we ought to build that first. Do you agree?'

Without giving Seton the chance to say anything or protest further, Brice changed tack.

'I was told you've been reporting to Mrs Kinross in my father's absence, is that correct?'

'Aye, in as much as it was possible, her being female and all.'

'You're saying she didn't understand estate matters?'

'Not really, no. And half the time she's sickly, as you must know. Mostly she gave me free rein.'

'I see. And you've been dealing with all the correspondence on her behalf?'

'What little there was, yes.'

'So you would have been the one receiving my father's letters?'

'There weren't many, as I recall. I did wonder at it myself, but then with things being the way they are here in Scotland, I thought perhaps they weren't getting through. Mrs Kinross remarked upon it as well.'

Brice frowned. 'My father told me he wrote to you at least four times a year.'

Seton shrugged again. 'I didn't receive anything near as many letters as that.'

Since he didn't believe him, Brice didn't comment on this. Instead, he changed the topic of conversation again rather abruptly. 'I had a quick look at the fields yesterday too – I'd say it will be time for the harvest within the next couple of weeks. What do you think?'

'Yes, although we need a few more sunny days.'

'Agreed. How about we make a start in, say, ten days?'

'We?'

Brice raised his eyebrows at the man. 'Yes, of course. It's all hands on deck during harvest time, is it not? At least where I come from.'

Seton goggled at him, then shook his head. 'You'll have to excuse me, my lord, but I'm past my prime and I injured my back not long since.'

'I see.' Brice thought he saw all too clearly, but decided against forcing the man to take part. He hid a smile. He hadn't expected anything else, although as far as he could see, there was nothing wrong with the factor whatsoever. In fact, he'd seldom seen a man his age in such good shape, apart from maybe his own father. 'Let's hope there are plenty of other strong men around then. You have enough scythes I take it or do I need to buy some?'

'Scythes? What for? The grain is simply pulled from

the ground so all you need are your hands.' Seton looked confused.

'Pulled from the ground? Roots and all?' Brice couldn't believe what he was hearing.

'Aye, that's how it's usually done. Then the grain is extracted from the ears by burning – *graddaning* we call it.'

'Preposterous! No wonder you have to slaughter so many animals each autumn. You'll have no straw for winter feeding.'

'Exactly.' Seton's expression indicated that he thought he'd made his point, whereas in fact he'd only made Brice more determined to have his way.

'Well, it's not how I'd like you to do it this year. We're using scythes. You'll humour me by trying my way, at least this once, won't you?' It wasn't really a question, they both knew that.

Seton scowled. 'On your head be it,' he muttered darkly.

'Indeed. Please tell the men to get started on the haymaking immediately then. I'll join them as soon as I can.' Brice nodded dismissal. 'I'll see you later.'

After Seton had left, Brice sat for a long time deep in thought. He'd have a hard time proving the factor had done anything wrong so more drastic measures were called for. He pulled a clean sheet of paper towards him and began to write a letter to his father.

He needed assistance.

'He's a strange carle, so he is.' Greine came into the kitchen, carrying a basket full of kale which she'd just washed in the loch. 'Don't know what to make of him.'

Marsaili, who was sitting by the kitchen table trying to make a note of all their new supplies in the household account book, looked up from her task. 'Who?'

'The laird, of course.'

'Why do you say he's a strange man? What's he doing now? Handing out more food?' Although she was joking about it, she knew it wasn't a laughing matter, but she was also aware her employer wouldn't be able to buy his tenants' affection simply by giving them things. *He should just comb their hair for them.* She squashed the unruly thought, but couldn't quite suppress a delicious shiver which trailed down her spine as she remembered how good his ministrations had felt earlier.

'No, he's making hay. Wielding a scythe as though he was born to it. And him the laird! That's not something I ever looked to see.'

Marsaili stared at Greine. 'Really? Well, I never.' It would seem he'd understood. A thought struck her and she smiled. 'Has he got Mr Seton helping out as well?'

Greine snorted. 'Hardly. Haven't seen hide nor hair of him since that meeting in the estate office this morn. Did you see him leave with his tail between his legs?'

Marsaili frowned. 'No, but I hope the laird knows what he's doing. Antagonising Mr Seton can be dangerous. He's likely to strike back.'

'Well, I didn't hear a stramash, so I'd guess the factor's just a mite put out not to be in charge any more. He'll come round. After all, he must have kennt it was going to happen one day.'

'Yes, but not so soon.' As he'd told her, not long ago.

'Anyway, you should go for a wee walk down the meadow,' Greine said with a twinkle in her eyes.

'Why would I want to do that? I have work to do.' Marsaili tried to look stern.

'Well, he's a fine figure of a man, and no mistake. A woman could do worse than look at him.' Greine laughed out loud as Marsaili picked up a nearby rolling pin to mock threaten her with.

'Honestly, is there anyone around here who's not set on match-making?'

But for the rest of the afternoon, she had to fight an overwhelming urge to go for a walk.

Only a few men answered the summons to help with haymaking, but Brice was pleased to see Sandy *Mor* and his son Rob among them. He knew if he could win the trust of the main tacksmen, the rest of the tenants might follow. Despite being short-handed, they finished by late afternoon. They'd cut as much grass as they could of the kind which grew in the wetter fields near the loch. Some of the township women had spread it out to dry and had promised to turn it regularly. It wasn't much, but it was a start. Brice could only hope more would grow before winter set in. He'd also been pleased to see Archie and some of the other children arrive at regular intervals with baskets full of grass they'd collected elsewhere.

'That's a great help,' he told them. 'Keep it up, then come to me for payment. Archie, you'll tell me how much I owe each child, won't you?'

'Aye, I will.' Archie beamed at him and scurried off.

Upon his return to the house, Brice washed and changed his clothes, then made his way to the north tower and knocked on the door to Ailsa's rooms. Flora opened it and smiled when she saw it was him.

'Come in, Brice. I'm sure Mother will be pleased to see you.' She added in a whisper. 'You've no idea how your arrival here has invigorated her. It's been ages since I've seen her this lively.'

'Then I'm glad,' he replied.

He had always liked Ailsa, although as a young boy he'd never quite understood why she was always so melancholy. His own mother was full of life and usually happy and smiling. The contrast between the two women couldn't have been more defined if they'd tried. Despite her air of sadness, however, Ailsa had treated him with kindness and it was therefore no hardship to pay her a visit and sit with her for a while. His father had also explained to him about Ailsa's marriage to Killian's cousin Farquhar, which had been far from happy and possibly violent. It was understandable this should have left a mark on such a gentle woman.

'Ah, dear boy, how lovely to see you,' Ailsa said, her face lighting up. He bent to kiss her translucent cheek and was assailed by the familiar scent of roses which enveloped her constantly. Kirsty was sitting by the window and he greeted her as well.

'And you. I trust I find you well?' he said to Ailsa.

'Never better. Your homecoming yesterday was so enjoyable. I don't remember when I last had such an entertaining evening. I've been waiting for you to come and claim your birthright for a long time and now you're finally here.' Ailsa sighed happily.

Brice wasn't sure he'd agree with her that the previous night's supper had been entertaining, at least not in the way she meant, but decided not to comment on her remark. Instead he said, 'Well, I have to admit that I haven't. Been waiting, that is,' he clarified when she looked confused. 'My father never mentioned my inheritance until a few weeks ago. I'm not quite sure why.'

'I'm certain he had his reasons. Killian was always a shrewd one. Unlike my late husband ...' Ailsa trailed off and the despondency seemed to come over her again, but soon after she shook her head and smiled at him. 'But we mustn't dwell on the past. It's all over now.'

'Indeed, although I sense some people around here are having a hard time forgetting certain things that have happened.' Brice didn't want to upset Ailsa, but he needed some answers and he knew she was cannier than she let on. He'd discovered that early on.

'I take it you mean our factor, am I right?' Ailsa queried, her mouth tightening a little.

'Yes, exactly. Do you know … did something happen to him personally to make him take against the English so? I mean, I know all about his family losing their holdings, my father told me, but surely there's more to it than that?'

'I don't think so. It's just that some people, Mr Seton included, are very proud of their heritage and consider themselves terribly hard done by. To be fair, his brother was the only one who declared himself a Jacobite openly, so I think Seton expected to take charge of Bailliebroch after Culloden. Sadly it didn't happen and he's a man who holds a grudge, is our Mr Seton.'

'I can well believe it.'

'Are you having problems dealing with him?' Ailsa asked. 'I'm afraid I've had as little to do with him as I possibly could.' A shadow crossed her features.

'Nothing I can't handle.' Brice decided to change the subject. He didn't want to distress Ailsa and it was clear she didn't like Seton. 'Now let's discuss more important matters – your wardrobe.'

'I beg your pardon?' Ailsa stared in astonishment and Brice laughed.

'I just meant, your clothing, or possible lack thereof. I took the liberty of buying some lengths of material for you in Edinburgh, but I'm not sure I chose the right colours. Also, there may not be enough since I didn't know my cousins would still be here too. I'll have it brought up, but will you promise to tell me if you'd like any of it returned or exchanged? You too.' He smiled at Flora and Kirsty, especially the latter whose eyes were shining with excitement.

'How thoughtful! Thank you. It's been a while since we

had new gowns. Any materials will be most welcome, no matter the colour, I assure you.'

'Good. Then perhaps you can also use some silks? I brought some back from my last journey to China and thought you might like to have a length each.' He tried not to think about the fact that he'd originally bought them for Elisabet. They didn't need to know that.

'Really, it's too much. You didn't have to bring us anything.' Ailsa looked almost overcome.

'Don't you dare refuse, Mama,' Kirsty laughed. 'I haven't had a decent gown for years and I for one will gladly accept. There is just one thing though, cousin …'

'Yes?' Brice saw her eyes twinkle with mischief suddenly and wondered what was coming.

'Would there be enough for our other sister too?'

It was Brice's turn to be surprised and he stared at Kirsty, then frowned. 'Forgive me, but I was told Mairie passed away. Is that not so? I was sure Father said she caught the smallpox …' He almost added that he'd guessed Flora had insisted on nursing her younger sister, then caught the disease herself, which would account for the marks on her face.

'Oh, I wasn't talking about Mairie, but Marsaili.'

'What? You've lost me now.'

'Kirsty,' Ailsa admonished quietly, but there was no force behind the word so Kirsty ignored her mother and told Brice the story of how the minister had come to tell them about their half-sister.

'How extraordinary,' Brice said when she'd finished. 'I was under the impression your father … that is to say, I'm surprised he'd care so much about any illegitimate child he'd sired.'

Ailsa's mouth tightened again. 'To be sure, he never did with any of the others.' At Brice's startled look, she smiled wryly. 'Oh, I'm not blind, Brice, nor deaf. Farquhar left quite a few children in these parts, but they were all girls, so he didn't bother to acknowledge them. It seems he was still hopeful of having a son, however, which is why he wrote that letter and spoke to the minister before he left on his last journey. And I, for one, am glad.'

'You are?' Brice reflected that this quiet woman continued to astound him. There was a steely core underneath the soft exterior which most people underestimated. 'How so?'

Ailsa smiled. 'Marsaili is a sweet girl and since she'd lost her mother and I a daughter of the same age – with a similar name even – it seemed like fate threw us together. Besides, she belongs here, she's kin.'

'Indeed. But what about the others?'

'None have come forward with a claim of kinship.' Ailsa shrugged. 'If they had, I would have done what I could for them.'

Kirsty interrupted. 'So is that a yes, then? Can she have some of the silk?'

Brice laughed at her enthusiasm. 'Of course, I can always buy more.'

Ailsa's expression became instantly more sombre. 'But there isn't the wherewithal to fund such purchases. We don't want to be a burden to you.'

'Don't worry about that. Now I'd best go and fetch the material for you so you can make a start on your sewing if you wish. I'll be right back.'

Chapter Thirteen

'Marsaili, come quickly. There's something you must see.'

Kirsty came rushing into the kitchen, where Marsaili was still checking on the supplies in their unusually full larder. She turned to see her half-sister almost bouncing up and down, excitement staining her cheeks pink. At least she didn't look as though the 'something' was bad news.

'Can it wait? I'm a little busy here.'

'No, it can't. Come on.' Kirsty grabbed her hand and pulled her towards the door.

Marsaili shook her head and laughed. 'Very well. What is it?'

'Wait and see.' Kirsty's eyes sparkled and Marsaili wondered what on earth she was up to.

She followed her up to Ailsa's rooms where the door stood open already. Marsaili stopped dead on the threshold, her eyes opening wide. It looked as if an entire draper's shop had suddenly been transferred to Ailsa's sitting room. There were bolts of striped cotton leaning against the wall, some basic bleached linen and several different shades of serviceable dark woollen material. What caught her eye the most, however, were the lengths of shimmering silk draped across Ailsa's knees and the nearby table and chairs. Marsaili put a hand up to cover her mouth, which had fallen open.

'How beautiful!' she exclaimed, then noticed that apart from the women, the room also contained Brice. 'Oh, I beg your pardon, I didn't see you there, my lord.'

He smiled and held up a hand. 'Please, don't mind me. I'm just a bystander.'

'Liar,' Kirsty said to him with a laugh. 'This is all his

doing,' she told Marsaili. 'He bought every one of these. Are they not splendid?'

'Indeed.' Yet again, Marsaili was surprised at his thoughtfulness, but perhaps his mother had had a hand in this. Or his sisters. Her gaze returned to the sumptuous silks. She'd never seen their like and couldn't take her eyes off them.

'Which colour do you like best?' Kirsty asked, lifting them up one by one to hold them in the light. 'I like this blue one, it's like a summer sky, and Flora is very taken with the lilac one.'

'No, the green is the loveliest,' Marsaili said without thinking. The stunning emerald seemed to shift to a much lighter mint every time Kirsty touched it and Marsaili thought she'd never seen anything so exquisite.

'Then you must have that one,' Ailsa said. 'For my part, the silvery grey is more to my taste.'

'Have it? What do you mean? These are yours, surely?' Marsaili came out of her trance and blinked at Ailsa.

'There is one for each of you,' Brice said, and added the word, 'cousin,' with a grin.

'But I ... no, I can't ... it's not seemly. I mean ...'

Ailsa held up a hand and spoke in a much firmer tone than usual. 'My dear, we've had this conversation before and you know my views on the matter. Brice is the head of the family now and he agrees with me. You are a daughter of this house and you have a right to be treated as such. Please accept this generous gift from your cousin.'

'Second cousin,' Brice winked at her. 'But who's counting? Apart from Iain.' He ducked with a laugh as Kirsty aimed a punch at his arm.

Marsaili was torn. She'd never been offered anything so fine in her life and it was extremely tempting, but it would make her beholden to Brice. What would he expect from her?

As if he'd read her mind, however, he smiled and said, 'If you all wish to give me something in return, then please make me a new cover for my bed. Every time I look at the one that's there, it reminds me of great-grandfather and I feel as though I'm trespassing.'

Ailsa laughed. 'Now that I can understand. The old curmudgeon is probably watching you and begrudging your use of his bedchamber.'

'Well, he wanted me to inherit this house, so he'll have to put up with it,' Brice said. 'But he can take his fusty old cover any time.'

They all laughed at this and somehow Marsaili didn't get a chance to protest any further about accepting the green silk and if she was perfectly honest, she didn't want to.

It was the finest gift she'd ever received.

Marsaili was one of the last people to enter the great hall for supper that evening. She knew the laird had issued another open invitation to everyone and this time the room seemed more crowded. There were at least fifty faces around the table, including the men, women and children who'd been helping with the haymaking. She headed for her usual place, but Brice's voice halted her in her tracks.

'Cousin Marsaili, you're to sit here from now on.' He pointed at the seat next to Flora, which was right opposite Seton.

'I don't think ...' she began, but to her surprise Ailsa interrupted her.

'No arguing, my dear. It's only right,' the older woman said, her voice firm. She'd declared she would take all her meals downstairs from now on, which was a small miracle in itself.

Marsaili wasn't at all convinced this was proper and neither was Seton if the look on his face was anything to go by. He glanced suspiciously between her and Brice, as if he thought there was some conspiracy going on. Or worse, maybe he thought she'd slept with the man to earn this favour? Marsaili felt her cheeks flood with colour. She didn't want to go against a direct command from Ailsa, however, so decided she had no choice.

'Oh, very well,' she said and went to sit down. No one else seemed to think there was anything wrong with this arrangement, but she couldn't help but feel awkward.

Flora, kind as always, whispered, 'Be glad you're not a boy. You'd have been envying Brice his position as the heir because you're born a month before him.'

'Am I?' Marsaili was momentarily distracted by this piece of news. She hadn't known how old he was exactly.

Flora nodded and added, 'Now think no more about it, please. You belong here with us.'

Marsaili tried to concentrate on her food and didn't contribute to the conversation. She smiled occasionally though because of the banter going on between Brice and his cousins. He teased them about how they'd attract all the eligible gentlemen in the Highlands once their new dresses were ready. Flora and Kirsty both answered back and Marsaili realised they treated each other like siblings. Neither of her half-sisters seemed to notice Brice as a man, although how they could fail to do so was a mystery. Perhaps because they were both older than him? Either way, for some reason she was happy about that, although why it should matter, she had no idea.

When she looked up at one point, she caught Seton staring at her with a thoughtful expression in his eyes. It was almost as if he was evaluating her anew and it made a shiver hiss down her spine. What was he up to now? She was very much afraid he'd thought of some new way of forcing his way into her bed. But what?

She turned pointedly away and swore under her breath. She mustn't forget to be on her guard. The wretched man could strike at any time.

Brice found he was actually enjoying the evening, greatly helped by his cousins who both seemed determined not to let the conversation flag. Some of the other people followed their lead, and when he threw a question at Sandy *Mor*, the man answered with equanimity.

'Coinneach Kinross? You don't remember the tales about him? Well, there's someone here who'd be only too happy to refresh your memory. Mungo? Did you hear that? You've actually got an attentive audience for once.'

He laughed and most of the others present joined in. It seemed to ease the tension in the room considerably and Brice was grateful. He smiled at Sandy, then nodded at the elderly man who stood up at Sandy's bidding. With skin dark and wrinkled by smoke and sparse hair which stood up in tufts from his domed skull, Old Mungo reminded Brice of a goblin. But there was nothing wrong with either his memory or his lungs, as they all soon found out. He obviously wasn't accounted the clan bard for nothing.

Mungo banged his hand on the table and called for silence. 'Listen all, fer I have a tale tae tell ye. A tale o' times gone by when the heid o' the Kinross clan was the first Coinneach and our ancestors fought by his side fer wha' was right. This is wha' happened and it's the truth, as weal ye ken ...'

Everyone listened to his story of hair-raising exploits, adventures, acts of vengeance on other traitorous clans and the bravery of Kinross clansmen through the ages. To Brice they sounded like a quarrelsome lot who liked to bear a grudge and who never hesitated to take revenge for the slightest provocation. This seemed to involve an awful lot of blood-letting, but not one of Old Mungo's listeners minded.

They were all as spell-bound as if they'd never heard his stories before in their lives and Brice had to admit he enjoyed them too.

He felt the kinship he shared with all these people more strongly with every word. He was MacCoinneach, the direct descendant of the man in the tales, and he owed it to him to take care of the clan. Their honour now rested with him.

When Old Mungo finished his stories, a couple of the other tenants, who were not to be outdone, fetched their instruments and regaled their new chief with further endless dirges about the heroic deeds of his ancestors. Marsaili had to admit the man bore it with fortitude, managing to keep his face straight even when the singer proved to be sadly out of tune as he'd had very little practice of late.

She found herself wondering if, some time in the future, such tales would be told of the present master. He certainly looked the part of a hero, his golden good looks emphasised by the glow of the candles. But did he have what it took on the inside?

That remained to be seen.

Marsaili was just about to take a tray of food to the estate office the following day, when a gaggle of children burst into the kitchen, all talking at once and looking very agitated. Greine had to shout 'Whisht!' and point her finger at one of them in order to make sense of what they were saying. 'You, Roy, take a deep breath and tell me what's the matter,' she said.

Young Roy did as he was told, then the words came tumbling out of him in Gaelic. 'We were playing over by the woods, Mrs Murray, and we were climbing up onto some of the branches of that really big tree and then Archie said as how he could climb the highest and no one would dare go as high up as him and we said he was just a braggart and wouldn't do it, but he did and now he's stuck and can't get down again and what are we going to do?'

Roy finally ran out of breath at the end of his long sentence and Greine got a word in edgewise. 'Are you telling me Archie's sitting up a tree?'

All the children nodded in unison and started babbling again. Greine turned to look at Marsaili. 'Lord help us,' she said. 'I'd best go see.'

'Hold on, let me just deliver this to his lordship and I'll come too.' Marsaili hurried off and ran into the estate office, forgetting to knock. She more or less dumped the tray in front of a startled Brice and turned for the door, muttering, 'Sorry, in a hurry.'

'Wait! Tell me what's happening, please?' His voice sounded imperious, so Marsaili quickly told him what was going on. To her surprise, he threw down his quill and jumped up.

'I'll help,' he said. 'Lead the way.'

She just nodded, too anxious about Archie to argue.

Greine had already left the kitchen and they caught up with her at the edge of the woods. It was really only a small copse of trees, not a forest by any stretch of the imagination, but that's what it had always been called for some reason. There was a particularly fine oak there, the only one for miles. It must have been hundreds of years old, Marsaili thought, and not far from the top of it sat Archie. From down below they could see he was clinging on for dear life, his face as white as death.

'Heavens, boy, have you no sense?' Greine scolded. 'What on earth possessed you?'

Archie didn't reply. He seemed to be beyond speech and closed his eyes.

Quite a few people had come running, but no one seemed

to know what to do. Marsaili bit her lip. The boy was so high up, if he fell, he might not survive even if the branches slowed his descent.

To her amazement, Brice started to take his shoes and stockings off, then shrugged out of his waistcoat. 'I'll get him down,' he said and shouted up to Archie, 'Just hold on, varmint, I'm coming. Don't let go, all right?'

Marsaili thought she saw Archie nod, but couldn't be certain. 'Are you sure you should be doing this?' she asked, but Brice only nodded and swung himself up onto the nearest branch.

Her heart leapt into her throat at the thought of him going up there, but after watching him for a few anxious moments, she had to admit it looked as though he knew what he was about. He made short work of the lower branches, which were stout and fairly evenly spaced. Higher up, he proceeded with slightly more caution which proved wise since once or twice a branch snapped off and made him lose his footing. A gasp went through the small crowd that was now gathered under the tree, but he seemed unconcerned and continued upwards.

'Nearly there,' he called up to Archie, who had his eyes shut again. 'Hang on.' This last admonition was plainly unnecessary, but Marsaili realised that by talking to the boy, Brice kept him from panicking. Her admiration for him rose a notch.

In what seemed like a relatively short space of time, even though it felt like for ever, Brice reached Archie and wrapped one arm around the boy's waist. 'I've got you, you can let go now,' he was heard to say. He had to repeat himself a few times until he penetrated the fog of terror the boy was obviously stuck inside. Finally, he made Archie comprehend that he had to put his arms round Brice's neck instead and hold on tight. 'I'll need both my hands to get us down safely, do you understand?' he explained.

Marsaili saw the pair begin the descent and felt a cold sweat break out on the back of her neck. Her stomach muscles were clenched so tight she could barely breathe and she hardly registered the low murmuring of the crowd all around her. She had eyes only for Brice.

He seemed to do everything with an easy grace, including tree climbing, and she watched, spellbound, as he used his powerful arms and shoulders to keep his balance. He lowered himself and his burden carefully from branch to branch until he was on the lowest one and could drop the boy down into outstretched arms. Finally, he jumped to the ground with the fluid movement of a cat out hunting. Marsaili couldn't take her eyes off him.

He looked up and met her gaze, then he smiled in that dazzling way. It seemed to her his smile was directed only at her, but then he turned to accept the congratulations from the bystanders and the thanks of Greine.

'I'm right sorry to have put you to so much trouble, laird,' the cook said. 'I'll skelp his backside for this, so I will.'

Brice ruffled Archie's hair. 'No, please don't punish him. I'm sure he's learned his lesson well enough already. I'd say he was very brave to make the attempt.' He winked at Archie. 'But next time, let me give you some lessons in climbing first, eh?'

Archie nodded and managed a weak smile. 'Th-thank ye fer g-getting me doun, sir,' he said in a small voice.

'Not at all. Now how would you like a ride on my shoulders back to the house?' Brice didn't wait for the boy's answer, but swung him up and sat him on his shoulders, then started walking. Archie squealed, but not with fear this time. He looked proud, like a hero returning triumphant from a battle and some of the colour returned to his cheeks.

Marsaili exchanged a look with Greine, who shook her head. 'The laird's too soft,' the cook muttered. 'But maybe he's right, Archie's had a fright, but he's haill. And after everything else that's happened to him ... Well, the least said the better. We'd best get back to our work.'

As they followed the cavalcade of excited children, running and jumping around Brice and Archie, Marsaili felt something inside her melt at the sight. It was a rare man who would treat a child so gently, especially one who'd done something so stupid.

She looked at Liath, who followed silently behind her as usual. 'I guess you're wiser than the humans here at Rosyth. You had his measure from the outset, didn't you? Wonder if he'll forgive the rest of us in time?'

Liath gave a short bark and looked as if he was grinning. Marsaili smiled back.

Chapter Fourteen

A week later, the morning dawned bright and sunny, and Brice was up early to make sure the harvest got under way. They'd had a run of warm, dry days, and the crops were ripe and ready – oats, barley and bere, the inferior kind of barley which grew on some of the less fertile fields. He knew they'd have to hurry if they wanted it all harvested safely. Any day now, it could turn rainy again, which would not be good.

He'd been perfectly serious about taking part and knew he'd already proved this by working with the men making hay. Helping with the harvest was something every able-bodied man, woman and child had to do at Askeberga and he didn't see why it should be different here. The strongest men would cut the grain with their scythes, the women walked behind, two assigned to each man. One laid the bundles ready, while the other tied them into sheaves. Children gathered up any left-over bits of straw and stooked the sheaves. It was teamwork, pure and simple.

'Anyone who doesn't take part won't get a share of the grain,' he'd told Seton the night before. 'Unless they have a very good excuse, of course.' He'd given the factor a pointed look, which had no effect since the man had skin as thick as shoe leather.

He was pleased to see that what looked like the entire population of the township had turned up and were being organised into teams by Seton. He allowed the factor to assign him to one such group and someone handed him a well sharpened scythe and a whetstone. The villagers were still a bit wary of him, but once the work got started, he noticed they relaxed a little. One or two of the men even dared a joke or two, comparing his technique to theirs.

'Is that how they Swedes dae it? Must tak'em till Yuletide.'

Since Brice could see well enough there was no difference, he answered in a like manner. 'On the contrary, you're the ones who'd be lagging behind,' he retorted with a smile.

Harvesting was hard work which needed strength and endurance. He knew he had both and actually enjoyed the physical exercise it entailed. It would also be satisfying to have the grain safely indoors in case the weather decided to turn, which was all too likely here in the Highlands. He'd had the men repair one of the barns so they had somewhere dry to store the harvest. Now all they had to do was bring it in.

All in all, he thought it was shaping up to being a good day.

Marsaili was in a different team to the one Brice had joined. Since Seton was in charge of organising these, she rather suspected he'd engineered this on purpose. He'd continued to dart suspicious glances between her and Brice at every meal, even though she made a point of not looking towards the head of the table unless she had to. She didn't want to cause trouble for the new laird unnecessarily and he hadn't singled her out again either.

She wasn't so far away along the field that she couldn't observe Brice, however, and she was pleased he was holding his own among the harvesters. He was right in the middle of the line of reapers, all swishing their scythes in wide arcs, working in tandem. Marsaili knew it was something that required quite a lot of skill, but she needn't have worried about Brice. He seemed to know exactly what he was doing.

It made her cross with herself that she cared, but since their meeting by the loch and his rescue of Archie, she had subconsciously begun to root for him. She knew he was going to have to prove himself here and she wanted him to become accepted. It may be silly, but if Liath liked him, he had to be a good man, she reasoned.

At lunchtime, everyone took a well-earned break and Greine and some of her helpers came up from the house carrying hampers of food. Pitchers of ale were also brought and everyone received their share. Marsaili sank down in the welcome shade under a small tree and rested her back against the trunk. To her surprise, Brice hunkered down beside her.

'May I sit with you?' he asked politely. She nodded assent and he lowered his tall frame to the ground and leaned against the same trunk. He was so close she felt his shoulder brush hers, but although she knew she should have protested, she didn't say anything. She discovered she liked having him near.

'I hope your, er ... swain won't mind,' he whispered, 'but I saw him go off to his own house just now so hopefully he won't notice. I've had enough of talking to the others for now.'

'M-my swain? Whatever do you mean?' Marsaili sat up straight and turned to stare at him. 'I'm not promised to anyone.'

'Oh? I was given to understand ... but perhaps I misunderstood.'

'You most certainly did.' Marsaili gritted her teeth to contain the anger welling up inside her. If Seton was going around telling people she belonged to him, it was the outside of enough.

Brice held up his hands. 'Fine, I believe you and I apologise. I didn't mean to cause offence.'

Marsaili settled back down and tried to calm herself. It wasn't Brice's fault after all, so she shouldn't take it out on him. 'No, I'm the one who should apologise. It's a bit of a touchy subject, is all.'

'I swear I'll never so much as mention it again,' Brice averred.

Marsaili just nodded, but after a short while she had to ask. 'What did he say?'

'What? Oh, no one said anything to me, it's just that from the looks I received whenever I talked to you, I gathered ... but obviously I was wrong. Really, I'm sorry.'

Marsaili was relieved to know Seton wasn't telling anyone he thought she'd soon succumb to him. It was bad enough him glaring at the laird when she was near him. One of these days, she'd have to make him understand she'd never be his. 'Please, forget it,' she murmured.

They munched on bread and cheese for a while and Marsaili felt strangely peaceful sitting here with Brice. She realised that apart from his first visit, he'd never ogled her the way other men did or made her feel uncomfortable. He did have a strange effect on her body, but not because he was consciously doing anything, except perhaps teasing gently.

'So when were you going to tell me we're related?' he asked, closing his eyes and leaning his head back when he'd finished his meal.

'I didn't think it was relevant. I've never thought of myself as your kin, no matter what Mrs Kinross says.'

'Well, you should. You *are* kin, she's right about that. And she clearly likes you, which in the circumstances is somewhat unusual.'

'She's a very kind woman.' Marsaili spoke from the heart. She'd never had a harsh word from Ailsa and certainly no reproaches for being who she was.

'Yes, indeed.' Brice turned to look at her and Marsaili drew in a sharp breath. He was so close, those heavenly eyes only inches from hers. They held her enchanted, she simply couldn't look away. If he leaned forward just a fraction more, his nose would touch hers and his lips ... She swallowed hard and blinked. His eyes crinkled at the corners and he smiled at her. 'I'm glad you chose the green silk, it will be perfect on you as it matches your eyes.'

Marsaili knew she was blushing, but an answering smile tugged at her mouth. 'Why, thank you, but ... I really shouldn't have it. You must have meant it for Mrs Kinross.'

'Can you keep a secret?' he asked and she noticed his gaze had turned serious all of a sudden. She nodded. 'To tell you the truth, all the silks were bought for someone else, but she didn't deserve them, so I just brought them with me when I left Sweden. I'm afraid I had no thought of being kind to Aunt Ailsa or anyone. Does that make you think badly of me?'

'No. At least you didn't sell them for profit and you've now made several people very happy by giving them away.'

'True. Still, it wasn't very noble of me to pretend I'd brought it for her and my cousins.'

'I think they'd forgive you.' Marsaili laughed. 'I should think any woman would forgive a man who gave them something so exquisite. Did you really buy them yourself in China?'

He nodded. 'Yes. I've been there twice and each time I purchased my fair share of goods, silk included.'

'Was that how you learned to climb, the way you did when you rescued Archie?'

'Yes. I was up and down the rigging with all the other sailors. My father thinks I'm mad, but I love it. The view from up a tall mast is incredible. Fair makes your stomach do somersaults.'

Marsaili shuddered at the thought. 'I don't think I'd like it. Going to China, though, that must have been wonderful. You are so lucky. To sail to faraway places and see the world ...' She sighed wistfully.

'And eat rotten meat and drink water with maggots in it

for weeks on end, oh, yes, lovely.' It was Brice's turn to laugh when Marsaili made a face. 'It's not as great as it sounds, but I admit the sights more than made up for all the hardships.'

'You're just teasing,' she accused.

'A little, but I'm serious too. I'm glad I went, but I have no wish to go again. From now on, I'll leave it to others.'

'Will you tell me about the good things some time?'

'What, like the giant squid with tentacles eight yards long that nearly capsized the ship?'

She punched him on the arm, which felt a bit like hitting a stone wall. 'Stop it.'

He chuckled. 'Very well. I'll tell you about my adventures whenever you like. But I may require some form of inducement, because it will be hard work remembering them all.'

'What sort of inducement?' She peered at him suspiciously.

He bent to whisper in her ear. 'One kiss for each tale.' Then before she had time to protest or even gather her wits, he jumped to his feet and called out that it was time to go back to work.

She could only be glad no one had been sitting within earshot of them.

Brice didn't know why he'd asked Marsaili for kisses. He knew very well he shouldn't get involved with her, especially now he'd found out she wasn't just a servant. Ailsa would have his hide if he tried anything. But there was no denying Marsaili was extremely beautiful and he felt drawn to her almost against his will.

Truth to tell, he'd been tempted to kiss her there and then, but of course he could do no such thing. It would have been tantamount to a declaration of intent and that was the last thing he wanted. He wasn't leg-shackling himself to any woman any time soon.

Thoughts of marriage inevitably made him remember Elisabet, but to his surprise the pain which usually accompanied the image of her in his mind didn't come this time. He frowned, then realised that when he closed his eyes it wasn't Elisabet he saw, but Marsaili. And if he compared the two, he didn't find his new cousin wanting.

That was odd.

He glanced over to where Marsaili was kneeling on the ground, expertly tying up a sheaf of barley. It was hard work, painful on the skin of the wrists and forearms, but she seemed oblivious and worked quickly. Her amazing hair flashed in the sunlight where it escaped the thick plait dangling across her shoulder. She moved with grace and there was strength in her capable hands and arms. As for her figure ... well, no man could complain about that. Although she was tall – much taller than Elisabet, who had been more like a small porcelain doll and fine-boned with it – she was perfectly proportioned. Brice turned away.

This wouldn't do. Women couldn't be trusted, no matter how lovely they were to look at. He'd learned that lesson now and he wouldn't forget.

Still, a little flirtation now and again couldn't hurt, could it? As long as he didn't go too far.

After a week and a half of hard work, the crops were all safely stowed indoors. Marsaili was bone weary, but felt a great sense of achievement as she made her way back from the fields on the final day with the others. Everyone was in a good mood, looking forward to the harvest feast Brice had ordered for the following day.

Brice himself walked at the front of the group, next to Seton who had taken no part in the harvesting other than as an overseer. Marsaili glared at the factor's back. She'd heard someone say Seton was pleading some aches and pains as an excuse for not helping, but she knew he'd consider manual labour beneath him. He'd never done anything menial for as long as she'd known him.

He and Brice appeared to be arguing and she lengthened her stride until she was within earshot.

'We're not *graddaning*. I told you, that's an appalling waste,' she heard Brice say. 'You know we need the straw this year.'

'But it's how things are usually done here,' Seton replied, his mouth set in a mulish line. 'Always have. I think you'll be hard put to find anyone willing to do anything else.'

'We're not burning anything. This year we're doing it my way, by threshing, and if it doesn't work, next year I'll listen to you.'

'They won't do it, I tell you.'

'They will if they wish to eat this winter,' Brice countered, clearly adamant. Seton opened his mouth as though he wanted to argue further, but Brice didn't give him the chance. 'Hold on,' he said and stopped abruptly, then jumped up to stand on top of the nearest stone dyke wall. 'A moment,' he shouted. 'Can I have your attention, please?'

Everyone came to a halt and shuffled closer, looking from Brice to the factor, whose expression was far from happy.

'Mr Seton and I disagree on the small matter of how to extract the grain. I say we should be threshing and winnowing, while Mr Seton would prefer burning as has apparently been the custom here.' There were a few perplexed looks, but also some nods from the crowd. 'Well, let me ask you this – would you do some hard work now for a couple of weeks and keep enough cattle alive over the winter to feed your families, or would you rather starve?'

There was an angry protest from Seton. 'Now see here,' he began, 'you can't just come and force your foreign ways on us willy-nilly.'

'I'm not,' Brice countered and gestured towards the people around them. 'I'm asking them to choose.'

Seton opened his mouth to protest some more, but before he could say anything else, one of the men spoke up. 'I'm for threshing,' he declared and took a step forward as if showing his solidarity with Brice. 'I'm tired o' seein' the weans go hungry.'

Another man nodded. 'Makes sense to me.'

'And me.' Sandy *Mor* joined them, as did his son.

Some muttering broke out among the other men, but most of them eventually sided with Brice. 'Aye, we'll dae it if ye promise we can hae our fair share.'

'I promise,' Brice said. 'I know it's a long, onerous job, but if we make sure the threshing barn is next in line to have its roof repaired, there's no rush. We can take turns after dark when all other chores are finished. Agreed?'

'Yes, I'll see to it.' Sandy nodded.

'Good, we don't want any water seeping in and ruining things. I'm not taking any chances, the grain is precious.'

Brice turned to Seton, who just shrugged. 'Be it on your head,' he said and strode off. Marsaili shivered as she noticed the dagger look Seton threw his new master before he left. It didn't bode well. She could understand why Brice was against *graddaning* since it was rather wasteful, but Seton had been correct in that it was the custom here. She only hoped Brice was right to insist on new ways.

The crowd dispersed and set off again. Those who were not returning to their homes in the township soon entered the courtyard of Rosyth House just behind Brice and found him standing next to a small, black-clad man by the steps to the main door. Marsaili felt her heart skip a beat, since she recognised him all too well. Mr Keil was a preacher who'd been shown the door the last time he'd visited and had been asked never to return to Rosyth.

Yet here he was.

It was obvious Brice had no idea who the man was or that he wasn't just an ordinary clergyman. He was talking to him politely and indicated he was welcome to enter the house. Marsaili wanted to rush forward and stop him, but decided it might be better if she warned Brice in private. She glanced at Seton, who seemed to have been waiting near the house. He had ordered the preacher to leave not two months previously, but he was keeping his mouth shut now.

Marsaili frowned. Something wasn't right.

She followed the others indoors, but instead of going to her room to wash and change, she waited until she saw Brice excuse himself and head for the master bedchamber. Making sure no one was looking her way, she followed him swiftly and caught up with him just outside his door.

'A moment please, my lord,' she whispered.

He turned, surprise in his eyes. 'Marsaili? What …?'

She put a finger to her lips and gestured for him to go inside. He smiled and did as she asked, closing the door behind them. 'I didn't realise you were so impatient for those stories I promised you,' he said with a grin. 'Or maybe it was the inducement you craved?' Before she could protest, his arms went around her and he pulled her close. She gasped and looked up at him, but in the next moment he stole her breath by putting his mouth on hers.

Marsaili forgot everything and just revelled in the feel of his lips caressing hers in the most wondrous fashion. She'd been kissed before, but always roughly and against her will. This was different. It was as if he was asking permission to continue by moving so slowly she could have broken it off any time. For some reason that only made her want more. She allowed him to nibble at her lower lip and stroke it with his tongue. He carried on, deepening the kiss and she reciprocated. It seemed her own tongue had a will of its own and it wanted to twine with his.

He tasted of ale and smelled like straw, dust and male. They were both filthy and hot after the long day's work, but she didn't care. Nothing mattered except the wonderful feeling of being held by him, worshipped with his mouth.

If only they could stay this way. If only she hadn't come to …

Her brain suddenly remembered the reason she had followed him and she tried to push him away, muttering 'No, wait, that wasn't why …'

He stopped kissing her and looked down on her, his gaze a bit unfocused. She noticed his breathing was ragged, but so was her own and her pulse was beating at least double its normal rate. He smiled, but didn't let go of her. 'That wasn't why what?' he asked, his voice a mere whisper.

'I just came to warn you, Brice. The man you welcomed into the house – you have to get rid of him. He's dangerous.'

His eyebrows shot up. 'A man of the cloth? Surely not.'

'He's not any old minister, he's a non-juring one.'

'Ah.' Brice's expression grew serious.

'You know what that means?' Marsaili had to make sure he understood the danger he was in.

He nodded. 'He's an Episcopalian clergyman, right? One of those who refused to swear the Oath of Allegiance to the English king. In other words, a hunted man.'

'Yes. The ministers of the old Scottish faith who won't swear the oath are constantly sought by the authorities,' Marsaili confirmed.

'I've heard of this, but I hadn't thought there were many left. I did wonder why a clergyman should turn up on my doorstep out of the blue like that, especially since I've already met the Presbyterian incumbent of the Rosyth parish. I understand now.'

Non-juring ministers were no longer allowed to preach and their meeting houses had been destroyed, Episcopal churches burned even. Anyone found harbouring such a man would be in breach of the law.

'You must make him leave,' Marsaili urged again, gripping his shirt front with both hands without thinking.

He shook his head, a thoughtful look in his eyes. 'No. I get the feeling he's here for a reason and I want to find out what it is.'

Marsaili blinked. 'Are you mad? The Redcoats could arrest you. Just having Mr Keil in the house is enough.'

'Then we must make sure they don't find him.'

'But …'

He put a finger over her mouth and she stopped talking. 'Listen to me. I smell a rat, but as long as I don't get caught harbouring the man, no one can do anything. I think I have a plan. Will you trust me on this?'

She nodded. Strangely enough, she did trust him. 'I want to help. What would you have me do?'

He smiled and bent to give her one last kiss, which she didn't resist. 'If any Redcoats come snooping, stall them outside for a few moments and I'll guarantee they won't find Mr Keil.'

'Very well, I'll do my best.'

'Good, then we'd better not keep him waiting.' He let go of her, but reached out a finger to stroke her cheek. 'And unless you'd like to share a bath with me, I suggest you leave now. I'll check that the coast is clear.'

Marsaili made her way to her own room soon after on legs which felt decidedly jelly-like. It wasn't from fear for Brice's safety, however, she trusted him when he said he was in no danger.

It was something else entirely which frightened her much more. Love.

Chapter Fifteen

'It would seem I was right. Like father, like son.' Seton wandered over to where the minister was sitting enjoying a tankard of ale while he waited for his host to return.

Keil looked up, a wary expression in his eyes. 'He appears friendly enough, but time will tell, I suppose.'

Seton noticed the minister was looking gaunt and haggard, as if he'd been having a tough time lately. There couldn't be many of them left now, hunted as they were by the Redcoats. He guessed it was proving more difficult these days for a man like Keil to hide and find shelter. He'd had a hard time persuading the man to come back, which wasn't to be wondered at. They'd exchanged some harsh words during the minister's last visit to Rosyth and it was only by chance he'd heard the man was in the neighbourhood.

He watched Brice when he came back from changing out of his work clothes. The way he spoke to Keil indicated he had no idea he was harbouring a fugitive, which was just what Seton had hoped. Brice had obviously had it instilled in him that hospitality was one of his main duties as laird and he didn't question the stranger too closely.

As a result, Seton spent the evening in a much better mood than he'd been in of late. Not only did he have Marsaili to look at across the table, but out of the corner of his eye he watched the new laird becoming the best of friends with Mr Keil. It was a very satisfactory state of affairs.

He couldn't wait for the morning, when things would become even more interesting. He smiled to himself. *At least from my point of view.*

Brice tried to act as though everything was normal. He

wasn't worried about the presence of Mr Keil, he could handle that. What was bothering him was Marsaili.

Or rather the way he'd reacted to her earlier.

Damn it all, he thought. *I shouldn't have taken advantage of her like that.* But how could he not? She'd been in his bedroom, so close he could smell the sweet scent of lavender and heather she used on her hair, and he couldn't resist. One kiss, he'd promised himself, but it just wasn't enough. He'd needed more.

She felt so good in his arms, so right. He wanted to crush her to him, hard, and never let go. Whenever he'd kissed Elisabet – and she'd allowed him to on quite a few occasions – he had held her carefully, as if she was a fragile doll. She was so small and ethereal, he always had the feeling she might break if he didn't handle her with kid gloves. With Marsaili, that thought hadn't even entered his mind. Although she was tall and slender, there was nothing frail about her. In fact, she was perfect.

He shook himself mentally. What was the matter with him? He had already decided to stay away from her, so why couldn't he? It didn't make sense.

He would have to try harder.

Marsaili had just returned from the kitchen the following morning when she heard the commotion in the courtyard. She'd gone to order more porridge for Brice and his guest, who were having an early morning discussion on the merits of religious tolerance, as far as she could make out. Seeing as they were alone at the table, there was no harm in it, but Marsaili was worried someone would overhear them.

Brice had obviously heard the noise as well. He looked up and met Marsaili's gaze, but he didn't look unduly worried. 'Excuse me just one moment, Mr Keil,' he said to the minister, then he stood up and went over to Marsaili.

'Do you remember what I said yesterday?' he whispered. At her nod, he continued, 'Excellent. Please, go then and try to stall whoever is outside for a little while. Pretend like you've never seen Mr Keil. And then could you go to the kitchen and gather up enough food and drink for a couple of days, plus fetch some blankets and a pillow and leave it all in the book room?'

Marsaili didn't understand this final request, but said, 'Very well.' She was sure he'd have a good reason for asking her to do it.

'Thank you. Now hurry, please, I need a little time alone with my guest.'

Outside Marsaili found a troop of Redcoats, led by a large, florid man whose scarlet coat strained across his corpulent middle. Beads of sweat stood on his brow, as if he'd ridden fast to get there, and both his boots and the horse's flanks were dusty. She wasn't surprised to see Seton talking to him and the expression on the factor's face was decidedly smug.

'Good morning, gentlemen. A fine day, is it not?' she walked across to where the captain and his men were dismounting, and stopped in front of their leader. She gave him her best smile and saw his eyes widen.

'A very good morning to you, Madam.' The man bowed. 'Captain Sherringham at your service.' His eyes strayed down over her curves, then back up to her face and she saw the familiar flame of lust light up his gaze. She pretended not to notice, but it galled her all the same. Honestly, men were so predictable, although for once this came in useful.

'I'm afraid the mistress of the house is indisposed, but I'm the housekeeper here. If you've stopped for some refreshment, I will order it brought immediately.'

'Er, no, Madam, although naturally a drop of something is always welcome.' Captain Sherringham cleared his throat. 'We've, uhm, received reports that a man of the cloth has been sighted around these parts and I was just asking permission of Mr Seton here for us to search the premises.'

'Oh, I see. Well, if you think it's necessary, then by all means, but I have to tell you I've been in the house since yesterday and I've seen no such person.' She widened her eyes at Sherringham, who frowned. Out of the corner of her eye, she also saw Seton's brows come down into a scowl.

'Now see here, Marsaili,' he began, but she turned to fix him with a glare that stopped him from continuing.

She turned back to Captain Sherringham, who cleared his throat again, a nervous habit which was already beginning to grate on Marsaili. 'I'm afraid I must insist, inconvenient though it may be, Madam,' he said. 'Shouldn't take us long.'

Marsaili sighed in an exaggerated fashion, but gave in with good grace. 'I suppose it's your duty, captain,' she conceded, wondering if she had stalled him for long enough. She didn't know how much extra time Brice needed, but hoped he had somehow whisked the minister out of the back entrance. The captain's next words made her insides freeze with fear, however.

'I've already taken the liberty of sending some of my men round the back. I hope you don't mind, Madam?'

'No, no of course not.' Marsaili tried to keep her expression innocent and clenched her fists underneath the apron she was wearing to stop from showing her nervousness. 'Step inside then, if you please.' She indicated the captain should follow her.

'Jones, Allder, you stay out here,' Sherringham barked at two of his men. 'Don't let anyone leave for now.'

The great hall was mercifully empty, but Marsaili couldn't help darting an anxious glance around. Was there anywhere a man could successfully hide in here, she wondered. *Not unless they climbed up inside the chimney.* Sherringham seemed to have come to the same conclusion and immediately ordered two men to search inside the flue.

'Nothing here, sir. Permission to continue with the rest of the house?'

'Yes, immediately.'

Captain Sherringham didn't seem disposed to take part in the search himself, but wandered round the room inspecting the faded hangings and old paintings with a faintly supercilious air. Seton stood by the door, watching the proceedings and Marsaili wanted to wipe the smug look off his face by clouting him round the ear.

'I say, what's going on here?' Brice came walking into the room, his gait unhurried and with an expression of surprise on his face. 'Are we being invaded?' The question was clearly meant as a joke, since he was smiling.

'Captain Sherringham, His Majesty's 5th Dragoons.' The captain bowed, although not with the same gallantry he'd afforded Marsaili. 'We're conducting a search of the premises, with the permission of this lady.' He nodded at her.

'I see.' Brice lifted his eyebrows at Marsaili, who shrugged apologetically.

'I'm sorry, my lord, I didn't think you'd object? The captain believes there may be a minister hiding in here, although I did say as how I hadn't seen anyone myself,' she said.

'Right, please carry on then,' Brice said. 'I hope you don't mind me continuing with estate matters?'

Sherringham nodded. 'By all means.'

Brice sauntered off and Marsaili excused herself as well. She remembered Brice's second request about the food and blankets, and hurried to gather together what he'd wanted. She took the items to the book room, which had clearly already been searched since some of the furniture was out of place. Dust motes danced around the window drapes as if they'd been pushed aside recently and some soot had fallen down into the fireplace where the Redcoats had obviously poked inside it.

She placed the food, blankets and pillow on the table, then jumped as she heard a voice whispering behind her.

'Thank you, Marsaili. Please could you close the door behind you and stand outside as if deep in thought for a moment? Then open it again and the food will be gone.'

Brice! Marsaili looked around, but there was no one there. Her gaze flew to the drapes, which were wide enough to hide a man, but she could see they weren't concealing anyone at the moment. She realised there must be a secret hiding place behind the walls and scanned them, wondering which one it could be. She saw nothing out of the ordinary, but nodded in the direction the voice had come from.

She did as he'd asked and when she opened the door again a short while later, the room was empty. She took a few steps inside, just to make sure, but she was alone. *So I was right*, she thought, *there is a secret chamber*. She'd heard of them, of course, but never imagined there would be one at Rosyth.

'Marsaili? What are you doing in here?'

She whirled around and put up a hand to still her heart, which had just done a somersault inside her chest. 'Mr Seton! I didn't hear you coming. I … er, was just checking to make sure the soldiers hadn't damaged anything in here.'

He grunted in reply and glanced quickly round the room. 'They haven't.'

'I know, so I'd better return to my duties. If you'd kindly step aside? I have much to do.'

Brice put his ear to the wall and held his breath. He'd heard Seton's voice soon after he closed the secret entrance and knew Marsaili was alone in the room with the man. Judging by her vehemence in denying any liaison between them earlier in the week, that was probably the last thing she wanted. But she was trapped and it was all Brice's fault. He swore silently.

He heard a change in Seton's voice as he answered her request to step aside. 'Oh, aye, you're always busy, but one of these days you'll make some time for me, eh?'

'No, I won't. I've told you before, there's no chance of that.'

There was a small thud and the wall next to Brice, which was quite thin at that point, shook slightly.

'You're not hearing me, Marsaili. I won't wait for ever and sooner or later I will take what I want, with or without your agreement.' Seton's voice was a hoarse whisper, vibrating with suppressed fury and also, Brice guessed, desire.

'Take your hands off me this instant.' Marsaili's clipped tone was equally angry and Brice frowned. What would he do if Seton forced himself on her? He couldn't stand by and let it happen, but neither could he reveal he'd been listening on the other side of the thin wall. And there was Mr Keil to consider as well. The preacher was in another part of the passages, but if the soldiers got wind of a possible hiding place, they'd leave no stone unturned until they found the man.

Hell and damnation! He waited with bated breath, his hands clenched into fists.

Marsaili solved the problem for him. She let out a shrill whistle, the kind any boy would be proud to produce, and Brice heard Seton utter an exclamation of annoyance at the same time as the sound of scrabbling claws came rushing down the corridor outside the room and through the door.

'Blasted hell-hound,' Seton swore. Liath growled and came to a noisy halt with a low, but threatening bark. 'Don't you dare touch me or else ...'

'You know he won't unless I tell him to,' Marsaili said,

sounding more than a little relieved. 'Now hadn't you better make sure the Redcoats aren't helping themselves to anything they shouldn't, Mr Seton?'

Seton muttered something which sounded like a coarse oath, but nonetheless he stomped out of the door. 'Haughty bitch,' was the last thing Brice heard the man say and then all was quiet for a moment.

Marsaili let out a sigh of relief and then murmured to the dog. 'Good boy, Liath, thank you. One of these days I'm going to let you savage him, so help me God … If only he'd give up!'

As she moved away, followed by the dog, Brice picked up the blankets and provisions and made his way along the dark passage towards the place where he'd left Mr Keil. His thoughts were all focused on what he'd just heard, however, and he realised he had been very wrong in his assumption that Marsaili was in collusion with the factor. It was clear Seton wanted the housekeeper, but she had refused. Several times, by the sound of things. And now he was threatening her if she didn't give in. How long had this been going on?

It certainly put his first visit to Rosyth in perspective and it was evident Marsaili had only been doing Seton's bidding as an employee. For some reason, that thought made him very happy. Then he drew in a sharp breath and stopped dead as he realised why.

He wanted Marsaili for himself.

Seton stormed into his own house and slammed the door shut so hard the rafters shook. He kicked an empty bucket which happened to be standing nearby and swore under his breath, but although the bucket made a satisfying din as it hit a wall, it didn't soothe him one bit. Captain Sherringham's parting shot hadn't exactly sweetened his temper either.

'I don't know whose idea it was to send for us, but you

can tell the dolt from me that I don't appreciate people wasting my time. I won't be coming here again without very good reason.'

Since Seton was the 'dolt' in question, he had a hard time not answering back. He managed to bite his tongue, but only just. Instead he vented his fury on Iain, who happened to come looking for his father soon after.

'I don't understand it,' he spluttered. 'How did the damned clergyman manage to escape? I made absolutely sure the English approached the house from two directions and still he evaded them. It's unbelievable!'

'It was you who called them out?' Iain stared at his father with a slightly disapproving frown. That was enough to make Seton even more annoyed.

'Of course. Who did you think it was? We want rid of the laird, I've told you before. If we can get him arrested, maybe he'll think twice about staying in Scotland.'

'The Sassenachs would never be able to convict him for housing a non-juring minister, surely? He's a foreigner and the Lord only knows what faith he belongs to. They can't blame him for that.'

'That's not the point, you fool. We want him scared off, running back to his own godforsaken country with his tail between his legs. Even if the Redcoats don't convict him of anything, they sure as hell won't treat him well while he's in their custody. We all know that.'

Iain was quiet for a while, then said, 'It's not right, Father. This estate belongs to him and you've taken more than enough of what's his already.'

'Have you gone soft in the head, boy?' Seton grabbed Iain by the shoulders and shook him hard, but Iain shrugged him off and glared at him.

'No, I think I'm coming to my senses. What you've been doing is wrong. As long as the laird was some stranger living far away, I didn't think about it. I thought he was an arrogant bastard who didn't care about his clan or his lands. Now I've met him, I know that wasn't so. He's a decent man, trying to make improvements and help his people. That changes things.'

Seton ground his teeth. 'No, it doesn't. Not for us. We still have our own lands and people to think about. They need us and the only way we can help them is by getting Bailliebroch back. How do you suggest we do that if we can't continue what I've started here? Think, boy, there *is* no other way. We'll never earn enough money otherwise unless we turn to highway robbery.'

'That's more or less what you're doing already,' Iain muttered.

'I'm doing it for you, for us!' Seton felt as if the rage would choke him and he wanted to punch his fist through the nearest wall. 'Can't you see?'

'All I see, Father, is that it's wrong and I want no part of it any more. Face it, we've lost Bailliebroch and we have to make the best of our situation. I for one am happy to stay here and be the factor after you. And Kirsty doesn't mind, she's not after being a grand lady.'

'Kirsty,' Seton spat. 'The stupid girl has turned your head to mush. I don't even know what you see in her. Insipid, blonde chatterbox –'

'Don't say another word or you'll regret it.' Iain's voice had enough menace in it to penetrate even Seton's fog of fury.

The two glared at each other for a moment longer, then Iain flung away and headed for the door. 'Do what you want, Father. But just so you know, I'll have no further part in it.'

'Yes, you will, or I'll tell the laird it was you who was stealing from him all along. He'll believe me, because no one in their right mind would denounce their own son unless it was true. And it is true, you were in on it from the very beginning. I can prove it.'

Iain stared at his father with eyes that shot sparks of fury. 'You're despicable,' he spat, before leaving. He slammed the door and Seton threw an ale jug after him. It shattered against the wood with a gratifying crash, but it didn't help cool his temper any more than kicking the bucket had earlier. He still wanted to murder someone, but he'd be damned if he'd give up this easily. This plan hadn't worked, too bad. He'd come up with another.

Chapter Sixteen

Thomas Sherringham was a man who'd been eminently suited to take part in the Duke of Cumberland's 'cleansing' operation in the Highlands. He hated the Scots with a vengeance and believed he had just cause – his only sister had died because of them. It made his blood boil just thinking about it.

Susanna had had her head turned by a Jacobite when the Young Pretender marched his troops into England. Believing herself in love, she'd followed the man back north and was never seen again. Sherringham later found out she'd died in childbirth in some Highland hovel and he'd taken great pleasure in killing the inhabitants and burning the place to the ground. In fact, he revelled in all the punishments he was able to mete out to suspected Jacobites, young and old, male or female. They were scum. An ideal world, to him, was one where the reprisals never ended, but unfortunately it was mostly coming to an end and the government easing up on their task.

It was not to be borne.

Sherringham knew the insurgency was far from over. These people were heathens, barbarians, totally without honour, in his opinion, and the Duke had been right when he refused to treat the Jacobites as normal opponents in a war. He agreed they were traitors to the crown, one and all, and not entitled to any rights or consideration even as prisoners. Sherringham was convinced they'd never give up their preposterous claims, even if outwardly they pretended to do so. The ferment was simmering just under the surface and all he had to do was scratch the top and it would come bubbling up.

He had recently been reassigned to the very edge of the Highlands where his superiors felt there would be less cause for him to punish anyone. He was determined to prove them wrong.

'There are Jacobites everywhere,' he declared to his troop. 'The people hereabouts may pretend innocence, but in their eyes I see defiance and deceit lurking. It's merely a question of rooting out the worst offenders by foul means or fair. Then we apprehend them and give them their just desserts.'

Instead of using only force, Sherringham now operated by stealth. He pretended to befriend a number of local men and waited for them to let slip some clues about their neighbours' proclivities. Often, he would join them for a dram or two of their infernal drink of choice, whisky, which he only tolerated because he had to. Men talked without constraint when under the influence of alcohol and he'd made use of this on a number of occasions.

Seton was different. He had actually sought out Sherringham of his own accord several times. Just recently he'd told him of the return of the heir to the Rosyth estate and his possible Jacobite connections. Sherringham immediately detected an ulterior motive, and this had proved to be the case. Seton wanted someone with connections to smooth his way towards buying back his own estate and he was willing to pay.

Seton had obviously thought information was enough to secure him a deal, but in that he'd been wrong. Sherringham wasn't about to sell his services for what might amount to nothing more than speculation. Instead, he demanded payment in gold and information.

'How much d'ye want then?' Seton clearly didn't like the idea of having to part with so much as a farthing extra.

'It will depend on how difficult I find it to convince them to sell you the land. Let's start with a down payment, shall we?'

And he'd made him pay several times now, which was perhaps why Seton had called him on this fool's errand today. Sherringham scowled as he rode away from Rosyth House. He didn't doubt there had been a preacher there, but the new laird was obviously too canny to get caught harbouring one under his roof. It was annoying, but not the end of the world. The man was newly arrived and if he really did have Jacobite tendencies, as Seton claimed, then it was only a question of time before he slipped up.

When that happened, Sherringham would be ready.

The harvest feast, or *ceilidh* as the villagers called it, was a great success. As the weather continued fair, they held the celebration in the courtyard outside Rosyth House and benches and make-shift tables were set out in one corner. Having seen their laird take such an active part in the harvest work, everyone seemed to have unbent towards him, at least a little. Marsaili heard quite a few whispered comments to the effect that perhaps the 'mon wasnae sae bad after a' and 'belike he was a bra' carle'. A good man? She couldn't agree more, but she also knew they still had a lot to learn about him.

He received more than his fair share of flirtatious glances from all the girls of marriageable age and even some of the older women. This wasn't surprising either, Marsaili thought, since he was a fine looking man. She couldn't help but feel a twinge of annoyance, however, because he wasn't discouraging them in any way. Whenever some girl smiled at him, he smiled right back. Marsaili found herself wondering if his deep blue eyes were as mesmerising to the other girls as they were to her. And did he look at them in the same teasing way?

She tried to banish such thoughts. They weren't good for her peace of mind.

When everyone had eaten their fill of the plentiful supply of food and some people had had a few too many cups of wine, strong beer or whisky, old Mungo got out his fiddle and one of his grandsons a whistle. 'Time for some dancing!' he shouted, and all the younger villagers present jumped up with alacrity to begin a reel with much clapping and stamping of feet.

Marsaili watched from the shadows, trying to keep out of Seton's line of vision. She knew he'd try to claim a dance whether she wanted to or not and she preferred to avoid this if possible. His hands wandered much too freely for her liking these days and nothing she did ever discouraged him. With any luck, he'd drink himself into a stupor soon. That had happened before.

'Are you not dancing?' The voice came out of the darkness behind her and made her jump. Brice materialised beside her and looked at her with eyes that glittered in the light from the nearby torches. He smiled and held out his hand. 'We can't have the most beautiful woman in all of Rosyth without a partner. There's another set forming, will you show me the steps, please?'

'I ... you don't know them?'

'It's been a while, my memory needs refreshing.'

She should have said no. This man was dangerous to her equilibrium and her conscience was telling her – no shouting at her – to stay away from him. But her body had other ideas. Putting her hand in his, she followed him over to where the other dancers were performing energetically. She gave Brice a short demonstration and told him what to do. He soon caught on, making her suspect he hadn't been entirely truthful.

'You, sir, are a liar,' she told him, but sweetened the accusation with a smile. 'You've done this before.'

He grinned back, unrepentant. 'I told you, it was a long

time ago. But I confess, I wanted to hear your voice describe the steps and watch you perform them first.'

'Why you –'

He didn't allow her to finish the sentence. Instead, he laughed and caught her round the waist, lifting her high into the air to swing her around. It wasn't part of the official steps, but she didn't care. She forgot about everything except the way his eyes danced with merriment and his hands felt so warm through the material of her clothes as they held her. Strong and capable, they almost encircled her waist completely and she revelled in the sensation.

'There's no need to lift me,' she protested half-heartedly. 'You're going to injure yourself. I'm not exactly a doll.'

A strange expression flitted across his face, but was gone almost as soon. He smiled. 'No, but you're perfect nonetheless.'

Marsaili didn't know what to say to that, except a mumbled, 'Thank you.'

When they stopped for some refreshment in the form of claret, she felt the wine humming through her veins. Or perhaps it was the excitement of dancing with him? Either way, it gave her the courage to ask him about the preacher.

'So what happened with Mr Keil?' she whispered, making sure she was leaning close to him so no one else could hear.

He came even nearer and she felt his breath fan her ear when he replied. A tremor of awareness shimmered down her back. 'I shouldn't tell you really,' he said. 'It's best you don't know anything about it, but he's gone so there's no need to worry.'

'He escaped despite the Redcoats?'

'Yes, they won't find him, I promise. And he's not coming back either, unless he's desperate. I gave him enough money to live on for a while and he said there were still places where he was safe.'

Marsaili nodded. It was good to know the danger was over, at least for now. 'It's a shame he can't be left in peace, but he's made his choice I suppose. Do you … I mean, are you one of his flock?'

'No. I was brought up in the Swedish church. It's slightly different, but not markedly so. To tell you the truth, I don't have strong feelings either way. I go to church like everyone else, where is immaterial. I believe God listens wherever I am when I'm praying.' He sent her a teasing glance accompanied by a lop-sided grin. 'Right now, I'm praying for another dance with you. Do you think he's listening?'

'For shame,' she hissed, but couldn't stop a giggle from escaping her lips. 'That's blasphemy, my lord.'

'Brice, remember? No one can hear you.'

'Brice …' She loved his name, loved the sound of it. Loved the owner? *No! Absolutely not.* She glanced up at him and found him staring at her with a strange expression in his eyes. It made her insides melt, but she told herself firmly it wasn't love and he wasn't for her. *Liar*, a little voice whispered inside her mind. She ignored it. Whatever the case, one more dance couldn't hurt, could it? She took a deep breath and reached out her hand. 'Very well, just one.'

'One what? Oh, yes.' He came out of his trance and took her fingers, pulling her back towards the other dancers.

They hadn't taken very many steps, however, when Marsaili was suddenly yanked out of Brice's grip. A strong hand encircled her wrist and pulled her away. 'My turn, I believe. You don't mind, do you, laird?'

Marsaili stared into the hazel eyes of Seton and suppressed a shiver. There was something lurking in their depths, a glimmer of menace which frightened her even though she knew he couldn't do anything to her here. She glanced towards Brice, wondering if he would make a scene, the way Iain always did whenever someone tried to dance with Kirsty.

Brice only bowed and smiled at her. 'Not at all. Thank you for your time, Miss Buchanan.' Then he melted back into the crowd. Marsaili forced herself not to stare after him, but she felt almost bereft at his leaving so suddenly.

Seton dragged her into the dance, performing his steps energetically and with much grace. It occurred to Marsaili that he was like a wildcat, his sinuous strength awesome, but terrifying to his prey. And she felt like prey, the way he'd pounced on her and claimed her. He had no right to do so without asking her first, and it was as though he'd been trying to show Brice that Marsaili was out of bounds. Only she was entitled to tell him though. This man had no authority over her whatsoever.

'So you're making eyes at the laird now, are you?' Seton sneered. 'Won't get you anywhere. He's been telling everyone he's not the marrying kind, so the only way you'll ever be a fine lady is if you marry me.'

'Are you asking me?' She couldn't quite keep the surprise out of her voice. He must be getting desperate if he was willing to wed her to have his way.

'I might be. The point is, the laird never will.'

She knew there was no point arguing with him or correcting his assumption that she'd thrown her cap at Brice. He would believe what he wanted to. She could and would refuse his offer, however, just as she always did. Although a marriage proposal showed more honourable intentions, she still didn't want him. Not on any terms.

'You may find this hard to believe, Mr Seton, but not all women wish to be fine ladies. Especially not if it means having to wed someone who is repugnant to them.'

He pulled her hard against him, even though the dance didn't call for such a move, and she was trapped for a moment. His body was firm and unyielding, a steel vice that made panic well up inside her. She tried to struggle against his grip, but stood no chance against his superior strength. 'Let go of me,' she grated out from between clenched teeth. 'You have no right to –'

'Repugnant, am I? We'll just see about that. I'm sure you're your mother's daughter and she wasn't hard to persuade. What you need is a real man as I'll soon prove to you.'

Marsaili gasped and flinched as if he'd hit her. She had known her mother had lain with several men before she finally married, but she'd never realised Seton was one of them. And for him to want to wed the daughter of someone he'd bedded long ago somehow made it all worse. She made an angry noise and kicked him hard in the shin. Thankfully it was enough to make him loosen his grip and she shoved him away. 'Leave me alone.'

'You little vixen,' he muttered, but she saw to her consternation that his gaze was still blazing with desire and he smiled at her. 'I shall enjoy taming you and it will be soon, I promise.'

He turned around abruptly and pushed his way through the crowd, heading for the drinks table. Marsaili was left standing among the dancers. She received a few pitying glances, but she didn't stay to endure them. With her head held high, she marched off towards the house and went straight to her room, followed by Liath who'd been waiting by the door. She lit a candle with fingers that shook, then threw herself down onto the bed and wrapped her arms around the dog's shaggy neck.

'Oh, Liath, what am I to do?' she whispered. 'Why won't he give up?'

The big canine whined softly as if he understood her turmoil and leaned into her, calming her with his solid warmth. He was her only protection, but could he keep Seton away for ever?

Not if Seton could help it.

Brice watched surreptitiously as Seton manhandled Marsaili into the dance. The man was an oaf who needed to be taught some manners, but Brice didn't think this was either the time or the place. Everyone was enjoying themselves and picking a fight with the factor would ruin the harmony of the evening. Most of his tenants seemed to have accepted Brice now, albeit cautiously, and he was reluctant to change their favourable opinion by asserting himself so blatantly.

But damn it all, the man was touching Marsaili as if he owned her.

Just as he thought he might have to intervene after all, judging by the furious look on Marsaili's face, she once again solved the matter herself. She kicked the man on the shin with considerable force. This was apparently enough to make him let go of her and then disappear out of sight. Brice saw her stand alone for a moment, in the grip of some strong emotion. Her fists clenched and unclenched, but then she noticed the curious glances being thrown her way and stalked off towards the house. He wondered whether to follow her and make sure she was all right, but decided against it. She would want to be left alone.

Feeling restless and not in the mood to dance with any of the women gazing at him with inviting looks in their eyes, he headed for the stables. He hadn't had time for any early morning rides during the harvest week, so he thought he'd check on Starke. The big horse was being given special care by Archie, but he still liked Brice best. Halfway to his horse's stall, however, he became aware he wasn't alone in the building. There were murmurings coming from a stall further along. A courting couple, he thought, and turned to leave. The last thing he wanted was to intrude on someone's privacy. Starke would have to wait.

A voice he recognised stopped him in his tracks. 'No, Iain, not like this. I'm not having it, I told you.'

Kirsty. Was she in trouble? Brice hesitated. If her beau was trying to seduce her against her will, he'd have to do something about it. Although they were as good as betrothed, it didn't give Iain the right to force her. Brice came to a decision – he'd have to at least find out what was going on.

He headed for the furthest stall and cleared his throat loudly. 'Kirsty? Is everything all right?' he asked.

A lantern hanging on the wall cast a soft glow over the scene and Brice saw his cousin blush bright red as he stuck his face round a wattle partition. Iain, who'd had one hand up her skirts, dropped them as if he'd been scalded, and scowled at Brice.

'We're fine,' he snarled. 'And if you don't mind, we're a wee bit occupied.'

Brice raised his eyebrows at the man. 'I was talking to my cousin. Kirsty, do you need rescuing?' He smiled at her to show that she need not feel embarrassed at being caught like this, but the colour in her cheeks deepened nonetheless.

She shook her head. 'No. Like Iain said, we're fine.'

'Good. You're both fine. I'm glad to hear it. I'll, er ... see you outside then. Or not.' Brice chuckled and turned to leave again, but Kirsty's voice stopped him.

'Wait. There is something.'

'Yes?'

'No, Kirsty. It's nothing to do with him,' Iain hissed.

'Maybe he can help. Please, Iain, we can't go on like this. You know that.'

Brice looked from one to the other and waited. Iain's mouth was set in a mulish line, but at another pleading look from Kirsty he shrugged and muttered, 'Oh, very well, but you're wasting your breath.'

Kirsty bit her lip. 'It's Iain's father. He's against our marriage for some reason and Iain doesn't want to go through with it until we have Mr Seton's approval. Can you help us persuade him? We've waited ages already.'

Brice almost laughed out loud. He was probably the last person on earth Seton would listen to on such a matter, but then the man would never take advice from anyone, of that Brice was sure. 'I'm sorry, Kirsty, but I don't think I should interfere between a father and his son.' He saw his cousin's shoulders slump and she blinked away threatening tears. 'Perhaps there's another way, though? How about if I let it be known I'm arranging a dowry for you, one big enough to tempt any man's family?' Brice gazed Iain straight in the eyes. 'Would that persuade him, do you think?'

Iain nodded, the sullen expression being replaced with dawning hope and perhaps even a measure of admiration. 'Money would sway him, definitely. But can you get your hands on a large sum?'

Brice grinned. 'I didn't say I was actually going to show it to him. We can put him off by pretending it has to be sent for from Sweden. In the meantime, we'll hint that you've anticipated your vows a little and the marriage needs to go ahead immediately. We'll have to hope your father is blinded by greed and gives his consent.'

'And if he doesn't? What if he insists we have to wait until the money arrives?'

Brice shrugged. 'Then I'll hand some of it over to you, enough to keep him on side. Once the marriage has been entered into, your father won't be able to have it annulled.' He smiled again. 'I'm sure you'll see to it all the legal requirements are met.'

Kirsty blushed once more and punched her cousin on the arm, muttering under her breath, but Iain and Brice exchanged a look of male complicity.

Brice sobered. 'After the marriage, you'll have to tell your father I'll be the one keeping the money safe for you. He'll have no claim to it.'

Iain nodded. 'For sure.'

'So is that agreed then?' He held out his hand and Iain took it and shook it firmly.

'Aye, it is.' Then he snatched up Kirsty and whirled her around. 'Now can I tell him to get lost?' he laughed.

'No, I will. Be gone with you, Brice, and wipe that smirk off your face before I do it for you.' Kirsty's eyes were sparkling with happiness and Brice shook his head at the sight.

'What a pair of lovesick fools,' he said, but he took the hint and made himself scarce.

Chapter Seventeen

Back outside the stables, Brice stood for a moment, debating whether to seek his bed or join the revellers for a while longer. Before he could make up his mind, a voice rang out and he saw someone walking towards him from the direction of the *ceilidh*. Seton. *Damn!*

'There you are, *laird*.' The last word was said in a sneering tone, as always, but Brice ignored this. His main priority was to steer the factor away from the stables, or he might stumble on Iain and Kirsty the way Brice had done. Then all hell would break lose.

'Were you looking for me?' he said and went to meet the man halfway.

'Yes, some of the men want you to join a little game. I hope you have a taste for whisky?'

'A drinking game? Why not.' Brice had been thinking of seeking a cure for his restlessness with a dram or two of the local brew, but he wasn't sure he wanted to do it in company with Seton. If there were to be others present, however, maybe it wouldn't be so bad. 'Lead the way,' he said and pretended not to notice the other man's smirk.

He soon found out what Seton had been grinning about. The game consisted of seeing how many cups of whisky a man could down and still walk along a narrow beam, which had been set up between two trestles, without falling off. The cups weren't huge and held only about three mouthfuls. But since most of the men present had already had more than their fair share, they lost their balance at the first or second attempt. Seton was as agile as a cat, however, and got as far as six, as did Brice and his childhood friend Rob.

Following his seventh cup, Seton's luck turned. Although

he almost made it to the end, he misjudged his last step and went tumbling off. 'Damn it all!' he bellowed, predictably a sore loser. He'd landed on the grass with a thump and swore long and hard while rubbing at various parts of his anatomy. Someone helped him up and he went and sat slumped on a bench.

There were shouts of, 'Robbie, Robbie!' and slightly less raucous ones of 'MacCoinneach, MacCoinneach!' as Brice and the other man took their turn. Both succeeded, making Seton glare from one to the other as if they had offended him personally. When Rob failed his next attempt, Seton just nodded. He then watched with narrowed eyes as Brice tipped his eighth cup down his throat and climbed up to attempt the balancing act yet again.

'Eight, eight, eight!' the onlookers chanted. 'MacCoinneach, MacCoinneach!'

Brice hid a smile. He was confident he could do it and he had the advantage of having been more or less sober when they started the game. There were two other factors in his favour as well – he was used to the even stronger Swedish *brännvin* and he'd had to balance on many a beam in rough weather while sailing to China.

'Go mon, go!' The voices grew louder, egging him on. He didn't want them to think he was showing off though, so he took it slowly, weaving a bit and pretending to almost lose his balance a couple of times. When he finally reached the end of the beam, the cheers were deafening. He accepted the congratulations and slaps on the back, but noticed Seton didn't come forward. The man had closed his eyes and feigned sleep.

Brice didn't care. 'Thank you all,' he shouted. 'If I can find the way, I think I'll seek my bed now. Goodnight!'

A few of the women called out to him as he made his way towards the house and he wondered if any of them would have offered to accompany him. He wasn't tempted though. He didn't want to acquire a reputation for seducing the local girls.

An image of Marsaili suddenly rose in his mind's eye and he stumbled slightly. *Damn it, but I don't want her either. Do I?* He stopped for a moment in the great hall as his head was spinning. He wasn't blind drunk, but neither was he sober and he cursed Seton, hoping the other man would wake up with a sore head. After his week of carousing in Gothenburg, Brice had vowed never to get into such a state again, but he'd had no choice tonight.

Thoughts of Seton brought him back to thinking of Marsaili. Was she really all right? What had the whoreson said to her to make her so angry? Perhaps he ought to check?

'Fool,' he muttered to himself. 'She doesn't need you.'

But was there really any harm in making sure?

Marsaili found it hard to go to sleep as the thoughts chased each other round and round inside her tired brain. Just as she was finally beginning to relax, however, there was a soft knock on her door. She sat up, instantly alert, and panic washed over her like a sudden cold squall, while her lungs constricted with agitation. Glancing at Liath, she noticed he wasn't growling. She frowned at him.

A low whisper came through the door. 'Marsaili? Are you all right?'

Her heart did an odd double beat, but she breathed a sigh of relief that it was Brice's voice and not Seton's. 'Yes, I'm fine,' she called softly. 'Thank you.'

'Are you sure? Only ... I noticed you and Seton had some sort of altercation. Would you like me to have words with the man? He's in my employ after all.'

Marsaili hesitated. She didn't doubt Brice could make Seton stop harassing her, but she knew the factor wouldn't leave it at that. He'd take some sort of revenge on Brice and for some reason she couldn't bear the thought of that.

'Marsaili? Talk to me.'

She took a deep breath. It seemed as though he wouldn't go away until he'd seen for himself that she was unharmed, but she knew opening the door probably wasn't wise. Still, if it made him leave faster ... She lifted the heavy bar and found him outside, frowning. The moonlight from a narrow window gave his features a strange glow.

'I didn't realise this was a fortress,' he said. 'Are we expecting invaders?'

Marsaili felt herself flush. 'I ... this part of the house is, uhm ... a little isolated. And I wouldn't want anyone to walk in unannounced in case it gave Liath the wrong idea.'

He looked past her at the big dog, who gazed back adoringly and thumped his tail against the coverlet. 'Oh, hello boy.' Brice smiled and turned back to Marsaili. 'It's nice to know you're protected. Should it be necessary, I mean.'

She nodded. A strong smell of whisky emanated from him and she wrinkled her nose even though he didn't appear particularly inebriated. Had he been swimming in the stuff, she wondered? Either way, caution was probably the better part of valour so she gripped the door and said firmly, 'Indeed. Now as you can see, I'm perfectly fine so perhaps you should go back to the *ceilidh*? I need to sleep if I'm to be up in time for my duties tomorrow. I'll bid you goodnight.'

Without warning, he reached out a hand and stroked her cheek with two slightly rough fingers. 'I thought everyone would have a rest day after working so hard this week. You deserve one too.'

His fingers were barely touching her, but she was aware of nothing else. The contact made her skin tingle and the breath catch in her throat. She wanted to wrap her own fingers around his strong wrist and pull his hand closer. The fumes of whisky, combined with the fresh smell of the outdoors and his own unique scent, washed over her. It was intoxicating. Closing her eyes, she managed to resist the impulse to touch him, but she didn't tell him to leave.

He must have taken this as an invitation, because the next thing she knew his mouth was on hers. Butterfly kisses, slow and languorous, were dotted across her lips, each one lasting a little longer than the next. He was gentler than the last time he'd kissed her, and only placed his hands very lightly on her shoulders. If possible, she found this even more enticing. She knew the sensible thing would be to push him away and close her door, but she didn't want to. Not yet. She was playing with fire, but it felt good. Wonderful, in fact, and she didn't want him to stop.

'This is a bad idea,' he murmured against her mouth, then contradicted himself by putting his arms around her to pull her against his hard, lean body. Although it was an echo of what Seton had done to her earlier, Marsaili felt none of the revulsion or panic the factor had caused. On the contrary, having the length of Brice touching her almost from neck to knee fired her blood.

'Yes, very bad,' she breathed, opening her mouth for his tongue to explore. At the same time, she couldn't resist running her hands up his broad back and shoulders, her fingers burned by the heat of him through his shirt.

She'd never liked whisky herself, but the tang of it made his kisses taste like heaven. Marsaili couldn't understand it. She ought to have been repulsed and disgusted, instead she couldn't get enough.

His hands moved down to caress her behind, pushing her against him. She felt the evidence of his desire, but even that didn't frighten her as much as it should have done. A wanton part of her wanted to rub herself against him like a cat and she was just about to do so when a low growl from Liath brought her to her senses. Brice must have heard it too, because he broke off the kiss. They both froze and listened.

Someone was coming up the spiral staircase.

Brice glanced around him and tried to make his brain function. The heady combination of too much liquor and Marsaili in his arms didn't help, but he managed to assess his options somehow. They were on a small landing which didn't lead anywhere except to Marsaili's room, since it was at the very top of the tower. There was only one thing to do, as far as he could see. He propelled Marsaili into the bedroom and shut the door as quietly as he could, sliding the stout bar into place. He saw her open her mouth to protest, but put a finger on her lips to shush her. They both knew he shouldn't be in here, but he wasn't staying long and no one would ever find out.

The steps could be clearly heard since whoever it was didn't even attempt to mask his or her progress. Marsaili stared at the door as if in a trance, her eyes huge with fear. Brice could see she knew who was coming and that it obviously wasn't the first time it had happened. He clamped his teeth together hard. *Well, it will be the last*, he vowed.

Liath was still growling, the sound growing in volume until it seemed to rumble round the small room. Brice gave the dog a pat of approval, then moved silently to stand behind Marsaili. He put his arms around her waist and pulled her against his chest. He could feel her trembling, but she relaxed slightly and leaned into him as if she trusted him to keep her safe. This made him draw in a sharp breath, but he didn't stop to analyse the protective instincts she was awakening. Time for that later perhaps.

A kick on the door announced the visitor's arrival outside. 'Marsaili? I know you're in there so don't pretend you're not. And that infra ... infr ... *infernal* animal too.'

Seton. Brice wanted to bare his fangs and growl, the way Liath was doing right now. A wave of anger washed through him, but he tried to keep it at bay. The man was obviously still drunk and there was no way Brice could confront him at the moment. That would compromise Marsaili beyond return. He hugged her closer and leaned his cheek against the top of her head. He was surprised to realise she fit against him perfectly, her soft curves moulded to him. It was as if she'd been made for him and him alone.

Seton's slurred voice interrupted his thoughts. 'Don't think you can 'scape me ... Y'know it's futile. You're mine. Always have been.' Seton laughed, a humourless cackle. 'Wouldn't be here if it wasn't for me. Sh'd thank me. Be a whore like your mother oth'wise. I made that lelly-liv ... lily-livered priest come see the widow. He'd told me 'bout your father years before.'

Marsaili's chest rose and fell quickly, showing Brice that the man outside the door was distressing her with his disclosure. He put a finger on her mouth again to indicate it was better not to reply. Engaging a drunk man in conversation only prolonged it, in his experience, and it was the last thing they wanted.

Seton gave one last bellow of frustration and thumped on the door with his fist. 'Sleep well, vixen. When you're mine, I'll be keeping you 'wake at nights, see if I don't ...'

The words trailed off and the door shook as if something heavy had fallen against it. Brice guessed Seton had passed out on the landing and he probably wouldn't be waking up any time soon. He swore inwardly, but dare not take the risk of rousing him, however, so he couldn't possibly leave that way. He was left with only one option.

Well, two, but he wasn't so far gone he'd contemplate the second one.

He pushed Marsaili gently out of his embrace and she turned to frown at him, consternation and anxiety clear in her lovely green eyes. Brice bent close to her ear and whispered, 'Don't worry. I'll leave now and I'll send someone to fetch Seton and carry him back to his house.'

'But what if he wakes when you step over him?'

'I'm not leaving that way.' He smiled and couldn't resist giving her one last kiss. 'But if you ever tell a soul what I'm about to show you, I'll have your guts for breakfast.' He was only half joking, since his father had impressed upon him the need for absolute secrecy.

Her eyes opened wide again, but in surprise this time, as he walked over to a small garderobe built into the outside wall. Searching with his fingers, he found the hidden catch and pushed at the stones on one side. It required some force, but with a scraping sound, they finally moved back to reveal a narrow opening which obviously hadn't been used for quite some time. Cobwebs fluttered at the top and a slightly mouldy smell wafted into the room, together with a cold draught.

Marsaili blinked, but he gave her no time to comment. He just smiled and waved, then stepped inside and onto the hidden staircase and closed the door behind him. After standing still for a moment to allow his eyes to adjust to the faint light, he made his way down the steep steps with a slight feeling of regret.

He knew he'd made the right decision. Although spending a night with Marsaili would not have been a hardship in any way, he knew it would have had consequences. Consequences he wasn't sure he was ready to accept as yet. He needed to think and with Marsaili in his arms, his brain didn't seem to work at all. Not to mention all the whisky sloshing round inside him. He was therefore very grateful to his ancestors for having the forethought to provide him with an escape.

Quite what he was escaping from, however, he couldn't decide.

Marsaili spent a sleepless night, going over what had happened in her mind and staring at the wall where the secret door was located.

Had Brice used it before? Had he entered her room while she was sleeping? The thought made her shiver, but she didn't think so. For one thing, Liath would surely have given some sign of Brice's presence. Even if he never growled at the man, he always greeted him with at least a tail wag and that would wake Marsaili.

But what did she really know about Brice? How could she be sure he was to be trusted? Now she was aware of the hidden door, there was nothing to stop him using it if he was bent on seduction. And the thing which scared her most was that she wasn't sure she'd be able to resist.

I wanted him.

There was no disguising the fact that she'd completely lost her head while he kissed her. She had been ready to act the wanton, to forget all her principles and allow him to do whatever he wanted. In no way had she stopped his hands from exploring at will. Instead she had reciprocated, running her hands over those broad shoulders, the taut muscles of his arms and ...

Dear God, what must he think of me?

She had sworn never to let a man treat her the way they'd behaved towards her mother. First her father, Farquhar Kinross, and then a string of others had used Janet, until that old goat Simon Grant decided to marry her. And he'd only done it to have a housekeeper and someone he could knock about whenever he felt like it. Marsaili felt loathing for her step-father well up inside her, but quelled it. He was dead, no point dwelling on the past.

I can't let it happen to me.

She had to make it clear to Brice that she was not like her mother and never would be. As soon as possible, she would seek him out. She had to make him stop playing games with her because she didn't trust herself not to respond.

Brice emerged from his chamber around noon and headed straight for the loch. The water was decidedly fresh, but it woke him up and cleared some of the cobwebs out of his fuzzy brain. It couldn't cure his sore head, however, but he knew it was just a question of waiting it out.

A hearty meal of cold left-over roast meat with bannocks helped, and a tankard of ale went some way towards easing the pounding behind his eyes. He didn't really feel ready to deal with the world though, so when Marsaili came over and requested a private word with him, he frowned at her. She was probably going to question him about the secret passage and he wasn't in the mood for explanations.

'Can it wait? Only I'm not exactly at my best right now and I was planning on returning to my room for a while.' He put up a hand and massaged his scalp, which felt good.

'It won't take long, I promise. I ... just wish to discuss something briefly.' There was an anxious look in her eyes, which was unlike her, and he noticed there were dark circles underneath them as if she'd slept badly.

He swallowed a sigh. 'Very well, follow me.'

He led the way into the old laird's book room and shut the door after she had passed through. She stopped almost immediately and turned to face him.

'How many rooms in this house have doors like the one you showed me last night?' she demanded.

'I'm not going to tell you that. It's a secret shared only

by my father and brother and I shouldn't have shown you the one in your room either. It was only because necessity forced my hand. I hope you haven't spoken of it to anyone? I did warn you to keep it to yourself.' He glowered at her, his head starting to ache more fiercely again. He'd thought he could trust her, but perhaps not?

'No, of course I didn't mention it, but you must see it doesn't make me feel very safe.'

He tilted his head to one side and pretended to misunderstand. 'On the contrary, it ought to be immensely reassuring. If Seton ever comes calling again and succeeds in battering your door down, you can disappear into thin air and he'll be none the wiser.'

She took a step towards him and pointed at him, green eyes narrowed and shooting sparks. 'It's you I'm worried about, not Seton. He won't get past the door and even if he did, Liath would deal with him. You, however, there's no stopping. I doubt my dog would attack you even if I told him to, the traitor.'

He crossed his arms over his chest and regarded her from under hooded eyelids. 'And what makes you think I'd come sneaking into your room at night? I'm a well brought up young man. I usually wait for an invitation.'

Marsaili snorted. 'Like you did last night?'

He allowed himself a grin. 'As I recall, you opened the door when I knocked and although I'll admit to pushing you inside later on, that was to protect your reputation, not destroy it.'

She glared at him. 'So that's why you kissed me?'

He laughed, even though it hurt his head. 'No, I kissed you because I couldn't resist and because I felt like it. You didn't tell me to stop so I assumed my advances weren't unwelcome.'

'Well, they are, so kindly desist in future. I'm a respectable woman and you can't bamboozle me with your charm, the way you do everyone else.'

'Hmm, would you like to put that to the test?' he asked, stepping closer and running a finger sensuously along her lower lip while he stared into her flashing eyes. He saw them open wider in dismay when he pointed out, 'You haven't moved away from me even now.'

She shook him off and turned her back on him. 'Don't, please. I ... would be grateful if you would keep your distance from now on. Go and practise your wiles on someone else. I'm sure there are plenty of girls around here who'd be only too pleased to warm your bed.'

'Perhaps I don't want them.'

She threw him a glance over her shoulder. 'That's not what I've heard. I was told you think all women are the same and none worth bothering with for long, but you'll have any who offer you temporary amusement.'

It was Brice's turn to frown. He recalled saying something of the kind jokingly, perhaps to one of the other men, but he hadn't meant it to reach female ears. He attempted a nonchalant tone. 'Well, you can always try to change my mind, you know,' he challenged. 'Could be I just haven't met the right woman yet. That's what my father thinks anyway.'

'Maybe I can't be *bothered*,' she countered, pronouncing the last word with considerable sarcasm.

He chuckled. 'No, maybe I'm not worth wasting your time on,' he agreed. 'Was there anything else or can I go back to bed now?'

'You haven't promised to leave me alone yet,' she pointed out, peering at him suspiciously.

'Indeed.' His grin widened, but he didn't say the words she was waiting to hear.

She made an impatient noise and flounced to the door. 'Oh, you're impossible. Just keep away from me, do you hear?'

'Yes, madam, loud and clear.' He executed an exaggerated bow, but didn't stop smiling. 'Too loud, in fact. Ouch.' He put up a hand to his aching head again.

In exasperation she yanked open the door with unnecessary force and stepped outside, but in the next moment she came flying back into the room as if she'd rebounded off something. She let out a little cry of surprise.

Brice looked past her and groaned. 'Great timing, as always,' he said.

Chapter Eighteen

Marsaili fought to keep her balance. She'd collided with someone who had his hand up, ready to knock. A stranger who looked as astonished as she must do herself. Dark grey eyes blinked at her from under darker brows and deep brown wavy hair that was slightly too long. She'd bounced hard off a wide chest, but although the man was a bit on the stocky side, he wasn't fat, just thick-set and muscular.

'I beg your pardon,' he said, 'but I was looking for Brice Kinross.' He looked up and caught sight of Brice. 'Oh, there you are.' A smile spread across his features. 'I'm sorry, I didn't realise you were entertaining a ... er, lady.'

The way he hesitated over the final word made Marsaili see red. 'If you don't mind, sir, I'm the housekeeper here and we were having a discussion about provisions,' she informed the man, staring him straight in the eyes to see if he dared to dispute this. He raised his hands in mock surrender, but she could tell he wasn't convinced because his eyes were still laughing.

Brice smiled and came forward to envelop the man in a bear hug. 'Ramsay, it's good to see you. And Alex and Ida too? Well, well, we are honoured indeed.'

Marsaili glanced behind the man called Ramsay and noticed belatedly that he wasn't alone. A teenage boy with masses of wildly curling black hair and merry honey-brown eyes was grinning at them all. Dimples either side of his mouth gave him an impish look, which was reinforced by his gangly, lean frame and turned up nose. Holding his hand was a small girl aged about four or five, with hair as blonde as Brice's and serious blue eyes.

Marsaili drew in a sharp breath. Brice was a father? She

didn't know why, but somehow this had never occurred to her before.

'Gentlemen, may I introduce Miss Marsaili Buchanan, my housekeeper, as she mentioned. Marsaili, this is Ramsay Fergusson, my uncle, and a young friend of ours, Alex Adair, both come from Sweden for a visit if I'm not mistaken. And last, but not least, Ida.' He hunkered down and held out his arms. 'Hello, my sweet. Do I get a greeting?' The little girl smiled at last before running towards him. Brice lifted her high up and swung her around, making her shriek with joy.

'Higher, please, higher!'

Marsaili felt as though there was a knot pulling her insides tight until they hurt. Since Brice wasn't married, this had to be an illegitimate daughter and she couldn't help but wonder about his relationship with the girl's mother. It was obviously good, if she allowed the child to travel this far to see her father. Surely Ida hadn't travelled alone with two men though? Marsaili craned her neck to look out of the door again and caught sight of a young girl sitting on a bench in the great hall. A nursemaid or the mother?

The man called Ramsay interrupted her thoughts by joking with Brice.

'You should know we've come for a visit. You sent for us,' Ramsay laughed. 'Although come to think of it, you don't look quite at your best today, so perhaps you've forgotten? Should I hazard a guess as to what you were doing last night?' He sent Brice a teasing glance.

'Is it that obvious?' Brice shook his head, then grabbed it as that clearly hurt. 'Damned harvest feast. The villagers practically forced me to partake in some drinking game. What could I do but humour them? I didn't want them thinking their laird a coward or worse.'

Ramsay laughed again. 'I doubt they had a hard time persuading you. But I'm pleased you're in tolerably good spirits, unlike the last time I saw you.'

A shadow passed over Brice's features, but he quickly masked the pain Marsaili glimpsed in his eyes. 'I'm fine, apart from a splitting headache of course.'

'Glad to hear it. I've brought you some letters, but perhaps you'd rather read them later when you stop seeing double.' Ramsay dug out half a dozen letters from a satchel and handed them over.

Brice flicked through them, glancing at the writing as if he knew each and every one. When he came to the last two, however, he froze for an instant, then held them out to Ramsay, his mouth tightening. 'These you can burn. I don't want them.'

'Are you sure? It might help to read what Elisabet and Jamie have to say –' Ramsay began, but Brice interrupted him.

'I'm not interested in any more excuses. Besides, it's in the past. It doesn't matter any longer.'

Marsaili knew Jamie was Brice's brother, but wondered who Elisabet was. She was obviously someone who had hurt Brice in some way, judging by the way his eyes darkened at the mention of her name. Ida's mother? A woman he loved? The thought sent more sharp pain knifing through Marsaili's innards, but she gritted her teeth against it. Why should it matter to her whether Brice loved someone? She didn't want him anyway. To stop herself from thinking about the matter further, she concentrated on her duties as housekeeper.

'I'd better see about rooms for your guests, my lord,' she said to Brice. 'Shall I put them near you?'

He nodded, his brow lifting. 'Yes, please. And send for some refreshment. I'm sure you're all parched, am I right?' This last was addressed to Ramsay, who nodded.

'Something to drink would be very welcome, thank you, and perhaps a biscuit or something for Ida.'

'Of course. I'll see to it right away.' She hesitated. 'Er, would you like the child to sleep in your room or an adjoining one?'

'What?' Brice's eyebrows shot up, then he started laughing. 'No, no, young Ida is Ramsay's daughter, not mine.' He shook his head at her and added sarcastically, 'You really do have a high opinion of me, don't you?'

'Well, I ...' Marsaili looked from him to the little girl and then to Ramsay, who was smiling at her mistake too. The knot inside her loosened up. Why it should matter that the child was Ramsay's and not Brice's, she didn't know and she shied away from analysing this feeling too closely.

'Her mother was blonde,' Ramsay explained, 'and my mother and sister are too. Lucky for Ida she didn't inherit my looks.' He nodded towards the girl outside the door. 'Ida will be fine sleeping with Kristina, her maid, if you have a room for them, otherwise with me. Thank you.'

As Marsaili escaped from the book room, her thoughts were in a whirl, but she refused to allow herself time to dwell on them. She had a job to do and that was her only function here at Rosyth. Brice and his family were nothing to do with her.

'He's giving her how much?' Seton felt his eyes almost stand out on stalks as he made his son repeat the alleged sum of Kirsty's dowry. 'Is he mad?'

Iain shook his head with a smile. 'No, just rich, I would guess. Or his father is, at any rate. The laird says the money has to come from Sweden, so we'll only receive a part of it for now.'

'But that's much more than the original ...' Seton stopped himself, but even so, Iain threw him a look of suspicion.

'The original what?'

184

'The sum I'd originally thought she'd be receiving before I found out she had nothing.'

'Oh, yes, well, you can have no objection to the match now, surely?'

'I suppose not.'

Seton was barely listening. His brain was busy calculating how much he would now have left over after he'd bought back Bailliebroch. It would be more than enough to restore the house to its former glory, despite the terrible state the Redcoats had left it in. The thought filled him with joy and for the first time in weeks, he felt at ease with the world.

'Father?'

He realised Iain had been speaking to him and shook himself mentally. 'I'm sorry, what did you say?'

'I said, can I go ahead and speak to the minister now then? Do we have your consent?'

'Yes, yes, by all means. The sooner the better.' He waved a hand to shoo Iain towards the door. 'Women are fickle things. Don't, whatever you do, let such a prize slip through your fingers. Go, go, what are you waiting for?'

'All right, I'm going. And then I'd best see about having a house built for Kirsty and myself. With all that money, we can have one as big as this, can't we? No expense spared, with stone walls and everything.'

Seton scowled at his son. 'Don't be daft, boy. You won't need to live in a hovel, we'll use the dowry to do up Bailliebroch of course. That's where you and your wife belong.'

'For the love of ... haven't you given up on that notion yet, Father? We won't get it back, so there's no point saving the money for it.'

'Oh, yes there is. Just you wait and see. Now go!'

As Iain hurried out of the door, Seton sat down, deep in thought. He'd go to his secret hiding place as soon as he could safely sneak away without anyone noticing. He had a sudden urge to count the stash of coins he'd already amassed, just to make doubly sure. Not that he thought it was necessary now, but for the sheer joy of contemplating the fact that he had almost reached his goal. He was so close. *At last!*

He couldn't stop a grin from tugging at the corners of his mouth and soon after, when he made his way over to the big house, he even said a cheerful 'good morning' to young Archie, who normally annoyed him no end. The boy seemed besotted by the new laird and Seton couldn't abide watching the boy's hero worship of a man he himself loathed. Today, however, it no longer mattered.

Soon, he'd never have to see either of them again.

'So you didn't mind coming to Scotland then?'

Brice was walking down by the loch with young Alex Adair, who was looking around him with shining eyes. No wonder, Brice thought. It was a crisp autumn day, with veils of mist hanging just above the still water and draping the summits of the nearby hills. The purple and lilac hues of the heather, interspersed with yellow gorse and the starkly pewter-coloured rocks, made a spectacular backdrop to the towers of Rosyth nearby. It was almost a magical setting.

'No, absolutely not, it's wonderful here!' Alex enthused. 'My father has told me so many tales of his homeland, I've wanted to come for ages, but he wouldn't let me go.' The youth grinned. 'But when your request arrived, he couldn't say no, especially since I was going with Mr Fergusson.'

Brice smiled back. 'That's what I thought.'

'But why me? I mean, Mr Fergusson'll be more use to you with running an estate and so on. Me, I'm being trained for trading.' Alex made a face. 'Not that I mind very much, but

I'd rather be on the open seas without having to learn all those numbers and things first.'

'I know you're to be a merchant, but as I recall, you have certain other, shall we say, "special skills" I might be in need of. That is, unless you've turned into a saint recently?'

Alex's grin widened. 'Not bloody likely. I'm as good as ever I was and I still practise now and then when no one's looking.'

A look of mutual understanding passed between them. The skills Brice was referring to were illegal and probably shouldn't be encouraged, but he'd learned from his father that sometimes unorthodox methods were necessary. Alex's father had at one time been a pickpocket and a thief, before Killian rescued him from a life of poverty and crime. Despite now being an upstanding member of Gothenburg's community, the older Adair had taught his son all the tricks of his former trade.

'You never know when it might come in handy,' he'd apparently said. 'So long as you only use it in extreme circumstances and never for your own gain. If you do, I'll tan your hide but good!'

Brice had found out about Alex's extraordinary skills when he'd caught the boy practising on one of his mother's locked chests. At first he refused to believe the youngster wasn't stealing anything, but when both Alex's father and Killian backed him up, he realised it was the truth.

'I don't know how much you've been told,' he said now, 'but there's a man here, the factor Colin Seton, who I suspect has been stealing from the estate. He's very canny, so I very much doubt he'd keep any ill-gotten gains hidden in his own home, but just in case, I'd like you to sneak in and have a look around. Would you mind?'

Alex shrugged. 'Sure, as long as you keep him occupied elsewhere.'

'I will. He keeps his door secured, but the lock is old and shouldn't prove too difficult for you. However, if there's nothing there, I'd be grateful if you could keep him under observation to see if he'll lead you to his cache. And perhaps try and sound other people out in case he's acted strange at any time. Any clues as to where he's hiding the money would be great.'

'No problem. Just point him out to me and I'll get started.'

'Thank you. I owe you a debt for this.'

'Not till I've found something,' Alex laughed. 'Then you can give me a percentage. I've just been learning about those.'

Brice pretended to cuff the youth. 'Cheeky beggar,' he muttered. 'Come on, let's go and see where Mr Seton is. I find I need him to look at the stable roof with me.'

Ailsa and Flora came down for the midday meal and Marsaili noticed they greeted the newcomers as warmly as Brice had done.

'Why, Ramsay, how you've grown,' Ailsa said. 'You were tall last time I saw you, but now you've filled out nicely too.'

Ramsay smiled and kissed the older woman's cheek. 'Not too much, I hope? My sister will insist on feeding me, as if that's the cure for everything.'

'I'm sure she's only concerned for you. Do I take it you're staying with her and Killian at the moment then?'

'Yes, we thought it best for Ida.' He sent his daughter an adoring glance, but the little girl was busy talking to Flora and Kirsty and didn't notice.

Marsaili had been watching this scene and jumped when Brice whispered behind her, 'Ramsay was widowed two years ago. His wife died in childbirth and the babe also.'

She looked up at him. 'How sad,' she whispered back. 'He seems to have come to terms with it though.'

Brice nodded. 'Yes, Ramsay's not the sort to mope around. And he still has Ida.' His gaze softened as it rested on the little one. 'I envy him.'

Marsaili raised her eyebrows at him. 'You'd like children of your own?' He didn't strike her as the marrying kind, so this surprised her. Although, to be fair, he did have a way with both children and animals.

'Yes, as many as possible, especially daughters.'

'Now you're bamming me.' In Marsaili's experience men always wanted sons, as witness her own father's behaviour.

'Not at all. I told you, I have four sisters, and I've observed how they all adore our father unreservedly. I think sons are much more critical. My father certainly hasn't had an easy time of it with my brother and myself.' He laughed.

'Hmm, well, I wouldn't know about such things.'

Brice sent her swift look of consternation. 'Forgive me, I didn't mean to …'

'It's all right, I don't mind. Honestly, from what I've heard, I was better off without my father. He definitely wished only for sons, so he wouldn't have wanted me around.'

'Sadly, that's probably true.'

Marsaili was recalled to her duties by one of the maids asking her where she should put a pot of beef broth and Brice went to take his seat at the head of the table. Marsaili moved down so Ramsay could sit next to Flora, with little Ida in between them. She didn't mind and it had the added advantage of her not being opposite Seton, although for some reason he looked like the cat that got the cream today. Marsaili bit her lip. This couldn't bode well.

As soon as everyone had sat down, Brice stood up again and banged his spoon against his ale tankard. 'May I have your attention for a moment please. I have a very important announcement to make.' He smiled at Kirsty and Iain, seated side by side as usual. 'Today a date has been set for the marriage of this couple and I am happy to tell you that Iain will make Kirsty his wife not this coming Sunday, but the next – they've waited long enough already. A toast to them, if you please – Kirsty and Iain!'

Everyone joined in and Marsaili noticed Seton was beaming. That didn't seem right, since he'd been so against the marriage from the very beginning. She couldn't help but wonder what had changed his mind, but soon avoided his gaze. He kept throwing her meaningful glances as if to say it would be their turn next.

Over my dead body, she thought.

Ida was chattering away to Flora and it soon became clear they were getting on like a house on fire. Ramsay turned to Marsaili with a smile and nodded over his shoulder, rolling his eyes. 'I'm sorry, there's no stopping the little madam when she has an attentive audience. Poor Flora will want her sitting elsewhere tomorrow.'

Marsaili smiled back. 'I doubt it, she loves children. It's a shame she doesn't have any of her own.' Since this wasn't really a subject she ought to discuss with a virtual stranger, however, she changed topic. 'So, uhm, are you really Brice's uncle? You don't look old enough, if you don't mind me saying so.' She guessed him to be in his late twenties or early thirties at most.

'It's a bit complicated, but my mother had me very late and with her second husband, so Brice's mother is only my half-sister. I'm five years older than him, we've always been more like brothers really.'

'I see.' It was clear the two enjoyed a good relationship, which made Marsaili wonder about the other brother. 'And Jamie? Do you get on with him and all the sisters as well?'

Ramsay nodded. 'Yes, I do, but ...' He hesitated, a questioning look in his eyes. 'I don't know how much Brice has told everyone here, but he and Jamie aren't on very good terms at the moment. It makes it difficult for me, of course, stuck in the middle as it were.' He shrugged. 'I can see both sides and don't want to fall out with either.'

'I can understand that. I'd feel the same if Flora and Kirsty were to argue.'

'Precisely, but hopefully they'll come to some sort of understanding with time.'

Marsaili didn't want to press him further about the estrangement. It was private and if Brice had wanted anyone to know, he would have told them. She did wonder what it could be though, because Brice didn't seem the type of man to either stay angry for long or become annoyed at trifles. Whatever Jamie had done, it must be serious.

Later that evening, Brice shut himself in the book room and retrieved the letters Ramsay had brought. He quickly read the ones from his parents and sisters, smiling at each one in turn. There was no momentous news, but they were all full of chatty anecdotes of everyday life which made him slightly homesick. It was good to know they were all well though and missing him as much as he missed them.

At the bottom of the pile, however, were the two letters from Elisabet and Jamie. Ramsay had insisted on handing them back after Marsaili had left the room that morning.

'Don't be an ass, Brice, at least see what they have to say,' he'd advised. 'You owe them that much.'

Brice wasn't at all convinced, but he'd taken them without a word. He hadn't wanted to argue with Ramsay when he'd only just arrived. Now the urge to throw the letters straight onto the small peat fire that was burning in the grate was still strong. He'd been thinking about the whole *débâcle* less and less these last few weeks and reading these messages would just rake up all the hurt again. *What's the point?* he wondered.

Then again, the memories and pain had come flooding back just by seeing their handwriting. And he had to admit to a morbid curiosity as to how they would justify what they'd done. He'd refused to listen to their explanations in Sweden. If he read what they had to say, then that would be the end of it and he could put them out of his mind once and for all.

'Damn them,' he muttered. He stared at the letters for a moment longer before making up his mind. 'Oh, what the hell ...' He slit open the one from Elisabet first and started to read, scanning the lines of text with mounting incredulity.

He wasn't sure what he'd expected, but some sort of apology certainly. Instead, what she'd written was more or less a litany of accusations, claiming his 'neglect' of her had driven her into the arms of his brother. His 'cruelty' in leaving her for years on end instead of being there when she needed him and his 'obvious indifference' since he hadn't cared enough to stay in the same country as her until she was old enough to marry.

Brice shook his head, laughed and crumpled the letter into a ball which he threw with unerring accuracy at the smouldering fire in the tiny fireplace near the desk. 'Good old Elisabet,' he murmured, 'I should have known I could count on you to twist everything to your advantage. Father was right – I do pity Jamie.' Not that it excused his brother's perfidy, however. That was another matter altogether.

At least her letter confirmed what he'd suspected for some weeks now, that she wasn't the girl he thought he'd loved. *What a relief!*

Taking a deep breath, he opened Jamie's letter, wondering if he too would try to justify his actions by blaming Brice. He hadn't. Brice found only a few sentences and gritted his teeth as he read them.

Dear Brice,

I know you think I have forfeited the right to call you brother, but I just wanted to tell you whatever happens, that is how I will always view you – as my brother, my best friend, the person I've always looked up to most in the world. I cannot adequately express how sorry I am about what has happened. However, there is no going back and I have to live with the consequences. I know you probably can't forgive me, and I don't expect you to, but if you should ever find it in your heart to do so, please believe I'd do anything to make things right between us again. Just say the word.

Jamie

No explanation, no excuses. Brice closed his eyes, overcome with emotion. Anger, sadness and regret warred inside him, but the wound was too raw and fury won. He couldn't forgive Jamie yet and perhaps he never would.

With a savage curse, he flung the second letter into the fire as well, then stared into the flames as they devoured the paper and quickly turned Jamie's words into ash. He wished he could do the same with his thoughts, so he could have peace of mind, but as yet, they wouldn't give him any respite.

Forgive and forget? Maybe one day, but not any time soon.

Chapter Nineteen

The marriage of Kirsty and Iain took place ten days later, with Brice giving the bride away and yet another feast afterwards. The dancing and singing went on long into the night. Even the groom's father seemed pleased with the proceedings, although Brice noticed he wasn't too happy when Brice declared he'd keep hold of the dowry for now just to be on the safe side. He reckoned it would only be a matter of days before Iain was sent to ask for at least some of it with one excuse or another as to why it was needed.

Seton soon had something else to annoy him, however.

Two days after the wedding, Brice had the men round up all the cattle and bring them into a pen on the lower hill. 'It's time to sell off the spare bullocks. Ramsay, Alex and I will take the animals to market tomorrow, so we need to choose which ones to keep and which ones to sell,' he told the factor.

'But I wasn't going to set off for Crieff until the end of the week,' Seton protested. 'There's no need to go this early.'

'There's every need,' Brice countered. 'We want to sell while the buyers are still eager and they should be keen and waiting now.'

'Well, I don't know if I can be ready to travel so soon. My back is giving me trouble again and …'

Brice held up a hand. 'Don't worry, I'd rather you stayed here to keep an eye on things in my absence. Wouldn't want anyone to cheat me while I'm gone. Ramsay and Alex are all the help I need, plus one or two of the men. No, you take it easy and rest your back. Let Iain do the hard work, once he surfaces from wedded bliss.'

He saw anger flash in Seton's eyes, but the man couldn't

very well countermand a direct order from his laird, especially when it was worded as concern for his health. Brice guessed Seton had hoped to pocket some of the profits from the sale of the cattle and didn't like to be thwarted. *Too bad!* he thought. *I've had enough of his thieving ways.*

On the way back to the house, Alex came to meet them. He drew Brice slightly to one side and whispered, 'A word if you please.'

Brice nodded and the two of them waited for everyone else to pass so they were out of earshot. 'Have you found something?' he asked.

The youth nodded, his mouth a grim line. 'Oh, yes. There's a tumbledown old hut in the forested area over there,' Alex nodded towards the east. 'That's where he's keeping his stash, under a big stone which used to be part of the hearth.'

'Great, thank you! How did you find out?'

Alex smiled. 'Well, your little friend in the stables has pretty sharp eyes and he told me he's often seen Seton going for walks in that direction, which he thought was odd since there's nothing there. So I lay in wait and followed the man. But don't you want to know what I found?'

'What, you looked?'

'But of course! What's the point of finding a man's hiding place if you don't know what's in it?'

Brice had to laugh at that. 'Go on then.'

'There's a small chest almost full to the brim with gold coins. No silver or lesser metals, all golden guineas and half-guineas. He must have been saving for years!'

Brice felt his jaw tighten. 'Damned impudence,' he muttered. 'It should all have been sent to my father or used for the tenants' benefit.'

'So do you want me to fetch it for you? I put it back for now, just in case the man went again before I had a chance to tell you.'

'No, leave it. We can't prove it's his unless we catch him with it red-handed. I'll tell Iain to make sure his father doesn't go anywhere until we come back, then we'll confront him on our return. At least he won't be adding to his loot any time soon, I'll see to that.'

Little Ida was left behind when the men took the cattle to the market. The child didn't seem too concerned about being without her father for a few days and since her Swedish nursemaid was also there, Ramsay had no qualms either.

'I just hope she doesn't make more work for you ladies,' he told Marsaili and Flora, who happened to be with her at the time. 'I've noticed she's taken to you especially, Flora, but if she's a nuisance do tell her off. I'm afraid she's been a little bit spoiled since everyone feels sorry for her, being without a mother. She's not above using it to her advantage.'

Marsaili was interested to note that her sister's cheeks were slightly flushed as she replied, 'Not at all. Ida is a delight and she's always welcome to spend time with my mother and myself. Mama is teaching her to sew.'

'Hmm, well good luck with that.' Ramsay laughed. 'I doubt she'll sit still for very long at a time. I appreciate your kindness towards her though, I really do.'

Flora's cheeks turned an even deeper pink. 'It's no hardship, I assure you.'

After he had left, Marsaili couldn't resist teasing Flora a little. 'You like him, don't you,' she said.

Flora avoided her gaze and answered in a breezy tone. 'He's very nice, but he's not for me.'

'Why ever not? He's a widower, perhaps he's on the look-out for a wife and like he said, Ida has certainly taken to you.'

'Maybe, but he wouldn't want me.' Flora turned slowly back towards Marsaili. 'Look at my face. No one would.'

Marsaili saw the raw anguish in her sister's eyes and compassion squeezed her heart. She reached out a hand and put it on Flora's arm. 'Of course they would. If someone really likes you, a few pockmarks aren't going to make any difference. Honestly, Flora, I doubt anyone notices them but you.'

This wasn't quite true, but Marsaili willed Flora to believe her. Apart from her pitted cheeks, Flora was every bit as pretty as Kirsty and Marsaili knew she had a kinder nature too. She'd be a perfect wife and mother.

Marsaili hoped Ramsay was the sort of man who could see past small imperfections, because if he did, she was sure he'd be amply rewarded.

Before they set off with the cattle, Brice organised the rest of the men and youths into teams of four or five.

'I want you to make a start on repairing all the huts, please, beginning with those that are most tumbledown. The smith has been busy making nails, so there should be enough, and I know you can find all the other raw materials around here. You can take as much timber from the forest as you like. If there are any problems, talk to Mr Seton.'

'He's never wanted us to repair onythin' afore,' someone muttered.

Brice glared at the man. 'He has no say in the matter this time. Do you really want your women and bairns to freeze this winter? I've seen the state of some of your homes and quite frankly, I'm appalled. If you don't want to do this, fine, but if I were you, I'd jump at the chance.'

'Some o' the huts'll aye need building from scratch,' someone else said quietly.

'Well, the sooner you make a start then, the better, surely?'

There were nods of approval and Sandy *Mor*, the most

important member of the community apart from Mr Seton and the smith, spoke up. 'You're right, MacCoinneach, we'll see to it right away. Thank you. Come on, men.'

'I don't understand why they were so reluctant,' Brice grumbled to Ramsay as they set off for market. 'Do they enjoy living in squalor?'

Ramsay smiled. 'I think they're just testing you. They still haven't quite accepted you as their laird and don't like being ordered around.'

'Hmph. That's plain daft when it's for their own good.'

Ramsay shrugged. 'Give them time, Bri, give them time. Now what do you say we go to Edinburgh for a couple of days after we dispose of the bullocks? I have a hankering for some decent ale and entertainment.'

Brice shook his head. 'I don't think so. I'd rather not leave Rosyth for too long at the moment, I can't trust Seton not to do something stupid behind my back. You and Alex go ahead though. Ida's fine where she is, so you can be away as long as you want.'

'Are you sure?'

'Absolutely.'

'Very well, then, we'll go for a day or two, but send for us if you need us.'

Seton stood in his doorway and watched the laird ride away, wishing the man would never come back. He was a thorn in Seton's side and since he'd taken over the day to day running of the estate, the factor didn't even have anything useful to do. Not that he'd done much before, other than extract money, but still …

The promise of Kirsty's dowry was another sore point – Iain hadn't seen so much as a single coin yet and Seton suspected he never would either. It had all been a ruse, although why it should matter to the laird who Iain married was beyond him. The boy should have done as he'd been told and waited to marry the daughter of someone important once they had Bailliebroch back, but he thought himself in love.

'Pah!' Seton spat on the ground. His son was as brainless as the stupid woman who gave birth to him. Fat lot of use she'd been, giving Seton only the one child and then living for years afterwards so he couldn't take another wife. At least she was gone now and soon he'd have Marsaili in her place. On that, he was determined and he'd not let the laird stop his plans.

He hadn't really planned on marrying her, but the more he thought about it, the more it made sense. Not only would she be completely in his control, as his wife, but no one else would ever be able to have her. Seton was well aware of how other men followed her with their eyes. To have sole rights to her would be very satisfying. Besides, he had to marry someone and now the laird had acknowledged her as kin she wasn't a nobody any longer.

He glanced along the stone dyke wall which ran by the side of his house and noticed a part of the top layer had fallen down. The tacksman Sandy was walking past carrying an armful of tools and Seton called out to him.

'See to that, would you?' He nodded at the wall. 'And quickly before any more tumble down.'

'Sorry, Mr Seton, but the laird has ordered us to repair all the huts. No one can be spared for trifles just now,' Sandy told him with a distinct smirk. They'd never seen eye to eye and it was clear the man relished being able to refuse to do Seton's bidding for once.

Seton glared at the man, but knew he was beaten for the moment. It strengthened his resolve to be rid of the laird, however, and since no one seemed to need him right now, he sat by his fire and hatched a plan.

This time he wouldn't fail.

Brice entered the courtyard at Rosyth feeling tired, but content. The bullocks had fetched a good price and although he hadn't had much cattle to sell since he was trying to increase his herd, not deplete it, the sum obtained was a welcome bonus. Young bullocks were no use in any case unless for slaughter, it was the females who were worth keeping.

Archie came running to take Starke's reins as soon as Brice had dismounted. Brice couldn't resist giving the little lad a hug and a smile before handing them over. 'All well here?' he asked.

'Aye.' Archie grinned. 'We've barely seen hide nor hair of Mr Seton so it's been very quiet.'

Brice laughed and ruffled the boy's hair. 'Glad to hear it.' He put his hand in his pocket and brought out a parcel. 'Here, I found you something at the market which I thought you might like. But be careful with it, right? I don't want any bloodshed.'

Archie unwrapped the packet with almost indecent haste and then shrieked with joy. 'A proper dirk, I don't believe it! Thank you, thank you so much, it's wonderful!'

He hugged Brice's middle again, his little face beaming. Brice had known the boy would like a new dirk, since his old one was so puny and very basic. He'd found a small but sharp one with a horn handle inlaid with silver swirls that had seemed perfect. 'You're very welcome. You've earned it by taking such good care of Starke. Now, I'd better go inside, but I'll see you later, no doubt.'

As he took the stairs up to the great hall two at a time, he realised he was happy and what's more, he hadn't thought about Elisabet since he'd burned her letter. He barely even remembered what she looked like. That part of his life was well and truly in the past and he'd resolved not to think about it any more. During his time away, it had been another face which invaded his dreams, one with lovely green eyes and a generous mouth just made for … He flung open the door and collided with the owner of those very attributes, who uttered a little shriek.

'Oh! So you're back then.'

He put his hands on her shoulders to steady her and noticed she didn't shrug them off, despite her previous admonition for him to keep his distance. This made him smile and before she had time to react, he bent and quickly kissed her full on the lips. 'Indeed,' he said, 'and very glad I am to be here.'

'I thought I told you –' she began, but he interrupted her with another kiss, lingering a touch longer this time.

'Yes, yes,' he murmured, 'I know, but it's your own fault for looking so delectable. You tempt a man sorely, Marsaili.'

'Well, really! I don't see how I can be to blame,' she protested, but there was a tinge of pink on her cheeks that told him she was pleased at the praise.

He watched with amusement as she tried to collect her wits, but he didn't give her a chance to think about it for too long. 'So you missed me then,' he said, leaning forward to pull her closer and nuzzle her neck, just below the left ear. Her skin was feather soft and he inhaled the familiar smell of heather and lavender that was so uniquely hers.

'No, I didn't,' she replied, the breath hissing out of her as he nibbled her ear lobe. 'Kindly don't …' She put both hands up and pushed against his chest, but in a very half-hearted way.

'What? Not even a little? For shame! And there was I, yearning for your sweet lips …' His mouth made its way along her chin and touched the corner of those lips. 'Aching to hold you, taste you …' He flicked his tongue along the plump fullness, making her open for him, and then dived in. He vaguely heard another hastily indrawn breath and then she capitulated, kissing him back. Her hands came up to tangle in his hair, caress his neck and shoulders, and he allowed his own hands to wander downwards as he deepened the kiss.

A loud bark and something heavy bumping into Brice's thigh pulled them apart. While Liath greeted him as enthusiastically as always, Brice muttered, 'We're going to have to work on your timing, boy.' But he couldn't help smiling and patted the hound. 'Yes, yes, lovely to see you too.'

'I, er, had better go.' Brice quelled a sigh as Marsaili backed away and headed for the kitchen. 'I'll see about some victuals for you,' she said.

'Excellent, thank you. And unless it's washing day again, do you think I could possibly have a bath? Please? I feel as if all the dust of Scotland is clinging to me.'

'Very well.'

Brice knew he could have gone down to the loch. The water temperature was still bearable, but only just. His muscles felt cramped from sitting in the saddle for so long though and the hot water would be much nicer. He smiled again to himself as he went to sit by the hearth where a peat fire smouldered quietly, the smoke drifting in lazy clouds up the chimney.

It was good to be back.

No sooner had he finished this thought, however, than the door burst open and the Englishman, Sherringham, came striding into the room without so much as a knock. Brice got to his feet in an instant, his body tensing.

'You, sir, are under arrest,' Sherringham announced. Some of his men had followed him into the room and he gestured for them to grab hold of Brice.

Brice drew himself up to full height, which meant he towered over the Redcoats, who were all shorter than him. 'I beg your pardon? On what grounds?'

Sherringham pointed a finger at Brice and narrowed his eyes. 'We've found your weapons hoard, *laird*.'

'My what?' Brice felt his eyebrows rise. He had no idea what the man was talking about. On the walls of the great hall hung a couple of rusty old rapiers, relics of times gone by, but when he glanced at them they were still there, so he assumed the captain was talking about something else.

'Broadswords, muskets, pistols, dirks ...' Sherringham ticked these items off on the fingers of one hand. 'Quite a little cache you had here, although perhaps you should have hidden them better. Hay is so easy to move, you know.'

'I have absolutely no knowledge of any weapons,' Brice stated. 'I've only just returned from a trip to the south.'

'So? They've likely been here an age, since the battle of Drummossie Moor in fact. As I'm sure you know, it's against the law to possess any such things. You are facing at least six months in gaol. I have no choice but to take you to Fort George in Inverness.'

'Now see here,' Brice was becoming very angry and shook off the hands that were still attempting to hold him, 'I don't own any weapons as far as I'm aware and if my tenants had any, you must take the matter up with them. Besides, I'm a Swedish citizen and you have no right to arrest me.'

'Swedish or not, you're the laird here, and as such, you're responsible for your people and their possessions. That makes you subject to our laws.'

Brice clenched his fists and glared at the pugnacious man. 'You're making a mistake, Captain Sherringham. I have friends in high places down in Edinburgh and they will vouch for me.'

Sherringham sneered. 'A likely tale. And be that as it

may, they're not here now, are they? Summon them for your trial, if you wish. For now, you're coming with us at once. Jones, Allder, bring him.' He snapped his fingers and turned towards the door.

The soldiers who'd been given the task of dragging Brice along complied with this request with smirks and mutterings of 'how the mighty have fallen'. Brice couldn't resist fighting them off again, but several of their comrades came to their aid and in the end he realised it was futile. He couldn't take on an entire troop of soldiers on his own. As they entered the courtyard he saw Seton standing by the English horses, looking mighty pleased with himself. Brice threw him a look of loathing, but said nothing. Instead he called Archie over. The boy was hovering by the stairs, obviously finished with his task of seeing to Starke.

'Archie, can you fetch my horse, please. It seems he's needed once more.'

'Not so,' Sherringham put in. 'You'll be walking. Prisoners don't ride.'

Brice gritted his teeth and took a deep breath to stop himself from saying something he might regret. His hands were swiftly tied in front of him and attached to a long rope held by one of the mounted soldiers. Archie's eyes opened wide with consternation and he ran over to fling his arms around Brice's legs. 'No! Ye cannae dae sic a thing' tae him! Tak it off,' he shouted, using Scots instinctively so that the Sassenachs would understand him.

Brice bent quickly and prised the boy off, whispering in Gaelic, 'Never mind that now. Go and tell Marsaili what's happened and make her write to a Mr Rory Grant in Edinburgh immediately. Got that? He'll know what to do. Rory Grant, understand?' He added directions to Rory's lodgings.

Archie nodded, his eyes filling with tears which he tried to blink away.

'Everything will be all right, you'll see,' Brice promised. 'Just do as I say.'

'I will.' Archie ran off and disappeared towards the back courtyard.

Brice turned to Sherringham. 'Am I not even to see the weapons I'm accused of having hoarded? How do I know you're not making this up?'

'Oh, you'll see them soon enough. At your trial.' Sherringham sniggered and ordered his troop to move forward. Brice felt a tug on the rope that bound him and started walking. He was so angry at the moment, any discomfort was forgotten. Sending Seton one last look which promised dire retribution, he concentrated on thoughts of revenge. They would keep him going for sure.

Chapter Twenty

Marsaili was in Brice's bedroom, placing clean drying sheets next to the large wooden tub which had been brought upstairs by one of the men. When Archie burst in through the door, her heart skipped several beats and she put up a hand to steady it.

'Good Lord, but you made me jump, bantling. What's wrong?'

She could see from the boy's face he was in the grip of strong emotion and his mouth opened and closed several times before he managed to get any words out. He ran over to clutch at her skirts, raising tear-laden eyes to hers.

'It's the laird ... been taken ... Redcoats,' he panted. 'Said, must write ... friend ... Edinburgh.'

'Whoa, what? Taken? What on earth for?'

'Weapons ... an awful lot of them ... hidden.'

'I don't understand.' Marsaili walked over to the window which faced the front of the house and gasped at the sight before her. She could see Brice, his hands bound, being dragged along the road out of the township. The troop of Redcoats weren't even riding particularly slowly in order to allow him to keep up. He was having to half run so he wouldn't fall. She clapped a hand over her mouth and whispered, 'Dear God!'

She turned back to Archie to ask him for further details, when suddenly the heavy door to the master bedroom slammed shut. A grating sound announced that the key had been turned in the lock from the outside and both Marsaili and Archie stared at it for a moment before being galvanised into action.

'No, wait! What is the meaning of this?' She ran to the

door and pounded on it, but she didn't really need to hear Seton's laughter from outside to explain what had happened.

'Since the pair of you are so fond of the laird, I thought perhaps you'd like to spend some time in the man's room,' Seton called through the thick planks. 'I can't risk having you mobilise anyone to help him, so prepare yourselves for a lengthy stay. You should be comfortable enough.' He chuckled again and Marsaili banged a fist on the door in pure frustration and fury.

'You'll not get away with this,' she shouted. 'When the laird comes back, he'll see you pay for this.'

Another chuckle. 'If he comes back,' came the reply. 'I hear English gaols aren't the best of places to spend half a year. You can catch all manner of diseases, especially when you're weakened by hunger.'

'You're despicable!' Marsaili kicked the door for good measure, but only succeeded in hurting her toes, which made her even angrier.

'Yes, well, I'll soon have you changing your tune when you're mistress of Bailliebroch.'

'For the last time, I'd rather die than marry you, you snake!'

There was no reply to this, however, as Seton's footsteps receded into the distance. Marsaili sank down onto the floor, with her back against the door, and Archie followed suit. 'Now what are we to do?' she muttered.

'I don't know, but the laird … what'll happen to him? Was Mr Seton right?'

'Not if I can help it. But first, please tell me exactly what happened.'

As the boy launched into his tale, Marsaili clenched her fists in her lap and tried not to panic. She didn't think to question her desperate urge to help Brice. It was the right thing to do, nothing more. The kiss they'd shared was neither here nor there.

He'd just been in a good mood, teasing her, and meant nothing by it. It made no difference either way. *I'd be as concerned for anyone else*, she told herself. But would she?

She shook her head. Perhaps she did have a partiality for the laird, but she'd never admit it and nothing would come of it. It didn't change anything though. What had happened was an injustice and she had to extricate him somehow. That meant she had to think of a plan. There had to be some way of freeing Brice, but how?

Nothing could be done until they themselves had been rescued. And how could they be when no one even knew they were locked in? The master bedroom was in a quiet part of the house. It wasn't likely anyone would go near it. Could they shout out of the window? Doubtful. It was high up and no one had any business being at the front of the house at the moment.

But wait, the men bringing hot water? A brief surge of hope coursed through her, but then she realised Seton would probably tell them it was no longer needed. The laird had been led away, he had no use for a bath.

'Damn!' she muttered. 'There has to be another way.'

But as Archie stared at her, eyes big and full of hope, she knew she was grasping at straws. They were well and truly stuck.

Brice had known he was in for an unpleasant time, but had underestimated the sheer cruelty of Captain Sherringham. The man seemed to revel in his prisoner's discomfort and made no allowance whatsoever for the fact that Brice had to walk while everyone else was on horseback. The pace, although fairly slow by riding standards, was punishing for someone trying to keep up. This was especially true over the uneven terrain they traversed towards early evening when they turned off the main road.

Somehow, Brice kept going, however, without uttering a single complaint. He was sure that had he done so, Sherringham would only have urged his men to go faster.

'We'll be stopping at an old castle ruin where there are a couple of rooms left with roofs,' Brice heard the captain tell his second in command. 'I can't abide the hovels the natives call inns hereabouts. I'd rather take my chances with the elements. At least you don't get bed bugs or stink of peat smoke for days on end.'

By the time the ruin in question hove into view, Brice was having to reach for his last reserves of strength. His leg muscles were screaming in protest and his feet ached where his boots were chafing from the long march. As the troop came to a halt, he tried not to show his fatigue and stood with head bent, trying to catch his breath. He had a feeling his trials were far from over.

'Not so cocky now, are you, laird,' Sherringham sneered. Brice looked up to find the captain standing right in front of him, fixing him with eyes full of disdain. As before, Brice drew himself up to his full height, thereby forcing the Englishman to look up to him. This made Sherringham's eyebrows come down in a fierce scowl. 'Think you're better than us, do you?' he asked. 'Well, think again. You're just another damned rebel and I'm going to show you exactly how we treat scum like you.' He turned to a group of his men who had been watching the exchange with avid eyes. 'Men, teach the prisoner a lesson, then put him in the pit.'

Brice drew in a deep breath, trying to prepare himself for what was to come. He didn't have long to wait. Some of the soldiers began to take turns to hit him, as if they were practising their punching techniques. Although he was able to block some blows, his bound hands prevented him from retaliating. He noticed it was only a few of the men who put any effort into it though and some hung back altogether as much as they could. *At least there are a few decent ones among them then*, he thought, but it was always thus. Soldiers were told what to do, but not all of them were as bloodthirsty and full of hatred as Sherringham.

A couple of his henchmen seemed to be of his ilk, however, and they took pleasure in doing their worst, which was bad enough. Whenever Brice was pushed to the ground, he had trouble scrambling to his feet. Each time he was knocked over, kicks rained down on him until he felt as if his insides were on fire. It was the worst beating he'd ever received in his life, since normally he'd at least be fighting back.

'Cowards,' he hissed. 'Untie my hands and we'll see if you're as brave.' But the soldiers ignored his goading and the few who were enjoying this sport continued until he lay still on the ground, curled up, just waiting for them to finish. The only thing that sustained him through the ordeal was the fury burning inside him at such injustice. He hadn't expected any favours along the road, but this went way beyond what was normal. These men were animals, their captain most of all.

'That's enough, surely?' Brice heard someone say and the blows ceased.

He felt hands lifting him by the arms and dragging him into the castle ruin. Daylight was fading fast, but he could see a hole in the floor of the room he was dragged into and knew immediately what it was. An old *oubliette*.

No sooner had the word passed through his mind than he was shoved into the black pit, hurtling through space for longer than was comfortable. He tried to brace himself, but landed awkwardly with one foot slightly twisted, wrenching the ankle.

'Hell and damnation!' he swore.

Luckily, the bottom of the pit was fairly soft with a layer of mud and leaves which had no doubt blown in through the broken castle walls. Brice thanked God for this small mercy as it meant he hadn't broken his leg at least, which would have been a real possibility had the bottom been made up of stones. He pulled himself upright and for a while he leaned on the stone wall while he tried to block out the pain that assailed him from every part of his body.

From deep inside, he dredged up the last remains of his rage and gritted his teeth. He wasn't going to put up with this a moment longer. He had to escape.

But how?

Marsaili tried not to let despair engulf her. It slowed her thought processes and she knew she needed all her wits if she was to come up with a plan.

'I wish there was something we could do or another way out,' Archie muttered, his dark eyes huge with misery and dejection. 'Perhaps I can climb out the window? If we tie the sheets together, you could lower me down, maybe?'

But Marsaili hadn't heard his question. Her mind grasped onto his first sentence and she turned to him with hope surging through her. 'That's it! I'll bet you anything there is.'

'Is what?' Archie frowned.

'Another way out. A secret one.'

Archie's eyebrows rose almost to his hairline. 'Like in the stories Auntie Greine tells sometimes, you mean? Ghostly passages?'

Marsaili smiled for the first time since they'd been locked in. 'No ghosts, I hope, but passages, yes.' She jumped to her feet and held out a hand to pull Archie up. 'Come, help me look for it. This is the master bedroom, the laird would be bound to want a way out in times of trouble.'

She walked over to the nearest panelled wall and began to feel her way along, tapping every so often with her fingers to check for any sounds of hollow spaces. Archie watched her with a dubious expression at first, but soon copied her. 'Are you sure?' he asked.

Marsaili nodded. 'I'd bet my last merk on it.' She glanced towards the door. 'But if you hear anyone approaching, stop at once. We don't want anyone to know what we're doing.'

It took them a while, but in the end their efforts were rewarded. Archie called her over to the far corner, next to the thick outer wall of the house, and pointed. 'It's maybe hollow here. Listen.' He knocked softly on that part of the panelling, then at another to show the difference.

'You're right.' Marsaili beamed at him. 'Now all we have to do is find the catch.'

It proved to be inside a small hole near the floor, which looked as though a mouse had made it. When Marsaili wriggled a finger inside, she encountered a catch which sprang loose, allowing the panelling to swing outwards. Stale air whooshed out, making dust motes dance in the light from the window. Behind the secret door was a narrow staircase leading down.

'Yes!' She turned to grab Archie by the hand, then thought of something else. 'Wait. We need to make sure no one finds out we've gone, at least for a while. Come, help me push something heavy in front of the door.'

There was a large, ornately carved chest at the foot of the huge four poster bed. Together they managed to alternately push and drag it over to the door, wedging it against the side of a small fireplace that was nearby. 'There, that should stop anyone from coming in.' Marsaili dusted herself down. 'Let's get out of here now, quickly.'

Archie needed no second bidding, but followed her into the secret passage. They pulled the door closed behind them and stood for a moment to allow their eyes to adjust to the darkness. 'It's not as bad as I thought,' Marsaili whispered. 'There's some light coming in.' Even so, they had to feel their way along carefully, so as not to go tumbling down the rough steps, and it took them quite a while to reach a small door at the bottom.

'Archie, you must swear never to tell anyone about this, anyone at all, do you understand? I only found out by accident and the laird wants it to stay a secret.'

'Don't fash, I'll not say a word.'

They listened carefully before opening the door, but it proved to be behind a large bush at the side of the house and they crouched underneath its branches while making sure no one was about.

'Are you going to send that letter now?' Archie asked in a hushed whisper.

'No, there's no time to lose. I'm going after the laird myself.'

'What? Are you sure? He said to write.'

'Yes, but who could we trust to take a letter to Edinburgh? Seton will be watching everyone. I'll tell you what though – if I'm not back in two days, you ask Kirsty to write to Mr Grant. The laird will need a lawyer to defend him in court if I can't free him, do you understand? Maybe I will too.' It was a lowering thought, but she refused to consider failure already.

'Aye.' Archie still looked doubtful, but Marsaili didn't give the boy time to think about it any more.

'I'll need Liath, a couple of *garrons* and some food and blankets,' she told him. 'If I go straight to the stables, do you think you could make it to the kitchen unseen and tell your aunt what's happening? She'll give you what I need, but Seton mustn't catch you.'

'I can do that. He never pays any mind to us children anyway, so I doubt he'd notice me unless he was looking for me. He thinks I'm upstairs.'

'Very well, but be careful. I'll go and saddle the ponies

213

and I'll meet you in the stables. If anyone comes, I'll hide in the hay loft.'

Their luck held and Archie soon came tip-toeing into the stables with Liath in tow. The dog was pleased to see her, as always, but seemed to understand the need for silence instinctively. 'Found him in the kitchen,' Archie whispered.

'Excellent, thank you.' Marsaili took the items he'd brought and stuffed the food into a saddle bag. 'I'm not taking the laird's horse, he's too fierce for me.'

'Not him, Starke's like a lamb, not crabbit at all.'

'Be that as it may, he'd be no use on Highland mountain paths and if I manage to rescue the laird, that's how we'll be travelling.' She rolled up the blankets and tied them to the back of the saddles. Archie had also brought a plain grey *arisaid*, the large woollen outer garment worn by Highland women. It was really nothing more than a very large blanket and could be used as such if necessary. Marsaili put it on by pleating about two thirds of it round her waist and fixing it in place with a belt, leaving a gap at the front. The left-over piece, she pulled up behind her and round her shoulders, fastening it with a crude pin. It would keep out the cold and if it rained she could pull it up over her head. 'Now can you make yourself scarce, Archie? I don't want Seton to catch you or even see you until I'm long gone.'

'I'll go back to Auntie Greine. She said as how I could sit in the larder.' He hesitated. 'Are you sure you shouldn't just go straight to Edinburgh yourself? Mr Seton wouldn't know.'

Marsaili shook her head. 'No, I have a feeling we'd never reach the laird in time. And I just know something awful would happen to him. You saw that captain, he was enjoying himself. There's no saying what he'll do to Br ... the laird.'

Archie nodded slowly. 'Aye, well good luck!'

'Thank you, Archie.'

As she led the ponies out of the entrance towards the

loch, Marsaili prayed no one would see her and tell Seton. She doubted many people were on his side, but she didn't want to take any risks. This was too important.

They made it into the small copse where the trees hid them from view. Here Marsaili found a fallen log to stand on in order to clamber onto one of the ponies, then gripped the reins tight. She wasn't used to riding much, but was sure she could manage. *I have to!* Out of her pocket she took a neckcloth she had grabbed on her way out of Brice's room. She hoped it smelled of him, even though it hadn't been worn for a few days. Holding it out to Liath, she bent down to whisper, 'Find him, Liath. Seek. Please, find him.' She knew he could do it. It was a game she'd played a lot with him when he was a puppy and which he'd always enjoyed. Liath's ears pricked up and his mouth opened as if in a grin, then he set off without hesitation.

Marsaili urged the ponies into a trot, following the dog's loping stride. *Please, dear God, help us find Brice quickly, before it's too late*, she prayed silently.

As soon as his eyes had adjusted to the semi-darkness of the pit he found himself in, Brice began to look for a way out. Since *oubliettes* were obviously supposed to be escape proof, he wasn't too hopeful. It was at least four yards from top to bottom, which meant that no matter how high he jumped, he'd never reach the rim. And with a hurt ankle, he couldn't jump much in any case. The circumference of the hole was also too large for him to be able to brace himself against opposing sides and thereby climb out. There was one thing in his favour though – it looked as though this particular castle had been a ruin for quite some time. That meant the elements had wreaked havoc with the original construction, and fortunately this proved to be the case in his primitive prison as well.

The walls were made out of stone, smoothed and mortared so as not to give anyone a handhold for scaling them. However, rain, wind and the occasional hardy weed had worked on the mortar and loosened it considerably in many places. Brice noticed one side of the pit in particular was crumbling more than the others. He went over to test it with questing fingers and then tried to climb a short way up.

'*Fan i helvete*,' he swore softly in Swedish when he put his weight on the damaged ankle. A red-hot streak of pain sliced through it and he had to grit his teeth in order to conclude his experiment. A short while later, there was no doubt in his mind he could escape that way with a bit of luck and perseverance. The wall held and if he searched with his fingertips, he was able to find enough of a hold to progress upwards. Thankfully, this didn't dislodge the actual stones of the wall, which seemed able to bear his weight.

The ankle was his main concern, because he needed both feet, but there was nothing he could do except try to endure the pain. To make it more bearable, he tore strips of material off the bottom of his shirt and tied the ankle securely. This strapping helped a little, although it made it difficult for him to put his boot back on. In the end, he succeeded by sheer force.

Now all he had to do was wait for an opportune moment. The soldiers would no doubt have a meal, then most of them would bed down for the night somewhere within the castle walls. They weren't stupid, they would leave someone on guard, but as long as he took them by surprise, it should be possible to take care of one or two men, Brice thought.

It had to work, because he sure as hell didn't want to stay here.

Marsaili felt as if she'd been riding for days and since her behind wasn't used to it, she was getting sore. There was no point thinking about it, however, because she wasn't going back until she'd found Brice and rescued him. Quite how she was going to do this, she had no idea. She was beginning to wonder if she hadn't been too hasty though, setting off on her own like this. There were men in the township who seemed to have accepted Brice and she might have been able to persuade them to help her.

'Well, it's too late now. I'll think of something,' she muttered to herself. If she turned back now, the soldiers would be too far ahead. Once they reached Fort George, there would be no chance of freeing Brice. She gritted her teeth. 'I'm not letting those accursed Redcoats treat him like a criminal.'

She had honestly thought the hunt for possible Jacobites and their weapons had come to an end. Most people she knew of were either just getting on with their lives or leaving for the Colonies far across the sea. It had been a long time since she'd heard of any Jacobite plotting and she knew well enough the charges against Brice were false. She was also in no doubt as to who lay behind his arrest. *Seton, damn him!* He couldn't have done it without the English captain though, and it seemed this Sherringham fellow was more tenacious than most.

'May he rot in hell as well,' she whispered. She'd like to have the pair of them horse-whipped.

At first, she had been riding along the new English road, which she knew made it easier for troops to reach the three forts strung out along the Great Glen to the north. She kept her senses on alert and rounded every bend with caution, but never caught so much as a glimpse of the troop. She guessed they must be travelling a lot faster than she was and they had a head start.

She continued even after it started to become dark as the moonlight made it easy to follow the wide road. After a while, however, Liath veered off to the right and Marsaili had to peer down at the ground to make sure she didn't send the ponies straight into a bog. The hound seemed to be following a narrow path, snaking up into the hills, and Marsaili wondered why. She didn't doubt his sense of smell. The dog looked like he was on a hunt and never wavered. She only hoped he wouldn't get over-excited if he did catch sight of Brice, thereby giving her away to the enemy.

'Easy, boy,' she admonished. 'Be quiet, all right? And slow down!'

At long last Liath came to a halt and stood sniffing the air, whining softly.

'Good dog,' Marsaili slid off her pony's back and patted the hound. 'You've found him? All right, hush now, hush boy.'

She peered through the darkness and saw what looked like an old ruined keep up ahead. Near a doorway she glimpsed a small fire and now and then people moving in front of it, blocking the light. She led the ponies round to the back of the ruins where she found a copse of trees that had perhaps once been an orchard belonging to the house. She tethered the *garrons* to a sturdy branch and then grabbed Liath's collar, setting off up the hill.

'Come on, Liath, let's see if we can come up with a plan.'

Chapter Twenty-One

Brice waited patiently until the sounds from the soldiers became few and far between. Then he waited some more and at last all was quiet apart from the hooting of an owl. He had found a largish stone to sit on, thus sparing him from the mud at the bottom of the pit, but it was uncomfortable and hard. His ankle was throbbing and he knew it was badly sprained. He had a feeling his boot would have to be cut off or else be stuck until the swelling went down.

'Could have been worse,' he told himself. If he'd broken his leg, he would have had no chance whatsoever of climbing out and escaping. At least now all he had to do was bear the pain.

When the soldiers had been silent for some time, he began the attempt to ascend the wall. It was hard going, but his arms were strong from climbing the East India ship's rigging and he knew he could do this. He refused to even contemplate failure. The pain in his ankle sliced through him and all the other cuts and bruises made him suck in a sharp breath each time he moved, but he blocked it out, concentrating on finding hand and footholds. It seemed to take him for ever, especially since he had to stop each time he dislodged a small stone or handful of mortar, in case the noise brought his captors to check on him. Nothing happened.

He was only about a foot away from being able to reach the top edge when suddenly an eerie howling noise echoed round the surrounding hills. All the soldiers scrambled to their feet, running this way and that, obviously startled out of their slumber. The sound rang out again and seemed to be coming from quite close by. It sent shivers down Brice's back.

'What in the name of God ...?' he muttered. He hadn't thought there were any wolves left in Scotland. The Redcoats obviously did, however. To a man, they stampeded outside the castle's courtyard, shouting and swearing.

'Where is it? Is it coming this way?'

'Shoot it! Over there, I see its evil red eyes!'

'Imbeciles! There are no wolves here.' That was the captain's voice, trying to sound firm, but not succeeding very well.

'But sir, you can hear it for yourself.'

'And Houghton saw something moving. There, sir, look.'

A couple of shots rang out, but the howling continued afterwards. Brice didn't wait to hear any more. Gathering all his strength, he pulled himself up the last few inches and grabbed hold of the pit's edge. He heaved his body over the side and rolled quickly away from the hole, into the deeper shadows of a wall. There, he got to his feet and moved stealthily towards the opening. As he glanced out, he saw the captain and his men all gathered outside the main building, still arguing while the howling went on. The noise seemed to be coming from a different direction now, confusing them and causing more dissension.

Brice hobbled into the next roofless room and turned left, hoping to find an opening in the back walls of the castle ruin. Just as he rounded the corner, he collided with something soft which emitted a small noise of surprise. *Damnation! Why wasn't this one outside*, Brice wondered. He didn't stop to ask though, instead he pushed the person around and twisted one of his arms up behind him. Brice then put his own hand over his captive's mouth. The man tried to bite him.

Brice drew in a harsh breath of surprise and the combined scent of heather and lavender assailed him, making him freeze momentarily. Taking his hand away, he turned the captive round and peered through the darkness. 'Marsaili?' he whispered.

'Yes. Now let go of me and let's get out of here,' she hissed back, giving him an impatient push.

Brice was so stunned at finding her here, of all places, he did as he was told. He felt her grab his hand and pull him along, back in the direction she'd come from. 'Is there a way out at the back?'

'Yes, but hurry. Liath won't keep them occupied for long.'

'Liath? The wolf?' Brice wanted to laugh out loud, but knew this was neither the time nor the place. He limped after her as fast as he could, once again gritting his teeth against the pain shooting through his ankle every time he set his foot on the ground. She was right, they didn't have much time.

A tumbled down stone wall appeared in front of them, the faint moonlight outside showing Brice he had a hill to descend now. He pulled air into his lungs, preparing himself for yet more pain while they clambered over the loose stones. Marsaili set off at a run, with Brice following as fast as he could, half running, half hopping on one leg. He saw her glance over her shoulder and stop to see what was taking him so long, but he motioned her on. If anyone was going to be caught, he didn't want it to be her.

Thankfully, there were no cries of *'prisoner has escaped!'* and at last Brice reached the small copse of trees where Marsaili waited. He was thrilled to find two ponies there as well and sent up a swift prayer of thanks to God. There was no way he could have continued much further on foot.

'What's wrong with your leg?' Marsaili whispered.

'Not my leg, twisted ankle. I'll tell you later.' He mounted one little horse while Marsaili untied the reins from a branch, then he watched her pull herself onto the other. 'How do we get Liath back?'

'I'll whistle for him as soon as we're halfway down the hill.'

'But the Redcoats will hear you,' Brice protested. He couldn't bear the thought of being caught again now he was so close to freedom.

'I doubt it. The sound I'll make is like that of a small bird. I've trained Liath to heed that, as well as a normal whistle.'

'Just like you taught him to howl on command?' The thought of her doing this amused him and made him realise how strong the bond was between her and the hound.

'Of course. It seemed like harmless fun at the time, I never knew it would come in useful.'

'Well, I hope he's as obedient to your whistling.'

This proved to be the case and Brice was relieved to see Liath come bounding after them a short while later. He swore he'd give the faithful hound a dozen juicy bones once they were back home again. He deserved that and more. And as for his mistress and her foolhardy rescue mission which could have gone so wrong ... well, he'd think about that later.

'Which way?' he asked as they reached the large road which headed north east towards Inverness.

'Straight across,' Marsaili said firmly. 'If they discover you gone, they'll think you've gone back home or to Edinburgh to find help, so we need to throw them off the scent. We'll take a long route, just to make sure, as high up the hills as possible.'

'Very well, makes sense.'

Brice urged his pony into a trot and crossed the road, heading what he guessed was south-west. Anywhere was better than the *oubliette* he'd just left.

Travelling in the Highlands could be treacherous even in daylight, so Marsaili knew they would have to be careful or they'd end up either falling down a hillside or stuck in a bog. Liath didn't seem to hesitate, however, so in the end they let him lead them along narrow paths only he could see in the darkness.

'I think we can trust him not to go anywhere unsafe,' Marsaili said to Brice and he agreed.

'Yes, he seems more intelligent than most hounds.'

All went well until Marsaili's pony stumbled on something and began to limp.

'Oh, no! Stop, Brice, I need to check the *garron's* hoof.'

She dismounted and tried to feel the pony's leg. He shied away from her hands and whinnied, turning to nip at her arm. 'Hey, none of that, if you don't mind.' To Brice she said, 'I think he's hurt. I can't quite see, but it looks like he can't put much weight on it.'

'Seems to be the night for sprained ankles,' Brice sighed. 'Do you think this one can manage to carry both of us? Otherwise we'll have to take turns walking.'

'I suppose we can try, they're strong little creatures.'

'Come on then, up you get. We can't afford to waste time.'

Brice helped her to mount up behind him and she wrapped one arm firmly around his waist while holding the reins of her own pony with the other.

'I hope he can at least walk without any weight on his back,' she muttered.

Brice's pony carried on, although at a slower pace. At one point he too stumbled, and Marsaili held her breath waiting to see if he'd been hurt, but he seemed fine. Instead she realised she'd heard a grunt from Brice, which made her frown. She squeezed his waist again on purpose and was rewarded with a curt, 'Don't!' Then he seemed to remember his manners and added, 'Please.'

'Why? Where else are you hurt? Did you fall over when they pulled you along?' Concern for him flooded through her, giving way to outrage once more at the treatment meted out to him.

Brice chuckled, but it was a rather strained sound. 'I ache everywhere,' he admitted. 'But I didn't fall.'

'You mean …?'

'The Redcoats decided to have some sport with me, yes. Before they pushed me into a very deep pit, which is how I came to twist my ankle.'

'Damned whoresons!'

Brice turned to peer at her through the gloom. 'Such language!' he teased, pretending to be shocked. 'And here was I thinking you were a lady. Tut, tut.'

'I don't care, it's what they are,' she muttered. 'What gives them the right to treat you like that? They've not even proved your guilt yet.' Which reminded her. 'You didn't hide any weapons, did you? I mean, I know your father's a Jacobite, but you never said …'

'No, I didn't. That's not to say I wouldn't, if my father asked me to, but in this instance, I'm innocent. I have a fairly good idea where they came from though.'

'I know. Seton,' she spat. 'He'll pay for this, so help me God.' And she told Brice what had happened after his departure.

Brice groaned. 'Damn it all, woman, the entire household will know about the secret tunnels soon. Then what will be the point of them?'

'It's not as if I had a choice,' she huffed, then heard another chuckle. 'Oh, you're teasing me again.' She punched him lightly on the arm, then remembered his injuries as he drew in a hissing breath. 'Oh, I'm so sorry! I forgot.'

'It's all right, just try to restrain yourself from now on, please.'

'Perhaps I shouldn't hold onto you?'

'Don't be daft. I'm not having you fall off. Besides, I like your hands just where they are. For now.' Another chuckle.

Marsaili muttered under her breath. 'Men, hmph.'

'Are you saying you don't like holding me now? That's not how it seemed when I came back from market.' She heard amusement in his voice and wanted to hit him again, but refrained.

'Think what you like. You surprised me, is all.'

'Hmm, long surprise, eh?'

'Hold your tongue, Brice, or I'll squeeze your ribs again.'

'Promises, promises, never anything else with you, is there,' he sighed.

'Brice!' She tried to make her voice sound threatening, but probably didn't succeed very well since he laughed again. He did stop teasing her though, and she allowed herself to just enjoy holding him tight. His stomach felt hard, yet warm, under her hands and it was very tempting to lay her cheek against his broad back. Eventually she gave in to the urge and didn't regret it. It was almost as though she belonged there.

'We'll need to stop soon,' Brice said eventually. 'The ponies have had a long day and night and must be very thirsty, as am I. Any suggestions?'

Marsaili thought for a moment. 'Shieling huts?' she ventured. 'If we go a bit higher up, there ought to be some and they should be empty. Everyone will have brought their *kyloes* down long since.'

'Good idea. Help me look then.'

Chapter Twenty-Two

It took them until the break of dawn, but eventually they came upon a couple of deserted shieling huts. Thankfully, they were also in the lea of a large outcrop of rock which shielded them from view.

'Unless Sherringham has tracker dogs, he'll never find us here,' Marsaili said.

'He'd have to go to the nearest garrison for those. I doubt he'd waste the time.'

Brice heard a small burn gurgling its way down the hillside and led the two ponies in the direction of this sound as soon as he'd dismounted. In the pale morning light, both he and the horses drank their fill of the cold water. Brice also washed his face and hands as best he could. He felt refreshed, but increasingly stiff and sore all over. He'd had plenty of time during the ride to assess his injuries and had come to the conclusion he had several bruised ribs and probably contusions everywhere else. It was nothing that wouldn't heal with time though and he was thankful for this.

'We'll have to leave the *garrons* outside, they'll never fit inside the huts,' Marsaili told him when he returned to her side. She was speaking in a low voice, even though it was unlikely the Redcoats were on their trail.

'No, they're not exactly big, are they?' Brice had to bend almost double to enter the nearest one and peer in. It contained only a small hearth on one side and a sleeping platform made of turf on the other, that was all. There was barely room to turn around, let alone bring in a horse.

The ponies didn't mind though. As long as they had grass to eat and the burn nearby, they were happy. Brice hobbled them, but knew the horses wouldn't wander far in any case.

'Liath will let us know if anyone approaches, won't he?' he asked, although he was sure this was the case.

'Yes, I've told him to be on guard. He knows what that means.' It was becoming lighter all the time now and she suddenly seemed to notice his face. 'Brice! Dear God, what ...?'

He held up a hand. 'It's not as bad as it looks, honestly. Nothing's broken, not even my nose, which is a minor miracle.'

She shook her head and put up a hand to touch his temple. He tried not to wince and guessed he probably had a black eye since the merest brush of her fingers hurt. 'How can you be so calm about it?' she said, her eyes filled with what he assumed was pain on his behalf.

He shrugged, even though it hurt his ribs to do so. 'No point being angry now. I'll make them pay later. First, we need to reach home safely, then I'll seek retribution. We both know who to blame and as for the Redcoats, I have friends in Edinburgh who will help me clear my name. Or my father does, at any rate.'

'Well, sit down while I find some bedding. You need to rest.'

There was a large, flattish stone outside one of the huts, which had obviously been used as a stool. Brice sank down onto it, happy to obey her this time.

Marsaili quickly gathered armfuls of heather and spread this over the sleeping platform, covered with a blanket. 'Come, lie down,' she urged and Brice made his way inside. He sank down onto the makeshift bed and groaned, leaning against the wall. 'Ah, that's better,' he muttered. 'At least it's not muddy.'

'Muddy?' Marsaili followed him into the hut.

'The bottom of the pit I was in. Very slimy.'

'Oh, right.' She grabbed a small pail someone had left behind. 'Wait there, I'll be right back.'

'What?' Brice stared after her, but she soon returned with the pail filled with water.

'Let me wash your wounds,' she said, kneeling on the sleeping platform next to him.

'It's not necessary. I'll live.'

'Don't be stubborn. Take off your shirt, please.'

Brice watched as she pulled up her skirt and ripped a piece of material off the hem of her long shift. 'Now there's a command I don't hear often enough,' he quipped. 'Not from beautiful ladies anyway.'

She narrowed her eyes at him. 'Liar. I'll wager the ladies fight over you wherever you go.' He watched her cheeks turn pink as she realised she'd just complimented him. 'I mean … not that I …' she stammered.

Brice smiled and came to her rescue. Sort of. 'You think I'm that good-looking, huh? You obviously haven't met my brother.' He pulled his shirt over his head with some difficulty, gritting his teeth against the pain.

'If he's anything like as contrary as you, I'm glad,' she retorted with spirit.

'Oh, no, he's charm personified,' Brice told her. 'No lady can ever resist him.' He waited for the familiar stab of anger to shoot through him at the thought of Jamie taking what wasn't his, but nothing happened. This surprised him, but then he realised he didn't care any longer what Jamie had done. His father had been right – Elisabet wasn't worth fighting over. At the end of the day, Brice and Jamie were still brothers, their bond unbreakable. Whereas Elisabet was a fickle creature, not really part of the equation.

A great sense of relief swept through Brice at this epiphany. He really had put the past behind him. Now it was time to move forward, live his life on his terms. And time to enjoy what he had. *Carpe diem.*

Marsaili dipped her makeshift cloth in the cold spring water and began to bathe his battered face and torso. He saw her hesitate a couple of times, as if she was afraid to hurt him further, but her touch was so light there was no risk of that. The cool liquid soothed his bruises and she washed away any traces of blood until he felt clean and almost whole again. As she worked, he regarded her from under his eyelids, but she refused to meet his gaze. He gathered she was shy about touching him like this and he wondered again why none of the men at Rosyth had managed to capture her fancy yet. It seemed incredible that someone so lovely should not have been loved.

'There, better?' she asked when she'd finished.

He nodded and pulled his shirt back on. 'Yes, thank you.'

She still wouldn't meet his gaze. Instead, she put the pail away and rooted around in the saddle bag she'd brought inside. She handed him a bannock and some goat's cheese. 'Here, you must be starving.'

'Ravenous.' Brice devoured his food, making appreciative noises, while she nibbled at a small piece of oatcake herself. 'Thank you for that. I'm not sure I approve of your rash actions in trying to free me from the Redcoats singlehandedly since it was extremely dangerous and foolhardy, but you have your uses, I must say.'

Marsaili turned towards him and as the morning light spilled in through the open doorway, he could see her clearly. Her expressive face showed him she was unsure how to take his banter, but she retorted with some spirit, 'Is that so?'

He grinned. 'Mm-hmm. Although I'm sure providing food isn't the only thing you're good at,' he added, grabbing her round the waist to pull her back against him.

'Brice!'

'What? I only want to thank you for coming to my rescue.'

He pushed her heavy plait to one side and kissed his way up her neck. 'I don't know what I would have done without you. I might even owe you my life.' Marsaili squirmed in his grip, but he noticed she wasn't straining away from him. Quite the opposite.

'Your bruises,' she protested feebly.

He smiled against her soft skin and allowed his mouth to travel round to the underside of her chin and up her cheek, dotting more kisses along the way. 'I told you, I'll live. And my gratitude makes me forget all about them.'

'There's no need to thank me,' she murmured. 'Anyone would have done the same for …'

'For whom? The man they can't resist?' he teased.

She turned to give him an outraged reply, but he took advantage of her open mouth and kissed her instead, properly, deeply. He knew he shouldn't be doing this. It wasn't gentlemanly. They were alone, far from home and he ought to be protecting her, not threatening her virtue.

But he couldn't resist.

And if she allowed it, then where was the harm? If she told him to stop, he would. If not, he'd take whatever she offered.

Pushing her down onto the soft, woollen blanket, he ignored the little voice inside him that told him to stop now, before it was too late.

As far as he was concerned, it was already too late.

Marsaili had no idea how she'd ended up in this situation.

She'd been determined to tell Brice she was going to sleep in the other hut, for the sake of propriety, and that he had to keep his distance. But she had to feed him first and see to his hurts. He'd seemed so exhausted and obviously in severe pain, she didn't have the heart to read him the riot act straight away. *And look where that landed me!*

It was hard to string together any coherent thoughts at all when he kissed her like this. She couldn't concentrate on anything other than what he was doing, how good it felt. Before she knew it, they were both lying down in the cramped space, with him leaning over her, his mouth working its magic on her lips. She'd never known sparring with someone else's tongue could be so pleasurable, nor that it would make little streaks of fire shoot down the rest of her body and gather in the pit of her stomach. Or perhaps slightly lower down. The thought made her face heat up.

Brice's hand cupped her cheek, then made its way down to skim her left breast. She felt her nipple harden even though he was touching her through the layers of her bodice and shift. She had that strange urge to rub herself against him again. Of its own accord, her body strained upwards, wanting more. He seemed to be of a like mind and with an impatient noise, he tugged at the fastenings of her bodice until they came loose and his hand could gain access to her skin through the thin linen of the shift.

'You're so beautiful, Marsaili,' he breathed, feathering kisses along her jaw line and continuing down inside her shift. 'Absolute perfection.' His tongue found her nipple and she gasped, shocked at the intensity of feeling. More streaks of lightning shot down inside her, but she discovered she wasn't content to just let him do this to her. She wanted to explore as well.

'Can I?' she whispered, while pulling his shirt out of his breeches.

He gave a low chuckle, which sounded as if it was mixed with pain. 'No need to ask. Do what you will, I'm all yours.' There was lazy amusement in his voice, but also something else, something she responded to instinctively. A challenge, daring her to go on.

She did.

He's mine, all mine. At least for now. But did she want all of him? Could she forget her principles and just enjoy the moment? For she had no doubt that when it was over, he'd no longer be hers exclusively.

It was a depressing thought, but by now her fingers had found the smooth contours of his chest and hard stomach and she forgot everything except how good it felt to touch him. She caressed each of his nipples in turn and was astonished to find they reacted the same way hers had. Enthralled, she came across the trail of golden hair she'd seen by the lake and followed it downwards, making him groan as her fingers ended up dangerously close to his waistband. There, he gripped her hand and slowly placed it further down as if he was testing her resolve.

'Can you feel how much I want you?' he whispered. 'Does it scare you?'

'No.' And that was the truth, she realised. Perhaps she was a wanton after all, just like her mother, but she didn't care. She wanted him as much as he desired her and she wasn't afraid. Not at all. She knew it would be glorious, being with him, and this may be her only chance to experience it. She shivered as anticipation shimmered through her.

'And is it what you want too?' he asked, his hand now pushing her skirts up, his fingers trailing softly along the inside of her leg, up to where she knew he wished to go. She didn't stop him, moved instead to accommodate him.

'Yes,' she breathed. 'Yes, Brice, I want you. All of you.'

Another shaky laugh. 'Then how can I refuse? Your wish is my command.'

His fingers had found their way further up and she moaned as they reached their goal. He touched her, teasing, drawing a response from her that she was only too willing to give, and then suddenly she plunged over the edge, crying out. 'Ah, Brice, I ... dear Lord!'

'Wait, my love, that was only the beginning,' he told her, his voice husky with promise and desire. And as his fingers began their teasing again, she was amazed to find the waves build up inside her once more. 'This time, I'm going with you,' he whispered, kissing her deeply as he came inside her.

The momentary pain was soon forgotten and Marsaili followed her instincts, moving to his rhythm. She wasn't disappointed. It was glorious, mind-bogglingly so. When the exquisite sensations washed over her again, it was with a much greater intensity and she heard Brice cry out too, before he stilled and leaned his forehead on hers. At that moment, she felt complete, at one with him.

'You, my love, are amazing.' He nuzzled her cheek, still breathing heavily.

Her own breathing was just as erratic and Marsaili felt as though her heart might burst out of her ribcage any minute, but when he gathered her close and pulled her against him, she closed her eyes feeling utterly content.

She knew she'd probably regret this later, but for now, everything was perfect.

Chapter Twenty-Three

Since no one enquired about Marsaili's whereabouts, Seton decided to let her and the brat stew overnight. They'd gone quiet fairly quickly and as long as they didn't attract anyone's attention, they weren't going anywhere.

He was quite pleased with his quick thinking in locking them in. It had been a spur of the moment decision when he'd seen Archie run off to the master bedroom to blurt out his tale to Marsaili. *Two birds with one stone, an inspired idea.*

He smiled to himself as he entered the great hall the following morning and made his way up the staircase to the laird's chamber. They must still be in there because he was sure Marsaili would have marched straight over to his house to give him a piece of her mind otherwise. That was one of the things he liked about her, her spirit, although naturally he would have to curb it once they were married. He was looking forward to it immensely.

He paused outside the thick door to listen, but all was quiet. Perhaps they had exhausted themselves trying to find a way out? The thought widened his smile. Softly, he put the key in the lock and turned it, then pushed inwards. Nothing happened.

His smile faded and he gave the door a shove, but it still didn't move. 'What the hell …?' How could they possibly have secured it from the inside when he had the only key? There was no bar on this door.

Seton began to smell a rat. Something wasn't right here. 'Marsaili?' he shouted, but there was no reply. Not so much as a stirring from within the room. Seton swore most foully. *How could she possibly have escaped? Damn the woman!*

He clattered down the stairs and outside again, peering up at the window, expecting to see a makeshift rope or something. There was nothing. Cursing again, he rushed along to the kitchen, where a tired-looking Mrs Murray stood by the range, stirring some porridge. She barely spared him a glance, but yawned hugely.

'Where's Marsaili?' Seton didn't see the point of beating around the bush. If anyone knew her whereabouts, it would be Mrs Murray.

'How should I ken? I've enough to do with looking after things here in the kitchen without worrying about everyone else. By rights, she should be here helping me. If you see her, you can tell her from me.'

Seton strode over and gripped the woman's upper arm hard, turning her to face him. 'She's flown the coop, hasn't she?' he asked, but it wasn't really a question, more a statement of fact.

Mrs Murray frowned at him. 'What coop? What are you blethering about Mr Seton? If you don't mind, I've had a long night of it with a bad toothache and now I need to get on with my work.' She stared pointedly at his hand.

Seton let go of her and his gaze went to the corner where Marsaili's stinking hound usually spent most of his time. The dog wasn't there either. 'A pox on it!' he shouted, then swept an earthenware jug off the kitchen table onto the floor. It made a very satisfying noise as it crashed onto the stone flags, shattering into a thousand pieces, but it didn't quell his anger much. He ignored Mrs Murray's outraged protest and crunched his way across the shards to the back door.

When he reached it, he turned and pointed at the woman. 'You'll regret this, I promise you.' Then he stomped outside and headed for the stables.

When he found two of the ponies gone as well, cold fury filled him to such an extent he wondered if he was going to be sick right then and there. He drew in a couple of deep breaths to steady himself and try to order his mind. He had to think. He couldn't believe the stupid woman had actually gone after the Redcoats. What did she think she'd accomplish by that?

This thought calmed him slightly. There was no way Sherringham would listen to a female, let alone a Scottish one, pleading for a man he thought of as a Jacobite. She'd get short shrift from him and might even be imprisoned herself. Seton's temper cooled further.

'That wouldn't be so bad,' he muttered. It might even play into his hands, if he handled his cards right. Yes, let Sherringham scare the living daylights out of her for a few days, then perhaps she'd be more than willing to let Seton rescue her. 'Hah!' he exclaimed. *She might even be grateful!*

His mood improved yet again as he walked back towards his own house. He'd have to pack a few necessities and set off after them so he could have a word with Sherringham. No doubt the man would be amenable to an arrangement with the right incentive, as always.

Just as he reached his front door, however, a rider came thundering through the township, skidding to a halt next to him. It was one of the Redcoats and he'd ridden his horse hard as the poor beast was lathered with sweat and grime.

'Mr Seton,' the man panted. 'Have you seen the prisoner this morning?'

'What?' Seton goggled at the man as his pleasant daydreams came crashing down.

'The prisoner, sir. He escaped last night and we assumed he'd head straight for home in order to obtain help. Have you seen him?'

Seton shook his head. 'No, he's not come back and there's no one here who would help him.' At least he hoped there wasn't. 'He must have headed straight for Edinburgh. After him, man! There's no time to lose.'

The Englishman glared at him. 'I'm aware of that, sir. Very well, I'd best report back to the captain. In the meantime, if you see the prisoner, kindly apprehend him and send word.'

'Aye, that I will,' Seton promised.

But he knew he'd lost this game as well. It was time for desperate measures. He needed the MacGregors.

When Brice woke up he was so stiff that at first he wasn't sure he could move at all. He groaned and tried to lever himself into a sitting position, but his bruised ribs screamed in protest and he had to make a supreme effort just to perform this simple manoeuvre. Marsaili stirred and blinked up at him, her green eyes full of concern yet again.

'Brice? Are you all right?' she asked, smoothing back a long red-gold tress which had fallen across her face. Her thick braid had come loose and the glorious mass of curls was spread out around her. Brice wanted to reach out and twine his fingers round the softness of it, but couldn't manage even that at present.

Instead he drank in the sight of her, all tousled and flushed from sleep. She'd looked even lovelier early that morning when he made love to her, twice, before they both fell into exhausted slumber. A certain part of his anatomy remembered this as well, but he was in no state to carry on where he'd left off, much as he would wish to.

He shook his head, even this small motion hurting like hell. 'No, I feel like I've been trampled by a herd of bullocks.'

She smiled slightly and sat up, reaching out a hand to touch his bare chest which was none too pretty in the light of day. He glanced at it and took in the bruises and contusions which mottled his normally golden skin. 'It will heal,' she said, 'but we need to get you home. I have salves that will help and perhaps a hot bath with certain herbs ... but there's nothing I can do for you here.'

He arched an eyebrow at her. 'Nothing?' he queried softly, raising his own hand to caress her smooth cheek. His muscles protested, but he ignored them. He couldn't resist touching her a moment longer. She was too beautiful for words.

She blushed crimson and turned away. 'For shame, you can barely move. How can you think about … about *that* at a time like this?'

'With you around, I think of nothing else,' he answered truthfully, but she seemed to think he was joking for she just shook her head and scrambled off the sleeping platform.

'I'll go and get the *garrons*,' she told him. 'Try and get yourself dressed and I'll help you mount. We really shouldn't tarry here any longer.'

When she'd ducked out of the hut, he sighed, but he knew she was right. This was neither the time nor the place to pursue what had happened between them. It would have to wait until he'd sorted out his other problems.

Trying to take only shallow breaths, he reached for his shirt.

They made their way along the narrow mountain tracks slowly, trusting Liath to alert them to any dangers. The ponies were sure-footed and nimble and Marsaili's mount seemed to have recovered enough for her to ride him. Even so, they got off to walk whenever they came to any dangerous parts, despite Brice's injured foot. Marsaili heard the little grunts of discomfort he made every so often and wished there was something she could do for him. But the best thing would be if they could reach Rosyth as quickly as possible.

Truth to tell, she was a little sore herself, although obviously it was as nothing compared to what he was suffering. She shifted her position so the saddle wouldn't chafe her nether regions. She could hardly believe the things she'd allowed Brice to do to her, but at the time, she'd been unable to help herself. He had completely enthralled her with his love-making and she'd forgotten all her promises to herself.

Fool! she thought. How could she have given in so easily?

As if he was thinking along the same lines, Brice glanced over his shoulder at her and said, 'Marsaili, about what happened ...'

She looked away. 'It's fine. Let's not discuss it now,' she said, trying to keep her voice flat and emotionless. She couldn't bear for him to tell her he'd only taken what she offered so freely. That in the cold light of day he regretted it and as laird he needed to look higher for a wife. There was no need to have it spelled out.

'But what if ...?'

'I'll inform you if there is to be a child,' she snapped. 'Please, I don't want to talk about it now. I'm bone weary and so are you.'

He frowned at her, searching her eyes with his, then he nodded. 'Very well, but we *will* discuss it when we're both rested.'

'Fine,' she agreed, but she had no intention of letting him bring the subject up ever again. He'd had his sport and that was all he'd get from her. If there was a child, she would make sure he paid for its upkeep, but otherwise, she'd forget anything had ever happened between them.

Remembering would be too painful.

They decided to approach Rosyth House from the opposite direction to that normally taken in order to make sure the Redcoats weren't lying in wait for them. They left the ponies in the small forest by the loch while they crept up towards the house and made their way to the secret door Marsaili had used to escape from the bedroom. It was almost pitch dark by the time they arrived and they neither saw nor heard anyone.

Brice's bedchamber was exactly as Marsaili had told him she'd left it, with the chest still wedged against the door. 'No one's been in here,' she whispered.

'Doesn't look like it, no.' Brice threw a look of longing at his bed, but knew he couldn't relax yet. They had to find out what was happening in the rest of the house.

With Marsaili's help, he silently moved the chest out of the way and tried the door. To his surprise, it opened and on the outside he found the key in the lock. He removed it and closed the door once more, locking it from the inside.

'What are you doing?' Marsaili breathed.

'I want you to stay here while I go and find out what's going on downstairs.'

'But …'

'You'll be safe in here and I won't be using the normal routes.' He gestured towards the secret entrance.

'Oh, I see.'

He put his hands on her shoulders. 'Promise me you won't venture out until I come back? I'm sorry I have to leave you in darkness, but it's better not to announce our presence just yet.'

'Very well, but please hurry.'

He headed back into the secret passageway, but instead of going down the stairs the way they'd come, he opened another door to the right, just inside the panelling. It too had been cleverly hidden and he doubted Marsaili had noticed it when she used the staircase the first time. Once through this door, he had access to the warren of passages which criss-crossed the house, and he made good use of them now, albeit walking slowly. *It's a good thing Father made me memorise all these routes*, he thought, *since I can't see a thing*. His body felt as if every part of him was on fire, the strain of riding for so long having taken its toll.

He was amazed to see no sign of either the Redcoats or Seton anywhere. Instead he spied Ramsay and Alex in the great hall, pacing back and forth, discussing what they should do. It was a relief to see that they, at least, had been left alone.

'We can't ride after them now, it's too dark,' Ramsay was saying. 'We'll have to wait until morning, else we'll just get lost. Then what use will we be?'

'But we can't sit around doing nothing,' Alex protested. 'The Lord only knows what they're doing to him!'

'I know, I know, but we can't risk leaving now. It wouldn't be any use without a guide.'

'Then let's find one! What about that Iain fellow?'

Ramsay snorted. 'He didn't look like he'd be much help. He didn't even believe Brice had been taken until the cook told him what was what.'

Brice didn't stay to hear any more. It was clear to him there were no enemies in the house at present and should they arrive, he could always hide in the passages again. He went back upstairs to collect Marsaili and told her what he'd heard. Together, they made their way to the great hall.

'Brice! And Miss Buchanan? What in the name of all that's holy …?' Ramsay was the first to catch sight of them. 'Dear God, but what's happened to you, man?' His eyes opened wide as he took in Brice's black eye and other cuts and bruises.

'I'll tell you in a moment, but first – have you seen Seton? Or any English soldiers?'

'No, none, and as for that factor of yours, he's gone off somewhere with part of his gold.'

'Part of his … how do you know?'

Alex looked slightly sheepish and lifted up a small casket from a nearby table. 'I checked,' he said. 'Most of it is still here, but he's definitely taken at least a pouch full.'

Brice smiled at the youth and shook his head. 'Thank you. I suppose you'd better give me that so I can hide it somewhere. I take it you've helped yourself to a "percentage"?'

Alex grinned. 'Only a very small one. You did say I could.'

Brice nodded, but held out his hand for the casket. He didn't want Alex to be tempted to take any more.

'Can we discuss all this at a later time?' Marsaili put in. 'Br … that is, the laird needs a hot bath and some bandages.'

'That bad, eh?' Ramsay frowned at him.

'I've felt better,' Brice admitted ruefully. 'But I need to be sure we're safe first. I can't risk those Redcoats surprising us again.'

'Don't worry, we'll fight them off. Go and have your bath.' Ramsay extracted a couple of pistols from his capacious pockets and laid them on a table next to a chair, before sitting down. 'You might want to leave the hound here too.'

Brice looked around and was surprised to find Liath sitting behind them, tongue lolling after his long run earlier. They'd left him outside so he must have found his own way in. A moment later Archie came running into the room and cannoned into Brice, throwing his arms around his legs. 'You're back! I saw Liath in the courtyard and hardly dared hope it was true.'

'Ouch!' Brice tried to loosen the boy's grip, but Archie had obviously been very worried and it was like trying to prise open a stubborn oyster. In the end, he picked the boy up and gave him a fierce hug. 'Yes, I'm here, but I'm none too clean so would you mind if I had a bath before I tell you about my adventures?'

Archie nodded and let go at last. 'Sure.'

'You can stay here and help my uncle and Alex to keep guard, agreed?'

'Aye, I will.' Archie took a seat next to Alex, trying his best to look fierce.

Brice winked at his friend. 'I'll see you all later then.'

Chapter Twenty-Four

'Will you stay and help me? Please?'

Marsaili hesitated by the door of Brice's chamber. She'd been about to follow the men who brought hot water, but she found herself unable to resist the pleading note in Brice's voice.

'I need to fetch the salve and some bandages,' she murmured.

'You can do that afterwards.' He was sitting on the edge of his bed and she saw the strain etched on his face. He'd been through quite an ordeal and she guessed he wasn't in the habit of asking for help. Beneath the tan he was almost ashen-hued with fatigue and although she was very tired herself, it was probably as nothing compared to how he was feeling. His feet were bare, but taking off the boots and stockings seemed to have finished his reserves of strength. Especially since he'd had to cut one boot to pieces with his dirk. She made up her mind.

'Very well.'

Closing the door, she walked over to him and began to tug his shirt over his head. She heard him draw in a harsh breath as he raised his arms to aid her, but knew there was nothing she could do about it. He'd feel better once he was in the hot water.

'Can you manage ...?' she said, nodding towards his breeches.

He closed his eyes as if it was all too much for him, but then nodded. 'Yes.' Slowly, he undid the buttons and pulled the breeches down. Marsaili averted her gaze, so as not to look at the part of him which had fascinated her so that morning, although she couldn't help a glance or two. Not that she had anything to compare him with, but she thought him incredibly well made. All of him. She gritted her teeth and turned away. She'd do best to forget about how he looked without his clothes on.

'Right, into the water with you.' She half pulled him off the bed and propelled him towards the large wooden tub where the water steamed gently. With a hand on his arm, she steadied him as he clambered in and sank down. He leaned his head back on the rim, closed his eyes and let out a sigh of pleasure.

'Aah, that feels good. Almost as good as ...'

'Here, have a wash cloth,' she interrupted him, afraid of what he might have been about to say.

He looked up at her, one eyebrow raised. 'I thought you were going to help me. Could you at least do my back, please? There's no way I'd be able to reach around at the moment.'

She detected a mischievous glint in his eyes and crossed her arms over her chest. 'Are you really that sore or is this another of your little tricks?'

His expression turned innocent, blue eyes wide and sincere. 'Tricks? I don't recall using any of those on you. And I truly do ache, I swear.'

'Hmph.' Marsaili wasn't sure she believed him, but she took the cloth out of his hands nonetheless and lathered it with soap. 'Lean forward then, if you can.'

His mouth twitched. 'Yes, madam.' He obeyed and presented her with another fine view – broad shoulders with muscles rippling under smooth golden skin in between the bruises and cuts. Marsaili stifled a sigh. Who was she fooling? She'd never forget the sight of any part of him, no matter how hard she tried. She swore softly.

'Do I look that bad?' She heard the amusement in his voice and had to resist the urge to pummel him instead of rinsing off soap.

'No, you look fine, as I'm sure you know.' She knew she sounded curt, but she couldn't help it.

'Then it must be the soap that's vexing you,' he said, glancing over his shoulder with laughing eyes. 'Damned slippery things, soap.'

'*Brice* ...' She gave him her sternest look. 'I agreed to help you because I thought you truly needed me, but if you're going to play games, I'm leaving.'

He held up his hands in surrender. 'I'll behave, I promise. Anyway, I was only making a comment.'

'Yes, that's what you said this morning. The next thing I know, you'll do something else,' she muttered. 'You're the one who's as slippery as an eel.'

'That's not what *you* said then.'

She threw the wash cloth into the water in front of him. 'I told you, I don't want to talk about it. What happened ... shouldn't have happened, but it's done now and I'd thank you not to refer to it again.'

To her consternation, he stood up abruptly, the water sluicing off him the way it had done when she'd seen him down by the loch. Only this time, he wasn't wearing breeches and before she could do more than stare at him with eyes wide, he'd grabbed her arms and pulled her close.

'Why shouldn't it have happened?' he demanded, scowling at her. 'You wanted it as much as I did.'

'I'm not disputing that,' she said. There seemed no point in lying.

'Then why are you afraid of me alluding to it? You enjoyed it, didn't you?' She nodded reluctantly. 'So there's no reason why it shouldn't happen again if we both want it to.'

'But that's the point – I don't!'

He held her slightly away from him and stared into her eyes, his blue gaze intense. 'Why?'

'I ...' Marsaili swallowed down the lump of misery which

245

rose in her throat. 'Because you don't love me. Because I'm not good enough for you. Because I don't want to be like my mother, damn you! So just leave me alone from now on, all right? Just leave me be ...' She flung away from him and marched off towards the door, trying to stem the flood of tears threatening to spill down her cheeks. 'I'll send someone up with the salve,' she added.

Then she yanked open the door and fled, running down the stairs as if all the ghosts of the past were after her. But there was only one spectre she really feared, that of her mother. Janet's worn, downtrodden features rose up before Marsaili, even when she closed her eyes. Janet, forever trying to please one man or another. Janet being beaten for her trouble ...

No! I will not end up like her. I'd rather die.

Brice stared after Marsaili for a long while before sinking back into the water. *What on earth was that all about?* he wondered.

He knew he hadn't told her he loved her, but then he wasn't sure he was capable of loving a woman again. Not after last time. That didn't mean he was entirely without honour. He was well aware he couldn't just take Marsaili like a common doxy without any consequences. If nothing else, Ailsa would have his hide.

He would have to marry her now.

A couple of weeks earlier, the thought would have filled him with horror, but in the aftermath of making love to Marsaili he'd realised he didn't mind. It was the price he'd have to pay and he was willing. But was she?

He shook his head and picked up the wet cloth, continuing where she'd left off with soaping himself. Women were strange creatures and no mistake. What had she meant by 'not good enough for you'? Socially, she wasn't his equal perhaps, but he didn't care about that. He'd never expected to be lord of anything, so it made no difference to him who his future wife was descended from or that she was born out of wedlock. Nor did he care about her lack of dowry. He had enough money for both of them.

Was he not to her liking? He'd certainly pleased her this morning, he was sure. She hadn't complained then.

The only comment of hers he truly didn't understand was the one about her mother. He would have to make enquiries, discreetly of course, to see what had befallen the woman that was so terrible. Whatever it was, he could make sure it didn't happen to Marsaili if she agreed to be his wife.

Another thought struck him. Perhaps she needed wooing? He smiled to himself. He hadn't exactly been subtle or courted her properly.

'I'll give her a gift,' he murmured. Something to show her how much he ... appreciated her. He couldn't bring himself to even think the word 'love', but he did care for her, he was certain. Enough to want to spend the rest of his life with her?

Yes. Either way, he had committed himself to that path when he made love to her and there was no turning back now.

The MacGregors were an unruly lot, but they were just what Seton needed. Outlawed by the king himself over a century earlier, forbidden to even use their name on pain of death, he reckoned these infamous clansmen would be desperate enough to do anything for money. Although officially they didn't exist, he knew quite a number of them could be found in the Rannoch area. Accordingly, this was where he headed.

Rannoch Moor was a bleak and desolate place, at least at this time of year, but it wasn't more than a day's ride from Rosyth if you knew the way. Seton had to ride carefully along tracks that wound their way through the wilderness between lochs, peat bogs and streams. The mist-shrouded landscape was eerie and forbidding, and he became jumpy and nervous, but he persevered. This was not the time to lose his courage. He had to be bold if he was to attain his goals and therefore he had no option but to go on.

And attain them, I will, he was determined.

Not that he knew exactly where to find the outlaws. He doubted they stayed in one place for very long since their lives depended on not being caught. However, he was sure they'd be watching for anyone approaching and sooner or later he'd be challenged. Then he would state his business and hopefully be taken to their leader.

He wasn't stupid, he knew he was taking a risk by coming here. But he'd brought a pair of loaded pistols and had hidden most of his gold in a secret pouch which he'd stowed where he hoped they wouldn't look.

All he could do now was pray they'd be willing to assist him and not just rob him of what little gold they could find and slit his throat.

'But Captain Sherringham, sir, no one thought it was possible to escape from that pit! And I swear I only left my post for a moment. He must have been spirited away by the devil himself.'

'Imbecile! I suppose you'll tell me next it was the wolf who carried him off.' Captain Sherringham was in a towering rage and clouted the hapless soldier who was supposed to have been guarding the laird of Rosyth. The man cowered before him, fear making him quake in his boots, but the captain wasn't moved. 'Do you really think such feeble protestations will save you from punishment?' he sneered. 'The devil indeed …'

Sherringham took great pleasure in personally overseeing the administration of fifty lashes. He hoped it would serve as an example to the rest of his men never to leave a prisoner unattended. Not that it made any difference. This particular one was still on the loose and he hadn't heard from Seton either, so he assumed the laird had headed straight for Edinburgh. This was bad news. Kinross had shouted something about having friends in high places, if only he could get word to them. Although he hadn't heeded him at the time, Sherringham remembered it now and ground his teeth with frustration.

But what was he to do? Ride after the man and arrest him again? He doubted it would be possible if he'd taken shelter with someone powerful.

'Damn these Scotsmen to hell!' he muttered over and over again as he paced his quarters, thinking furiously.

But wait – if I can't get to the man directly, there must be some other way of catching him out. The woman! What was her name? Oh, yes, Miss Buchanan.

Sherringham remembered her. Lovely smile and a buxom figure. Fine if you liked country girls, but a bit too tall and strapping for his liking. He'd seen the looks which passed between her and the laird though. There was a man who was smitten, if he wasn't mistaken. Even if he wasn't, she was under the man's protection, so if Sherringham captured her, Kinross ought to come to negotiate her release.

Sherringham stopped his pacing and smiled. It was definitely worth a try and if no one came to the girl's rescue, well then he'd just have some sport with her before giving her to his men. She was a Jacobite whore and deserved nothing better.

His good mood somewhat restored, he called for his horse.

'So what's the matter with you then? You're like a bear with a sore head today.'

Kirsty was regarding Marsaili across the kitchen table where they were once again chopping vegetables. There was a speculative glance in her half-sister's eyes that Marsaili tried to avoid. Kirsty saw far too much sometimes and now she was happily wed herself, she seemed to want everyone else to share the same kind of joy.

Marsaili brought the knife down with more force than was really needed. 'Nothing. I'm tired and sore, that's all. We rode for nearly two days and a night altogether, and if you must know, my backside is rubbed raw.' She thwacked an onion in half, before taking a steadying breath. It wouldn't help for her to cut a finger off.

'Riding, was it?' Kirsty smirked. 'Are you sure that's all you did?'

Marsaili glared at her. 'Do you want me to show you? I'll wager it's not a pretty sight.'

If Kirsty noticed that she hadn't actually answered the question, she didn't say anything. Instead she laughed and held up a hand. 'No, thanks. I've had quite enough of seeing Brice's many bruises. He insisted on having me apply the salve you sent up since you wouldn't do it yourself.'

'I haven't the time to pander to the man. I have work to do,' Marsaili muttered. Brice had spent the better part of the day in bed, recuperating, and had asked for her, she knew. But she had no intention of going anywhere near him unless she had to. For her own sanity, she had to stay away because she didn't trust herself not to give in to his persuasive logic.

In a way, he was right. The damage was already done, so what did it matter if she allowed him to make love to her again? But there was a small chance she'd escaped becoming with child, and as long as she wasn't certain, she could cling to the hope.

Besides, she was very much afraid she was in love with him and she couldn't bear the fact that he didn't feel the same way. Quite how it had happened, she had no idea, but she'd reached this conclusion during the long ride home. There could be no other reason for her idiotic behaviour at the shieling hut. Why else would she have lost all reason?

'He'll come and find you, you know.'

Kirsty's statement, uttered with amusement tingeing her voice, drew Marsaili back to the present. 'I thought you said he was too sore to rise today.'

'That's what he wants us to believe, but he's probably just wanting your sympathy. If you don't go to him, he'll soon tire of that game.'

'Hmph. Well, he's the laird, I can't stop him from roaming his own house, but if he thinks I'll drop everything for his sake, he's much mistaken.'

'Is he now? I wonder …' Kirsty's infectious laugh gurgled out.

'Kirsty, I'll thank you to mind your own business. I'm too tired to argue with you.'

'Very well, have it your way. If you want to fool yourself, go ahead, it's your prerogative.'

'I'm not fooling myself about anything,' Marsaili said through gritted teeth. 'On the contrary, I'm the only person around here who can see anything clearly.'

On that parting shot, she dumped the chopped onions into the waiting pot and left the kitchen abruptly. It was bad enough when her own thoughts wouldn't give her any peace. If she had to endure Kirsty's teasing as well, she'd likely go mad.

What she needed was to be alone.

Chapter Twenty-Five

'Archie, have you seen Miss Buchanan?'

Brice had given up hoping Marsaili would come to see how he was and was now dressed and standing in the courtyard. He'd searched the entire house without finding hide nor hair of her, and he was becoming worried. With Seton missing and Redcoats about, there was no saying what might happen. He'd have to tell her to stay close to the house for the foreseeable future in order to keep safe.

Archie had been playing outside with some of the other children, but as always he came running when he spied Brice. 'Aye, laird, I saw her heading to the loch a while back. She didn't see me, even though I waved at her.'

'Really? Did she ... seem upset?' Brice knew the boy was perceptive and trusted his judgement. It was as well to know what he was up against before he faced Marsaili again. Since she hadn't come even when he'd asked for her specifically, he gathered she was still agitated. And he didn't want her to be.

Archie wrinkled his freckled nose, as if considering carefully, then he shook his head. 'No, don't think so. Just lost in thought.'

Brice smiled at the boy. 'Thanks, Archie. I'll go and see if she needs help with anything.'

It wasn't long before he found her, sitting in her favourite spot on the little jetty, staring out over the loch. She was wearing her *arisaid*, as there was a distinct nip in the air today, and she was huddled into it, slightly hunched over. Liath lay next to her, his head resting on the powerful front paws, but he raised it and banged his tail on the planks at the sight of Brice. Marsaili didn't turn around, but he knew she was aware of his presence because he saw her back stiffen ever so slightly.

He sank down behind her, close but not touching, and patted Liath when the dog moved closer. 'Marsaili, I'm sorry. I didn't mean to vex you yesterday,' Brice said. She made no reply, but he heard a small sigh.

'I want you to know I didn't make love to you on a whim,' he continued, determined to have things out in the open. 'It was something I'd wanted to do for quite a while now.'

'You and everyone else,' she muttered. 'It's the only thing anyone's ever wanted from me, ever since I first started growing curves.'

He heard the hurt in her voice and finally understood why she'd been so prickly. With a rueful smile in his voice, he replied, 'You can't really blame them, you know. You are extremely tempting to look at, but I promise you I see more than your face and figure. I see a spirited woman, and a kind and honest one. Well, I do now. It wasn't always so.'

'What do you mean?' She half turned and glanced at him at last.

'The first time I came here, and for some time after, I wasn't sure if you were in cahoots with Seton.' He shrugged. 'It certainly seemed that way and I heard you both talking about English spies.'

'*He* was talking about them, I just did as I was told.'

'Yes, I see that now. Also, you weren't to know I was harmless.'

'I'd hardly call you that,' she said, her voice so low he barely caught the words.

'Marsaili, look at me, please.' Reluctantly she turned towards him, her eyes still wary. 'I'm not a threat to you in any way and if you'll have me, I'd like you to be my wife.' He moved so he was on his knees in front of her, rather than sitting, then he smiled. 'I'm sorry, but you're making it very difficult for me to kneel before you. Unless you stand up, this is the best I can do though.'

She blinked. 'Your wife? But ... you can't marry me. I'm nobody, I have nothing. Surely your parents have already selected a suitable match for you?'

He shook his head. 'No, they trust me to choose for myself.' He looked away for a moment. 'I will be honest with you and tell you I had already done so, before coming here, but ... let's just say my suit didn't prosper. Therefore I'm a free man and I don't need you to bring anything to our marriage other than yourself. That's enough for me.'

She searched his eyes. 'You still love the woman you hoped to marry?'

Brice didn't hesitate. 'No. She's not worthy of my love. I'm not even sure now that I did love her, nor what love really is.' He reached out and took her hands, encouraged when she didn't snatch them back. 'If it means caring for someone, wanting to protect them and keep them safe, wishing them by your side and in your bed, then that is what I feel for you.'

He saw a shadow cross her features, but she didn't look away. 'Perhaps you're right,' she whispered.

He let go of her hands and instead cupped her cheeks, pulling her face to his so he could kiss her beautiful mouth. It was a soft kiss, but one full of promise. 'I don't want to rush you into a decision,' he said. 'I want you to choose me, the way I've chosen you.' He reached into his pocket. 'In the meantime, I would like you to have this. It was given to me by my mother's Chinese friend Mei and it is a charm for good luck.'

He held out a gold chain with a small green pendant in the shape of a disc with a golden Chinese symbol on either side. Marsaili stared at it as if in a daze. In the morning sunlight, the green material shone, reflecting its rays, but at the same time it was somehow see-through.

'Thank you, it's lovely. What is it made of?'

'It's jade, a stone much valued by the Chinese. It can be quite fragile, but they manage to shape it into objects as big as bowls sometimes.' He fastened the pendant around her neck and smiled again. 'There, it suits you much better than it did me. I've no idea why she thought I'd want to wear a necklace.'

Marsaili returned his smile, but her gaze was still troubled. 'Brice, I ...'

He put his fingers up to cover her mouth. 'No, don't say anything more now. I want you to have time to think. But please believe me when I say I truly want you to be my wife.'

He knew he was taking a risk by allowing her time to mull it over. He could probably have persuaded her here and now if he'd pressed his point, not to mention reminded her of the possible consequences of their actions the previous day. She was an intelligent woman, however, and he trusted her to make the right decision. Just in case she needed swaying in his favour though, he pulled her into his arms and kissed her properly. She responded without thinking, which made him believe he'd almost won the battle.

Sometimes it paid not to charge in like a bull.

Marsaili didn't know what to do. She allowed herself to enjoy Brice's kiss for the moment, because she couldn't think with him so close. It was easier just to feel and save any deliberations for later. Her need for him seemed mindless and it frightened her, but she couldn't fight it, not right now. She would think about what he'd said, consider her answer. He was right though, she needed time and she appreciated him allowing her the freedom of choice.

Unlike some people.

Brice's mouth moving over hers melted her bones, even more so now she knew exactly what these sensations led to. She leaned into him, wanting more, craving his touch. His strong arms crushed her to him and her breasts reacted to the contact between them. She shivered at the delicious pleasure even this small friction gave her, then wondered if she had lost all reason. Because she wanted him to take her, right here in full view of the house. She didn't care if anyone saw them, didn't give a damn about anything other than this urgent need for him.

She must be mad.

Liath broke the spell with a series of short, sharp barks, heralding danger. Dazed, Marsaili looked up and blinked to clear her vision. The next thing she knew, Brice had pulled her onto her feet and along the jetty. She stared towards the nearby forest and fear coagulated in her gut at the sight of six fierce-looking ruffians approaching. Dirty and unkempt, she at first took them for robbers of some kind, perhaps come to steal cattle. If so, they were in the wrong place though and she soon noticed they had their eyes fixed squarely on Brice. That didn't make sense, unless he had some enemies she knew nothing about, but there was no time to think about it. He thrust her behind him and hissed, 'Run, Marsaili, back to the house! Fetch Ramsay and Alex. Now!'

She obeyed without even hesitating for a second. She trusted him to hold these men at bay until he could get help and it was up to her to find it.

I have to save him!

The thought pounded through her mind in time with the rhythm of her feet as she ran for all she was worth. She glanced behind her only once and saw the men advancing on Brice, but none of them had followed her. The sight gave her feet added impetus and she burst into the house, tearing along the corridors. The jade pendant bounced on her chest and she remembered Brice had said it was fragile.

She reached up to unclasp it as she ran, clutching it in one hand to keep it safe. Out of breath, she erupted into the great hall. That was where Ramsay and Alex were usually to be found, but not today.

As she came to a halt just inside the door, her heart stopped beating altogether and if she could have made her limbs work, she would have run back the way she'd come. Unfortunately, she was frozen into immobility, unable to move so much as a muscle. All she could do was stare.

'Ah, Miss Buchanan, just the person I wanted to see. Take her, men.'

Captain Sherringham. *Damn him!*

Her legs began to move at last and she backed away, shaking her head. A side table halted her progress and she knew it was too late to make a run for it. She clenched her fists, which made the jade pendant dig into the palm of one hand, reminding her she was still holding it. *No! I'll not let them take that too!* Slowly, so as not to alert the men to her actions, she reached behind her and fumbled for a bowl she knew should be there. When her fingers found it, she placed the pendant at the bottom, then pretended to bolt for the door.

Sherringham's men moved swiftly and she didn't get far. In a few strides, they reached her. One of them lifted the butt of his pistol and she was vaguely aware of it coming down in an arc towards her head. The next thing she knew, everything went black.

Brice drew a dirk out of its sheath at his belt and prepared himself for a fight. He had no idea who these desperate-looking men were, but he could see they weren't here to talk. Out of the corner of his eye, he saw Liath come to take a stand next to him and his innards twisted with fear for the dog. He knew the assailants wouldn't hesitate to hurt him.

'Go, Liath, back to the house!' he hissed. 'Go on, leave!' But the dog ignored him and bared his fangs at the attackers, growling deep in his throat.

In the next instant, the men surged forward, dirks at the ready. Some dim recess of Brice's mind wondered why they hadn't just brought pistols to threaten him with, but apparently that wasn't how they fought. He didn't wait for them to fall on him *en masse*, but launched himself at the nearest man as fast as he could. Liath did the same, but although the dog managed to take one man down and make him howl with pain as he sank his teeth into flesh, he was no match for a dagger.

Brice winced when he heard the hound give a loud yelp, then a keening noise, knowing he'd been hurt, perhaps even mortally wounded. There was nothing Brice could do at the moment though, he had to defend himself. He made short work of the first man, feinting left, then right, before hitting the assailant with a powerful blow to the chin. The man had obviously been expecting a thrust with the dagger and therefore didn't see Brice's fist coming. He toppled to the ground and lay motionless.

The other four were cannier and came at him from different sides at once. Although he did his best, Brice couldn't fight them all, especially with his body still sore and several bruised ribs. He wondered what was taking Ramsay and Alex so long, but didn't have time to think about it too much. He could only pray they'd come to his assistance soon. He managed to get in a few punches and slashed one man's arm quite badly, but when one of the assailants cut Brice's own forearm, the sharp stab of pain made him drop his dirk. After that, it was only a question of time before he was overpowered. No one came to his aid.

With his arms twisted up behind him, they made him walk towards the forest.

'Who are you? What do you want with me?' he snarled, trying to dislodge the painful grip without success.

'The name's MacGregor and as fer wha' we want, ye'll find oot soon enough.'

Brice didn't bother asking any more questions. He doubted they'd reply in any case so he was just wasting his breath. He glanced over his shoulder and saw Liath lying on the ground. *Damn it all to hell!* Marsaili was going to be crushed to find her beloved dog dead and he wished he could have spared her that pain. There was absolutely nothing he could do about it, however, and he had tried to tell the stubborn hound to leave. He was moved by the dog's loyalty and sent him a silent message of thanks, wherever his spirit was.

Just before the group reached the edge of the forest, Brice heard a shout behind them. He turned to see Iain Seton come rushing out of the house, pulling his dirk out. 'Hey, stop! What do you think you're doing?'

The man next to Brice tsk-ed and shook his head. 'Wheesht, is he a loon or wha'?' the MacGregor muttered. Brice wondered the same thing, but hoped Iain wasn't by himself and that his arrival on the scene heralded more help. It was a bit late in the day, but still better than nothing.

Iain didn't remain alone for long, however. His father was suddenly standing next to him, grabbing him by the arm and holding him back. Brice could see they were arguing, but couldn't hear what was being said. A suspicion took root in his mind and he noticed the MacGregor men all ignored Seton as if he was no threat to them.

'He hired you for this, didn't he?' Brice asked, but he already knew the answer. He could feel it in his gut, this was Seton's doing. 'Whatever he paid, I can give you more,' he growled, anger filling him almost to overflowing. Was he never to be rid of the man? He should have hunted him down while he had the chance.

'Tha's wha' he seid too,' the nearest MacGregor smirked. 'Sae save yer breath. Ye're goin' tae need it.'

'Don't even think about running to his aid,' Seton hissed at his son, gripping Iain's arm firmly. 'Have you no sense? It's our last chance.'

Iain shook him off and scowled at him. 'No sense? You're the one who's lost all reason!' he exclaimed. He glanced at the group of men rapidly heading into the forest, soon to be lost from sight. 'Who are they? What idiotic plan have you hatched now?'

'It's not idiotic at all, I'll have you know. It's perfect. Those are some of the MacGregor outlaws and I've paid them to rid us of the laird and his friends once and for all.'

'What, you're stooping to murder now? That's definitely taking things a step too far. I'm not having any part of this.'

Iain was about to take off at a run after Brice, but Seton pulled out a pistol from behind his back and cocked it. The soft click behind his left ear made Iain freeze and he turned incredulous eyes on his father.

'You move and I won't hesitate to shoot, boy,' Seton answered the unspoken question. 'I won't kill you, but I will make sure you can't go very far for the foreseeable future.' He gritted his teeth and hoped Iain couldn't tell he was bluffing. He wasn't at all sure he could shoot his own son, but hopefully the boy wouldn't realise that. Besides, too much was at stake so perhaps he'd be able to pull the trigger if he had to.

Something which looked suspiciously like pure hatred flashed in Iain's gaze. Seton knew there wasn't anything he could do about it right now, but when they had Bailliebroch back and were restored to their rightful position in society, he was sure the boy would thank him.

'Now get back into the house and stay there. If I catch you

setting so much as a foot outside in the next hour I won't hesitate to use this.' Seton nodded towards the weapon.

A muscle jumped in Iain's jaw, but he did as he'd been told. 'You'll regret this, Father, mark my words,' he gritted out.

'I doubt it, and neither will you,' Seton said. He watched the boy go indoors and slam the door, then walked off towards the forest. He wasn't going with the MacGregors, but he had to pay them the rest of the sum he'd agreed and that meant fetching more gold from his hidey-hole.

Once they'd been paid, he hoped never to set eyes on them or Kinross again.

Chapter Twenty-Six

'I thought the mon seid Glasgae? Wha' are we doin' here then?'

Brice lifted his aching head and listened to the bickering MacGregors. He was sitting inside an old carriage on the quayside at Leith, the port just outside Edinburgh. He couldn't see much because the windows were shuttered, but there was a hole big enough for him to recognise the place he'd arrived at himself not so long ago. Unfortunately, he couldn't call out since he'd been gagged. The foul rag in his mouth was making him thirsty as hell, but so far no one had offered him either food or drink. He doubted they cared whether he lived or died.

The first MacGregor was answered by one with a much more cultured accent. 'I don't care what he said. We'll do whatever we bloody well please. He'll never know. Edinburgh was closer and although they'll have to make a small detour, they'll be sent to the colonies eventually, as agreed.'

'Are ye sure ye can trust the captain o' this here vessel?'

'Yes, I've dealt with him before. He knows what will happen should he fail me. Go find the others and let's get this over with. I don't want to stay here a moment longer than I have to.'

Brice glanced at the two dark shapes lying on the carriage floor next to where he sat propped against one side. Ramsay and Alex, unconscious. He'd been appalled to find them slung over a pack pony each as he left the forest with the MacGregors the previous day. He assumed they'd been ambushed before he himself was captured, but how or where, he didn't know. Neither was aware of their discomfort, however, which was a blessing, and when they finally stirred, they were gagged just like him so there was no chance to find out what had happened to them. Just before reaching Leith, someone had clouted all three of them over the head again and Brice was the first to stir. He obviously had the thicker head, which was only scant consolation since it was throbbing like the very devil.

Damn Seton to hell! Brice clenched his fists behind his back, where they were securely tied together. He would make the man pay for this, if it was the last thing he did, he swore. It may take him a long time, since he'd gathered from the MacGregors' conversation with each other that he and his friends were being sent to the Americas. It would be his goal from now on though and no matter what it took, he was determined to return and take his revenge.

His thoughts turned to Marsaili and something inside him lurched. He couldn't bear to contemplate her marrying Seton, which was probably what would happen. The devious whoreson would force her somehow, perhaps with the help of more MacGregors. The notion made Brice want to scream. She was his and she might be carrying his child.

He went cold all over. *My child!* Dear Lord, and he might never see it.

We have to escape.

In a blinding flash he realised he couldn't wait years before seeing Marsaili again, couldn't allow Seton to get his hands on her. *I love her!* What a fool he'd been. He shook his head at himself. He couldn't believe he'd fallen for a woman again, had let his heart become ensnared once more, but somehow he knew this was different. Marsaili wasn't Elisabet. If she ever promised him anything, she'd keep her word. He trusted her. If only he'd had the sense to realise that he loved her earlier, then perhaps she would have sworn to become his wife. Once she'd spoken those words, he knew she'd rather die than marry anyone else.

That's my Marsaili.

Somehow he had to find a way out of this situation. For now, all he could do was bide his time, but when Ramsay and Alex woke up eventually, they'd put their heads together and come up with some plan.

They simply must.

Seton didn't think he'd ever been so angry in his life, but as he marched back towards Rosyth House he literally saw red. His kist of gold was gone. The money he'd so patiently hoarded for years had disappeared and there were only two alternatives. Either Iain had taken it or the laird had. No one else could have even guessed it existed. Whoever it was, he would find out.

As he came out of the forest, he was astonished to see Iain and his new wife slowly making their way towards the house from the loch, carrying that infernal hound of Marsaili's on a blanket. He rushed over and brandished his pistol once more.

'What in the name of all that's holy do you think you're doing? Leave the flea bag and get back inside this instant! Didn't I tell you to stay in the house?'

Iain shot him a look of disdain. 'He's wounded and needs treatment. My wife would like to nurse him and her word is my law. Shoot me for it if you want, I no longer care.'

Seton was speechless at such defiance, but since the pair were heading back towards the house in any case, it didn't make much difference whether they brought the mangy hound or not. He didn't look to be long for this world. *And good riddance!*

'And where's my gold? Did you take it?' he demanded. 'I suppose you thought you'd stop my plans by removing the kist, but I'll thank you to give it back. It'll be yours one day, but not yet.'

Iain turned to glare at him with a frown. 'What kist? What are you talking about?'

'You know very well what I mean. The money I've been saving up for Bailliebroch. Now give it to me.'

Iain shook his head. 'I don't have any money, you know that. Kirsty's dowry hasn't been paid out yet and you've never given me so much as a merk unless you had to.' He and Kirsty had reached the stable yard now and carried the large dog into the nearest loose box where they placed him on some hay. They were both panting and red in the face from their heavy burden. Seton still couldn't understand why they'd go to such efforts for a mere dog.

'I'll go find Flora,' Kirsty said quietly, without looking at Seton. 'She'll know what to do if he needs stitching.'

'Stitching? Have you gone mad? He's not worth the effort,' Seton spat.

Kirsty fixed him with a narrowed gaze. 'I'll be the judge of that, Mr Seton. This hound is my sister's and I'll not have him die unless he has to. Are you going to stop me?'

Seton was too astonished by her open challenge to reply. She waited a moment, then left on her errand. 'You'll need to curb that tongue of hers,' he muttered to Iain, but his son stood up and marched over to face him.

'I like her exactly the way she is, so just you leave her alone, d'you hear? Now what's this nonsense about a stolen kist? You shouldn't have mentioned it in front of her, you know. She'll tell the laird and then where will you be?'

'Hah, he won't be hearing any tales for a long time, if ever. He's not coming back in a hurry. I told you.' The thought of Kinross sailing across the vast ocean towards the colonies cooled his temper somewhat and almost made him smile. Until he remembered his missing hoard. 'But if you didn't take my gold, then he must have. Find out from your wife where he might have hidden it. Or better yet, ask Marsaili.'

'Marsaili? I can't ask her, she was taken away by the Redcoats not half an hour ago. Why else do you think she's not here caring for her dog? Wild horses wouldn't keep her away normally.'

'Taken by the Redcoats?' Seton felt his heartbeat stutter. What did this mean? And what on earth was Sherringham playing at? He scowled at his son. 'Why didn't you stop them? She hasn't done anything.'

'I know that well enough, but what was I to do? One man against a whole troop of Sassenachs? That captain of theirs said he had a warrant for her arrest and everything. I went looking for the laird immediately, but that's when I found him being taken away as well, on your orders. Anyway, I thought you were in cahoots with the Redcoat so I assumed he was acting on your behalf. Another ploy to make her marry you? Scare her into thinking you her saviour?' Iain sneered.

'No, I had nothing to do with it. We must get her back, immediately.' He considered his son's words and remembered he'd had the same idea once before. 'Although come to think of it, that's not a bad notion. She ought to be glad to see me for once.'

'Well, good luck with persuading the Englishman to release her. I'd rather talk to the devil than have anything to do with that fellow. He's a nasty piece of work and no mistake.' Iain spat on the ground for emphasis.

'No, you don't understand. You'll have to come with me and help rescue her from their clutches. I don't know what he's up to, but I doubt he'll release her unless he feels like it. He won't listen to me.'

'I thought you said you had him exactly where you wanted?' Iain challenged.

'Not with regard to Marsaili. She was never part of the equation. The man's supposed to smooth my way towards buying back Bailliebroch, nothing more. Apart from

266

arresting Kinross, of course, but that didn't work out too well.'

Iain shook his head. 'So you're telling me Marsaili really is at the mercy of the Redcoats?'

'Aye, isn't that what I've been saying? We must go after them. Saddle the *garrons*.'

Iain glanced at the dog, who was whimpering slightly and panting. Seton couldn't believe his son would care what happened to the animal. He was probably only doing it to please his wife. Seton shook his head. One of these days Iain would be ruled by his head instead of what was in his breeches.

'Leave him, your wife can take care of him.'

Before Iain could reply, Kirsty returned, closely followed by Flora. She was frowning and carrying a note. She held it out to Seton. 'This is addressed to you. I found it in the great hall.'

Seton swore under his breath, but unfolded it quickly.

Seton, I have Kinross's wench. Kindly tell him that unless he gives himself up, I'll have no option but to keep her entertained for a long while. I'm sure he'll know what I mean. And if he tries anything or involves any of his high and mighty friends, he won't see her alive again. See to it he understands or our deal is off as well.

Sherringham

'Damn and blast it!' Seton threw the note at Iain, who caught it and read it, with Kirsty and Flora looking over his shoulders. Seton swore some more. It wasn't his fault the laird had escaped. And now Sherringham was ruining everything. It was not to be borne. 'Come, Iain, leave the women to deal with the mutt. We need to leave now if we're to have any chance of catching them. And find us some weapons.'

'I thought you handed those over to the Sassenach.'

'No, he left them behind. Hurry!'

Iain looked at Kirsty, who nodded. 'If you're going to save Marsaili, go, but keep an eye on him.' She glanced meaningfully at her father-in-law. 'I don't trust him. Especially not now I've read that note.'

Iain kissed her hard on the mouth, then bent to whisper what Seton assumed were sweet nothings in her ear before he finally went to do his father's bidding.

Seton shook his head. The boy was going soft.

The first thing Marsaili saw when she came to was something red which flickered in front of her eyes. She blinked to try and clear her vision, while registering that her cheek was being rubbed against scratchy material. This proved to be the back of an English soldier's jacket, which explained the red. She'd been leaning against him because someone had tied her to him, presumably so she wouldn't fall off the back of his horse.

She lifted her cheek as far away from him as possible and wrinkled her nose at the smell of wool. The soldier himself wasn't too fragrant either, but she had to suffer this as she couldn't put any distance between them. He turned his head to glance at her and nodded. 'So you're awake at last. That's good.'

Marsaili wasn't so sure. 'Where am I?' she croaked, her throat feeling as parched as a dirt road on a hot summer's day. 'And where are we going?'

'To gaol, of course. Where else d'you think prisoners end up?' The fellow sounded very cheerful and if she'd had full use of her limbs, Marsaili reckoned she would have tried to throttle him. As it was, she found her hands well trussed too, so there was no hope of her doing anything of the sort.

'I don't understand what it is I'm supposed to have done,' she complained. 'Surely you can't go around arresting people for no reason.'

'The cap'n has a warrant says you're a suspected Jacobite,' the soldier informed her. 'You'll have to prove otherwise, but it might take weeks before your case is 'eard. Meanwhile, you'll enjoy a spell in 'is Majesty's finest accommodation.' He chuckled and Marsaili had to grit her teeth to stop from saying something very unladylike.

'How come you were given the honour of my company?' she asked sarcastically. She saw several lascivious glances coming her way from the men in front of and beside them, but this one seemed unmoved by her nearness. *Thank the Lord for small mercies!*

''Cause I'm the only one the cap'n can trust with a woman on account of the fact I don't like 'em. I'll keep you safe for 'im.'

'What?' Marsaili didn't understand at first, but then something scandalous she'd once heard about men who preferred the company of young boys surfaced in her brain. She felt her cheeks turn scarlet. 'Oh.'

'Precisely.'

Marsaili drew in a deep breath and hoped the colour in her face was subsiding. She decided to change the subject and looking around her, she suddenly realised they weren't riding along the English road, as she'd expected, but a narrow Highland track. 'So we're going to Fort George then? Or one of the others, Fort William maybe?' She suppressed a shiver. She'd heard many a tale about what could happen to anyone taken there.

'No.'

'Where then?' She was surprised at his answer.

'You'll see soon enough. Now cease your prattle. I'm not s'posed to talk to you at all.'

Marsaili decided there was no point prolonging the conversation in any case. Besides, she felt nauseous from a severe headache and the motion of the horse. Swallowing hard she concentrated on keeping the contents of her stomach where they were.

'Ouch, my head! What the hell happened?'

The voice that came out of the darkness, accompanied by a groan, was unmistakeably Ramsay's. Brice felt him move and heard another muffled protest as he obviously bumped into Alex.

'You were knocked out,' Brice said. 'Again.'

'*Fan också*,' Ramsay swore in Swedish. He sounded very aggrieved and who could blame him? If Brice's head was sore, his uncle's had to be twice as bad.

'I agree,' came Alex's voice. 'But where are we?'

'Can't you smell it?' Brice asked. 'Salt water. We're on a ship, bound for the Lord only knows where.' He tried to tamp down on the vexation that was threatening to choke him. It wouldn't do any good to bemoan his fate. He needed to keep his wits about him. 'The bad news is we're being sent to the colonies, presumably as indentured servants.'

'What?'

'No! That means we'll be gone for years, if not …' Brice could almost hear Ramsay's thought process as the enormity of the situation hit him. 'Ida! I must get back to her. What will she think? I …'

'Wait, calm down.' Brice lowered his voice, in case anyone was listening to them. 'The good news is that I heard our captors talking about us having to change ships somewhere in order to get there. That means this is a smaller vessel, not an ocean-going one, so it will have to put in to port somewhere for us to be transferred. When that happens, we have to be ready.'

'What do you mean, ready? Oww, my skull …'

'Never mind your skull, Ramsay, it's as thick as granite.' Brice didn't know how much time they had to hatch a plan, and therefore there was no room for sympathy at the moment.

'Insensitive beast,' Ramsay muttered.

'I know, but listen, we need to find something in here to cut our bonds with. If we could free ourselves, we can try to overpower whoever comes to fetch us. Help me search. There must be something sharp.'

'And how do you suggest we do that?' Ramsay's voice was sarcastic. 'I don't know about you, but my hands are tied behind my back. Or at least I think they are, there's no feeling in them so I can't be sure.'

'Oh, stop moaning. You should be able to get onto your knees, unless they've tied your legs? Mine are free. Then you can crawl around and feel behind you along the walls. Alex, are you with us? Can you help?'

'I'll try. Just promise to stop bickering, please. The slightest noise is like a nail through my brain.'

Ramsay muttered something under his breath, then he and Brice both fell silent, since their heads were just as painful. Brice managed to get onto his knees and began a slow exploration of the space they were in, presumably a part of the hold. It was damp and stank of brine, rotting substances and something dead. A rat perhaps. Brice tried not to breathe too deeply, although he was becoming used to the odours by now.

He found nothing useful at knee-level, so with some effort he succeeded in pushing himself upright by using the wall as leverage. As he made his way along the wall, he was becoming more and more despondent. The cabin or whatever it was seemed entirely empty. There was nothing they could use, not even a nail sticking out of the timbers.

In the next instant, however, his head connected with something and he saw stars. 'Ow! What the ...?' He'd no doubt collected yet another bruise, this one to his forehead, but he reckoned it might just have been worth it. 'I've got something,' he hissed.

The other two stopped moving. 'What?' Ramsay asked.

'I think it's a lantern. Hold on, I'm going to try and knock it down with my head. If it has glass sides, it will shatter, and we should be able to use the shards to cut each other loose. If not, it may have sharp edges.'

'You'll make an awful racket. What if someone comes?'

'It's a risk we have to take. As soon as I've knocked it down, let's all dive to the floor and try and grab a piece of glass. Hide it somewhere quickly, then even if they come and clear up the mess and search the cabin, we'll still have one piece. Agreed?'

'Fine. Do it.' Alex's voice was curt and still laced with pain.

Brice didn't hesitate to put his plan in motion. Steeling himself against the impact, he head-butted the lantern from underneath, hoping it would come unhooked from whatever it hung on. Luck was with him and it did, crashing to the floor in an explosion of sound.

Immediately, he crouched down and felt behind him on the floor for some glass. He secured a large shard and scuttled over to the nearest wall where he pushed the glass in between two planks, leaving just a tiny bit sticking out. He hoped the other two men were doing the same. Then they waited for someone to come and investigate what they were up to.

No one came.

Brice sighed with relief. 'Maybe they're all busy sailing the ship?' he speculated. 'Or perhaps the wind is so loud up on deck they didn't hear us? Either way, let's get to work. Ramsay, come over here and I'll start on your bonds.'

Chapter Twenty-Seven

'You're sure Captain Sherringham isn't here?' Seton peered at the guard outside Fort William, frustration building up inside him. He didn't know how to tell whether the man was speaking the truth or not.

'Hasn't been here for days. Now d'you want to see anyone else? Otherwise clear off, you're blocking my view.'

'Come on, Father, let's go,' Iain hissed and pulled on Seton's sleeve.

'Oh, very well.' They walked off, away from the forbidding edifice which housed His Majesty's troops, and Seton had to admit to a sense of relief. This wasn't a place where he wanted to linger. 'How do we know he wasn't lying though? What if Sherringham is playing games with us?'

'I doubt it,' Iain said. 'He told you what he wanted in the note, he just didn't say where the laird should go. What other places could he take a prisoner?'

'Don't know. Let's ask around.'

After engaging several locals in conversation, they came up with a likely destination.

'Inveraray gaol,' Seton said. 'Yes, I've heard of it. They hold court sessions there too, so it would make sense. Although why he'd bother going all that way is beyond me.'

'It was probably to keep Marsaili as far away from Brice as possible,' Iain speculated. 'And throw him off the scent.'

'Brice is it now?' Seton groused, unaccountably annoyed at hearing his son talking about Kinross in such a familiar way. 'Anyone'd think the two of you were the best of friends.'

'He's not so bad and besides, we're kin now through marriage.'

'To hell with that! He's the enemy, as I keep telling you. The sooner you get that into your feeble mind, the better.'

Iain seemed about to protest, but Seton held up a hand. 'Never mind now. We'd better go straight to Inveraray to check if Marsaili is there. No time to lose. A pox on that slippery whoreson, Sherringham!'

Iain said nothing, only followed his father back to where they'd left their ponies. There was no need for words, they both wanted the same thing – to find Marsaili – although Seton didn't tell his son they may be after her for different reasons.

Time enough for that later.

They had taken turns to sleep for a while in order to try and rid themselves of their headaches and Brice felt much better for it. His ankle and his other cuts and bruises were healing too, apart from the ribs which would no doubt take a good few weeks. Either way, he was as ready for their escape attempt as he'd ever be.

He'd had a lot of time to think as well. Not just about Marsaili and the fact that he loved her, but also about his brother and the letter he'd sent. Brice shook his head in the darkness. *I should have trusted him when he told me he was set up*, he thought. *Jamie would never willingly have hurt me.* He was right, they'd always been the best of friends, there for each other. And unless Jamie's personality had undergone a spectacular change during the time Brice was away, marriage had been the furthest thing from Jamie's mind. He wouldn't have wed Elisabet if she'd been the prettiest girl in the world. No, the entire episode had to have been Elisabet's doing, somehow. Amazing how he could see this so clearly now, when he might never get the chance to tell his brother.

'Idiot,' he muttered. *I have to let him know I understand.*

He came to a decision. If they managed to free themselves and escape the fate Seton had planned for them, he'd write to Jamie as soon as he could and invite him to come and stay at Rosyth. *But not Elisabet, he's probably ready to murder her by now!* The thought made him smile ruefully. Yes, Jamie could probably do with a breathing space – being leg-shackled would be purgatory to someone as wild as him – and Brice needed to apologise for being so hasty.

Please God, give me that chance, he prayed.

There was so much more than revenge at stake here. They simply had to succeed.

'I think we've come into a harbour,' he whispered to the other two, after shaking them awake a little while later. 'I can only feel the ship bobbing gently up and down, none of the roiling motion we had earlier. Do you agree?'

'Yes, you're right.'

There was also muffled shouting which could be heard up above them, and footsteps running, as well as the creaking of block and tackle.

'We must be ready for them,' Brice said. 'Ramsay, you and Alex stand one either side of the door. Take off your coats and throw them over the head of whoever comes in first, then tackle them to the floor. I'll stand opposite, ready to take on anyone else. If possible, we should try to keep the noise down as much as we can so as not to alert anyone to what's happening.'

'Good plan. Then what?'

'We'll have to improvise after that.' Brice thought for a moment. 'If we're in a harbour, we could try rushing up on deck and just throwing ourselves into the water. We should be able to swim to safety before they react enough to lower a boat and go after us. You're both strong swimmers, right?'

Ramsay and Alex agreed. 'But if there aren't too many people on deck, let's take the dry route,' Ramsay added. 'No point getting drenched if we don't have to. This is one of my best coats.'

Brice chuckled. Only Ramsay could make jokes at a time like this. He was glad to have his two friends with him. Without them, he doubted he'd have been able to break free. At least with three of them, they stood a fair chance. 'Get into position then,' he urged. 'We must be ready to strike.'

Their plan went off without a hitch. Only two men came to fetch them and they were taken completely by surprise when they stepped inside the door. Brice grabbed the broken lantern and used it to knock the men out. Since they both had a coat over their heads, he didn't think they would suffer any lasting effects, other than the kind of sore head he'd had himself.

'You'd better not have got rust on this,' Ramsay muttered, pushing his arms into the sleeves of his garment as they checked for any signs of life outside the door.

'To hell with your coat! I'll buy you an even better one.' Brice grinned. 'Now come on.'

He'd been right in thinking they were in a store room on the lower deck. A ladder led up to the next level and he peeked cautiously out of the hatch before climbing up completely. There was no one there, just a collection of hammocks slung from beams and a few sailors' chests. Another shorter ladder flanked a larger hatch where moonlight filtered down from above.

'Ah, it's night time,' Brice whispered. 'I wasn't sure. That helps though. Come on, we'll have to be quick now so we surprise them.'

Repeating his earlier manoeuvre, he hesitated a fraction before launching himself out of the hatch and running across the deck. A gangplank led onto a large quay on the starboard side of the ship and he headed straight for it. There were four or five men, coiling ropes and making knots, while one who was dressed better than the others stood watching. Brice had to pass him, but by the time one of the sailors raised the alarm, he was already alongside the man. He saw the astonished expression on his face and the reflex action of reaching for a weapon, but the man didn't have a chance to bring it out. Brice simply gave him an almighty shove, all the harder since he had momentum from running, and sent him flying over the side and into the water.

Pandemonium broke out, but most of the sailors didn't know whether to rescue their captain, lean over the rail to look or tackle the escapees. Brice and the others didn't hang around for them to make up their minds. They headed for the gangplank, fighting off two men who belatedly tried to stop them, and then ran off along the quay as fast as their legs would carry them, ignoring any shouts coming from behind.

Weaving in and out of various alleys, where drunken sailors and ladies of the night were carousing, they finally came to a halt in a particularly dark spot. Brice leaned against a house and tried to catch his breath. 'We made it,' he panted. *'Tack gode Gud.* But ... where the hell ... are we? I thought I heard Dutch, can that be right?'

'Yes, Amster ... dam,' Ramsay replied, huffing and puffing even harder. 'Recognised ... the harbour. Been here ... before.'

'Damn! I didn't think we'd gone as far as that. We need to find a ship to take us back to Scotland immediately, but we have no money. The MacGregors searched my pockets and took everything.'

'Doesn't matter. Wait.' Ramsay took a while longer to get his breathing under control. 'I know some merchants here. I came with Killian once, trading. If we could find them, I think I can persuade them to lend us some money. We'll have to wait for daylight though. We need a place to hide till then.'

'How about a warehouse?' Alex had been quiet up until that point, but now joined the conversation. 'If we find a big one, I should be able to pick the lock quite easily and we could hide behind whatever is in there. No one will think to look for us in a place like that, surely?'

'Good idea,' Brice said. 'But what will you use to pick the lock? You don't have any of your usual tools.'

Alex laughed. 'We'll have to persuade one of the doxies to part with a hairpin or two. Shall we have a bet to see who can do it first? My money's on you, Brice. The ladies like you, I've noticed.'

'Cheeky son of a ...' But Brice couldn't help but smile. It was wonderful to be free and at least they had a plan of sorts. He hoped it would work.

It must, because the alternative didn't bear thinking of.

'Welcome to Inveraray,' the soldier Marsaili was with said cheerfully.

She looked about her. After more than three days of riding in the most uncomfortable way possible, and freezing cold nights huddled on the ground wrapped only in her *arisaid*, she was almost beyond caring where she ended up. But tired and sore though she was, she had to admit this was a beautiful place. Situated on the western side of Loch Fyne, which she'd been told led out to sea, the little town was mostly just a collection of humble cottages, with one or two larger houses. However, they had a most spectacular backdrop of glorious, forest-clad mountains, reflected in the mirror-still waters of the loch. On a day like this, when the skies were blue with only the odd fluffy cloud, it was utter perfection.

To one side of the town, there was building work going on and the soldier informed her the Duke of Argyll was in the process of rebuilding his castle there.

"E's takin' an awful long time about it, but no doubt it'll be very grand when it's finished,' the man commented. Marsaili assumed he was right, a Duke would build only the finest of dwellings.

Soon she forgot all about the lovely sights as they progressed into the town. The soldier was in a chatty mood and told her, 'This 'ere's Front Street and we're 'eadin' for the Town House. That's the court house to the likes o' you, and that's where the gaol is too, on the ground floor 'neath the court room. Look, there it is now.'

Marsaili glanced in through shutter-less windows to see inmates shuffling around an open space in front of what must be the holding cells. There were so many miserable faces, it was as if their collective despair was seeping out and into the street. She swallowed hard. Why had Sherringham brought her here? She soon found out as he rode down the line and stopped next to her and the man she'd been riding with.

'You'll await your trial here,' he said curtly. 'I like this place, the despondency quite lifts my spirits. I hope you'll feel the full measure of it until it's time for you to leave for a better place.'

Marsaili stifled a gasp. *A better place?* Surely he couldn't have her hanged without any evidence whatsoever?

He must have seen her alarm, however, because his mouth turned up at the corners. 'I'm talking about the penal colonies,' he clarified. 'If you survive the journey, that is.' He turned away from her towards his men. 'Take her away. I'll go and speak to the warden.'

As she was led inside the stinking gaol, Marsaili felt her skin crawl with both fear and disgust. Not only was this place filthy, but it seemed to contain some desperate looking people.

How was she to survive in here?

Oh, Brice, where are you? she wondered. Would he come to her rescue, the way she had his, or was he already dead? She remembered the six, fierce-looking men, and realised he wouldn't have stood a chance. Bile rose in her throat. She couldn't bear the thought of him hurt again or worse ... But if not him, then who could she turn to for help? Brice's friend in Edinburgh? Or even Ailsa?

She had no way of contacting either one. She was on her own.

'So are you going to try and find Sherringham and offer him another bribe?' Iain asked, as they finally rode into Inveraray. 'If Marsaili's really here, that is.'

Seton had thought about this long and hard, but had decided talking to the Englishman was useless. He obviously had his own agenda now and Seton wasn't even sure the man would keep their previous bargain. Although if he didn't, he'd find himself with a dirk in his back, Seton swore. *Lying, cheating bastard ...*

'No,' he said now. 'Let's go in search of the gaol and see whether it's possible to bluff Marsaili out of there. A bit of gold greasing the right palms might smooth our way. Not that I have much left at the moment, since you allowed the laird to steal what was ours from right under your nose, but ...'

'Me? I didn't *allow* him to do anything!' Iain glared at his father. 'I was busy with my wife, not watching Brice like a nursemaid.'

'Aye, and therein lies the root of the problem,' Seton muttered. 'And stop calling him that. I told you.'

'And what's that supposed to mean? Am I not to enjoy the married state like any other newly-wed? You denied us long enough.'

'Well, what was to stop you from tupping the girl and

have done with it?' Seton didn't understand his son's attitude to females. The boy certainly hadn't learned it from him. To Seton's mind, women were there to be taken and enjoyed whenever the mood came upon him. Marriage was for gain, nothing else, and as for love, that was a load of nonsense.

'Unlike you, I have principles,' Iain informed him, tightening his jaw. 'And Kirsty was worth waiting for.'

'I'm glad to hear it,' Seton replied sarcastically, 'but if you could stop thinking about her for just a moment, you can help me come up with a good story as to why Marsaili should be set free.'

Iain glowered at him, but thought for a while before suggesting, 'We could pretend she's my wife and that it's a case of mistaken identity? Let's say I have a cousin who's a known Jacobite and Sherringham thought she was married to him? Perhaps if she has a sister who looks a lot like her or something?'

'Hmm, yes, not bad. It's a start.'

They were riding down another street now and came level with a big building which was obviously the gaol. A large number of wretched people were milling around a sort of courtyard behind unshuttered windows and it was clear from the state of them most had lost all hope. Some were emaciated, most were filthy and to Seton, they all seemed pathetic.

'Dear Lord, would you just look at them,' he muttered. 'This is definitely the right place.'

'Look!' Iain hissed, pointing to one side. 'There's Marsaili, sitting in the corner. I'd recognise that hair anywhere.'

Seton scanned the prisoners until his gaze found her and something suddenly twisted inside him. It wasn't right, a woman like her sitting among such misery. She had a queenly presence, by rights she ought to grace the table of a laird. *No, not just any laird's table, mine!* She was like a jewel thrown into a midden heap, gleaming too brightly. 'Damn it,' he muttered, 'we have to get her out of there. Now!'

Iain glanced at him as if he was surprised at the vehemence in his father's tone. 'I know. But do you really think our plan will work?'

'I'm not sure. We'd better go and take a room at an inn first and perhaps have a drink or two with the locals to find out what's what. It's always best to be well informed.'

With a last regretful look at Marsaili, he turned his horse away. He would free her, if it was the last thing he did. Quite why he felt so strongly about it, he didn't want to consider, but he knew one thing – she didn't belong in there.

Marsaili sat with her back to the wall because somehow the sensation of cold stone behind her felt safer. She knew there was no such thing as safety here, but at least this way no one could come at her without her noticing.

She'd been accosted the moment she was pushed in through the door. Several miserable looking crones had rushed forward, pawing her and searching her pockets. When they came up empty-handed, they keened in frustration, but they'd left her alone since. Marsaili wasn't sure whether to be glad or not that she had nothing of value for them to take. On the one hand, she would have been angry if they'd stolen from her, but on the other, they all seemed so desperate it might have been a kindness to be able to alleviate their suffering temporarily.

Either way, she thanked God she wasn't wearing the jade pendant Brice had given her. She very much hoped it was still in the bowl where she'd put it and that no one else found it while she was gone and appropriated it.

It might be the only thing of his she'd ever have. If she even returned, that was …

The thought made her blink furiously to stem the tide

of tears that threatened. She couldn't endure the nightmare vision of never seeing him again, being held by him, kissed so passionately. His marriage proposal may not have been all she could have wished for, since he obviously didn't love her the way she loved him, but she knew she would have said yes. No matter what, she wanted to be his wife.

She hung her head. There was no hope of that now.

Someone sank down next to her and squeezed her arm. Marsaili looked up into the kind face of a woman of about her own age or perhaps slightly older. It was hard to tell as the light was fading fast and the woman's face was covered in grime. 'There now, ye'll get used tae it. It's a wee bit of a shock at first, bein' in here, but we women stick thegither. I'm Eilidh.'

'Marsaili.'

'What're ye here for? Stealin'? Whorin'?'

Marsaili shook her head. 'No. I've been told I'm a suspected Jacobite. That's just a trumped up charge though. I've naught to do with such things.' She hesitated. 'Do you ... do you know what the punishment for that is?' She wasn't sure she really wanted to know, but sometimes it was better to be aware of what was coming.

'Well, depends on how involved ye've been, or wha' they can prove. I'd say six months in here at the very least, but ...'

Marsaili felt relief. If there was a chance of getting out eventually, she could stand anything. 'So definitely not hanging then?' she said.

'No, no, shouldnae think so. Now come alang, I see the warden beckoning. It's time tae go inside for the night. Stay close by me, ye'll be fine.'

Marsaili wasn't as certain about that as her new friend, but since it was the best offer available, she obeyed.

Chapter Twenty-Eight

'Brice, I think it's morning. We need to leave before too many people are out and about.'

Alex's sharp hiss woke Brice from a half-slumber and he raised his head from the lumpy sack of grain he'd been leaning against. 'How can you tell?' He squinted into the gloom, but realised it wasn't quite as dark inside the warehouse as it had been when they entered the night before.

'Up there, see? A small window or opening. There's pale light.'

'Right, yes, well, you'd better wake Ramsay then. Let's go.'

Brice stood up and stretched, trying to ease the kinks out of his back and neck which were both stiff as planks. His ribs still ached like the very devil whenever he breathed in too deeply, so he took it slowly, massaging the back of his neck with his hands. The aches and pains in his body were as nothing to the icy fear that gripped his heart, however.

What if we're already too late? What if Seton has forced Marsaili into marriage somehow and had his way with her? Damnation, I'll kill him with my bare hands!

Brice tried to steer his thoughts away from such thinking. It didn't help and he needed to keep his wits about him, not mope around like a love-sick fool. He gritted his teeth and turned to his companions. 'Are we ready? Then tell me who we're looking for and I'll find the way.'

'How?' Alex asked. 'This is a large town, surely? It'll be like looking for a needle in a haystack, unless Ramsay remembers the way.'

'No,' came Ramsay's voice, gruff with lack of sleep. 'I stayed with the ship so I have no idea where to find them.

Killian brought the merchants to see the cargo, which is how I met them, but that was all. Sorry.'

'It doesn't matter, I'll just ask until we find them.'

'Oh, of course, I hadn't thought of that. Brilliant!' Ramsay clapped Brice on the back. 'I'd forgotten you speak Dutch.'

'Well, not quite fluently, but enough to ask something so simple. Who are we looking for?'

'Johannes Bruggen and Willem Visser.'

They exited the warehouse as if they'd had every right to be there, and although there were people going about their business outside, this ploy worked. No one paid any attention to them as they made their way along the nearest canal towards what they hoped was the centre of the town.

Amsterdam reminded Brice of Gothenburg, since the latter had been built in imitation of the Dutch city, albeit on a much smaller scale. Whereas Gothenburg's canals were more or less laid out like a grid, however, in Amsterdam they seemed to form concentric semi-circles which abutted the river Ij. In between the main canals were smaller ones, connecting the larger ones to each other. He'd heard it was a bustling commercial centre and he could now see that for himself. From the mixture of languages all around him, he also gathered there were lots of foreigners here.

There were bridges everywhere, and rows of neat brick houses, richly decorated with cornicing, faced the canals. Although no two houses were the same, most of them had distinctive looking gables, which were very attractive. Adding to the overall aesthetic impression were lots of trees that grew along the canal sides.

Brice stopped quite a few passers-by to ask directions and struck lucky with the fifth one.

'Oh, you mean the merchants? Yes, you need to turn here, then …'

They memorised the convoluted instructions and

somehow managed to find their way to the right *straat*. Here Brice stopped a maid on her way to market, and she pointed to a house on the right hand side of the nearest canal. 'That one, over there, *mijnheer*.'

'Thank you.' Brice gave her his best smile, which made her blush, and they went to knock on the door. 'I hope you're right, Ramsay, and they remember you.'

Ramsay grinned. 'What, you don't think I'm memorable? Just you wait and see.'

'Hmm, well, if you're wrong, Alex is going to have to turn to his father's former profession, because I'm not staying in this place a moment longer than I have to, nice though it may be.'

Marsaili didn't think she'd ever be able to sleep in the crowded gaol. Fear kept her from relaxing and there were moans and mutterings all round which kept her awake the first two nights. On the third one, however, she was so exhausted that somehow she must have dozed off eventually, only to wake with a start when a heavy hand descended on her shoulder. She tried to jerk away from it, towards the safety of Eilidh who was next to her, but the fingers held fast.

'Marsaili Buchanan?' a deep voice whispered.

'Y-yes,' she stammered, trying not to let her terror show too much.

'Come with me, your friends are waiting.' Marsaili was just about to ask which friends, when the man continued, 'They told me one word would make you believe me – Liath.'

Marsaili relaxed. She doubted Sherringham knew the name of her dog, only someone from Rosyth would. Scrambling to her feet, she felt Eilidh standing up beside her and realised she couldn't leave the woman behind after she'd shown such kindness. 'My maid is coming too,' she stated boldly, in a tone that brooked no argument.

'I wasn't told about her. That'll be an extra payment,' the deep voice grumbled. 'Oh, very well, come along then and be quick about it.'

Marsaili grabbed Eilidh's hand and followed the man. There were some protests as she tripped over people's legs and a few hands reached out to try and snatch at the hem of her skirts, but somehow they made it to one of the entrances to the prison. Outside, she saw two shadowy figures and as the gaoler hurried them through the doorway, these came forward.

'That'll be ten guineas. You didn't say nothin' 'bout a maid,' the man hissed.

'Ten? But …?'

Marsaili recognised Seton's voice and her heart sank, but she definitely didn't want to go back inside. *Better the devil you know*, she thought. 'Pay it, please, I'll reimburse you,' she whispered. Muttering under his breath, Seton did so.

The other shadow turned out to be Iain, which made Marsaili feel slightly better although she wasn't sure what his reasons for being there were. 'Come on,' he whispered, 'we must leave immediately.' Taking her hand, he pulled her swiftly down the street and since she was still holding onto Eilidh, she came too. Marsaili noticed Eilidh hadn't said anything, but assumed she was too pleased to be away from the gaol to care where they were going.

On the outskirts of the little town, two ponies waited and Seton and Iain mounted one each. Seton held out his hand to Marsaili, 'Here, you'll have to ride behind me,' he said. She hesitated only for an instant. This wasn't the time or the place to argue about details. Iain took Eilidh up behind him and they set off.

'How did you manage to bribe the gaoler?' Marsaili asked as soon as they were away from the town.

'It wasn't all that difficult. Some of the townspeople take turns guarding the gaol and we met him earlier at the inn. Didn't bat an eyelid when I offered him a small "reward" for helping us. Apparently lots of people escape from here. The judge isn't too pleased about it, I hear.'

'I imagine not.' Marsaili breathed in deeply of the cold night air, revelling in the fresh smell of pine.

'Who's the woman?'

'A friend,' Marsaili said simply. 'I couldn't leave her behind, I'm sorry. I'll pay you back, I promise.'

'Aye, you will.'

His words seemed to hold a double meaning which made Marsaili shiver, but she had no regrets about going with him. Anything had to be better than Inveraray Gaol.

'Thank the Lord for favourable winds!' Alex was striding along beside Brice, away from the port at Leith and in towards Edinburgh. Ramsay lagged slightly behind, looking tired and worn.

'Amen to that,' Brice replied with feeling. 'And for my father's foresight in dealing with such efficient and kind people.'

The Dutch merchants, Bruggen and Visser, had proved very understanding and accommodating. As soon as Brice explained the situation to them, they'd acted quickly and decisively. Passage to Edinburgh on a ship leaving the same day was found for the three of them, clean sets of clothes lent to them and a bath arranged for each. Brice had felt like a new man. *Mijnheer* Bruggen had also taken him aside and handed him a pouch of money.

'For any unexpected expenses during the journey,' he said with a smile. 'Don't worry, I'll make sure your father pays me back.'

'I can't thank you enough for your kindness.' Brice had liked both men immediately, but this one in particular. Of about his father's age, *Mijnheer* Bruggen was small and round with an almost completely bald head and a distinct twinkle in his eyes. He was calm and seemingly unperturbed by the arrival of three virtual strangers asking for help and Brice had the impression that behind the smiling façade lay a very shrewd brain. Killian had made a great choice of trading partner with this man.

As he strode towards Edinburgh now, Brice tried to emulate the Dutchman's unruffled demeanour, even though inside he was seething with impatience. They were back on Scottish soil, true, but there was still a long way to go. And even when they reached Rosyth, they may be too late. He refused to admit defeat until he knew for sure though.

'Do you have to walk so fast?' Ramsay grumbled. 'You may have slept for a while on that damned ship, but I didn't. I feel sick as a dog.'

'You know where we're going,' Brice flung over his shoulder. 'Just follow me to Rory's house at your own pace, if you want.'

'No, I'm not losing sight of you now.' Ramsay's mouth tightened and he hurried to catch up. 'We're sticking together or there's no saying what will happen. I just didn't think we needed to hurry quite so much.'

'Well, you're wrong. Every moment counts. Marsaili's at that devious man's mercy and I'll never forgive myself if … oh, never mind.'

Ramsay gave him a lopsided smile. 'You're really smitten, aren't you? And there's everyone back in Sweden thinking you're suffering from a broken heart. I can't wait to tell them different.'

'I was, damn it, but I know better now.' Brice glared at Ramsay. 'I thought I loved Elisabet, but it wasn't the real woman I idolised. I put her on a pedestal and never bothered to see whether I actually liked her or not, nor what was behind the pretty mask. I suppose I was just blinded by her beauty, like everyone else.'

'And how do you know you're not doing the same thing now with this Marsaili woman?'

'Because she doesn't pretend to be something she's not. She's honest, real and vibrant and … it feels different. I love her.' He shrugged, then threw Ramsay a speculative look. 'Just as you love Flora, I suspect.'

'What? No! I mean … she's a fine woman and all, but not for me, no,' Ramsay blustered.

'And why not? I've seen the way she looks at you.'

'You have? I mean, no, why would she? I'm a crusty old widower with a child – isn't that what you called me? No woman would want to take me on.'

'Rubbish. And you know well enough I was joking.' Brice grinned. 'Ask her and I'll wager a hundred guineas she says yes.'

'A hundred … are you out of your mind?'

'No, I'm saner than I've ever been. Alex, back me up here?' Brice smiled at Alex who'd been walking along silently, but obviously listening.

'I don't have that much money, but if I did, I'd bet the same,' Alex nodded.

'You're both insane,' Ramsay muttered, but his cheeks had taken on an interesting hue of pink which reached all the way to his ears.

Brice and Alex exchanged a look, but didn't say any more. It was up to Ramsay to act on their observations if he wished, but Brice for one hoped his uncle would make Flora a proposal. It was time his second cousin had a life of her own, instead of living in the shadow of her mother.

As for himself, he very much hoped he wouldn't end up living the rest of his life alone. Because if he couldn't have Marsaili, he would.

He truly wanted no one else.

'Warden, fetch a woman named Marsaili Buchanan if you please.'

Sherringham was seated opposite the Inveraray judge and had asked to see the Jacobite bitch to make sure she looked suitably wretched. He'd waited three days, to make sure she was thoroughly cowed. The worse her aspect, the more he hoped Kinross would be moved to give himself up in her stead. Even if the man arrived incognito in the town, he'd see her through the bars of the prison which was all to the good. That was one of the reasons why Sherringham had chosen to bring her here – at Fort William or any of the others she'd have been out of sight. He rubbed his hands together in anticipation, this should be interesting.

After a lengthy wait, the warden came back huffing slightly and with reddish cheeks. 'I'm sorry, your honour, but it seems she's gone missing.'

'Missing?' Sherringham sat up straight in his chair, but the angry tirade he was about to utter was drowned out by the judge who beat him to it.

'Another one! For the love of God, man, how many times do I have to tell you this is not acceptable? I thought you took on more staff to guard the prisoners?'

The warden shuffled his feet and stared at the floor. 'I did, sir, but ...' he shrugged, 'there's no knowing if they're trustworthy, is there? I did warn ye against employing townspeople.'

'You'll damn well *have* to make sure. I'm holding you responsible!'

The judge turned to Sherringham, apologetic but still visibly angry. 'I'm terribly sorry, but it seems there has been some dereliction of duty.' He glared at the warden again, but the man was still making a careful study of the floor.

Sherringham took a deep breath and clenched his fists so hard on the armrests of the chair his knuckles cracked. He could shout and bluster all he liked, but he knew it wouldn't help. The woman was gone. *Damn and blast!* Now he'd have to start all over again. He tried to compose himself and think.

'When did she go?' he asked curtly. 'Do you keep any sort of check on the inmates at all?'

The warden looked up. 'Yes, sir, they were all counted before being locked away for the night. She must have been there then as she wasn't reported missing at that point. And I was here myself until midnight, so she can't have left before then.'

'Hmm. Thank you.' Sherringham got to his feet. It was still early morning and if the laird only had a head start of a few hours, he might be able to catch up with them. Either way, he had to try.

And when he caught them, he'd make the scum pay.

Chapter Twenty-Nine

'Kirsty? And Flora! I'll be damned. What are you doing here?'

Brice was shown into the parlour of Rory Grant's lodgings and stopped dead at the sight which greeted him. He felt Ramsay and Alex bump into him from behind and then try to peer under or over his shoulders respectively. Ramsay drew in a sharp breath, but it was drowned out by the squeals of delight that echoed round the room.

'Brice, you're all right! And you two as well, oh, this is capital.' Kirsty rushed forward with her usual impulsiveness, while Flora stood up and blinked at them in surprise. Rory too got up from his chair and smiled when he saw who had arrived.

'Well, thank the Lord for that,' he said. 'We had begun to fear the worst and none of our enquiries have met with any success. You'd disappeared without a trace.' He came over to shake hands with all three men and clapped Brice on the shoulder. 'Come in and have a seat. Tell us what on earth happened to you.'

'We will, but first, why are my cousins here? Is something amiss at Rosyth? Ailsa? Marsaili? Ida?' Brice regarded the ladies with a slight frown, wondering what new calamity had befallen his family. There seemed no end to them at the moment and he felt anxiety churning his gut.

'Oh, you have no idea!' Kirsty began to wring her hands, further alarming Brice who now expected to hear the worst.

'Kirsty, let me explain. You're too melodramatic.' Flora came forward and put a restraining hand on her sister's arm. She sent Ramsay a shy smile and a nod before turning to Brice. 'We are here because Marsaili has been arrested by that Englishman who took you away. Kirsty's husband has gone with his father to try and have her released, but they weren't sure they'd manage it. Iain therefore charged Kirsty with going to Edinburgh to enlist the help of your kind friend here.' She nodded at Rory. 'He thought perhaps Mr Grant could stop any legal action against her. Naturally, I couldn't let Kirsty travel alone, so here we both are.'

'Yes, and a good thing too,' Kirsty added, 'because after Iain and his father left, Archie told us he'd heard the Englishman give his men orders to head for Inveraray. So they won't know she's there until they return home. Mr Grant had just proposed to travel straight there himself to see what he could do in the meantime.'

Brice waited until they'd finished, but while they spoke he felt his insides turn to ice. *Marsaili, taken by the Englishman! Dear God ... and with Seton in pursuit, that's not much better. He might find out her destination somehow and then ...* He tried to draw air into lungs which suddenly seemed too small. 'Thank you for your efforts. This makes it even more urgent, however. We had thought to ask Rory for the loan of some horses, so we could go north immediately. It sounds as if we need to press on as fast as possible, but heading west instead.'

He quickly related what had happened to them and why he was afraid for Marsaili. 'So you see, this may all be part of Seton's plan. Either way, if he manages to free her from gaol, she'll be in his clutches.'

'Not so,' Kirsty objected. 'My Iain's with them, remember?'

'I've nothing against your husband, cousin, but because he's a nicer man, he's not as ruthless as his father. Believe me, I doubt Seton will let his son stand in his way. He means to have Marsaili and now he thinks I'm out of the way, he'll stop at nothing to achieve his aims.' He rubbed his face to try and erase some of the tiredness and tension he was feeling. 'Any idea where he'd take her if he wanted a speedy wedding ceremony? If he's managed to spring her out of gaol, that is.'

'Bailliebroch,' said Flora without hesitation.

Brice stared at her. 'Why? I thought it was a ruin and it doesn't even belong to Seton any more.'

'The people there are still loyal to him, I've heard tell. He's their laird. That would include the priest, who owes his appointment to Mr Seton's late brother.'

Brice stared at Flora with new respect. 'That makes sense. Thank you.'

Colour rose in her cheeks, making the pockmarks less noticeable. Brice saw Ramsay staring at her and nudged his uncle to bring him out of his trance. 'Come on then, let's be on our way. There's no time to lose. We'll go north, then west, in the hope of meeting Seton along the way. We'll have to try and travel his journey, but in reverse if we can.'

'Huh? Oh, yes, very well.' Ramsay stood up, then hesitated. 'You go and see about the horses. I, er, just want a quick word with Miss Kinross about Ida. Make sure she's fine, you know.'

Brice grinned and cuffed Ramsay on the arm. 'Oh, I know all right. But don't be long.'

He ignored Ramsay's glare and headed for the door.

'Deuce take it! We'll have to stop, father. My *garron*'s gone lame.' Iain's voice cut through the silence of the late afternoon and made both Marsaili and Seton turn to look at him.

'Oh, for the love of ... I don't believe it.' Seton swore under his breath.

'Well, I told you this old nag wouldn't make it far. He's had to carry a double burden for two days now. Is it any wonder he's tired?'

'And I told *you* we should have stolen another one when we had the chance.'

Marsaili heard the impatience in Seton's voice, but couldn't help being glad about the interruption to this seemingly interminable journey. She hadn't wanted to say anything, in case she angered Seton, but she was exhausted and parched. Not to mention starving.

'I'm not a thief, unlike some people,' Iain retorted, jumping down from his horse and helping Eilidh off the rump. 'We could have bought one, or at least part-exchanged this for another.'

'We needed the money for other things. Would you have us leave Marsaili in that stinking place?'

'I'm sure there was enough for both matters,' Iain maintained stubbornly, then added, 'Why don't we stop here for the night? Since I assume we can't risk going into any of the towns, here's as good as anywhere. And maybe my horse will have recovered by morning.'

Seton shook his head. 'No, we haven't gone far enough yet, we need to press on. But perhaps a short rest will do the trick.'

'But it'll be dark soon,' Iain protested.

'So? There's almost a full moon tonight.'

Marsaili's heart sank. Dusk wasn't far off and to her it felt as if they'd been riding for ever. Her entire body was sore from being bumped up and down continuously and her fingers stiff from holding onto Seton so she wouldn't fall off. She really didn't want to continue.

They left the track they'd been following and entered a small forest, weaving among the trunks until they came to a clearing where a burn burbled its way along the middle. Marsaili jumped off the horse, stumbling slightly since her legs had gone a bit numb as well, then stretched her cramped muscles.

She glanced at Eilidh, who had walked a few steps behind

Iain without complaining. Away from the prison, Marsaili could see even clearer what a terrible state the poor woman was in. Her clothes were in tatters, filthy and mud-stained, and her hair hung about her face in listless hanks. Marsaili longed to dunk her, clothes and all, in a tub of water and scrub for hours, the way she would the laundry at home.

To his credit, Iain hadn't complained, even though Eilidh stank to high heaven. She must have been aware of this herself, because Marsaili heard her mutter an apology to him. 'I've tried no' tae sit too near ye. Wouldnae want ter ruin yer clothes, an' all.'

'It is no matter,' Iain said, smiling kindly. 'I'm glad if we managed to save another soul from such a hell-hole. No one should have to suffer that. Just out of interest, what did you do to be put in gaol, if you don't mind me asking?'

Eilidh sank down onto a nearby stone, as if her legs were too weak to hold her. Without proper nourishment for weeks on end, they probably were, Marsaili thought. 'I stole a couple o' bannocks,' Eilidh admitted, her head bent. 'But I swear it was only because I was desperate. I hadnae eaten for twa days and couldnae find work onywhere.'

'Oh, wonderful, now we're harbouring a criminal too,' Marsaili heard Seton mutter, but thankfully she didn't think his words reached Eilidh, who was closer to Iain.

'Don't worry, Eilidh,' she said to her new friend, 'I'm sure we can find you some work at Rosyth, can't we Mr Seton? The laird won't turn anyone away.'

'She can go there herself and ask,' Seton replied. 'You and I won't be going anywhere near Rosyth if I can help it.'

'What do you mean?' Marsaili raised her head to stare at him, a feeling of foreboding rising inside her.

Iain frowned at him as well. 'Yes, what are you talking about, Father? Of course we're going to Rosyth. I promised Kirsty we'd bring Marsaili straight back.'

'What do I care about your promises?' Seton sneered. 'Your wife can come and join us at Bailliebroch if she has a mind to, but she'll have to live under my rules there.'

'Not that again.' Iain groaned. 'Father, we've been over this and you won't get it back. Especially not now the Englishman has double-crossed you. Do you honestly think he's to be trusted?'

'There are others who can be bribed as easily. Be that as it may, Bailliebroch will be mine. I'll just have to find where the laird hid my money.' He cast a sour look in Marsaili's direction. 'You'll know, no doubt, so you can show me.'

'Me? Why would I know? And I've no idea what money you're talking about anyhow.'

Seton walked up to her and backhanded her across one cheek. 'Enough! Do you take me for a fool, woman? I saw the way the laird was making sheep's eyes at you and do you deny going off to rescue him from Sherringham and his men? You and that mangy hound of yours.'

Marsaili was too stunned by the slap at first to respond. Then anger welled up and she put her hands on her hips as she replied, 'How dare you hit me, you miserable excuse for a man? Even if I did know anything, which I don't, I wouldn't tell you.'

'We'll just see about that.'

Iain, who seemed as shocked as Marsaili at this turn of events, stepped forward with a scowl. 'Now see here …,' he began, but was cut off by the sight of his father taking one of his pistols out of his pocket. Seton aimed it straight at his son's heart.

'This is where you choose your allegiance once and for all, Iain,' he said, his voice deadly serious. 'Either you want your inheritance, in which case you'll do as I say and not interfere, or I shoot you now. If you're not completely committed to your birthright, you're no longer my son and no use to me. Do you understand? It's your choice.'

Marsaili waited with bated breath for Iain to come to a decision. She didn't want him to be like Seton, not now he was married to Kirsty, but on the other hand she definitely didn't want him dead.

It was an impossible choice.

'Wait, captain, there are fresh hoof marks here on the verge. And look, horse droppings too. They may have gone this way.'

Sherringham turned his horse and rode back to where one of his men was pointing at the ground. They'd been riding for the best part of two days, with only two confirmed sightings of the Buchanan woman and her rescuers. He was tired of this chase and wanted a meal and a comfortable bed for the night, but he wouldn't rest until he had her back.

'You could be right,' he conceded. Silently he added to himself, *Thank the Lord the woman has such vivid hair or we'd have missed that last turning.* The yokel they'd spoken to had said he couldn't be mistaken and it would seem he was correct.

'Very well, dismount and proceed with caution. I want to follow the hoof prints in the soft moss if possible. They can't have gone far. Complete silence from now on, that's an order.'

He'd find the bitch if it was the last thing he did. And then he'd deal with the arrogant Jacobite.

'Are you sure this is the way he'd take to Baillie-whatever-it's-called?'

Alex rode up next to Brice and peered at him in the deepening gloom. The day was nearly over and Brice knew they would have to stop soon or they'd risk injuring the ponies. He swore silently.

'Yes, Kirsty's directions were clear, but we're still a fair way off. We have to press on for just a bit longer. I'm sorry.'

'Don't worry, I was only making sure.' Alex never complained and Brice thanked God for this small mercy at least. The youth had certainly proved his worth during the last few days and when this was all over, Brice hoped Alex wouldn't leave in a hurry. He'd come to appreciate his company.

They'd headed north first, then west past Rosyth and Bailliebroch, stopping only to ascertain that Seton hadn't arrived at either destination yet. Kirsty had told them there was a highland path that led south-west from the edge of the Bailliebroch lands, straight towards Inveraray.

'If Seton's in a hurry, I'm sure he'd travel that way,' she'd said. Brice sincerely hoped she was right.

'Brice, this is madness.' Ramsay rode up on his other side. 'We don't even know if the man was heading this way. Shouldn't we have gone to the gaol first to check if Miss Buchanan is still there?'

Brice shook his head. 'No, Seton will have found a way to get her out. He wants her badly. If he was in cahoots with the Englishman, he'll have her free in no time. If not, he'd spring her out somehow. Trust me, I know the man by now.'

Ramsay sighed. 'Very well, but I hope you know what you're –'

He was interrupted by the loud crack of a pistol shot and all three of them stopped to listen as it was followed by a piercing scream. Brice pointed to the left. 'It came from over there. What if it's …?'

'Don't be daft, man. If Seton wants her as much as you say, why would he shoot her?'

Brice spurred his mount into a gallop and headed for the nearby trees. Ramsay was right, but he had to check just to make sure. And if it wasn't Marsaili, then some other poor soul was in deep trouble.

Chapter Thirty

Marsaili stared in dawning horror at the large patch of red staining Iain's shoulder. Eilidh screamed again, clearly frightened out of her wits, but Seton aimed his other pistol at her and told her to shut up. 'If you don't, you'll be next,' he warned. Poor Eilidh blinked, but closed her mouth, only emitting a series of hiccoughing sobs.

Marsaili rounded on Seton. 'Have you lost your mind? Your only child? How could you?'

She'd admired Iain for standing up to his father, although she guessed he'd never imagined Seton would actually pull the trigger. But then, neither had she.

'He's no son of mine, I told you. He has no pride in his clan, no loyalty, no guts. I doubt there's any Seton blood in him at all. My wife must've been unfaithful.' A low growling noise came from Iain's direction and Marsaili saw him stagger to his feet, his expression murderous.

Seton waved the pistol in his direction. 'Stay back,' he warned. Iain hesitated, then sank back down onto a nearby rock.

Marsaili shook her head at Seton. He was clearly mad, but also dangerous. She tried to edge away from him, but he was quick to turn the pistol on her. 'Don't even think of moving,' he snarled. 'This time you're coming with me. We'll be married as soon as we reach Bailliebroch. I've waited long enough.'

'Never,' she hissed back. 'I've told you my answer and I won't change my mind, no matter what you do. You can't force me into wedlock, the minister says a woman has to be willing. I'm not.'

'There are ways and means,' Seton smirked.

Marsaili ground her teeth in frustration. 'I don't understand why you can't take no for an answer. What's the point of marrying someone who doesn't want you? Where's the joy in that?'

His eyes turned darker with desire as he raked her with his gaze from head to toe and back again. 'But there's none so bonny as you, is there? You're a prize worth having and since I don't want to share, marriage it'll have to be. Besides, it's the principle of it now. You've defied me for too long. As my wife, you'll have to do what I tell you for the rest of your life, I'll make sure of it.'

She shook her head. 'I won't agree, I tell you. If you try to force me, I'll kill myself.'

'I won't give you the chance.' He walked over and grabbed her arm, pulling her towards his pony. 'Come on, we'll leave these two here. We don't need them. You,' he pointed at Eilidh, 'help him if you want, or go, I don't care. But don't you dare follow us.'

He was just about to mount up, when a voice rang out across the clearing. 'Well, well, so it wasn't Kinross who snatched the lady from under my nose, it was you. I should have guessed. Mind you, it makes it so much easier, because now I can put you behind bars as well. Two birds with one stone. Perfect.'

'You!' The one word was filled with loathing and Marsaili felt a shudder pass through Seton. 'Filthy, double-crossing son of an English whore.' He muttered an oath in Gaelic.

Sherringham shrugged. 'My parentage is not the issue here. I rather think yours is more important, Jacobite as they were. And as for our little agreement, that came to an end when you allowed someone to free Kinross from my clutches.'

'I didn't *allow* anything,' Seton spat. 'This stupid woman took it upon herself to do so, more's the pity.'

302

Sherringham's eyebrows rose. 'The woman, was it? I'll be damned.'

'That you will. I sincerely hope hell is where you're going.' Seton aimed his pistol at the Englishman. 'Now leave, or I'll have no choice but to shoot you.' He nodded in Iain's direction. 'I've already shot my fool of a son, so don't think I'll hesitate.'

The captain regarded him through narrowed eyes. 'Don't be an imbecile, Seton. There are at least ten muskets trained on you at the moment.' He indicated a number of dark shapes moving among the trees. 'My men won't miss and I'll wager they're faster than you. Now hand over the woman and the money you owe me and I might let you live.'

'Never, she's mine,' Seton hissed. 'I'd rather shoot her than give her to the likes of you.'

'Another suitor for the lady's hand? How touching. But I wasn't asking, that was an order. Hand her over or you die. *Now.*'

It was Marsaili's turn to tremble at the menace in the English captain's voice. She didn't know which was worse – being forced to go with him or staying with the clearly insane Seton.

She was spared the choice, since in the next instant complete chaos broke out in the little clearing. Several new dark shadows came tearing out of the line of trees, horsemen riding at full tilt. The first one knocked the captain off his mount with an almighty tackle, then grabbed at the nearest soldier's musket before he had time to fire it. Some of the other soldiers suffered a similar fate and several shots rang out, followed by the dull thud of bodies falling to the ground or screams of pain.

Seton turned his head to see what was going on and Marsaili took her chance to try and snatch the pistol from his hand. He was stronger than she'd thought, however, and began to wrestle it back from her. It was all she could do to keep it pointed away from her head and she feared it might go off at any second.

'Bitch!' Seton panted. 'Think you're too superior for a man like me? I'll show you ...'

But just as Marsaili thought she couldn't hold out any longer, a pony came charging towards them and the rider's booted foot kicked the pistol out of both their grips. It flew through the air and she saw Iain rise with an effort and catch it. He wasted no time, but aimed it straight at his father. 'Hah! My turn, I think.' There was no mistaking the triumph in his voice.

Seton stilled and Marsaili ducked away from him, intending to run for cover. She only managed three steps before he caught her skirts with a surprisingly strong grip, pulling her backwards and hard against his chest. She kicked out and hit his shin, making him swear and loosen his grip for a fraction of a second. Before he had time to grab her again, the shadowy rider charged at them once more and bent down to snatch her out of Seton's grip. She heard the sound of material ripping apart, then landed hard on the man's lap. Twisting around, she looked up into his face and gasped.

'Brice? You're alive! I thought ... Oh, thank God!' She wrapped her arms around his torso while he galloped deeper into the forest. He didn't go far, but pulled the horse to a halt.

'Marsaili, my love, are you all right? Did he ...?'

'No, I'm fine, I swear.'

He hugged her to him fiercely, almost squashing all the air out of her lungs, but she didn't mind. He was alive. That was all that mattered. And he'd come for her.

'I must go back and make sure the soldiers are all gone and Iain has his father under control. Please, wait here. I'll return in a minute.' He lowered her to the ground.

'I'll be here,' she promised. She wasn't going anywhere until she knew he was safe too.

Brice returned to the clearing and was relieved to see all was quiet. Ramsay was holding on to an English soldier he'd captured, whose right arm he had twisted up behind his back. The man wasn't struggling and seemed resigned to his fate, possibly because he was wounded. There was blood flowing down his left hand, Brice noticed. Thankfully, Sherringham was still lying on the ground where he'd fallen.

'Hasn't moved so much as a muscle,' Ramsay confirmed. 'Probably broke his neck when he fell off the horse.'

'Good.'

Brice glanced at Iain, who sat on a rock while a filthy-looking young woman did her best to staunch the flow of blood from a shoulder wound he'd sustained. This didn't stop him from pointing a pistol at his father with his right hand, which was obviously unharmed. Seton stood glaring at his son, but didn't look as if he dared move.

'Where are the other soldiers?' Brice asked.

Ramsay nodded in the direction of the track. 'Fled for their lives. There weren't as many as we thought, only five or six at the most. A couple of them were wounded, but not mortally I think. Alex is pursuing them a little way, just to make sure they don't turn back, but I doubt they will. Why should they risk their lives for nothing?'

Brice dismounted and crouched next to Sherringham. It was too dark under the trees to see whether he was breathing, so he grabbed the man's shoulder to turn him over. Before he'd got very far, however, the Englishman moved of his own accord. With the speed of an attacking snake, the man twisted and tried to stab Brice with a dirk which had been hidden underneath him as he lay on the ground. The blade glimmered briefly as it arced through the air, but Brice had been poised for trouble and reacted even faster. He managed to recoil just far enough so the blade only slashed the skin of his abdomen very slightly. He swore and blocked a second thrust by hitting Sherringham's arm. He didn't have his own dagger, because he'd already used it in the earlier fray and hadn't had time to retrieve it.

The captain tried to get to his feet, but Brice hooked a leg behind the man's knees and he came crashing to the ground once more. His knife blade sliced through the air maniacally, coming very close several times, but Brice managed to duck or feint and thereby avoid another cut. Sherringham slithered away like a greased eel and jumped up once more. Finding himself near Seton, he lashed out in his direction as well, catching the latter unawares and inflicting a cut to the upper arm.

Seton screamed and turned to defend himself against this unexpected onslaught. 'Shoot him!' he screamed at Iain, while pulling out his own dirk. 'Are you going to let this scum kill your father?'

'I should,' Iain muttered, 'but ...' He raised his voice. 'Put your dirk down, Sassenach, or I'll shoot you now,' he called out to Sherringham.

The Englishman paid him no heed and it was doubtful if he'd even heard him. He was trying to fight two men at once, as Seton was advancing on him from one side and Brice the other. 'I'm warning you, you'll pay for this. Harming an officer of His Majesty's army ... That's a hanging offence.'

'Not if we don't get caught, scum,' Seton snarled.

'Here, Brice, catch!' Ramsay threw Brice a lethal-looking dirk, handle first so he could catch it easily. Without pausing, Brice swung it round and pretended to attack Sherringham with it, but while the man concentrated on the oncoming blade, Brice kicked him in the knee so that his leg buckled. He staggered, but just as Brice was about to follow up with a hard fist to the chin, Seton threw himself at the Englishman with a blood-curdling yell.

Thanks to this, Sherringham had enough warning and swivelled round, bringing his dagger up for a deep thrust which caught Seton under the ribs. With a gurgling sound, he stopped dead and lifted a hand to the wound, looking down in surprise. 'Curse you,' he mumbled, then fell to his knees before slumping to the ground.

'No!' Iain's anguished shout was drowned out by the report of the pistol as he pulled the trigger at the same time. It was Sherringham's turn to look astonished when he too froze in mid-stride to glance down at himself. A huge, dark stain spread rapidly across his abdomen and with a long drawn-out sigh, he fell face first into the mossy undergrowth.

'Oh, hell!' Brice rushed forward at the same time as Ramsay, and they each turned a man over. Staring up at Brice were two lifeless eyes and when he glanced over, Ramsay was looking at the same on Seton's face. Just to make sure, Ramsay touched the side of first Seton's neck, then Sherringham's.

'No pulse,' he said, shaking his head. They both looked at Iain, who was standing motionless, the pistol just hanging from his hand.

'I didn't mean to …' he began. 'I was just …'

Brice got up and went over to him, taking the pistol out of his grip. 'It's all right. It wasn't your fault.' He put a hand on Iain's uninjured shoulder and shook him a little. 'The man was trying to kill your father and you acted in self-defence. No one can prove otherwise.'

'I'll swear tae that,' the filthy woman suddenly said, startling them both.

'And who might you be?'

'Eilidh Beattie. I'm a friend o' Marsaili's. From Inveraray.'

'Right. Well, thank you, your help will be most welcome.'

'I'll bear witness too in your favour.' The captured English soldier, who could have fled if he'd wanted to, Brice realised, stood where Ramsay had left him.

'You will?' Brice couldn't quite hide the surprise in his voice.

'Yes. He was a bastard, was Cap'n Sherringham, and I'll be damned if I let anyone hang for his sake when it was all his own fault. Draggin' us round on this stupid goose chase for days on end because he had a bee in his bonnet about Jacobites. Didn't like to be thwarted and was as mad as anythin' when he found the red-headed lady gone, but really, it wasn't up to him to pursue her, was it? No one asked him to.'

'Thank you, Mr …?'

'Moore, sir. Corporal.'

'Corporal Moore. Would you mind coming with us back to Rosyth? I'll tell your superiors you were wounded and needed treatment.' Brice nodded at Moore's left hand which was still bloodstained. 'Then I can summon a lawyer to take your sworn statement.'

Corporal Moore nodded. 'Don't mind if I do.'

Brice bent to search Sherringham's pockets. 'I'd better take care of any warrants he's carrying so that my friend knows what charges there were against us and can prepare a defence.'

'But that's just it, there weren't none,' Moore said.

'What?' Brice looked up at the man.

'He didn't have no warrants. Made that up. No one thought to ask to see them, just took his word for it on account of him being a captain and all.'

'Son of a bitch …' Brice muttered. 'I suppose that solves one problem at least. Thank you for telling me, Corporal Moore.'

Brice beckoned Ramsay over and pushed Iain gently in his

direction. 'Can you take care of things here for a moment, please? I must go back and fetch Marsaili, but I'll be right back.'

'Yes, go,' Ramsay nodded. 'Alex should be returning any minute, we'll be fine. I'll see to everything.'

Brice didn't need any more encouragement. He vaulted onto the nearest pony and took off into the forest as if all the demons of hell were after him. He couldn't wait another second to make sure Marsaili was still all right and where he'd left her.

She had to be. He couldn't bear to lose her now.

Marsaili heard a shout and then the sound of another pistol shot. Panic swept through her like a tidal wave and she put a hand to her mouth to stifle a scream of pure terror.

Brice! Brice, where are you?

He'd told her to wait and she knew she had to obey. Not because he had the right to command her in any way, but because she understood that if he had to worry about her, he wouldn't be able to concentrate on defeating their enemies. So the best thing she could do was to stay put. But dear God, it was the hardest thing she'd ever had to do.

She paced back and forth, stopping every now and then to listen for any threatening sounds. It was possible there were still Englishmen about and she didn't want to be caught unawares. Several times, she thought she heard a twig crack as if footsteps were approaching and her nerves felt as tightly strung as the strings of a harp. Finally, her ears picked up the drumming of hooves on the ground and she hurried to hide behind a large tree trunk, trying to blend in with the shadows. A horse and rider rushed by, then stopped and turned so quickly, the horse reared up and flailed its front legs in the air.

'Marsaili? *Marsaili!*'

The word was bellowed so loud she thought she might have heard it all the way back at Rosyth, which made her smile. She'd recognise that voice anywhere and stepped out from behind the tree, her legs trembling with relief. 'I'm here, Brice. No need to shout.'

He jumped off the pony's back and ran towards her, pulling her to him in another crushing embrace. 'Marsaili! Thank God for that. I thought I'd gone the wrong way. It's so damned dark here among the trees.'

He was breathing hard and she could feel his chest rising and falling against hers. It was a wonderful sensation and she briefly leaned her cheek on his shoulder, feeling like she had come into a safe harbour. 'I just thought I'd better be careful, in case it wasn't you,' she explained, looking up at him. 'I wasn't sure you'd come.'

'Of course I'd come. If it was the last thing I did, I'd always come for you,' he whispered. He stared into her eyes, searchingly, and asked, 'If you'd want me to, that is. Do you?'

Although she knew he probably couldn't see her all that clearly, she put her heart and soul into gazing back, then nodded. 'Yes, most definitely,' she breathed.

He closed his eyes in relief, then pulled her even closer and kissed her with almost savage intensity. His warm lips claimed hers as though he wanted to brand her, but she didn't mind. It was what she wanted too. She was his, had been from the first time he'd kissed her, she thought. There had been no going back after that. She kissed him with equal ferocity, revelling in the feel of his tongue, the taste of him, the thrills which raced through her at his touch.

He broke off when she made a small noise of satisfaction, obviously misinterpreting it. 'I'm sorry, am I hurting you? I don't mean to, it's just ... I've been so afraid.' He buried his face in her hair and stroked the back of her head and neck. 'I thought I'd never see you again and that Seton had won.'

'No,' she kissed his stubbled jaw line, her lips enjoying the soft bristles which tickled in the most delicious way. 'I would have died rather than marry Seton. I told him so. I'd have gone through with it too because I thought you were dead. Those men, there were so many of them and their expressions ...' She shuddered.

'I know, but they hadn't come to kill me. Seton couldn't persuade them to do that, apparently, so they abducted me instead. I was to be sent to the colonies as an indentured servant. Ramsay and Alex too.'

'But you managed to free yourselves?' She cupped his face between her hands, her heart beating hard with the realisation of how close to disaster they'd come.

'Yes, but it's a long story so I'll tell you later. Let's go back to the others now. I don't want to leave them for too long. There was some bloodshed, Seton and the Englishman are dead. I hope you're not squeamish?' He put a hand up to cover one of hers and turned his face to kiss the palm of her hand. Even this small contact sent a frisson of delight through her, right down to her stomach.

'No, I'll be fine. And ... I'm relieved.' She'd been about to say 'glad', but realised she wasn't. She hadn't wanted Seton's death, only for him to be punished for what he'd done. As for the Sassenach, he was unimportant.

'Come, then.' He took her hand and held on to it as though he'd never let go ever again. With his other one, he caught the horse's bridle. Thankfully the animal hadn't gone far and was a docile creature. Brice mounted and pulled Marsaili up behind him, making sure she was holding onto him before he set off.

'Don't worry, we'll soon be on our way home.' Then he laughed. 'Home! How wonderful it sounds and how strange that the word now makes me think of Rosyth straight away instead of Sweden.' He shook his head. 'I hate to admit my father was right when he said I'd like it here, but even he could never have realised how much.' He threw Marsaili a smiling glance over his shoulder. 'And it's all thanks to you.'

'Me?'

'Aye, *mo cridhe*,' he said in perfect Gaelic. 'Where you are will always be home to me. That is, if you've decided to accept my proposal? It seems so long ago now, I'd almost forgotten you have yet to give me an answer.'

Marsaili didn't hesitate, but hugged him tight. 'The answer is yes.'

Brice grinned at her. 'Excellent!'

Chapter Thirty-One

It was a very weary group that entered the courtyard of Rosyth House two days later, drawing a collective sigh of relief. Their journey had been slow, partly due to the fact that two of the ponies had to carry two riders each, and partly because they'd taken it easy so Iain's and Corporal Moore's wounds wouldn't bleed too much.

The moment the horses' hooves touched the cobbled stones, however, the door to the great hall was thrown open and Kirsty came rushing out, closely followed by Flora, Ailsa, Archie and a whole host of other people. Last, but not least, Liath limped out wagging his tail furiously. Brice saw him and felt a great weight lift from his chest. He sent up a swift prayer of thanks to God.

Kirsty reached them first, just as Ramsay helped Iain off his horse, and she let out a cry of alarm. 'My love, you're hurt!'

'It's nothing, a mere scratch,' he hastened to reassure her. 'A bullet grazed my shoulder, but I was lucky, it didn't lodge in there.'

'Thank the Lord. Come, we must get you cleaned up and I'll fetch some healing salve and ...' Chattering, she led her husband away, without noticing the smiles that followed the couple.

After letting Archie greet them with fierce hugs and a million questions, Ailsa came forward and took Brice's hands, covering them with her own. 'Welcome back, dear boy. Do I take it all is well now?'

He nodded. 'Yes, everything will be fine I think. I'll ask my father's friend Rory to make sure of it and we have witnesses whose statements should clear all our names. The

English captain didn't actually have any warrants for our arrests and Iain told me the weapons horde the Sassenach found was left behind here with Seton for safe-keeping. He knows where it is so we'll get rid of it as soon as possible. And as for Seton, I'm afraid he won't be bothering anyone ever again. Neither will the Englishman.'

Ailsa squeezed his hands. 'That is probably a good thing, sad though it may be. Now come indoors, all of you. We'll have water ready for baths in a trice, although you'll have to take turns, and there is food and drink. My daughters told me we had to be ready for every eventuality.'

'Thank you, it all sounds most welcome.' Brice turned to Marsaili. 'Would you like to have the first bath?'

'Yes, please.' She glanced at her friend, who had ridden with Ramsay so as not to nudge Iain's shoulder. 'And I think Eilidh would be glad of one too. You're sure you don't mind her staying?'

They had discussed the woman briefly on the way home and Brice had agreed to employ her. 'No, of course not, she's very welcome.' To Ailsa he said, 'Could I have some food and drink brought up to my room, please? I'm too tired for anything else right now.'

'Of course. Go and rest, we'll see you tomorrow.'

He headed for the house, just as a small whirlwind came flying out. Little Ida must have heard the commotion too and ran down the stairs to throw herself at her father. Brice laughed when she shrieked, 'You're home, you're home! Did you buy me anything? Flora said you did.'

Ramsay looked confused and sent Flora an enquiring glance, but when she nodded imperceptibly, a smile tugging at the corners of her mouth, understanding dawned. 'Well, if Flora says it's true, it must be,' he said. He lifted his daughter and began to walk towards the house. Flora stayed where she was, but then Brice saw Ramsay turn and hold out his hand to her. 'Aren't you coming? I'm relying on you to, er ... show me what it is *I've* bought.'

Shyly, Flora reached out to put her hand in his. The last thing Brice heard before entering the house was Ramsay asking Ida, 'Do you like Flora? Because I do and I've been thinking it might be good idea to ask her to come to Sweden with us. What do you say?'

And then Ida's enthusiastic reply, 'Oh, yes, Papa!'

Marsaili headed straight for her room and was glad when she didn't have to wait long for the tub and hot water to arrive.

'Will that be all?' the maid who'd brought drying cloths and soap asked.

'Yes, thank you. I can manage now.' She just wanted to be left alone, have her bath and go to sleep.

She was bone weary, but it was a relief to pull off the clothes she'd worn for the best part of two weeks now. They were covered in dust from travelling and grime from the prison and she thought she could probably smell the scent of Seton on them too, which made her shudder. It was all she could do not to throw them straight into the fireplace and burn them. She knew they would always remind her of this ordeal.

Sinking into the hot water was bliss and she leaned her head back, closing her eyes with a small moan. It felt so good and she never wanted to come out.

'There was I thinking you'd only make noises like that for me from now on, but I see hot water will do just as well,' a voice said from behind her, startling her into sitting bolt upright. She turned around, sloshing water everywhere.

'Brice! How did you ... I mean, what are you doing here?' She stared at the opening near the garderobe, knowing just how he came to stand in her room. 'You weren't supposed to use that,' she added with a frown.

'I'm sorry, I didn't mean to startle you.' He grinned and came over to kneel by the side of the tub, his eyebrows rising at the sight of her half out of the water. 'I'm glad I came though. I wouldn't have missed this for anything.' She hurried to sink down, but it wasn't much better.

'Brice, you shouldn't be here,' she tried to sound stern, but her pulse was racing and she knew she didn't mean it.

'I just thought you might need some help, seeing as you looked so tired when you left me earlier.' He picked up the soap and began to apply some to her back, while leaning forward to rain kisses along her collar bone and up her neck.

'Did you really? I think you had a much more selfish reason for coming,' she said, her voice sounding breathless even to her.

'Hmm, you may be right.' He continued to caress her back with one hand, while moving her long hair out of the way so his lips could work their way up to her cheek and from there to her mouth. 'Do you mind?'

'Since you're asking so nicely, no,' she whispered.

'Good. Then perhaps there's room for two in there?' Without waiting for her reply, he stood up and pulled off his shirt and breeches, giving her a view that made her totally speechless. She took in the full glory of him, all hard muscles, golden skin and fading bruises. Then he lifted her bodily so he could sit down in the tub with her on his lap. It was quite a big tub, but Marsaili doubted it had been designed for two. She found herself extremely close to him.

'Brice!' she protested, but she was distracted by the nearness of his still-bronzed chest and couldn't stop herself from touching it.

He chuckled and pulled her round so she was straddling him, then he kissed her again, more thoroughly this time, while using the soap as an excuse to caress the rest of her. When he came up for air, he murmured, 'I had another reason for coming, but seeing you in the tub almost made me forget.'

'Oh, and what was it?' Marsaili didn't really want to talk right now, but then the thought struck her that perhaps he'd changed his mind and didn't want to marry her after all. In which case, she shouldn't be doing this. She leaned back and looked at him, taking in the look in his eyes, the light blue darkened by desire. Just reading his thoughts so clearly made her feel weak.

'Down by the loch, when I proposed to you,' he said, 'I was an ass.'

Marsaili blinked. He *had* changed his mind. The thought was like a bucket of cold water thrown over her head. 'How so?' she asked, her voice a hoarse whisper. She swallowed hard. She didn't want to hear his answer because she knew it would hurt. *Like hell!*

He smiled at her, a languorous grin that stirred something inside her, despite her doubts. 'I told you I didn't know what love was. That I wasn't sure such a thing really existed.' He leaned forward to put the tip of his nose against hers and whispered, 'I was wrong. Completely and utterly. I was deluding myself.'

She gasped, but was too stunned to reply.

'Love is when you realise a part of you will die if you can't be with a certain someone. That life isn't worth living if you can't share it with that special person. That you want to kill, with your bare hands, anyone who comes between you. *That* is how I feel about you, Marsaili. I love you, with every fibre of my being, and I always will. Can you forgive me?'

'For what?' Marsaili wasn't quite sure what he was asking.

'For making you such a crass proposal, telling you I wanted you as my wife because I "cared" about you.' He shook his head at himself. 'I'm surprised you didn't clout me. I deserved it.'

Marsaili breathed more easily at last and managed a shaky smile. 'Of course I forgive you, especially after such a pretty speech.' She ran her fingers down his cheek, rasping his stubble with her finger nails. He squirmed and smiled at her. 'I think you've redeemed yourself, but you can always try a little harder to prove it to me.' She moved provocatively on his lap and saw in his half-closed eyes that he took her meaning. His fingers started roaming again, distracting her from words.

'Gladly, but not until you tell me what I want to hear,' he said, his voice husky with promise.

'And what is that?' She drew in a sharp breath as he found a sensitive spot which had her melting against him.

'You haven't told me if you love me in return. Is this to be a one-sided marriage? I can live with that, because I'm not letting you go no matter what, but I'd much prefer an equal partnership in every way.'

He kissed her eyelids, her nose, her cheek, the corner of her mouth, tantalising her, but not giving her enough. She made an impatient noise, turning her lips up to his, but he just shook his head. 'No more, not until you tell me what I want to hear. It's only fair, I've bared my soul to you. Or are you as cruel as you are beautiful?'

'Very well, I'll confess – I love you too. Have loved you, probably from the moment I first set eyes on you. You're gorgeous and irresistible and you know it. There, happy now?'

He grinned, looking satisfied in a very male sort of way. 'It'll do for a start. But when I'm through with you, I'm expecting to hear a lot more of your confession.'

He finally kissed her properly again, the way she craved, and she knew he was right. She hadn't told him the half of it – that she simply couldn't live without him and when he touched her, she'd do anything he asked. Anything at all.

But she had a sneaking suspicion he'd soon know anyway. There was no need for words.

About the Author

Christina lives in London and is married with two children. Although born in England she has a Swedish mother and was brought up in Sweden. In her teens, the family moved to Japan where she had the opportunity to travel extensively in the Far East.

Christina is an accomplished writer of novellas. *Highland Storms* is her third novel.

www.christinacourtenay.com
www.twitter.com/PiaCCourtenay

More Choc Lit

From Christina Courtenay

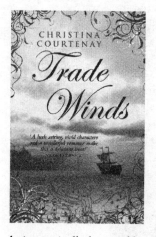

Trade Winds

Short-listed for the Romantic Novelists' Association's Pure Passion Award for Best Historical Fiction 2011

Marriage of convenience – or a love for life?

It's 1732 in Gothenburg, Sweden, and strong-willed Jess van Sandt knows only too well that it's a man's world. She believes she's being swindled out of her inheritance by her stepfather – and she's determined to stop it.

When help appears in the unlikely form of handsome Scotsman Killian Kinross, himself disinherited by his grandfather, Jess finds herself both intrigued and infuriated by him. In an attempt to recover her fortune, she proposes a marriage of convenience. Then Killian is offered the chance of a lifetime with the Swedish East India Company's Expedition and he's determined that nothing will stand in his way, not even his new bride.

He sets sail on a daring voyage to the Far East, believing he's put his feelings and past behind him. But the journey doesn't quite work out as he expects …

Prequel to Highland Storms

Visit www.choc-lit.com for more details including the first two chapters and reviews, or simply scan barcode using your mobile phone QR reader.

The Scarlet Kimono
Christina Courtenay

Abducted by a Samurai warlord in 17th-century Japan – what happens when fear turns to love?

England, 1611, and young Hannah Marston envies her brother's adventurous life. But when she stows away on his merchant ship, her powers of endurance are stretched to their limit. Then they reach Japan and all her suffering seems worthwhile – until she is abducted by Taro Kumashiro's warriors.

In the far north of the country, warlord Kumashiro is waiting to see the girl who he has been warned about by a seer. When at last they meet, it's a clash of cultures and wills, but they're also fighting an instant attraction to each other.

With her brother desperate to find her and the jealous Lady Reiko equally desperate to kill her, Hannah faces the greatest adventure of her life. And Kumashiro has to choose between love and honour ...

Visit www.choc-lit.com for more details including the first two chapters and reviews, or simply scan barcode using your mobile phone QR reader.

Why not try something else from the Choc Lit selection?

The Silver Locket
Margaret James

*Winner of CataNetwork Reviewers'
Choice Award for Single Titles 2010*

If life is cheap, how much is love worth?

It's 1914 and young Rose Courtenay has a decision to make. Please her wealthy parents by marrying the man of their choice – or play her part in the war effort?

The chance to escape proves irresistible and Rose becomes a nurse. Working in France, she meets Lieutenant Alex Denham, a dark figure from her past. He's the last man in the world she'd get involved with – especially now he's married.

But in wartime nothing is as it seems. Alex's marriage is a sham and Rose is the only woman he's ever wanted. As he recovers from his wounds, he sets out to win her trust. His gift of a silver locket is a far cry from the luxuries she's left behind.

What value will she put on his love?

First novel in the trilogy

Visit www.choc-lit.com for more details including the first two chapters and reviews, or simply scan barcode using your mobile phone QR reader.

The Golden Chain
Margaret James

Can first love last forever?

1931 is the year that changes everything for Daisy Denham. Her family has not long swapped life in India for Dorset, England when she uncovers an old secret.

At the same time, she meets Ewan Fraser – a handsome dreamer who wants nothing more than to entertain the world and for Daisy to play his leading lady.

Ewan offers love and a chance to escape with a touring theatre company. As they grow closer, he gives her a golden chain and Daisy gives him a promise – that she will always keep him in her heart.

But life on tour is not as they'd hoped, Ewan is tempted away by his career and Daisy is dazzled by the older, charismatic figure of Jesse Trent. She breaks Ewan's heart and sets off for a life in London with Jesse.

Only time will tell whether some promises are easier to make than keep …

Second novel in the trilogy

Visit www.choc-lit.com for more details including the first two chapters and reviews, or simply scan barcode using your mobile phone QR reader.

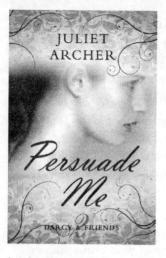

Persuade Me
Juliet Archer

When it comes to love, Anna Elliot is stuck in the past. No one can compare to Rick Wentworth, the man she gave up ten years ago at the insistence of her disapproving family. What if she's missed her only chance for real happiness?

Since Anna broke his heart, Rick has moved on – or so he thinks. Out in Australia, he's worked hard to build a successful career – and a solid wall around his feelings.

The words 'forgive and forget' aren't in Rick's vocabulary. The word 'regret' is definitely in Anna's. So, when they meet again on his book tour of England, it's an opportunity for closure.

But memories intrude – the pure sensuality of what they once shared, the pain of parting … And she has to deal with another man from her past, while his celebrity status makes him the focus of unwanted attention.

With Anna's image-obsessed family still ready to interfere and Rick poised to return to Australia, can she persuade him to risk his heart again?

This contemporary re-telling of Jane Austen's last completed novel is the second book in Juliet Archer's Darcy & Friends series, offering fresh insights into the hearts and minds of Austen's irresistible heroes.

Visit www.choc-lit.com for more details including the first two chapters and reviews, or simply scan barcode using your mobile phone QR reader.

All That Mullarkey
Sue Moorcroft

Revenge and love: it's a thin line …

The writing's on the wall for Cleo and Gav. The bedroom wall, to be precise. And it says 'This marriage is over.'

Wounded and furious, Cleo embarks on a night out with the girls, which turns into a glorious one night stand with …

Justin, centrefold material and irrepressibly irresponsible. He loves a little wildness in a woman – and he's in the right place at the right time to enjoy Cleo's.

But it's Cleo who has to pick up the pieces – of a marriage based on a lie and the lasting repercussions of that night. Torn between laid-back Justin and control-freak Gav, she's a free spirit that life is trying to tie down. But the rewards are worth it!

Visit www.choc-lit.com for more details including the first two chapters and reviews, or simply scan barcode using your mobile phone QR reader.

Please don't stop the music
Jane Lovering

How much can you hide?

Jemima Hutton is determined to build a successful new life and keep her past a dark secret. Trouble is, her jewellery business looks set to fail – until enigmatic Ben Davies offers to stock her handmade belt buckles in his guitar shop and things start looking up, on all fronts.

But Ben has secrets too. When Jemima finds out he used to be the front man of hugely successful Indie rock band Willow Down, she wants to know more. Why did he desert the band on their US tour? Why is he now a semi-recluse?

And the curiosity is mutual – which means that her own secret is no longer safe …

Visit www.choc-lit.com for more details including the first two chapters and reviews, or simply scan barcode using your mobile phone QR reader.

Turning the Tide
Christine Stovell

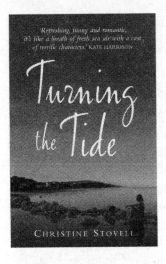

'Refreshing, funny and romantic, it's like a breath of fresh sea air with a cast of terrific characters.' KATE HARRISON

CHRISTINE STOVELL

All's fair in love and war? Depends on who's making the rules.

Harry Watling has spent the past five years keeping her father's boat yard afloat, despite its dying clientele. Now all she wants to do is enjoy the peace and quiet of her sleepy backwater.

So when property developer Matthew Corrigan wants to turn the boat yard into an upmarket housing complex for his exotic new restaurant, it's like declaring war.

And the odds seem to be stacked in Matthew's favour. He's got the colourful locals on board, his hard-to-please girlfriend is warming to the idea and he has the means to force Harry's hand. Meanwhile, Harry has to fight not just his plans but also her feelings for the man himself.

Then a family secret from the past creates heartbreak for Harry, and neither of them is prepared for what happens next …

Visit www.choc-lit.com for more details including the first two chapters and reviews, or simply scan barcode using your mobile phone QR reader.

The UnTied Kingdom
Kate Johnson

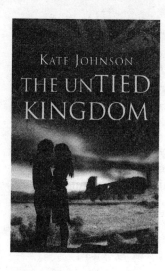

The portal to an alternate world was the start of all her troubles – or was it?

When Eve Carpenter lands with a splash in the Thames, it's not the London or England she's used to. No one has a telephone or knows what a computer is. England's a third-world country and Princess Di is still alive. But worst of all, everyone thinks Eve's a spy.

Including Major Harker who has his own problems. His sworn enemy is looking for a promotion. The general wants him to undertake some ridiculous mission to capture a computer, which Harker vaguely envisions running wild somewhere in Yorkshire. Turns out the best person to help him is Eve.

She claims to be a popstar. Harker doesn't know what a popstar is, although he suspects it's a fancy foreign word for 'spy'. Eve knows all about computers, and electricity. Eve is dangerous. There's every possibility she's mad.

And Harker is falling in love with her.

Visit www.choc-lit.com for more details including the first two chapters and reviews, or simply scan barcode using your mobile phone QR reader.

Want to Know a Secret?
Sue Moorcroft

Money, love and family. Which matters most?

When Diane Jenner's husband is hurt in a helicopter crash, she discovers a secret that changes her life. And it's all about money, the kind of money the Jenners have never had.

James North has money, and he knows it doesn't buy happiness. He's been a rock for his wayward wife and troubled daughter – but that doesn't stop him wanting Diane.

James and Diane have something in common: they always put family first. Which means that what happens in the back of James's Mercedes is a really, really bad idea.

Or is it?

Visit www.choc-lit.com for more details including the first two chapters and reviews, or simply scan barcode using your mobile phone QR reader.

Introducing the Choc Lit Club

Join us at the Choc Lit Club where we're creating a
delicious selection of women's fiction.
Where heroes are like chocolate – irresistible!

Join our authors in Author's Corner, read author interviews

Withdrawn *ms.*